AOHARU×KIKANJU Volume 12 ©2017 NAOE/ SQUARE ENIX CO., LTD. First published in Japan in 2017 by SQUARE ENIX CO., LTD. English translation rights arranged with SQUARE ENIX CO., LTD. and Yen Press, LLC through Tuttle-Mori Agency, Inc., Tokyo.

English translation ©2018 by SQUARE ENIX CO., LTD.

Yen Press
1290 Avenue of the Americas
New York, NY 10104

Visit us at yenpress.com
facebook.com/yenpress
twitter.com/yenpress
yenpress.tumblr.com
instagram.com/yenpress

First Yen Press Edition: August 2018

Yen Press is an imprint of Yen Press, LLC.
The Yen Press name and logo are trademarks of Yen Press, LLC.

The publisher is not responsible for websites (or their content) that are not owned by the publisher.

Library of Congress Control Number: 2016946057

ISBNs: 978-1-9753-5483-1 (paperback)
        978-1-9753-8212-4 (ebook)

10 9 8 7 6 5 4 3 2 1

WOR

Printed in the United States of America

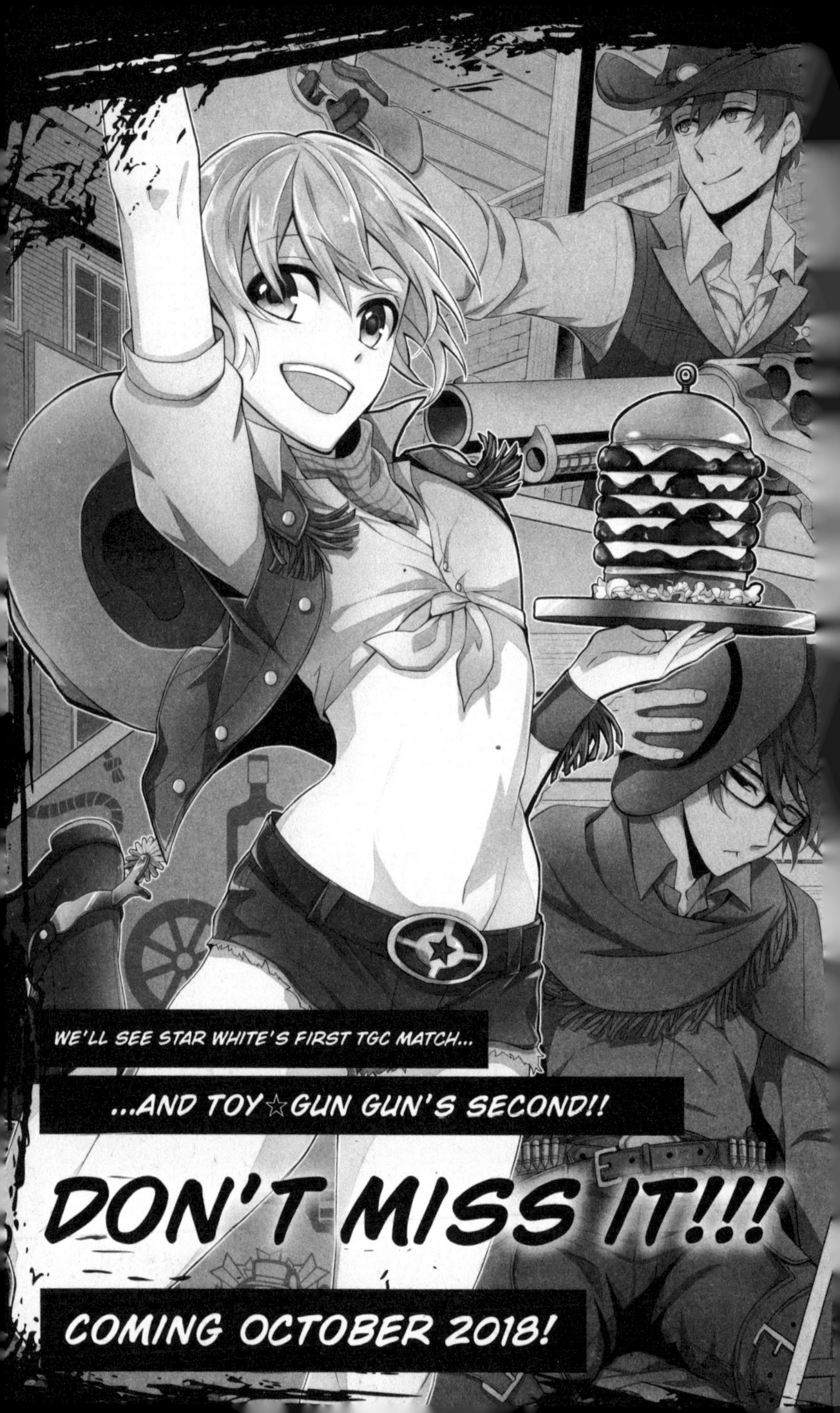
WE'LL SEE STAR WHITE'S FIRST TGC MATCH...
...AND TOY☆GUN GUN'S SECOND!!
DON'T MISS IT!!!
COMING OCTOBER 2018!

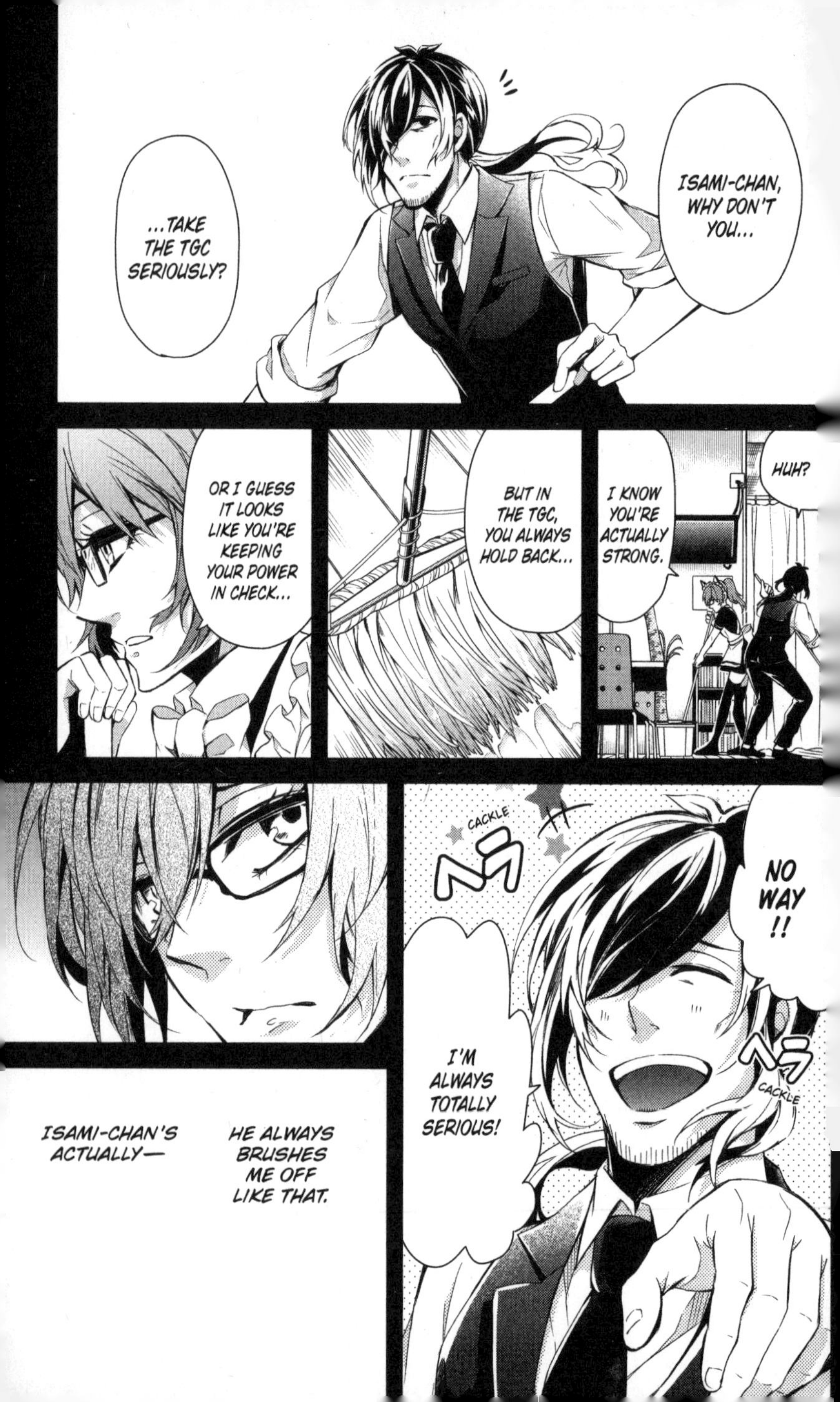
ISAMI-CHAN, WHY DON'T YOU...
...TAKE THE TGC SERIOUSLY?
HUH?
I KNOW YOU'RE ACTUALLY STRONG.
BUT IN THE TGC, YOU ALWAYS HOLD BACK...
OR I GUESS IT LOOKS LIKE YOU'RE KEEPING YOUR POWER IN CHECK...
NO WAY!!
CACKLE
I'M ALWAYS TOTALLY SERIOUS!
CACKLE
HE ALWAYS BRUSHES ME OFF LIKE THAT.
ISAMI-CHAN'S ACTUALLY—

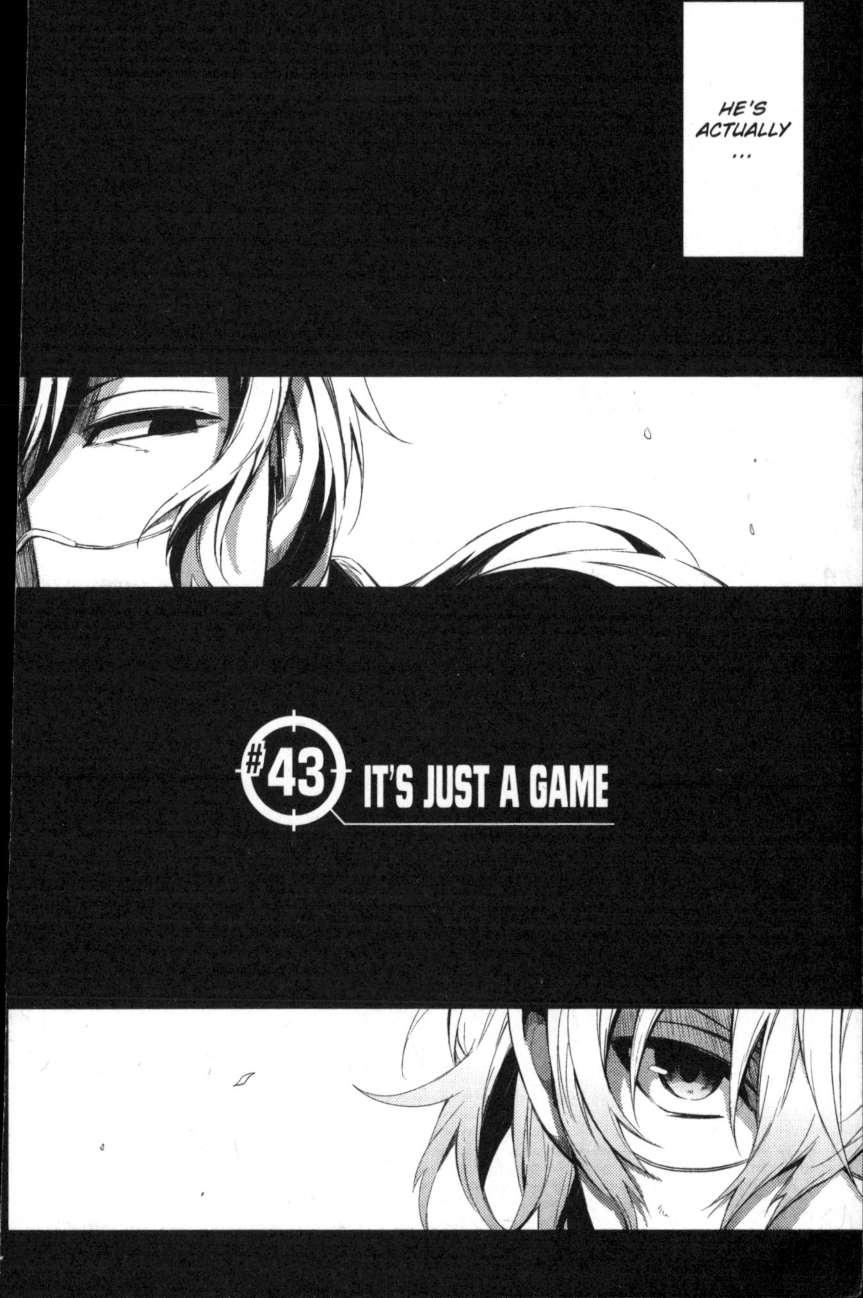
HE'S ACTUALLY ...
#43 IT'S JUST A GAME

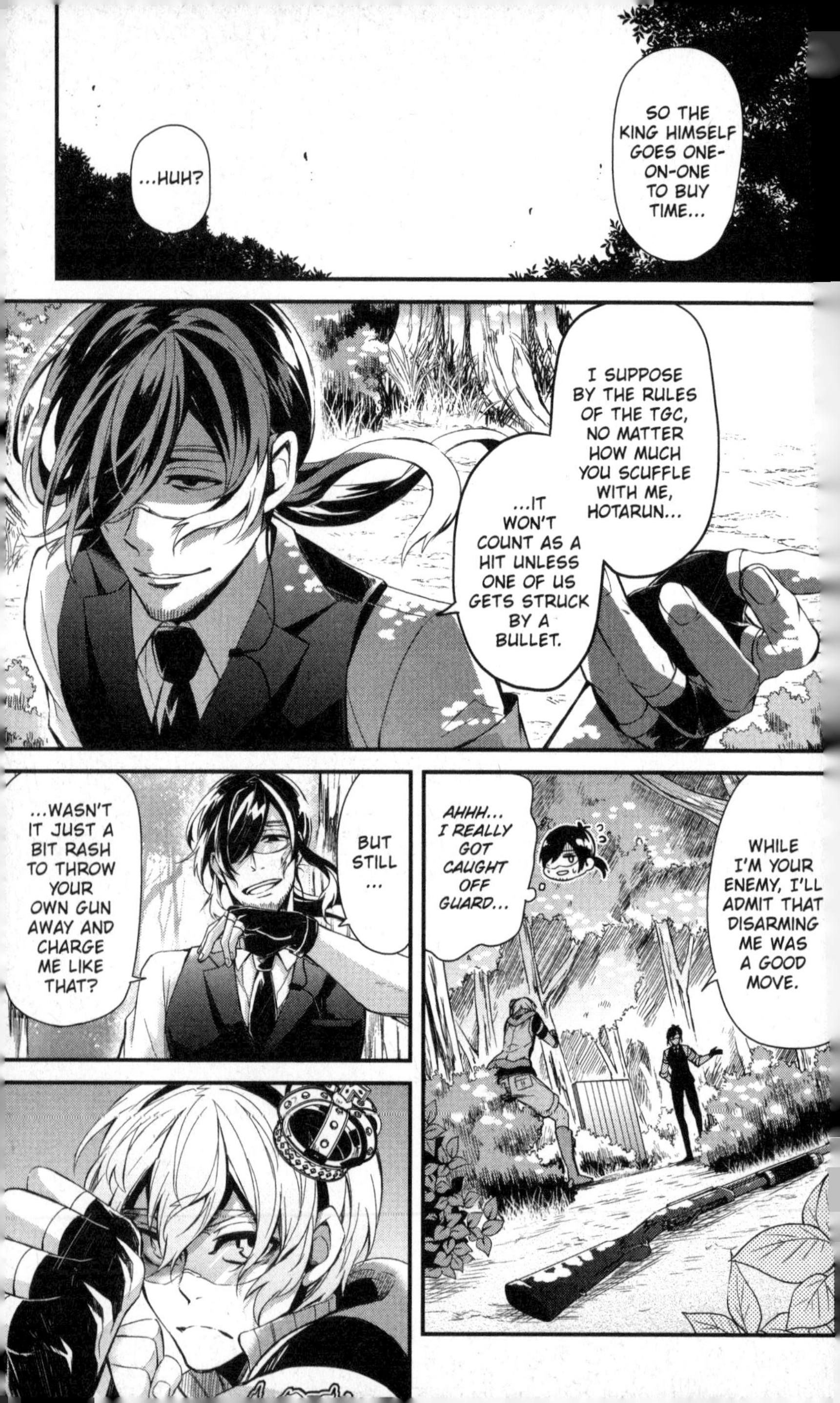
SO THE KING HIMSELF GOES ONE-ON-ONE TO BUY TIME...
...HUH?
I SUPPOSE BY THE RULES OF THE TGC, NO MATTER HOW MUCH YOU SCUFFLE WITH ME, HOTARUN...
...IT WON'T COUNT AS A HIT UNLESS ONE OF US GETS STRUCK BY A BULLET.
WHILE I'M YOUR ENEMY, I'LL ADMIT THAT DISARMING ME WAS A GOOD MOVE.
AHHH... I REALLY GOT CAUGHT OFF GUARD...
BUT STILL ...
...WASN'T IT JUST A BIT RASH TO THROW YOUR OWN GUN AWAY AND CHARGE ME LIKE THAT?

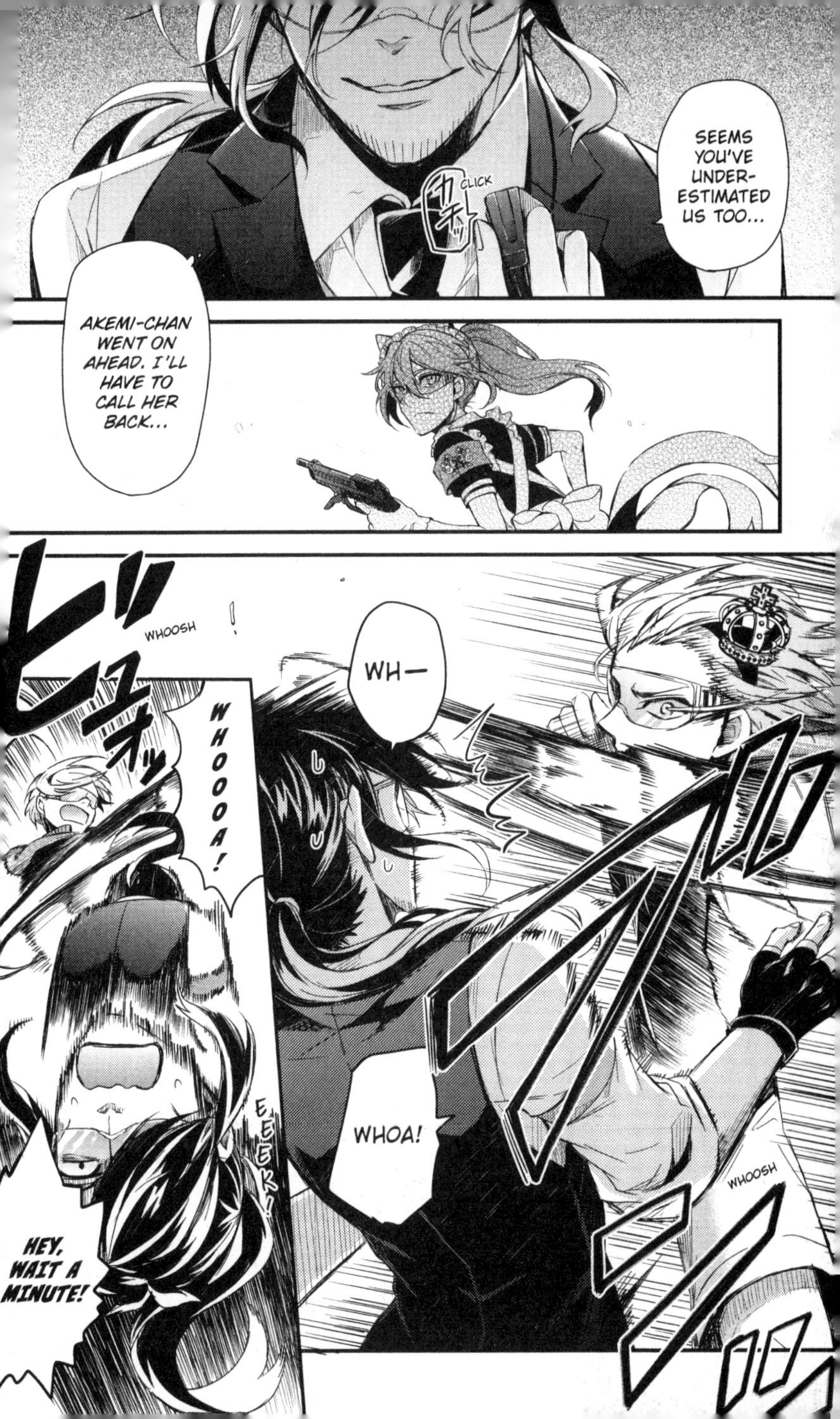
CLICK
SEEMS YOU'VE UNDER-ESTIMATED US TOO...
AKEMI-CHAN WENT ON AHEAD. I'LL HAVE TO CALL HER BACK...
WH—
WHOOSH
WHOOOOA!
WHOA!
WHOOSH
EEEEK!
HEY, WAIT A MINUTE!

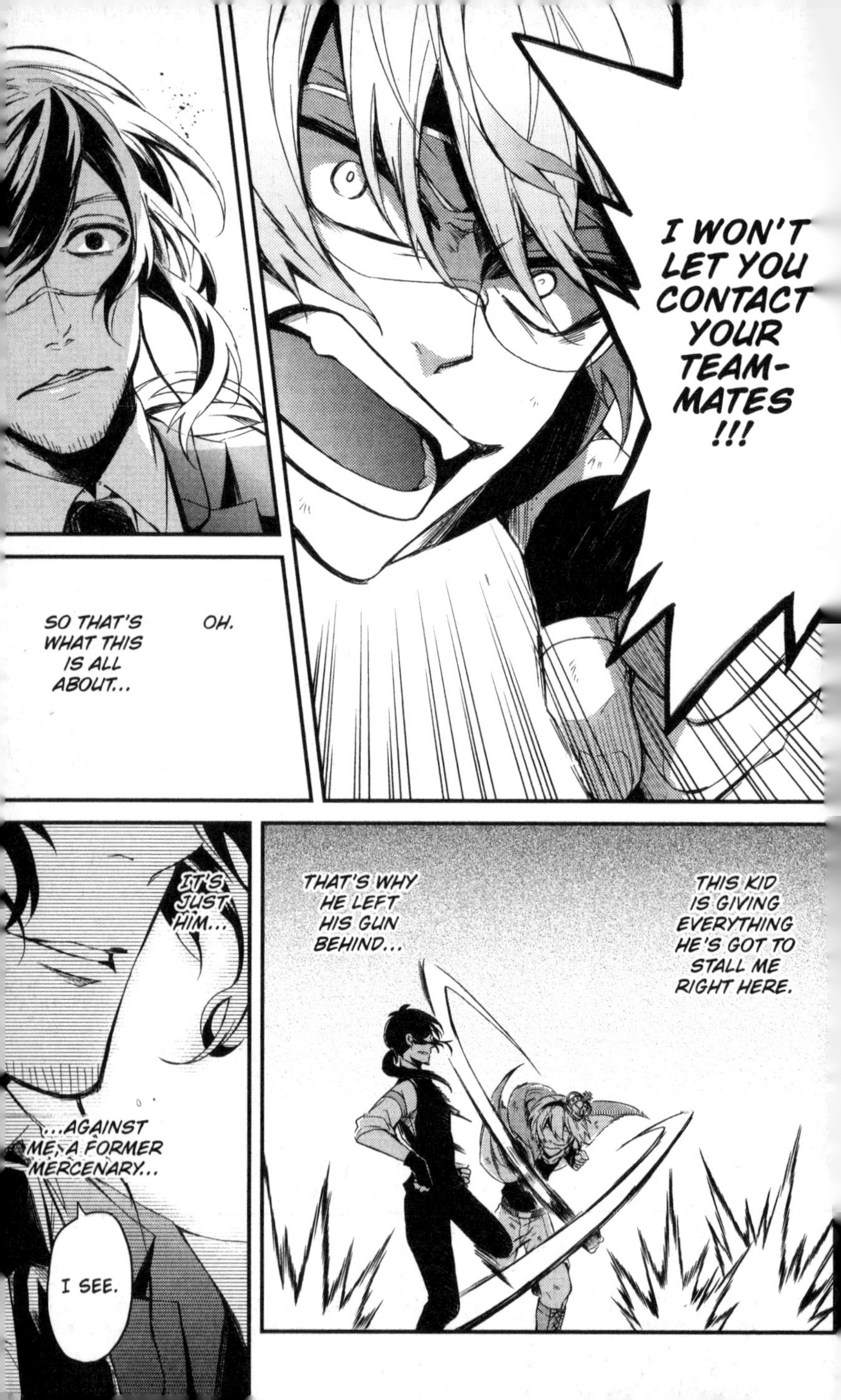
I WON'T LET YOU CONTACT YOUR TEAM-MATES!!!
OH.
SO THAT'S WHAT THIS IS ALL ABOUT...
THIS KID IS GIVING EVERYTHING HE'S GOT TO STALL ME RIGHT HERE.
THAT'S WHY HE LEFT HIS GUN BEHIND...
IT'S JUST HIM...
...AGAINST ME, A FORMER MERCENARY...
I SEE.

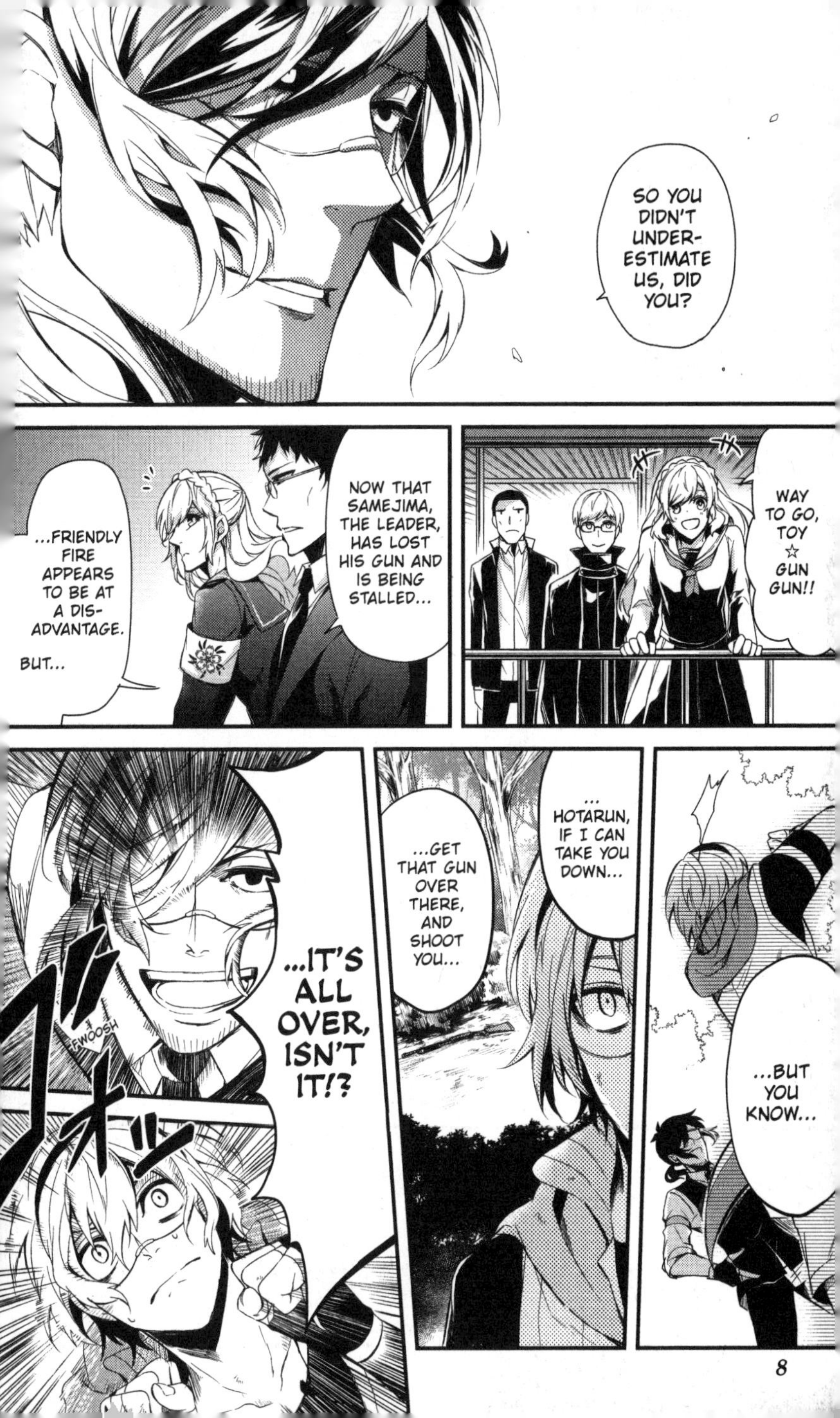
SO YOU DIDN'T UNDER-ESTIMATE US, DID YOU?
WAY TO GO, TOY ☆ GUN GUN!!
NOW THAT SAMEJIMA, THE LEADER, HAS LOST HIS GUN AND IS BEING STALLED...
...FRIENDLY FIRE APPEARS TO BE AT A DIS-ADVANTAGE.
BUT...
...BUT YOU KNOW...
... HOTARUN, IF I CAN TAKE YOU DOWN...
...GET THAT GUN OVER THERE, AND SHOOT YOU...
...IT'S ALL OVER, ISN'T IT!?
FWOOSH

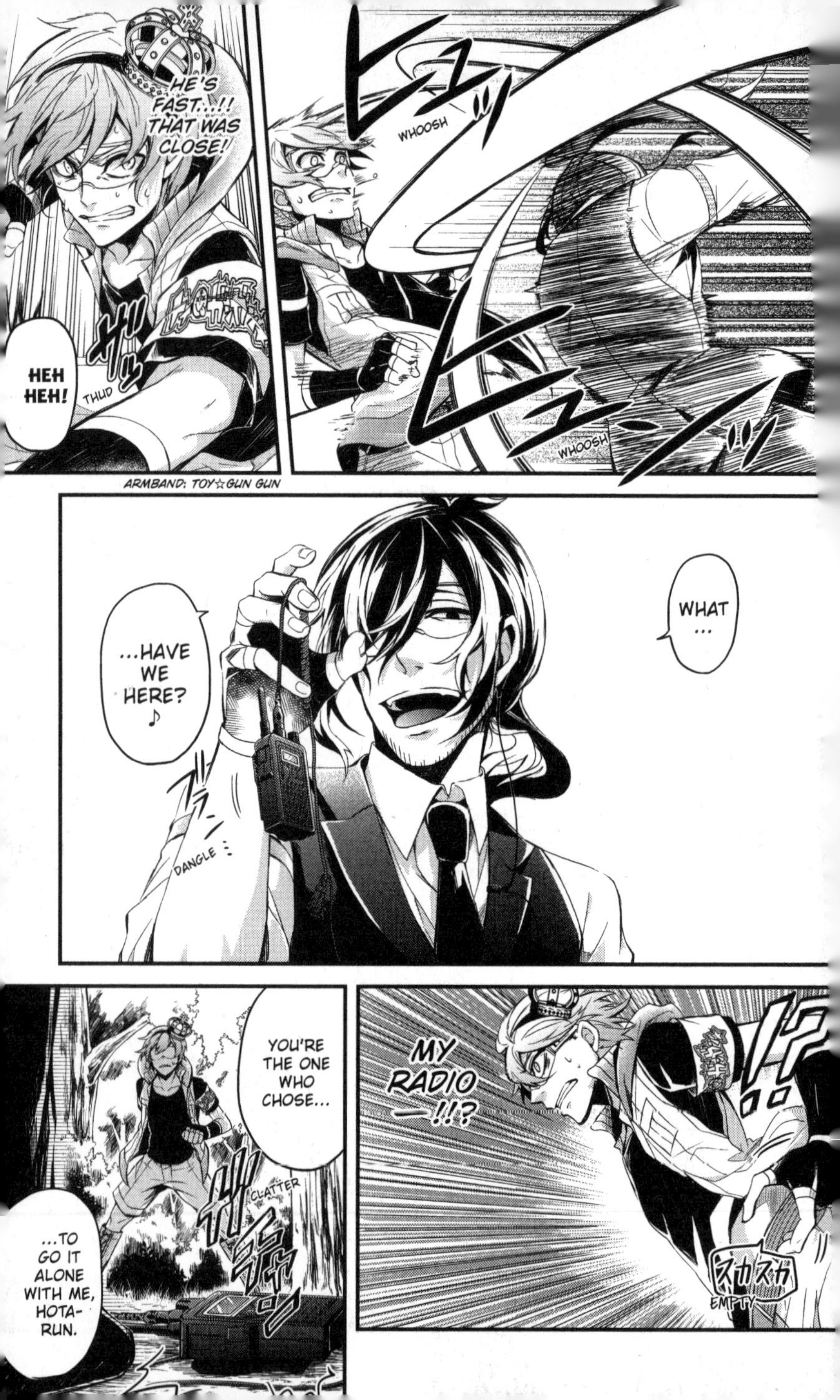
WHOOSH
WHOOSH
HE'S FAST...!! THAT WAS CLOSE!
HEH HEH!
THUD
ARMBAND: TOY☆GUN GUN
WHAT ...
...HAVE WE HERE? ♪
DANGLE
MY RADIO —!!?
スカスカ
EMPTY
YOU'RE THE ONE WHO CHOSE...
CLATTER
...TO GO IT ALONE WITH ME, HOTA-RUN.

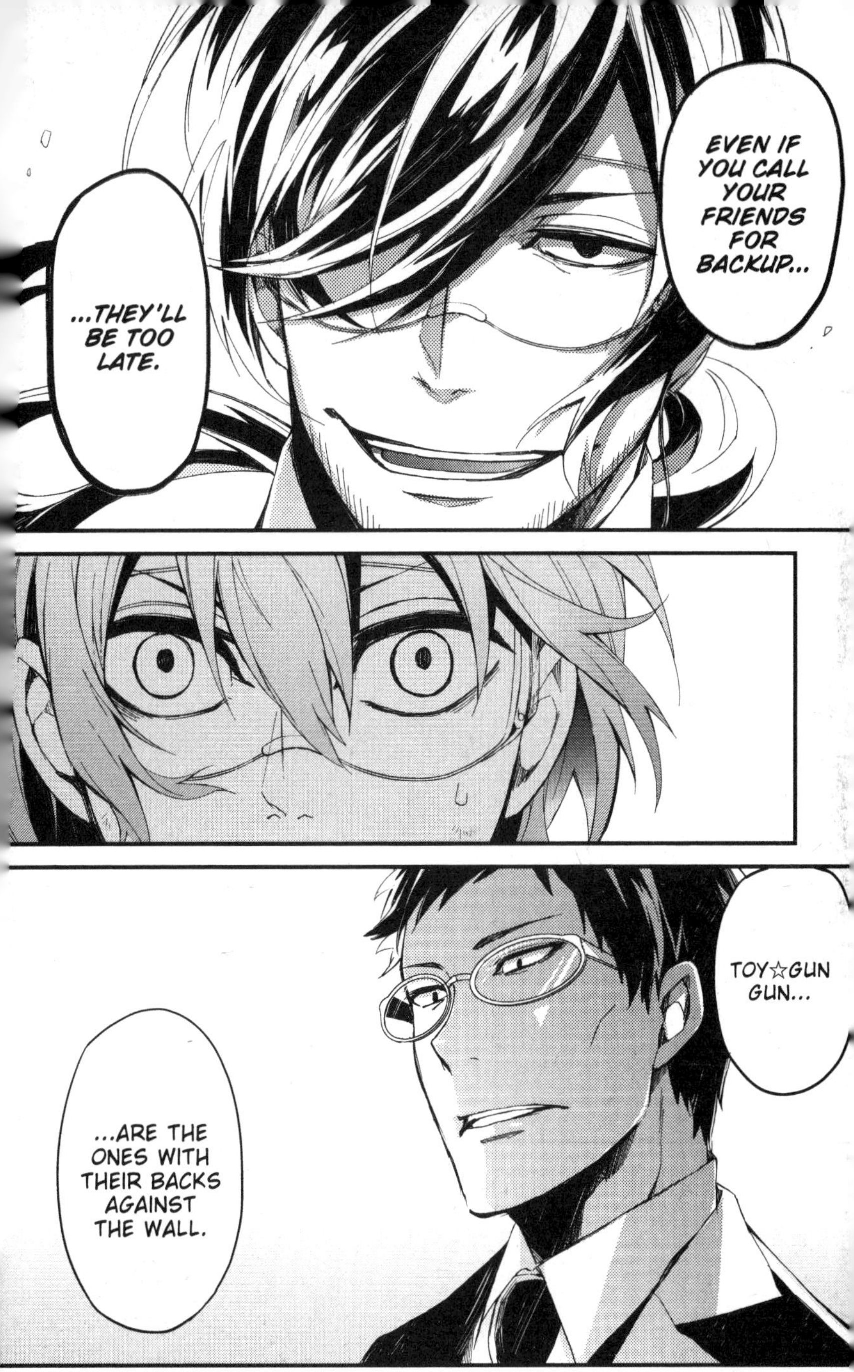
EVEN IF YOU CALL YOUR FRIENDS FOR BACKUP...
...THEY'LL BE TOO LATE.
TOY☆GUN GUN...
...ARE THE ONES WITH THEIR BACKS AGAINST THE WALL.

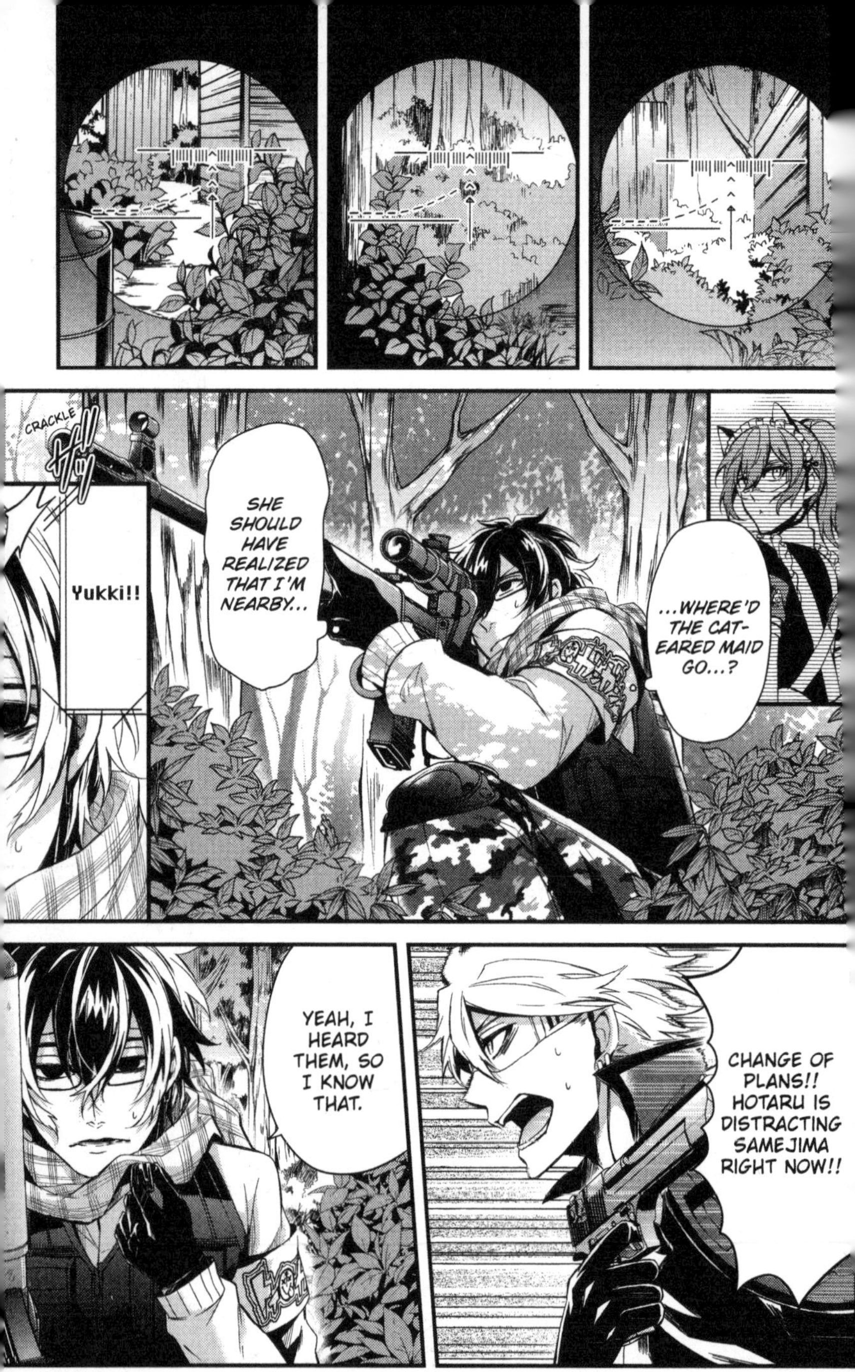
...WHERE'D THE CAT-EARED MAID GO...?
SHE SHOULD HAVE REALIZED THAT I'M NEARBY...
CRACKLE
Yukki!!
CHANGE OF PLANS!! HOTARU IS DISTRACTING SAMEJIMA RIGHT NOW!!
YEAH, I HEARD THEM, SO I KNOW THAT.

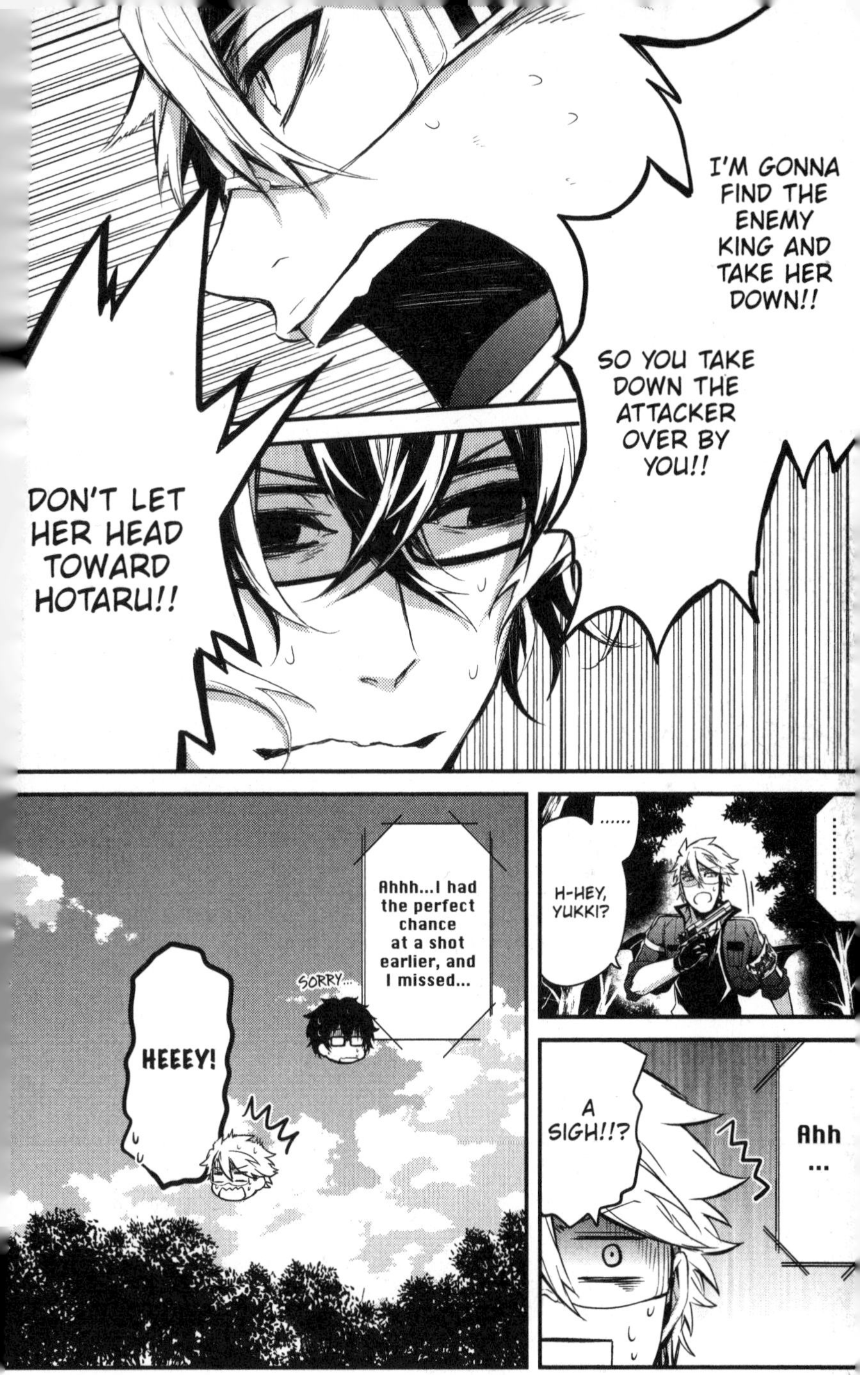
I'M GONNA FIND THE ENEMY KING AND TAKE HER DOWN!!
SO YOU TAKE DOWN THE ATTACKER OVER BY YOU!!
DON'T LET HER HEAD TOWARD HOTARU!!
......
......
H-HEY, YUKKI?
Ahh ...
A SIGH!!?
Ahhh...I had the perfect chance at a shot earlier, and I missed...
SORRY...
HEEEY!

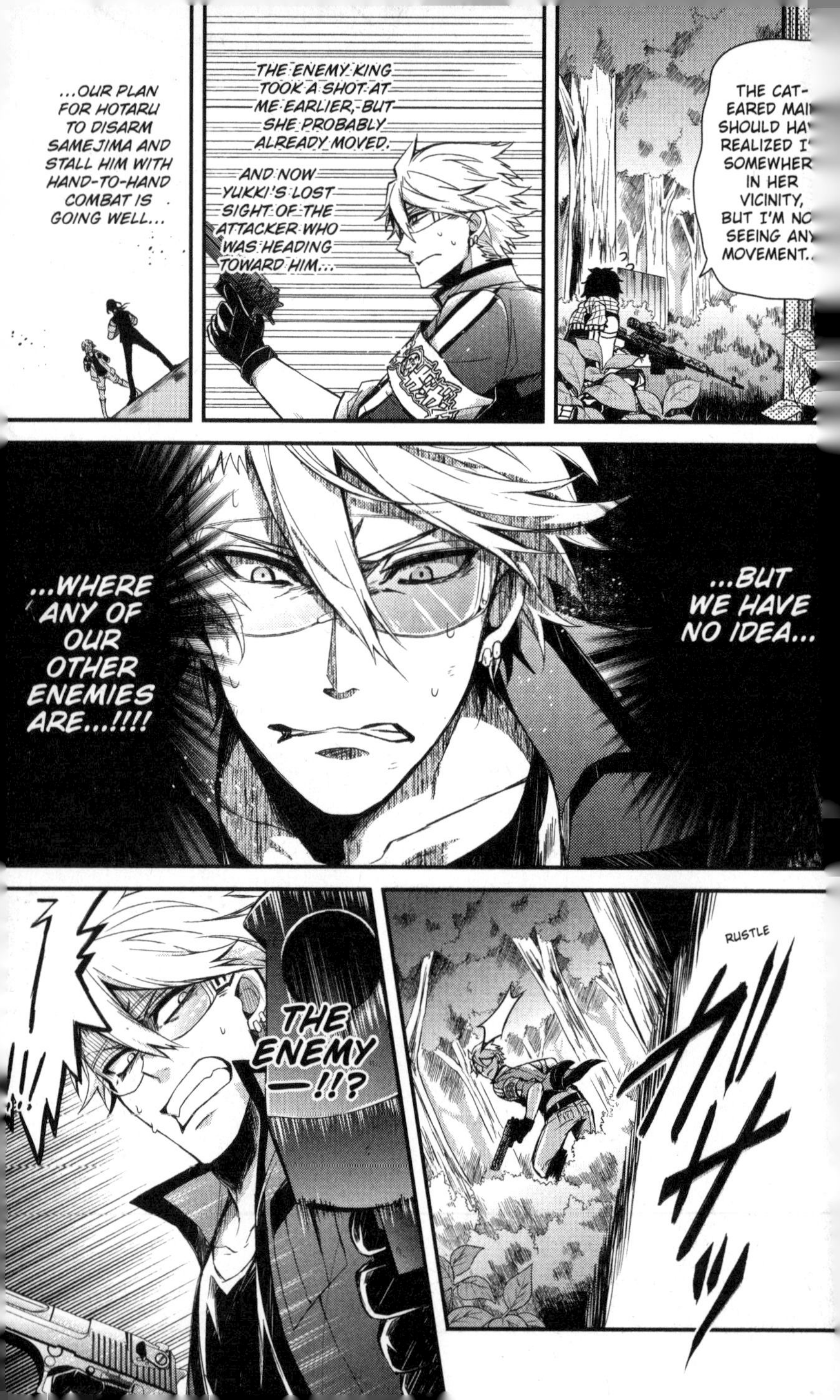

THE CAT-EARED MAI SHOULD HAV REALIZED I' SOMEWHER IN HER VICINITY, BUT I'M NO SEEING ANY MOVEMENT..
THE ENEMY KING TOOK A SHOT AT ME EARLIER, BUT SHE PROBABLY ALREADY MOVED.
AND NOW YUKKI'S LOST SIGHT OF THE ATTACKER WHO WAS HEADING TOWARD HIM...
...OUR PLAN FOR HOTARU TO DISARM SAMEJIMA AND STALL HIM WITH HAND-TO-HAND COMBAT IS GOING WELL...
...BUT WE HAVE NO IDEA...
...WHERE ANY OF OUR OTHER ENEMIES ARE...!!!!
RUSTLE
THE ENEMY—!!?

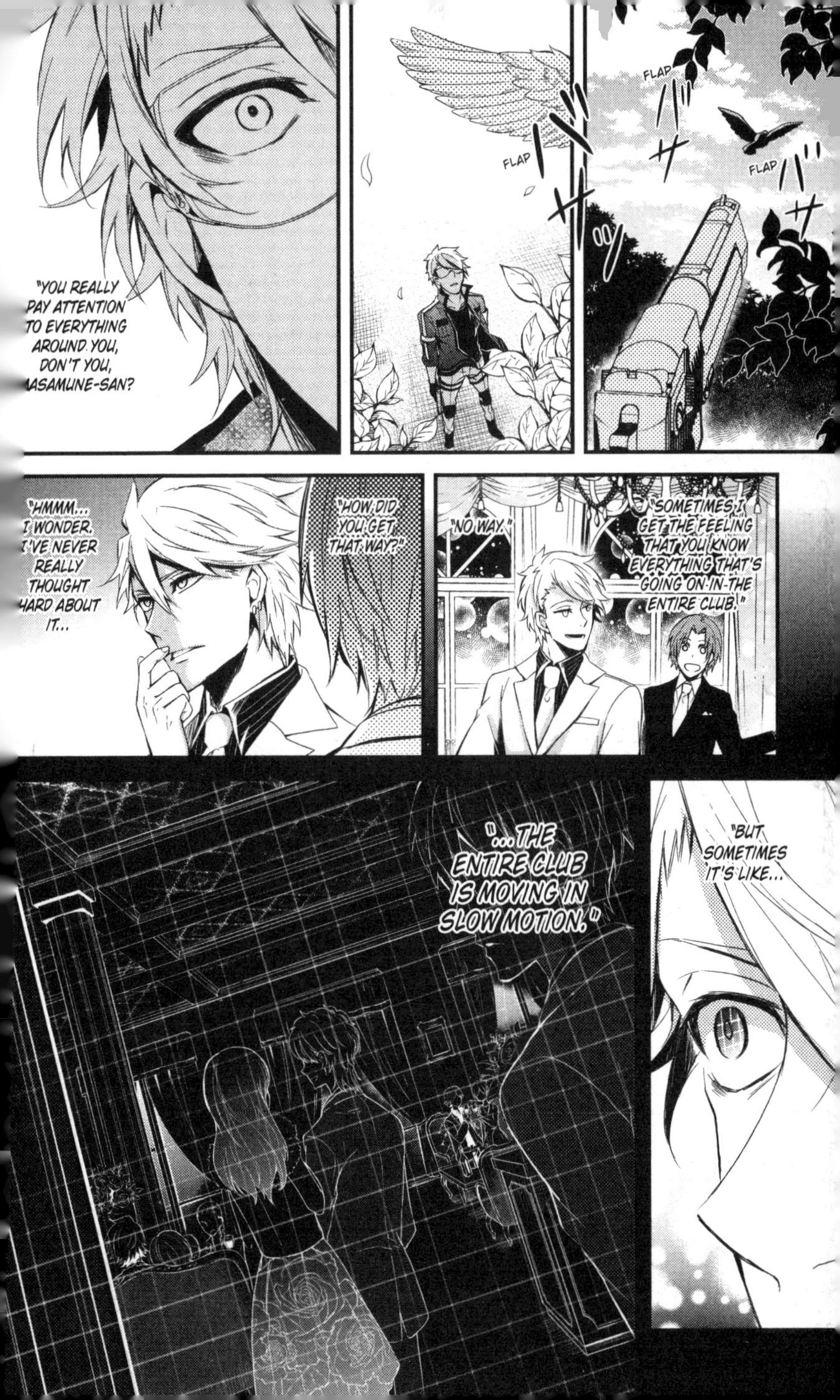
FLAP
FLAP
FLAP
"YOU REALLY PAY ATTENTION TO EVERYTHING AROUND YOU, DON'T YOU, MASAMUNE-SAN?
"SOMETIMES I GET THE FEELING THAT YOU KNOW EVERYTHING THAT'S GOING ON IN THE ENTIRE CLUB."
"NO WAY."
"HOW DID YOU GET THAT WAY?"
"HMMM... I WONDER. I'VE NEVER REALLY THOUGHT HARD ABOUT IT...
"BUT SOMETIMES IT'S LIKE...
"...THE ENTIRE CLUB IS MOVING IN SLOW MOTION."

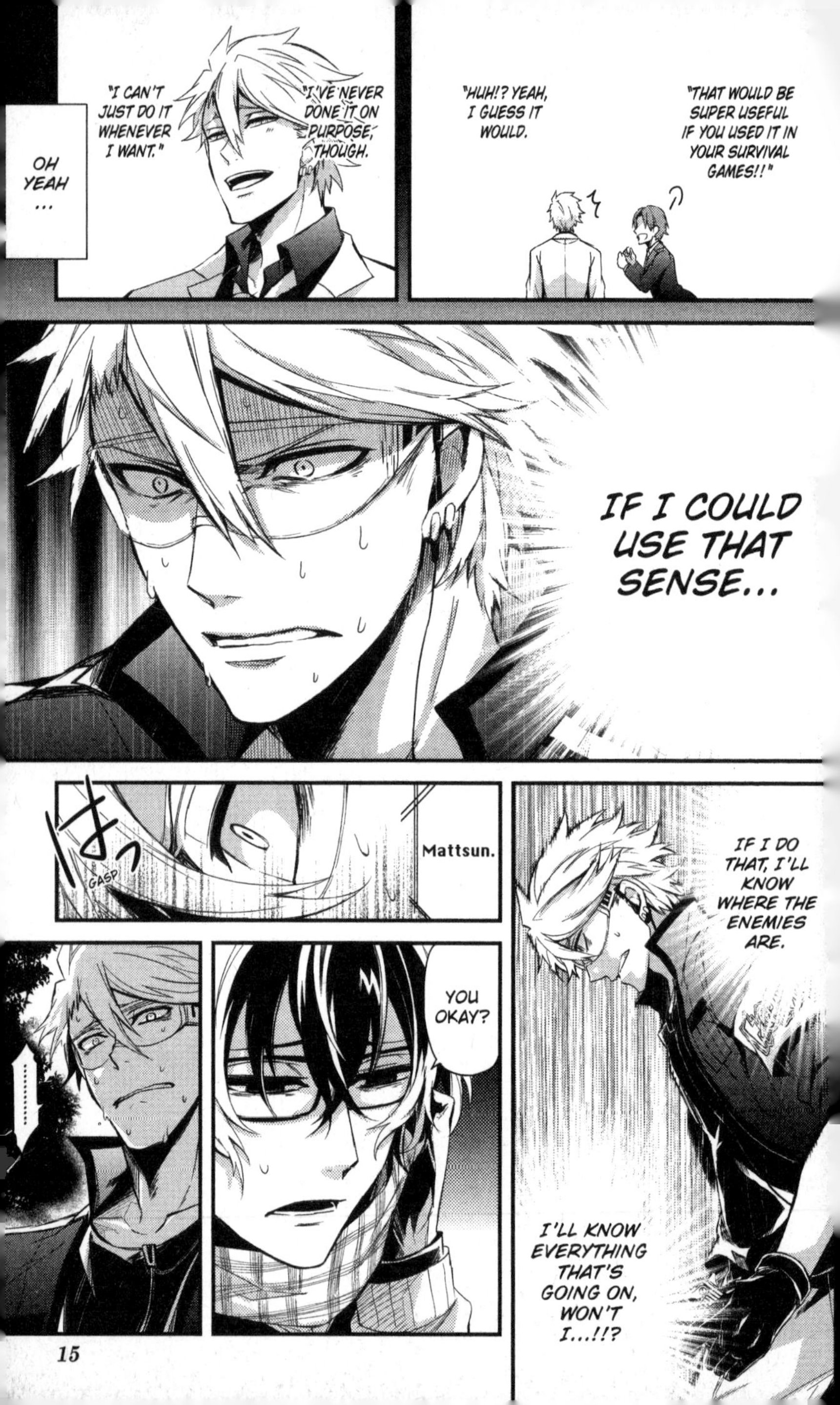
"THAT WOULD BE SUPER USEFUL IF YOU USED IT IN YOUR SURVIVAL GAMES!!"
"HUH!? YEAH, I GUESS IT WOULD.
"I'VE NEVER DONE IT ON PURPOSE, THOUGH.
"I CAN'T JUST DO IT WHENEVER I WANT."
OH YEAH ...
IF I COULD USE THAT SENSE...
IF I DO THAT, I'LL KNOW WHERE THE ENEMIES ARE.
I'LL KNOW EVERYTHING THAT'S GOING ON, WON'T I...!!?
Mattsun.
はっ
GASP
YOU OKAY?
......

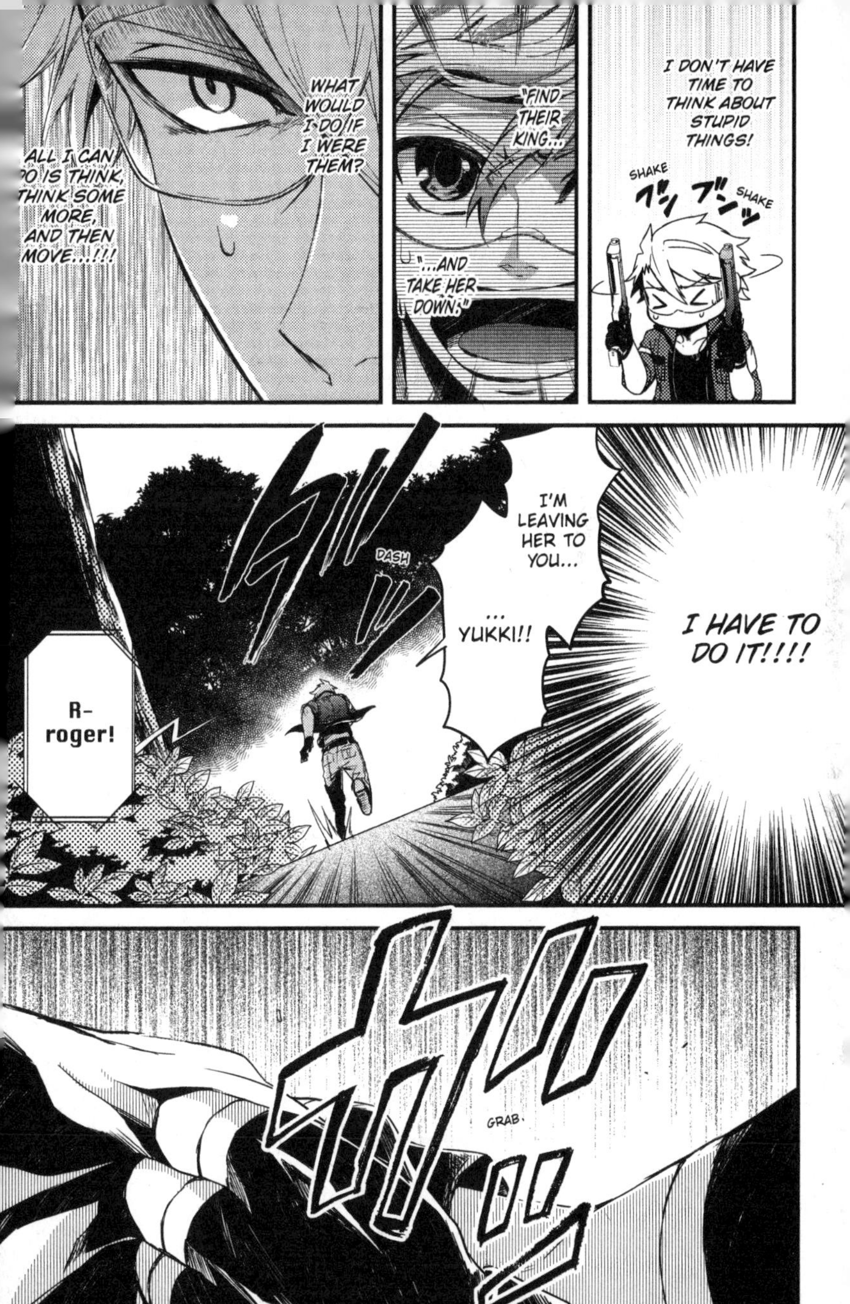
I DON'T HAVE TIME TO THINK ABOUT STUPID THINGS!
SHAKE
SHAKE
"FIND THEIR KING..."
"...AND TAKE HER DOWN."
WHAT WOULD I DO IF I WERE THEM?
ALL I CAN DO IS THINK, THINK SOME MORE, AND THEN MOVE...!!!
I HAVE TO DO IT!!!!
I'M LEAVING HER TO YOU...
...YUKKI!!
DASH
R-roger!
GRAB.

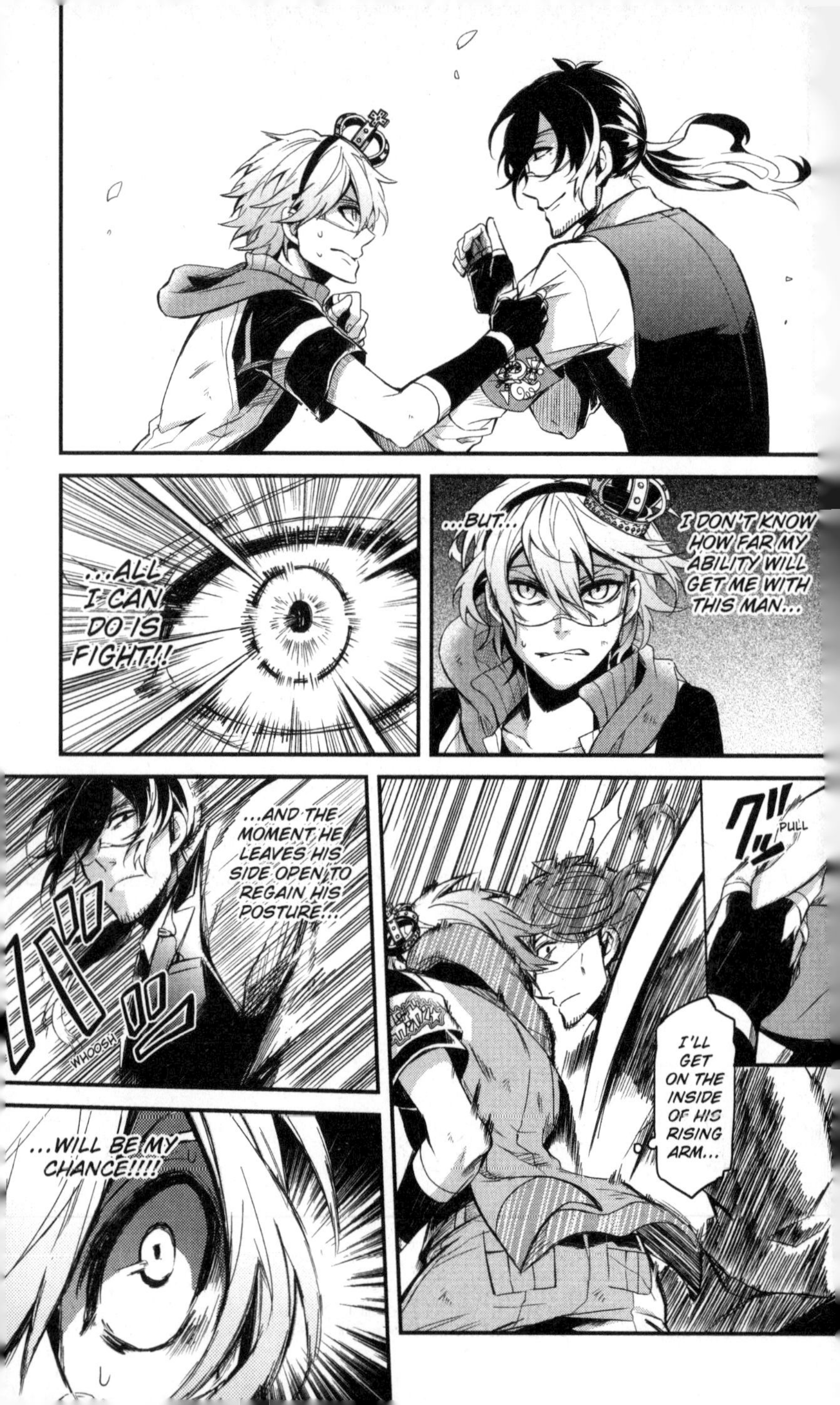
...BUT...
I DON'T KNOW HOW FAR MY ABILITY WILL GET ME WITH THIS MAN...
...ALL I CAN DO IS FIGHT!!
PULL
I'LL GET ON THE INSIDE OF HIS RISING ARM...
...AND THE MOMENT HE LEAVES HIS SIDE OPEN TO REGAIN HIS POSTURE...
WHOOSH
...WILL BE MY CHANCE!!!!

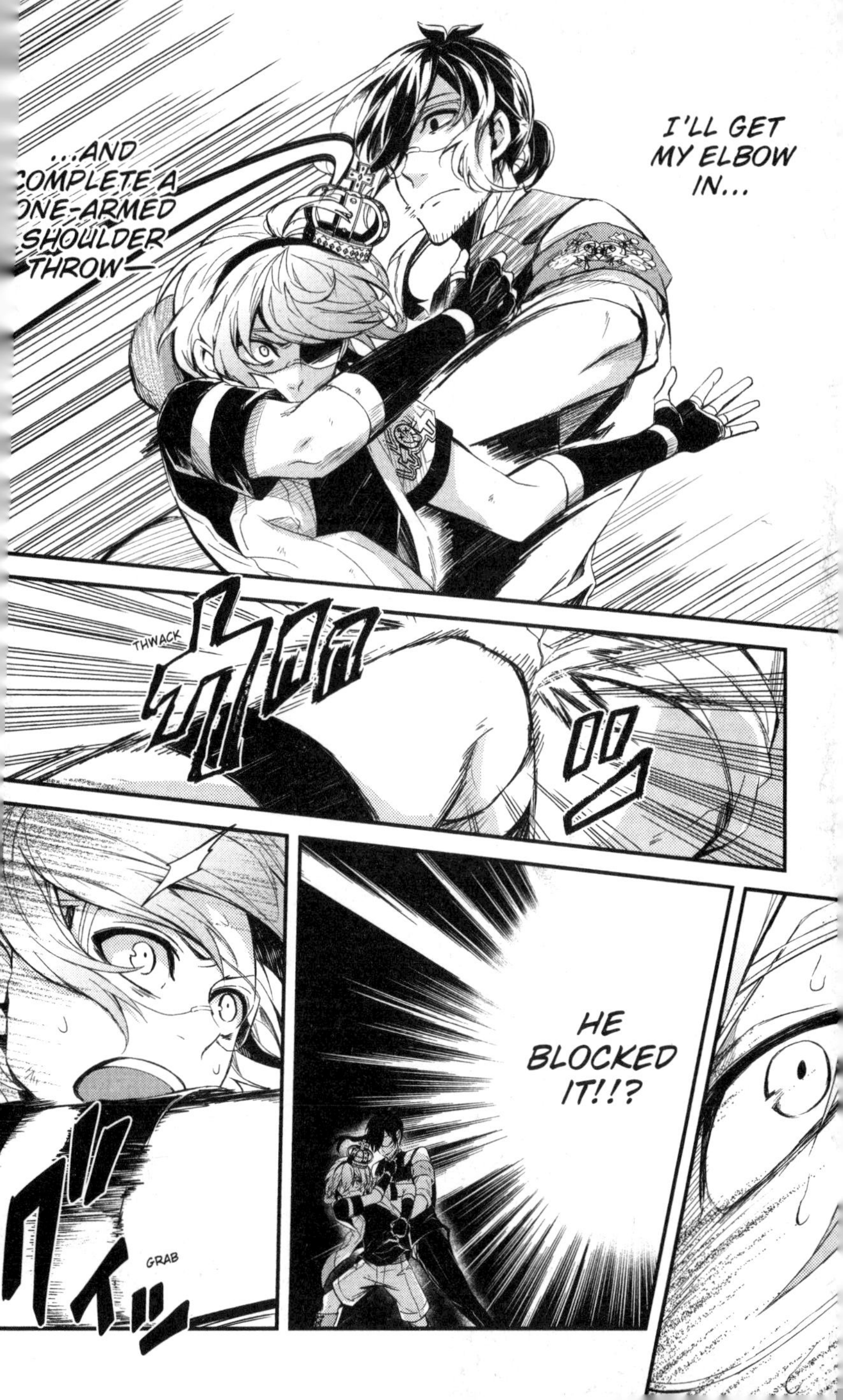
I'LL GET MY ELBOW IN...
...AND COMPLETE A ONE-ARMED SHOULDER THROW
THWACK
HE BLOCKED IT!!?
GRAB

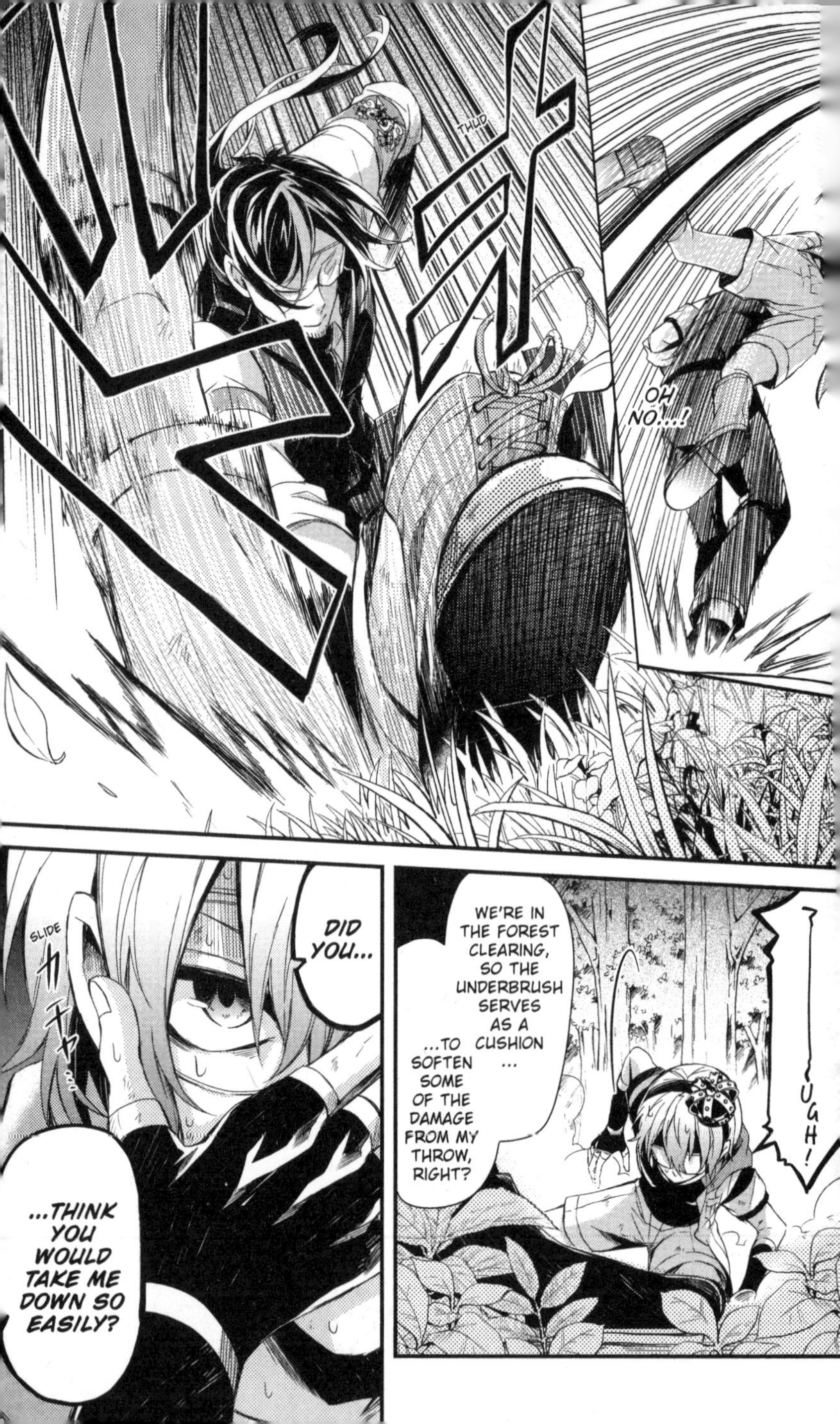
OH NO...!
THUD
UGH!
WE'RE IN THE FOREST CLEARING, SO THE UNDERBRUSH SERVES AS A CUSHION ...
...TO SOFTEN SOME OF THE DAMAGE FROM MY THROW, RIGHT?
DID YOU...
SLIDE
...THINK YOU WOULD TAKE ME DOWN SO EASILY?

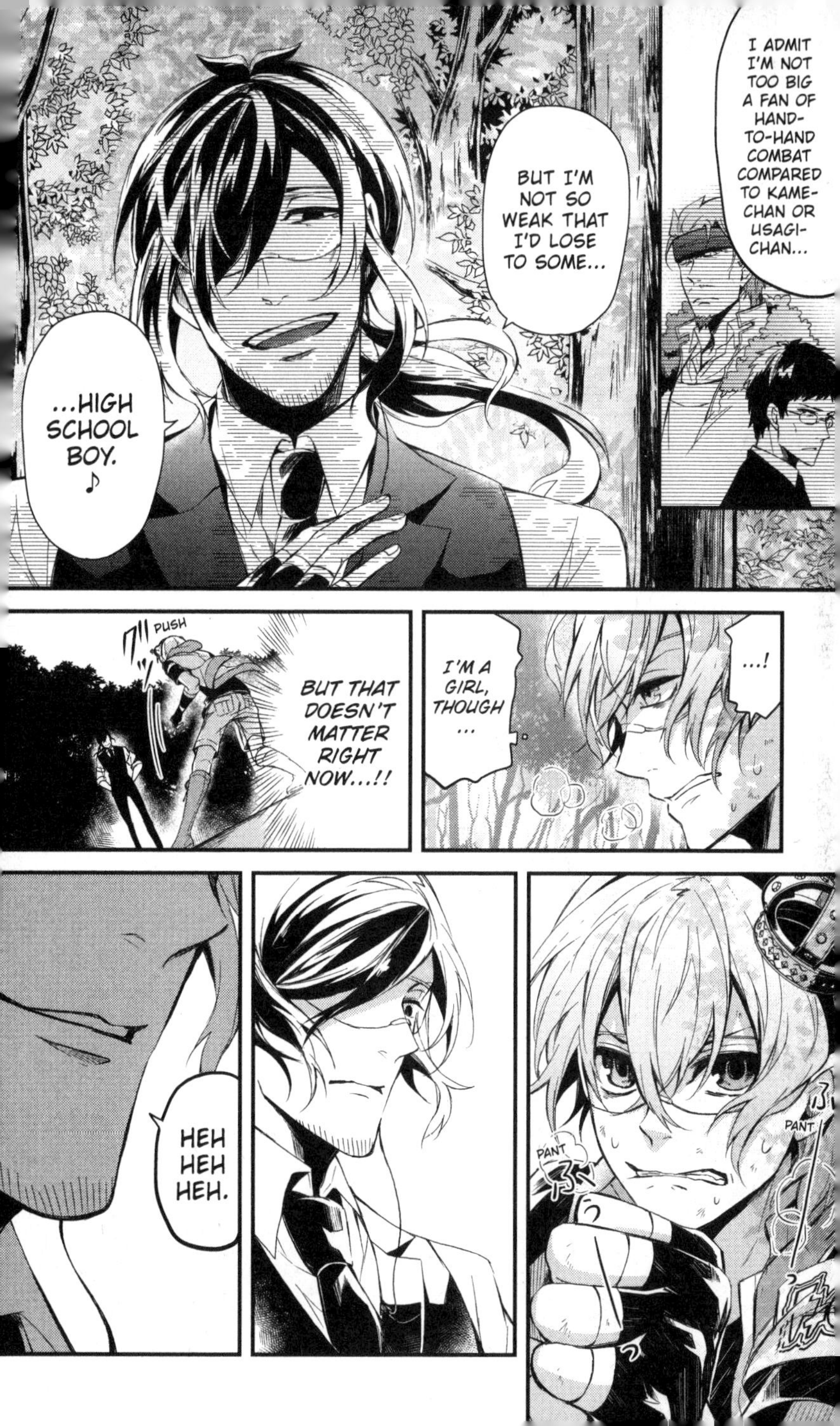
I ADMIT I'M NOT TOO BIG A FAN OF HAND-TO-HAND COMBAT COMPARED TO KAME-CHAN OR USAGI-CHAN...
BUT I'M NOT SO WEAK THAT I'D LOSE TO SOME...
...HIGH SCHOOL BOY. ♪
...!
I'M A GIRL, THOUGH...
BUT THAT DOESN'T MATTER RIGHT NOW...!!
PUSH
PANT
PANT
HEH HEH HEH.

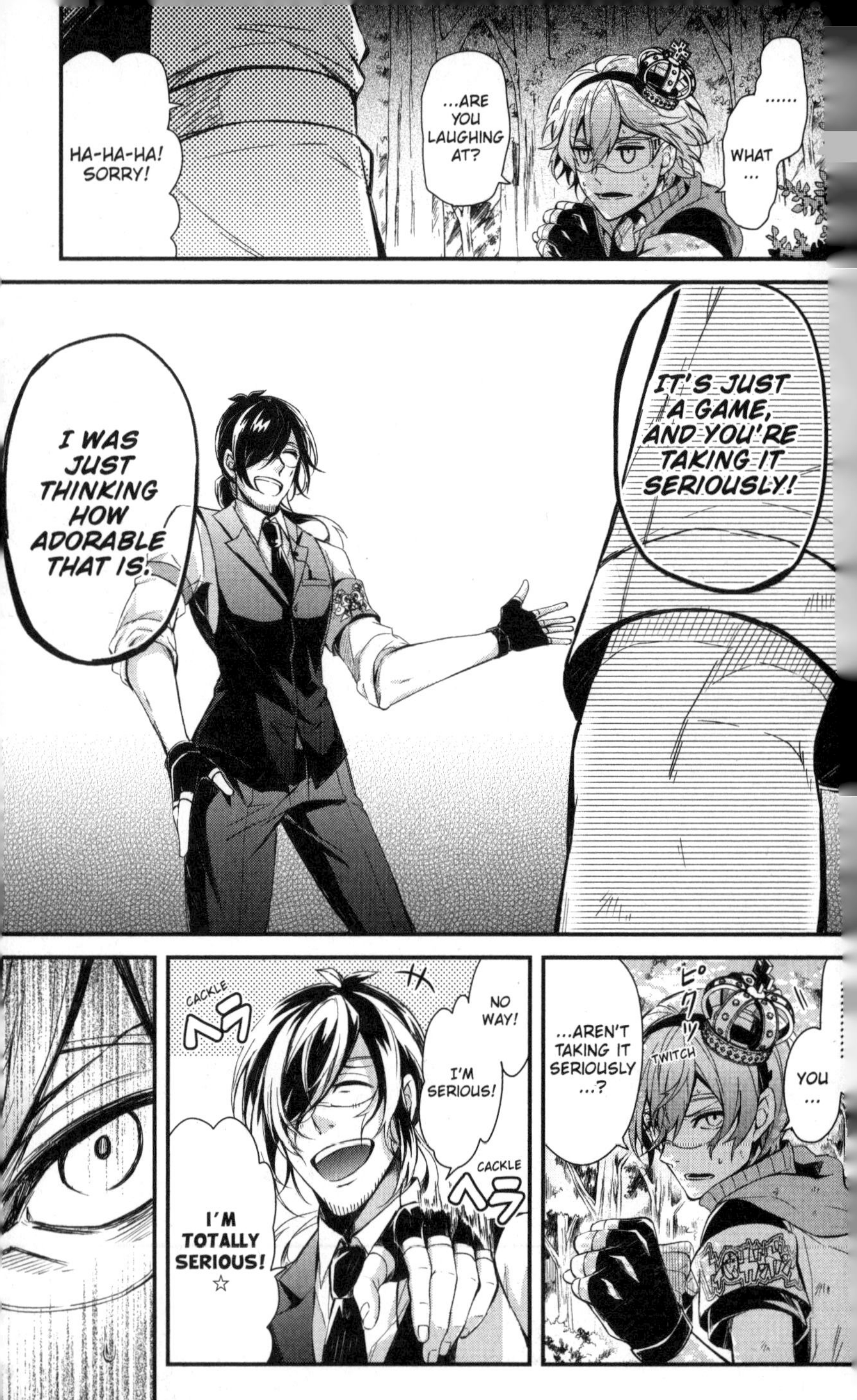

......
WHAT ...
...ARE YOU LAUGHING AT?
HA-HA-HA! SORRY!
IT'S JUST A GAME, AND YOU'RE TAKING IT SERIOUSLY!
I WAS JUST THINKING HOW ADORABLE THAT IS.
YOU ...
TWITCH
...AREN'T TAKING IT SERIOUSLY ...?
NO WAY!
CACKLE
I'M SERIOUS!
CACKLE
I'M TOTALLY SERIOUS! ☆

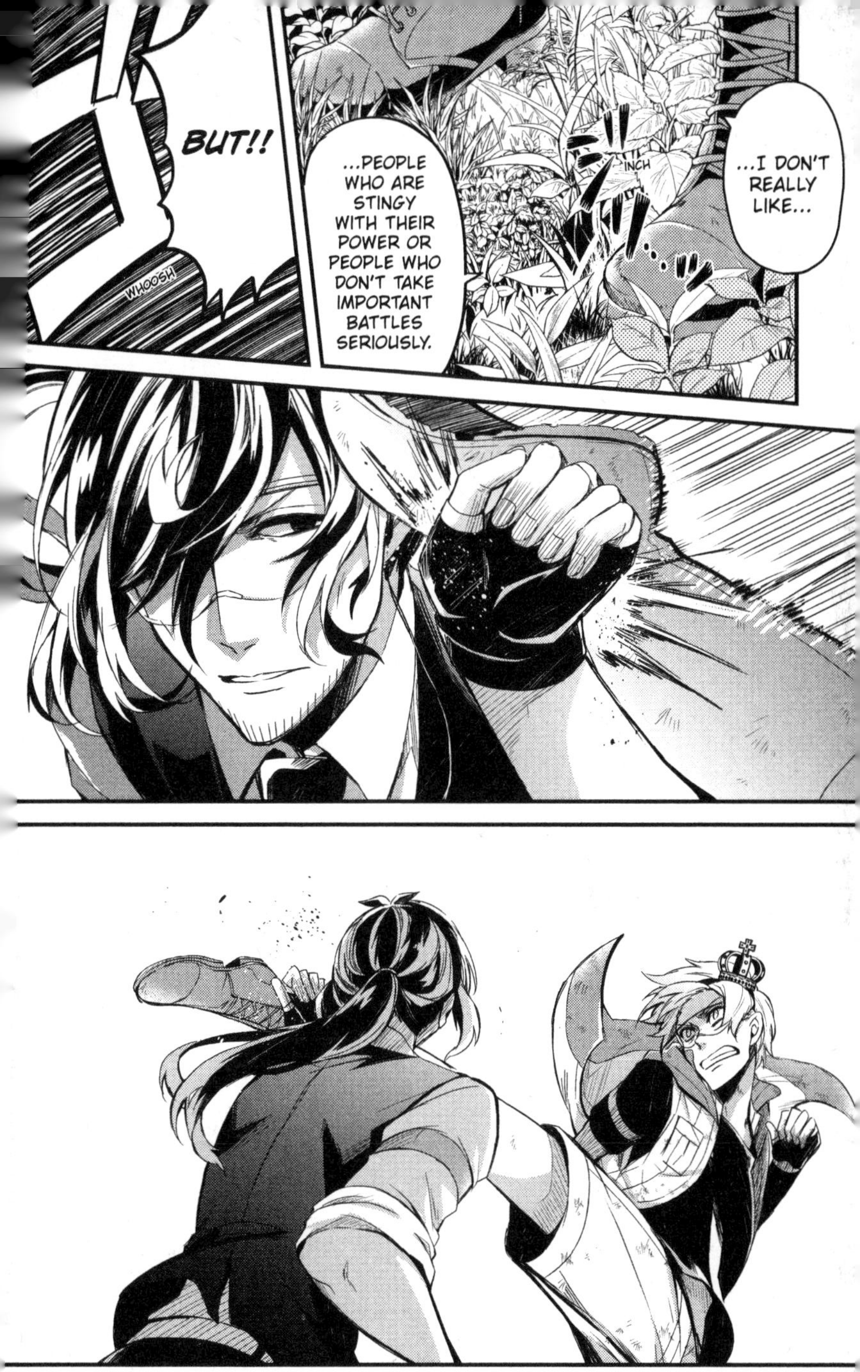
...I DON'T REALLY LIKE...
INCH
...PEOPLE WHO ARE STINGY WITH THEIR POWER OR PEOPLE WHO DON'T TAKE IMPORTANT BATTLES SERIOUSLY.
BUT!!
WHOOSH

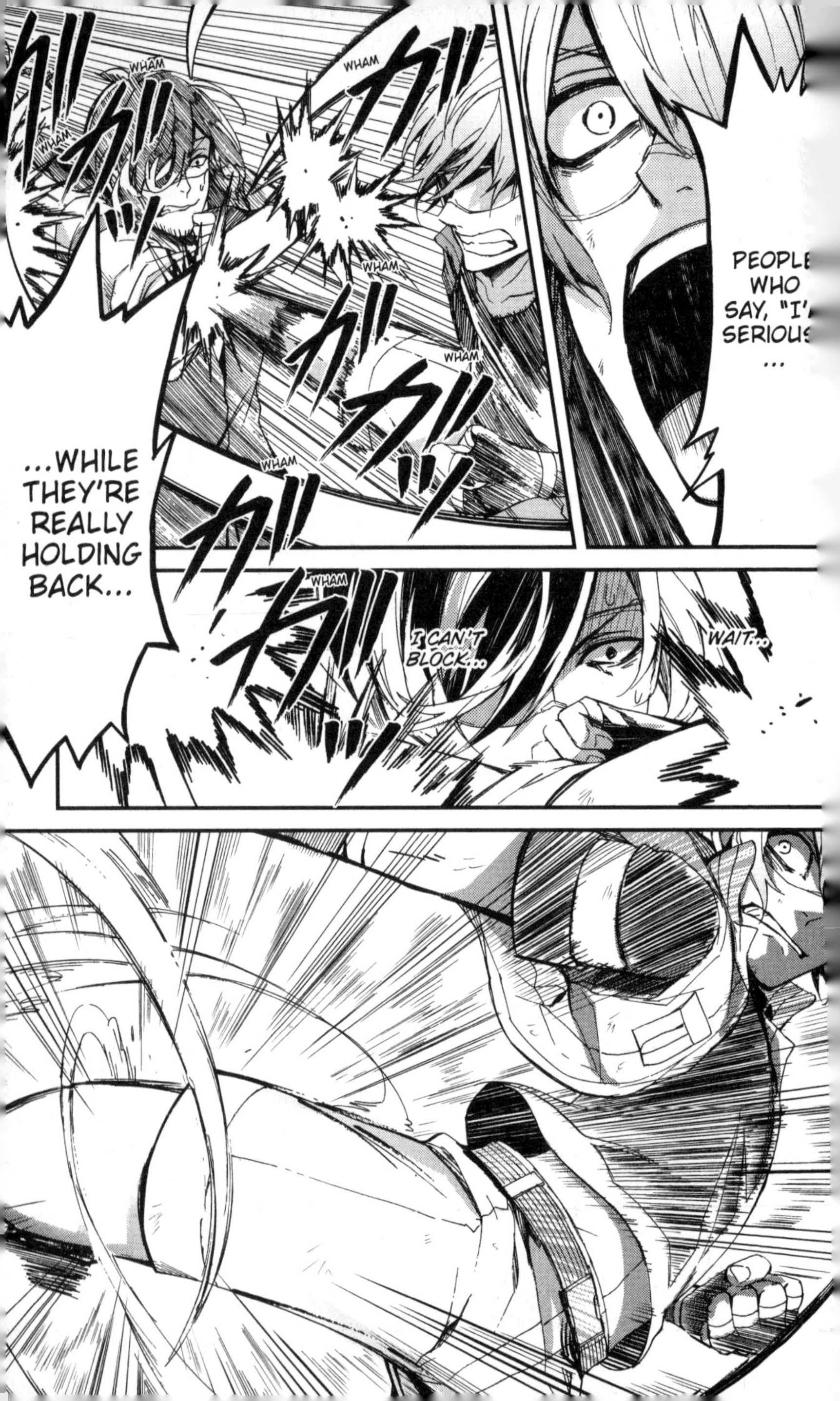
PEOPLE WHO SAY, "I' SERIOUS ...
WHAM
WHAM
WHAM
WHAM
WHAM
WHAM
...WHILE THEY'RE REALLY HOLDING BACK...
WHAM
WAIT...
I CAN'T BLOCK...

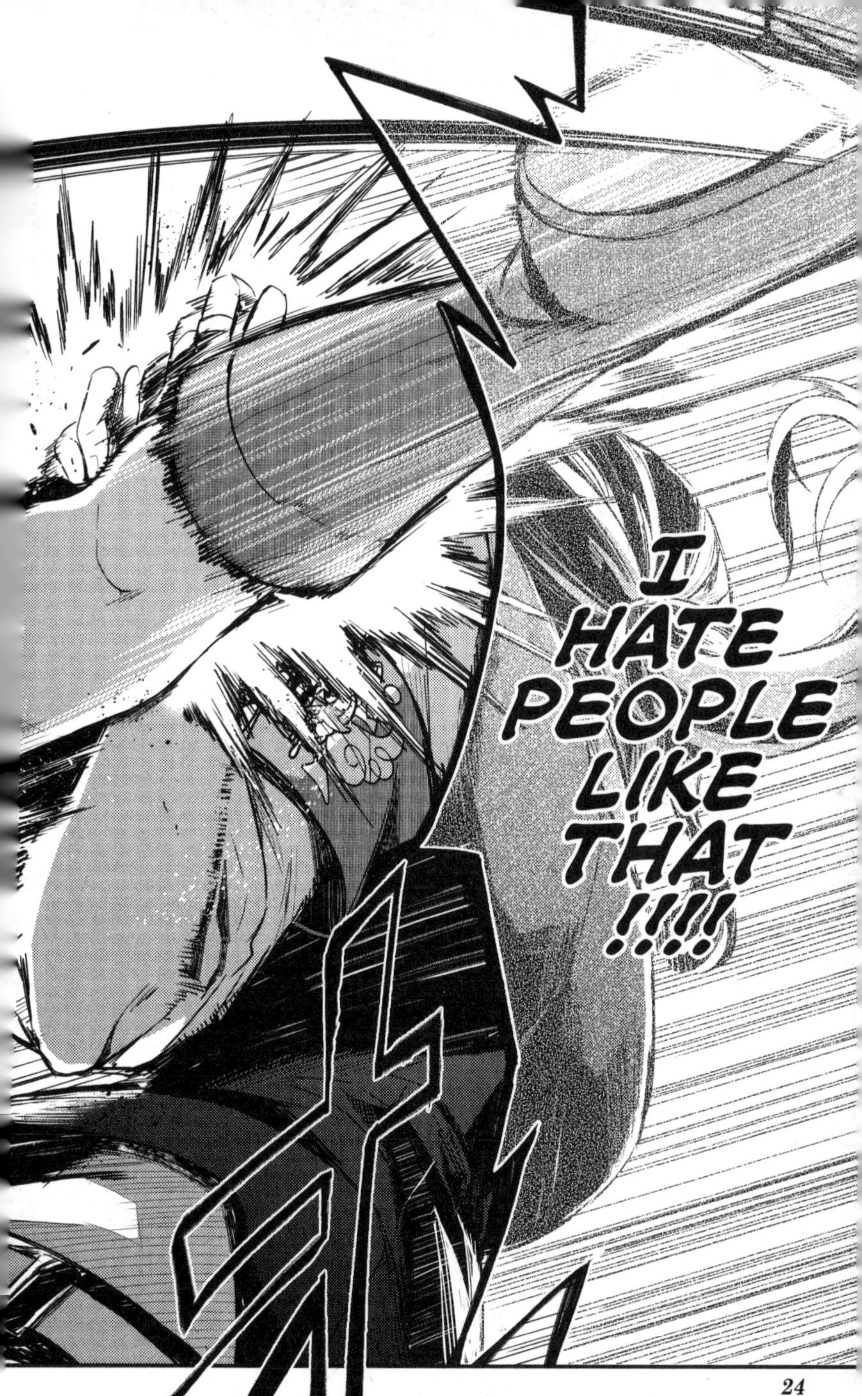
I HATE PEOPLE LIKE THAT !!!!

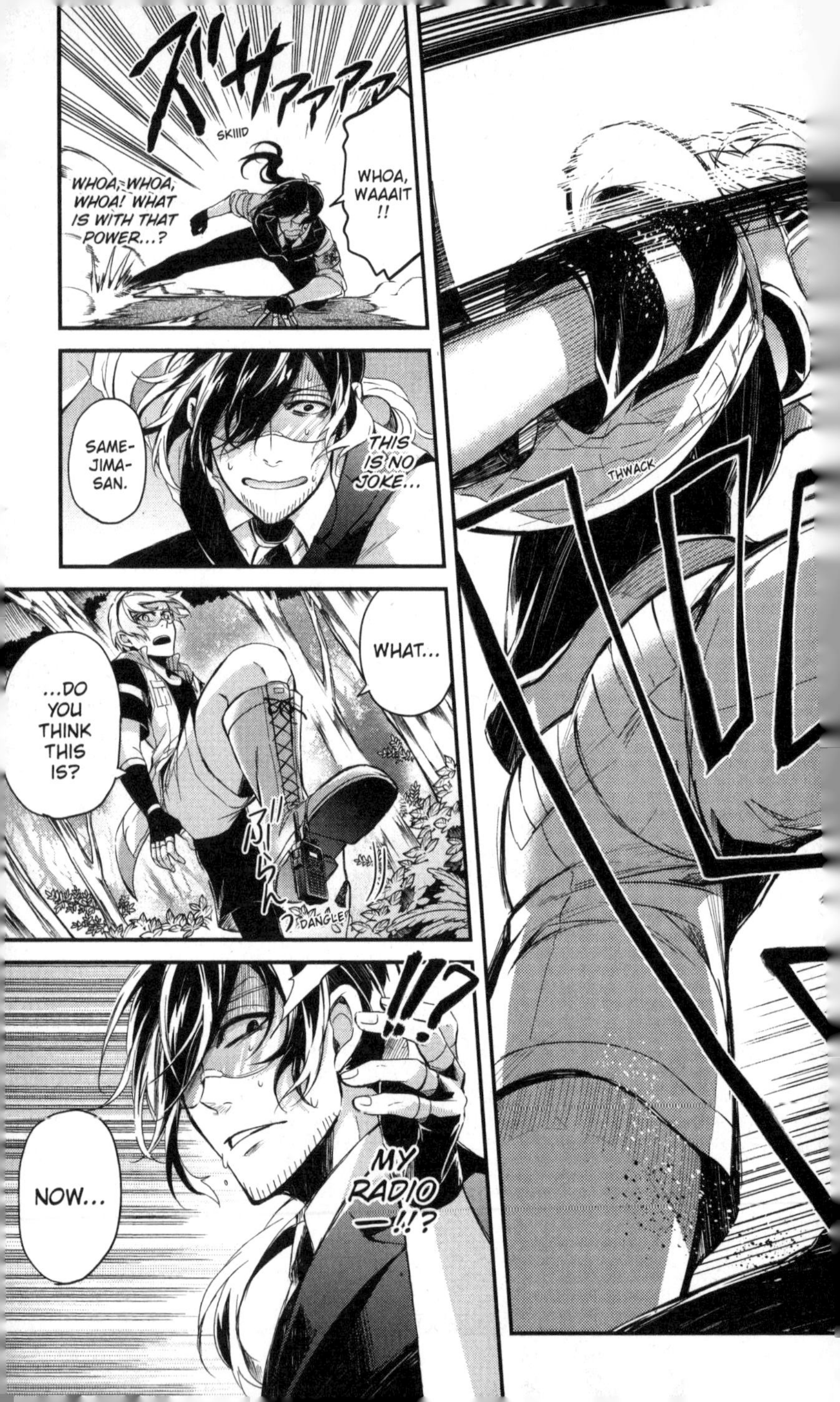
THWACK
ズサァァァ
SKIIID
WHOA, WAAAIT !!
WHOA, WHOA, WHOA! WHAT IS WITH THAT POWER...?
THIS IS NO JOKE...
SAME-JIMA-SAN.
WHAT...
...DO YOU THINK THIS IS?
ぶらん
DANGLE
!!?
MY RADIO —!!?
NOW...

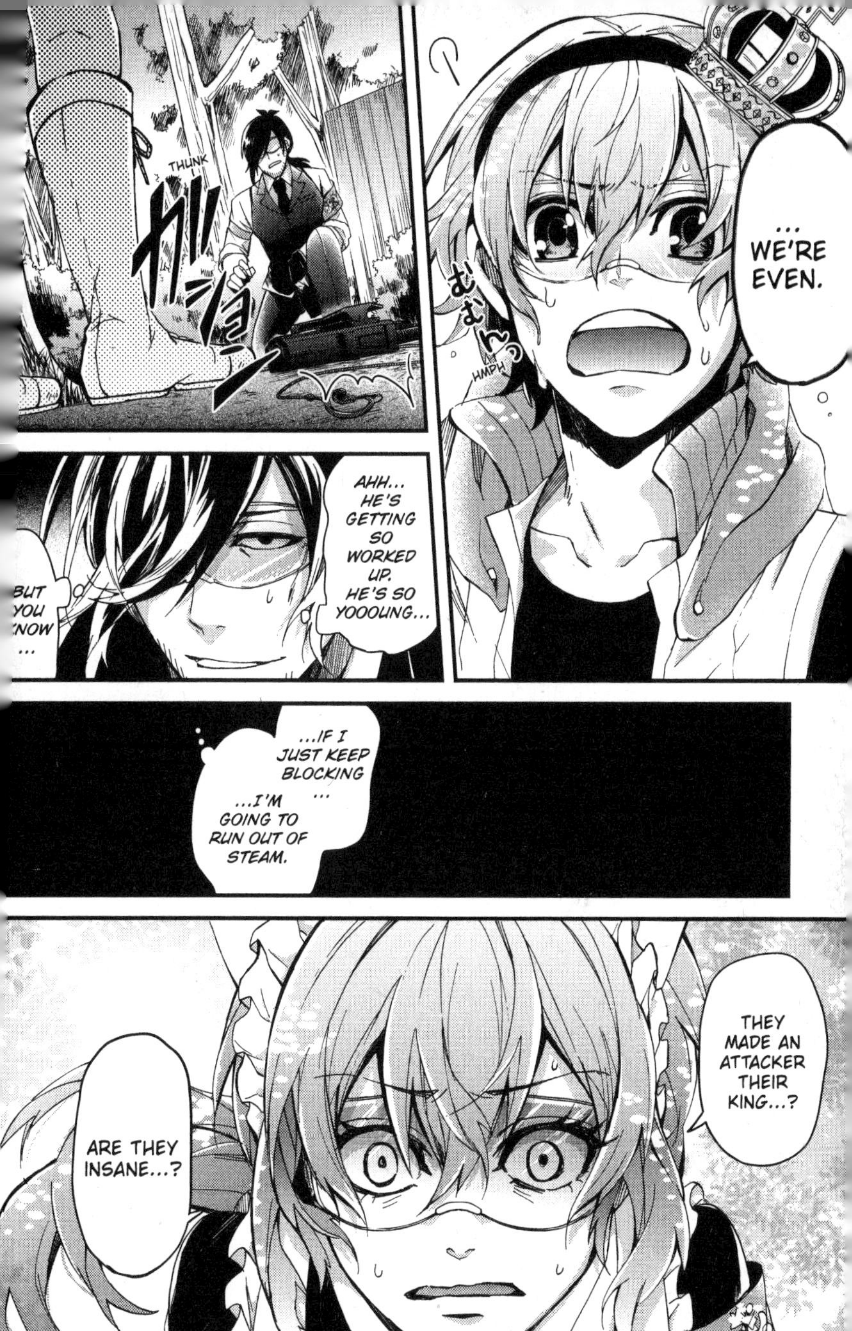

... WE'RE EVEN.
むむ〜っ
HMPH
ガション
THUNK
AHH... HE'S GETTING SO WORKED UP. HE'S SO YOOOUNG...
BUT YOU KNOW ...
...IF I JUST KEEP BLOCKING ...
...I'M GOING TO RUN OUT OF STEAM.
THEY MADE AN ATTACKER THEIR KING...?
ARE THEY INSANE...?

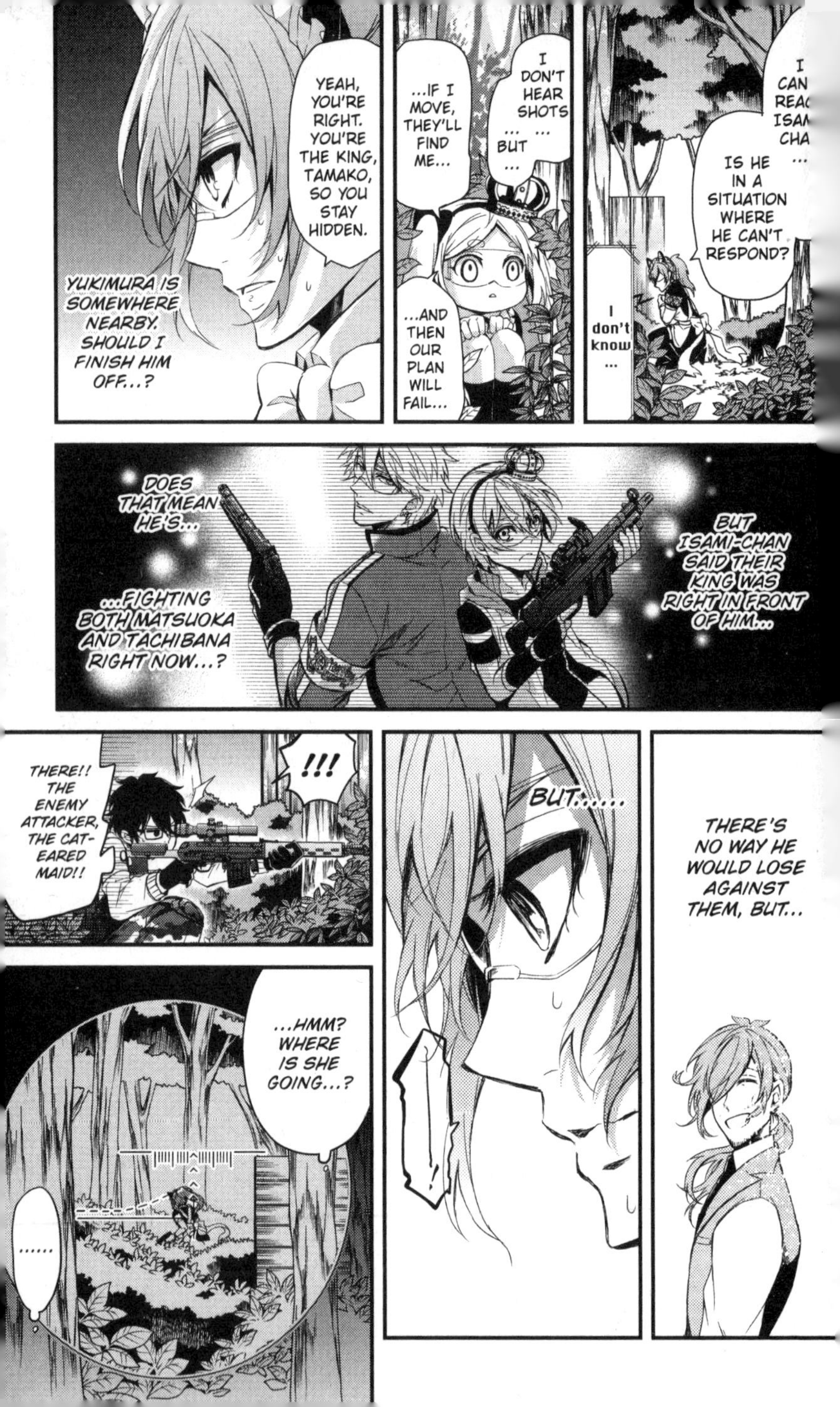
I CAN REAC ISAM CHA ...
IS HE IN A SITUATION WHERE HE CAN'T RESPOND?
I don't know ...
I DON'T HEAR SHOTS ... ... BUT ...
...IF I MOVE, THEY'LL FIND ME...
...AND THEN OUR PLAN WILL FAIL...
YEAH, YOU'RE RIGHT. YOU'RE THE KING, TAMAKO, SO YOU STAY HIDDEN.
YUKIMURA IS SOMEWHERE NEARBY. SHOULD I FINISH HIM OFF...?
BUT ISAMI-CHAN SAID THEIR KING WAS RIGHT IN FRONT OF HIM...
DOES THAT MEAN HE'S...
...FIGHTING BOTH MATSUOKA AND TACHIBANA RIGHT NOW...?
THERE'S NO WAY HE WOULD LOSE AGAINST THEM, BUT...
BUT......
!
!!!
THERE!! THE ENEMY ATTACKER, THE CAT-EARED MAID!!
...HMM? WHERE IS SHE GOING...?
......

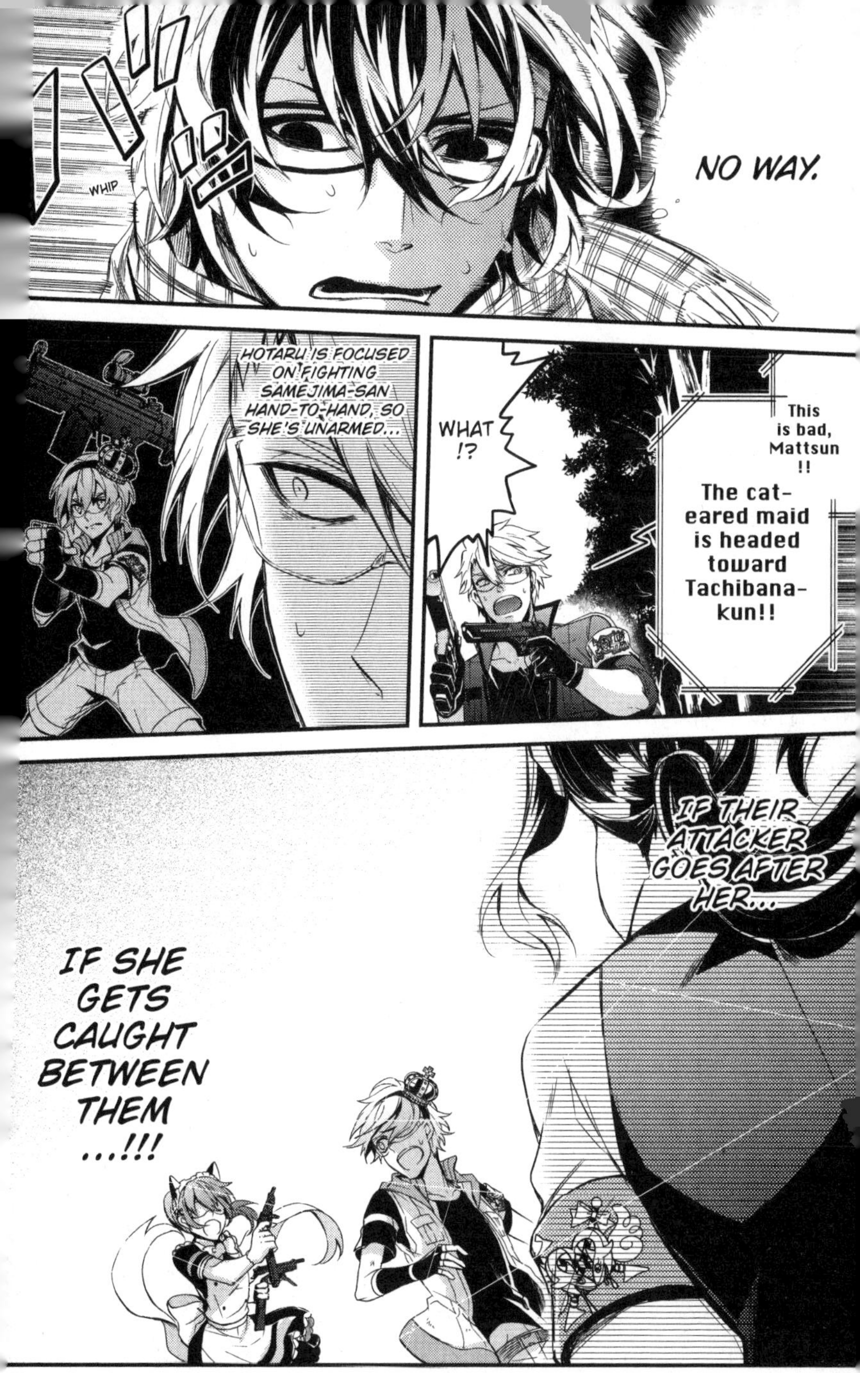

NO WAY.
WHIP
This is bad, Mattsun !!
The cat-eared maid is headed toward Tachibana-kun!!
WHAT !?
HOTARU IS FOCUSED ON FIGHTING SAMEJIMA-SAN HAND-TO-HAND, SO SHE'S UNARMED...
IF THEIR ATTACKER GOES AFTER HER...
IF SHE GETS CAUGHT BETWEEN THEM ...!!!

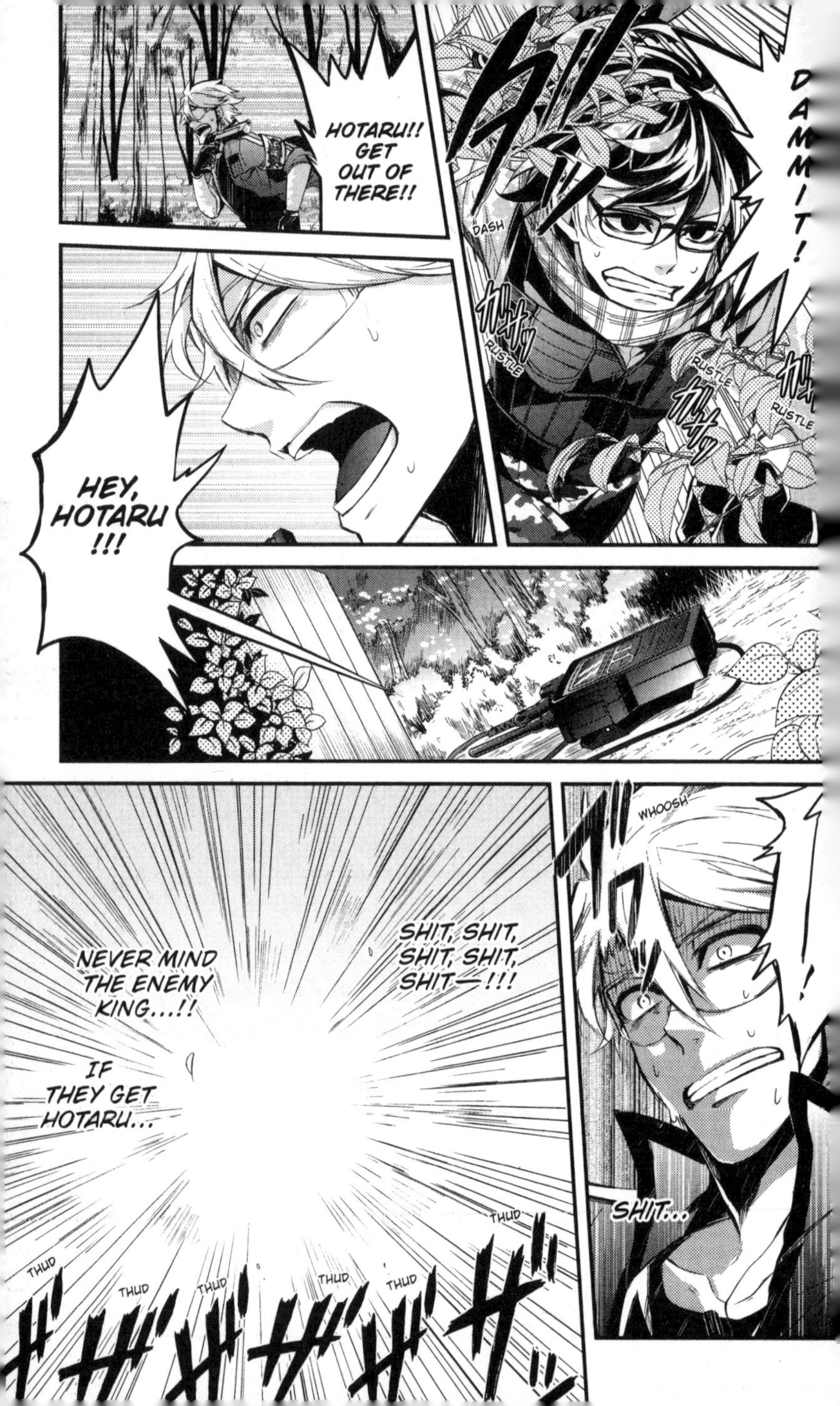
DAMMIT!
DASH
RUSTLE
RUSTLE
RUSTLE
HOTARU!! GET OUT OF THERE!!
HEY, HOTARU!!!
WHOOSH
SHIT...
SHIT, SHIT, SHIT, SHIT, SHIT—!!!
NEVER MIND THE ENEMY KING...!!
IF THEY GET HOTARU...
THUD
THUD
THUD
THUD
THUD
THUD

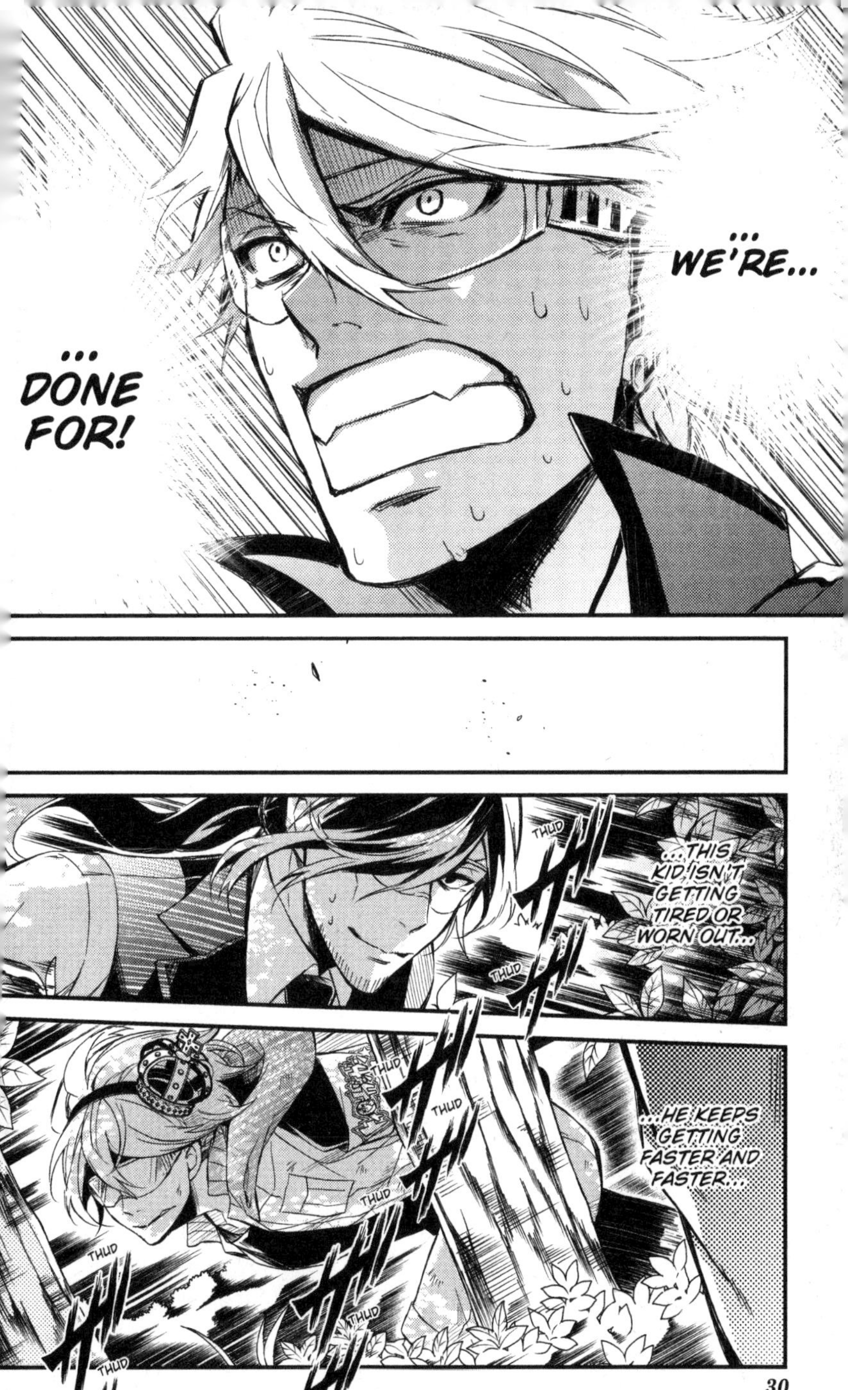
...WE'RE...
...DONE FOR!
THUD
...THIS KID ISN'T GETTING TIRED OR WORN OUT...
THUD
THUD
THUD
...HE KEEPS GETTING FASTER AND FASTER...
THUD
THUD
THUD
THUD

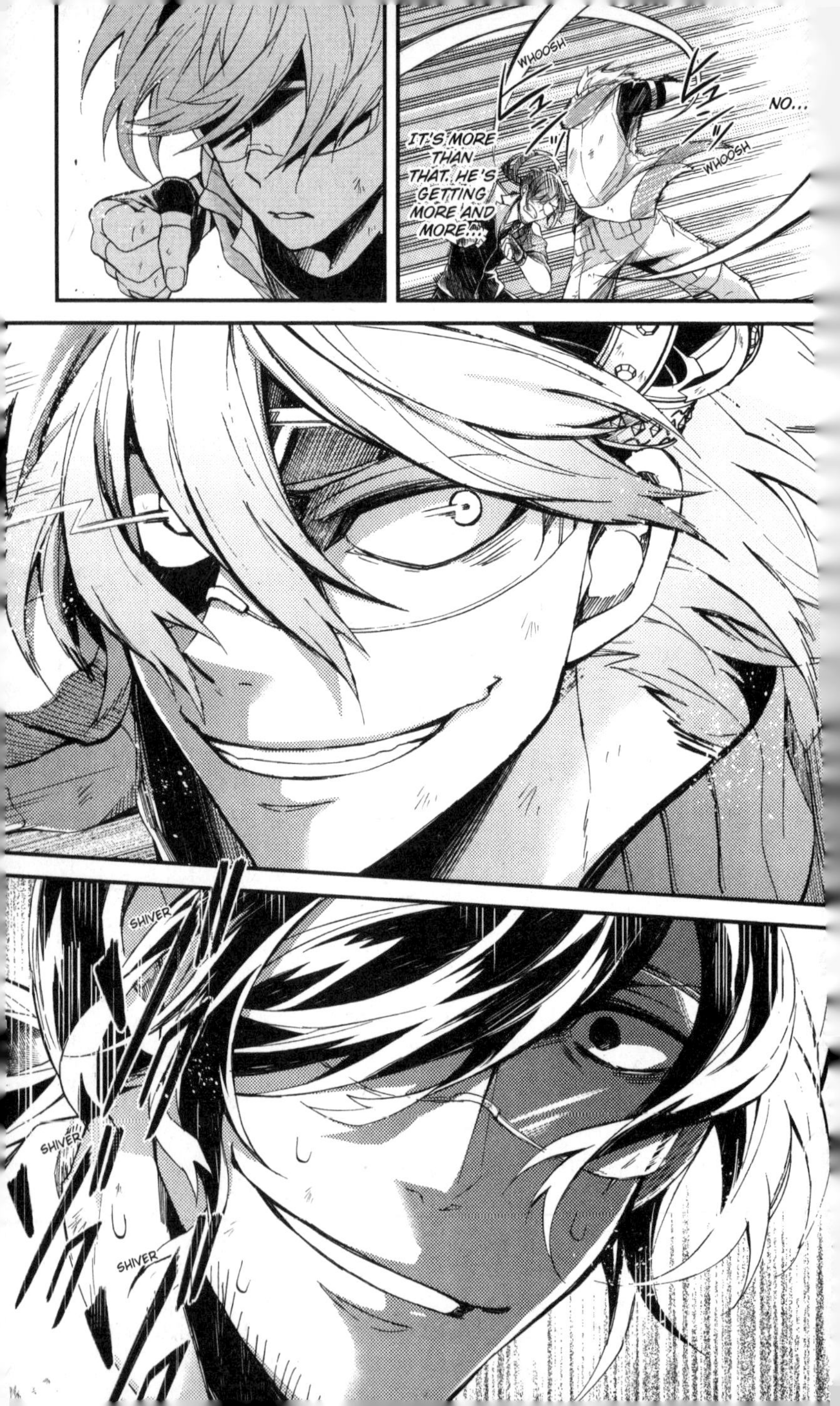
WHOOSH
NO...
WHOOSH
IT'S MORE THAN THAT. HE'S GETTING MORE AND MORE...
SHIVER
SHIVER
SHIVER

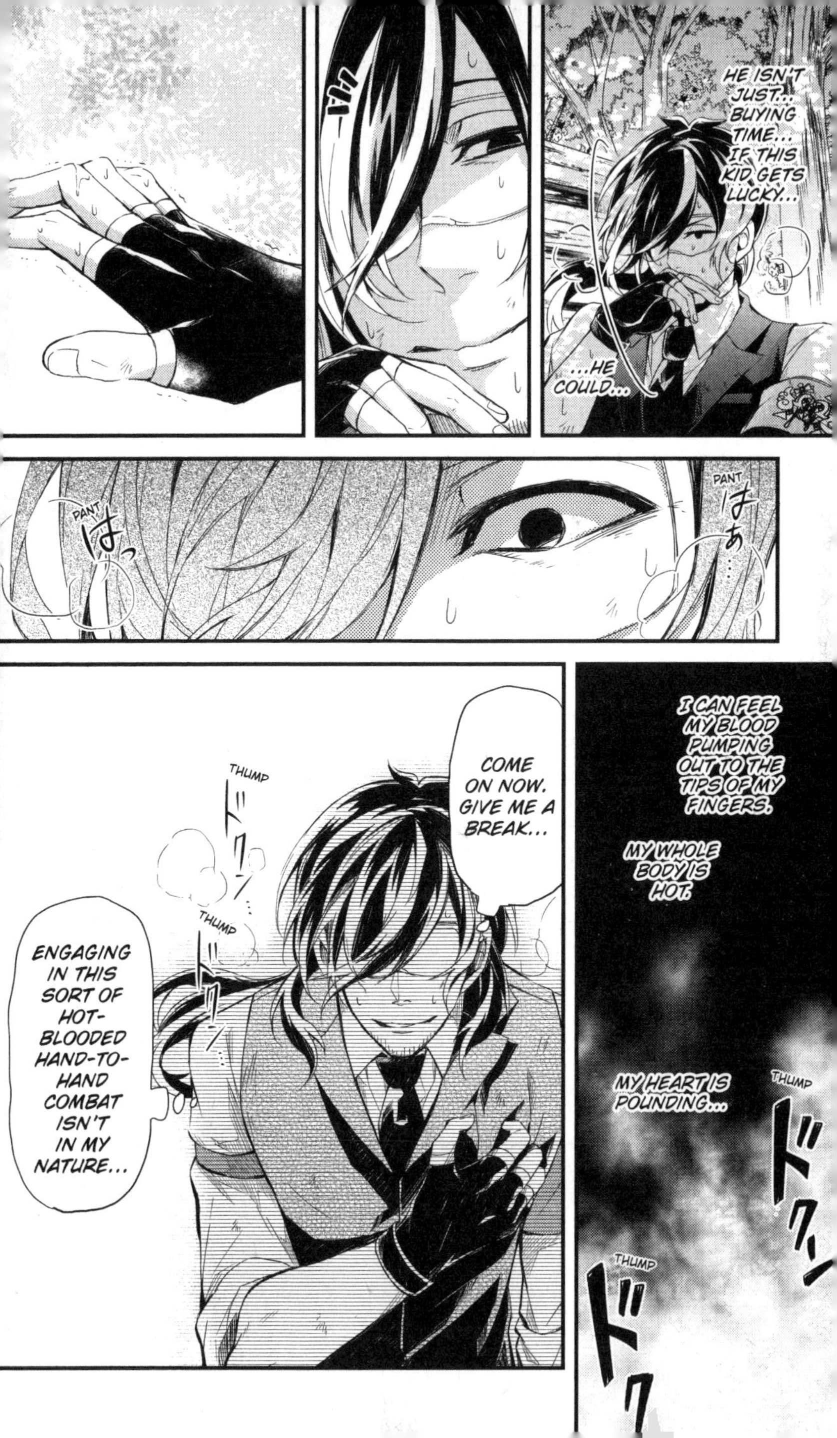
HE ISN'T JUST... BUYING TIME... IF THIS KID GETS LUCKY...
...HE COULD...
PANT
はぁ…
PANT
はっ
I CAN FEEL MY BLOOD PUMPING OUT TO THE TIPS OF MY FINGERS.
MY WHOLE BODY IS HOT.
MY HEART IS POUNDING...
THUMP
ドクン
THUMP
ドク
COME ON NOW. GIVE ME A BREAK...
THUMP
ドクン…
THUMP
ドクン…
ENGAGING IN THIS SORT OF HOT-BLOODED HAND-TO-HAND COMBAT ISN'T IN MY NATURE...

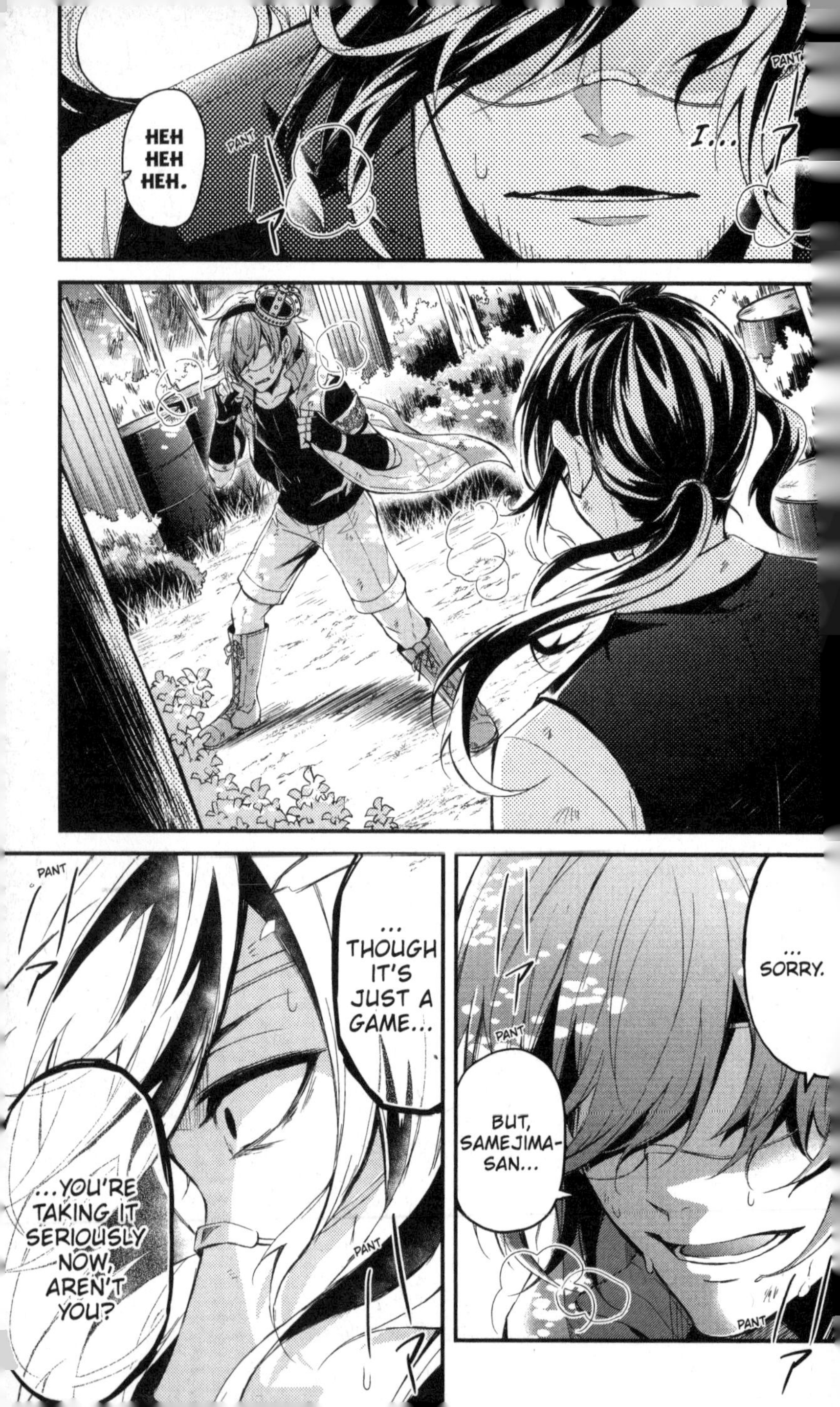
PANT
I...
PANT
HEH HEH HEH.
...SORRY.
PANT
BUT, SAMEJIMA-SAN...
PANT
...THOUGH IT'S JUST A GAME...
PANT
...YOU'RE TAKING IT SERIOUSLY NOW, AREN'T YOU?
PANT

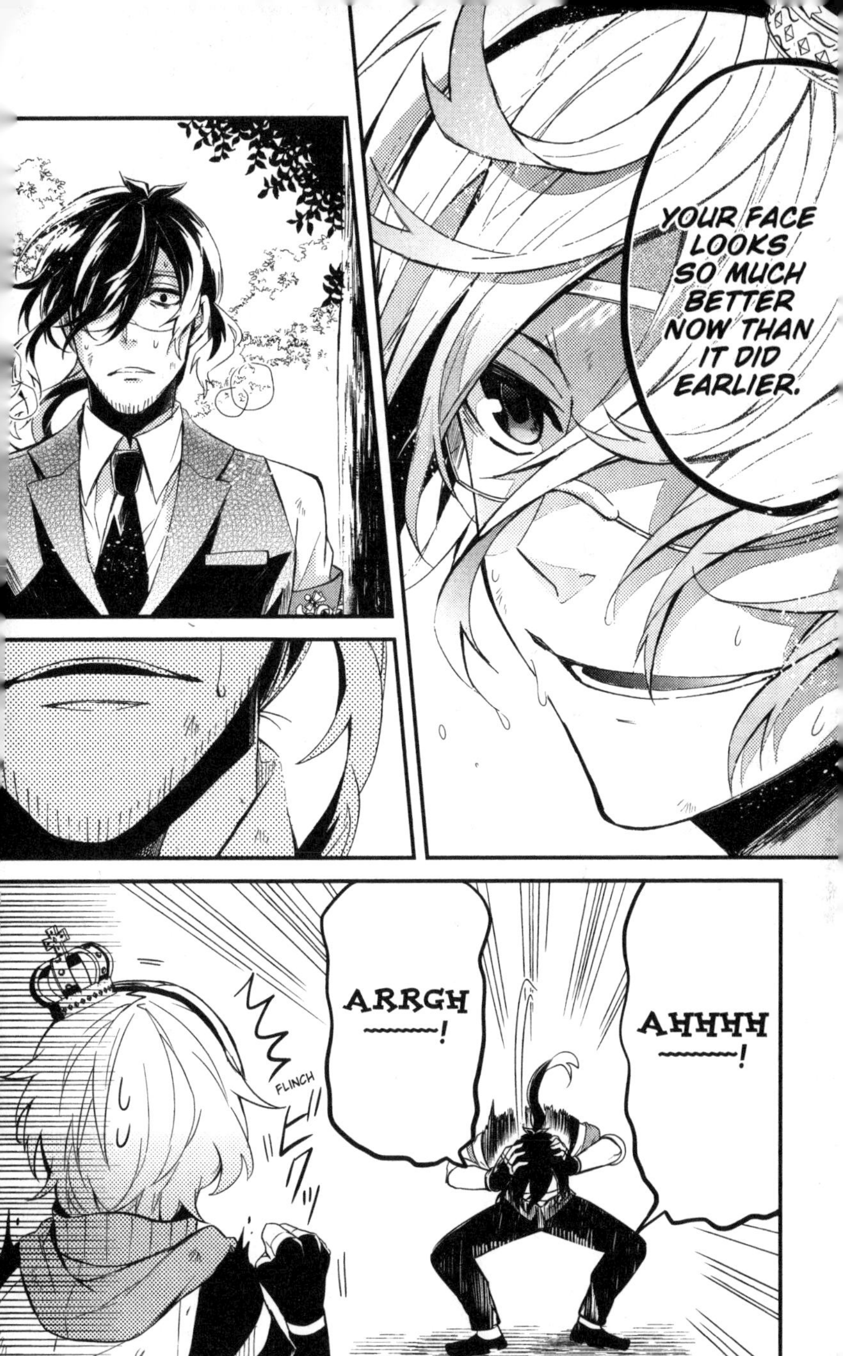
YOUR FACE LOOKS SO MUCH BETTER NOW THAN IT DID EARLIER.
AHHHH ————!
ARRGH ————!
FLINCH

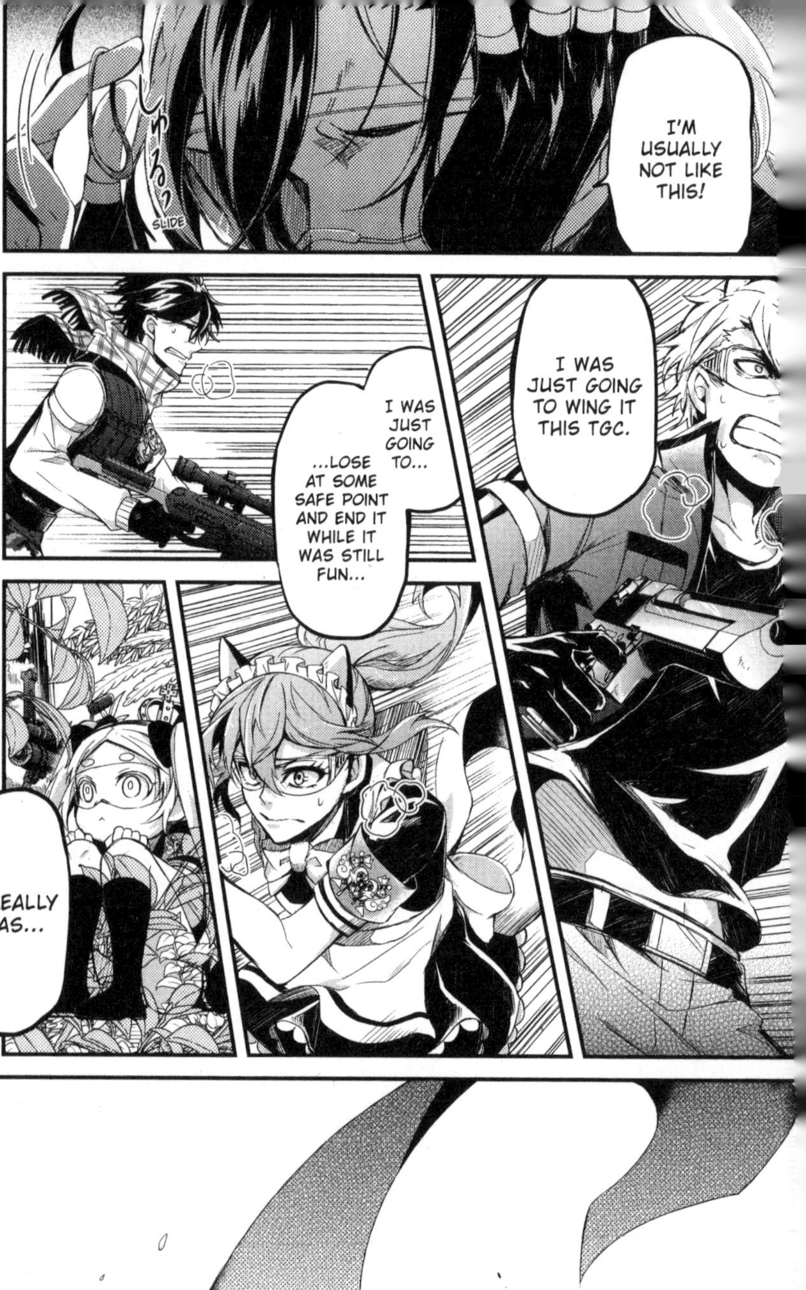
I'M USUALLY NOT LIKE THIS!
SLIDE
I WAS JUST GOING TO WING IT THIS TGC.
I WAS JUST GOING TO...
...LOSE AT SOME SAFE POINT AND END IT WHILE IT WAS STILL FUN...
I REALLY WAS...

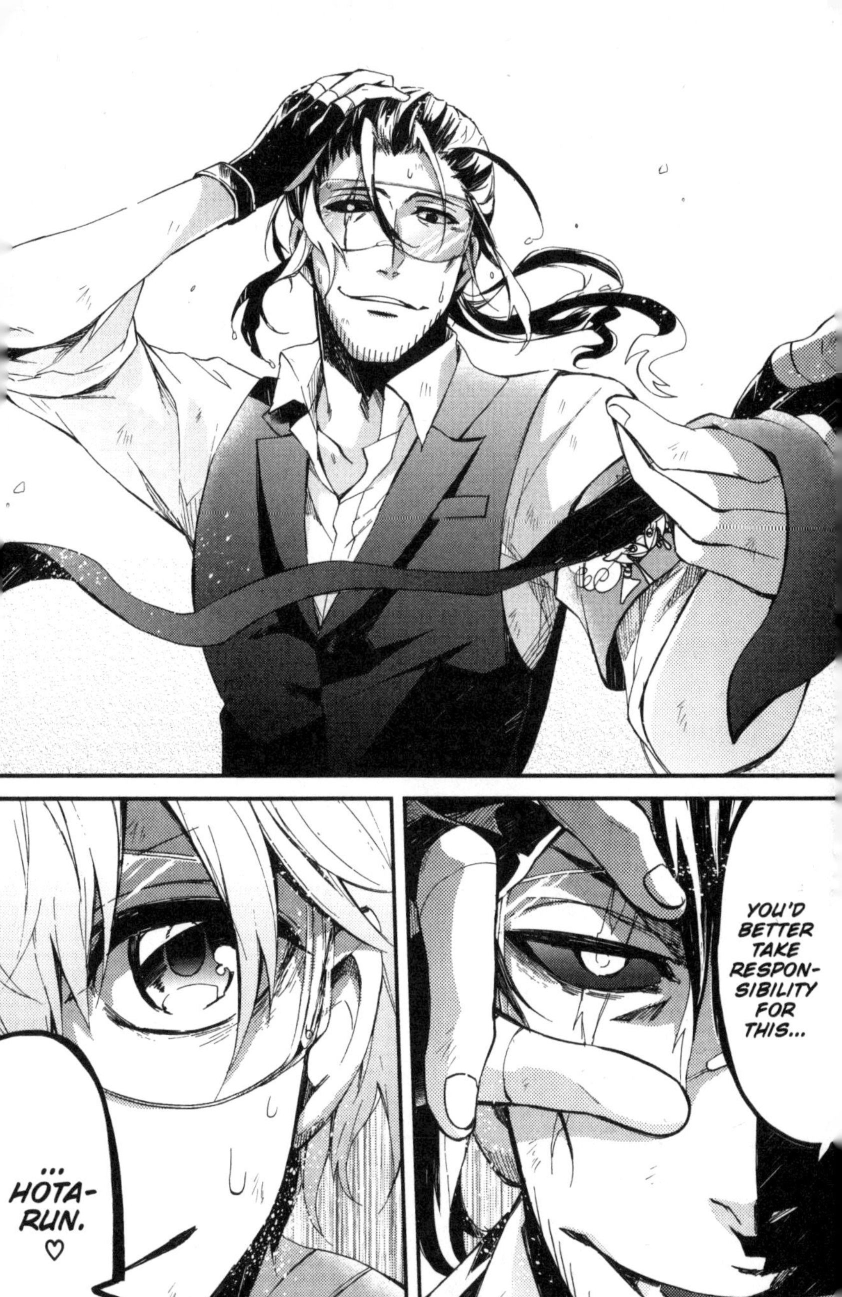
YOU'D BETTER TAKE RESPON-SIBILITY FOR THIS...
... HÖTA-RUN. ♡

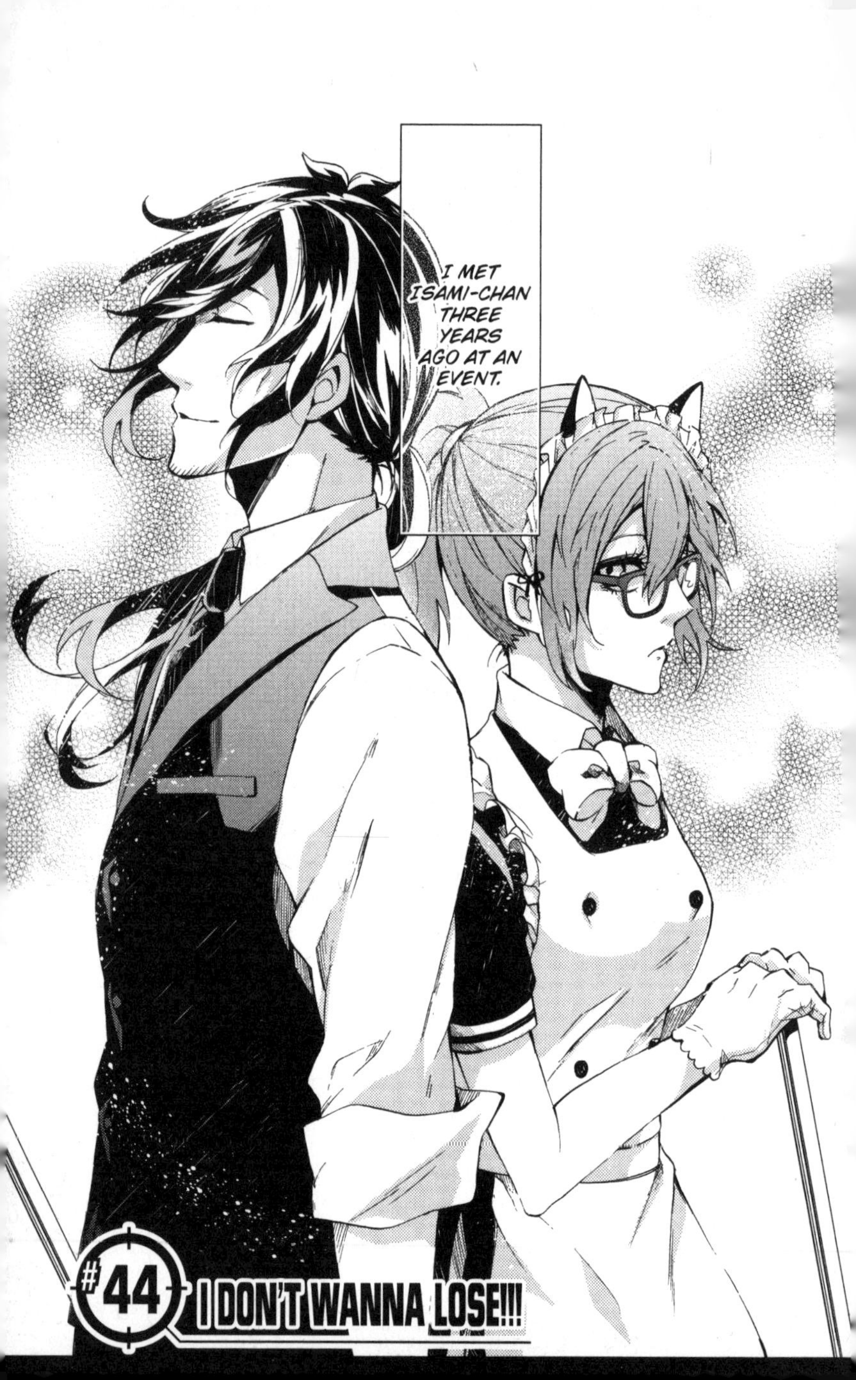
I MET ISAMI-CHAN THREE YEARS AGO AT AN EVENT.
#44 I DON'T WANNA LOSE!!!

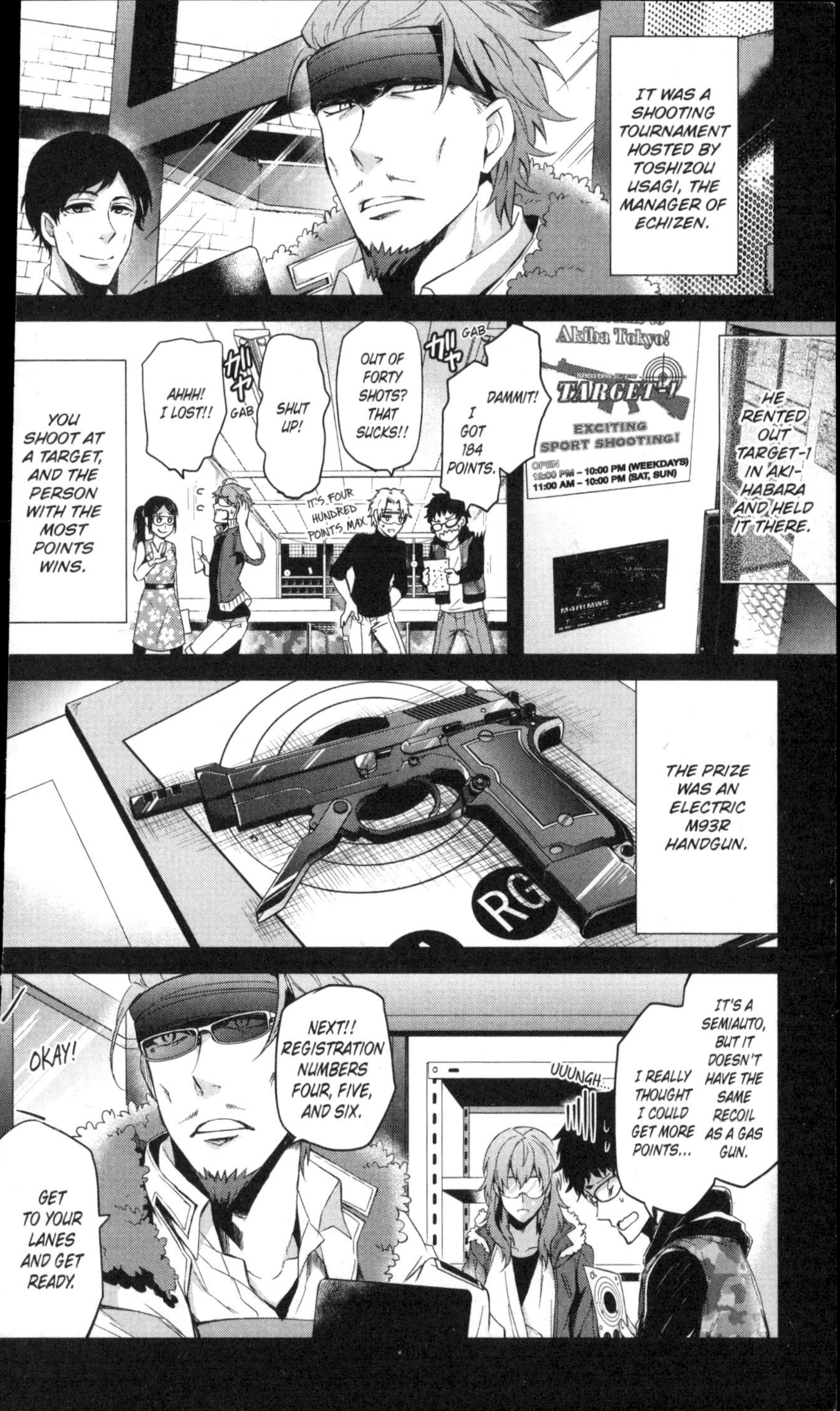
IT WAS A SHOOTING TOURNAMENT HOSTED BY TOSHIZOU USAGI, THE MANAGER OF ECHIZEN.
HE RENTED OUT TARGET-1 IN AKIHABARA AND HELD IT THERE.
Akiba Tokyo!
TARGET-1
EXCITING SPORT SHOOTING!
OPEN 12:00 PM – 10:00 PM (WEEKDAYS) 11:00 AM – 10:00 PM (SAT, SUN)
DAMMIT! I GOT 184 POINTS.
GAB
OUT OF FORTY SHOTS? THAT SUCKS!!
IT'S FOUR HUNDRED POINTS MAX.
SHUT UP!
GAB
AHHH! I LOST!!
YOU SHOOT AT A TARGET, AND THE PERSON WITH THE MOST POINTS WINS.
THE PRIZE WAS AN ELECTRIC M93R HANDGUN.
RG
IT'S A SEMIAUTO, BUT IT DOESN'T HAVE THE SAME RECOIL AS A GAS GUN.
I REALLY THOUGHT I COULD GET MORE POINTS...
UUUNGH...
NEXT!! REGISTRATION NUMBERS FOUR, FIVE, AND SIX.
OKAY!
GET TO YOUR LANES AND GET READY.

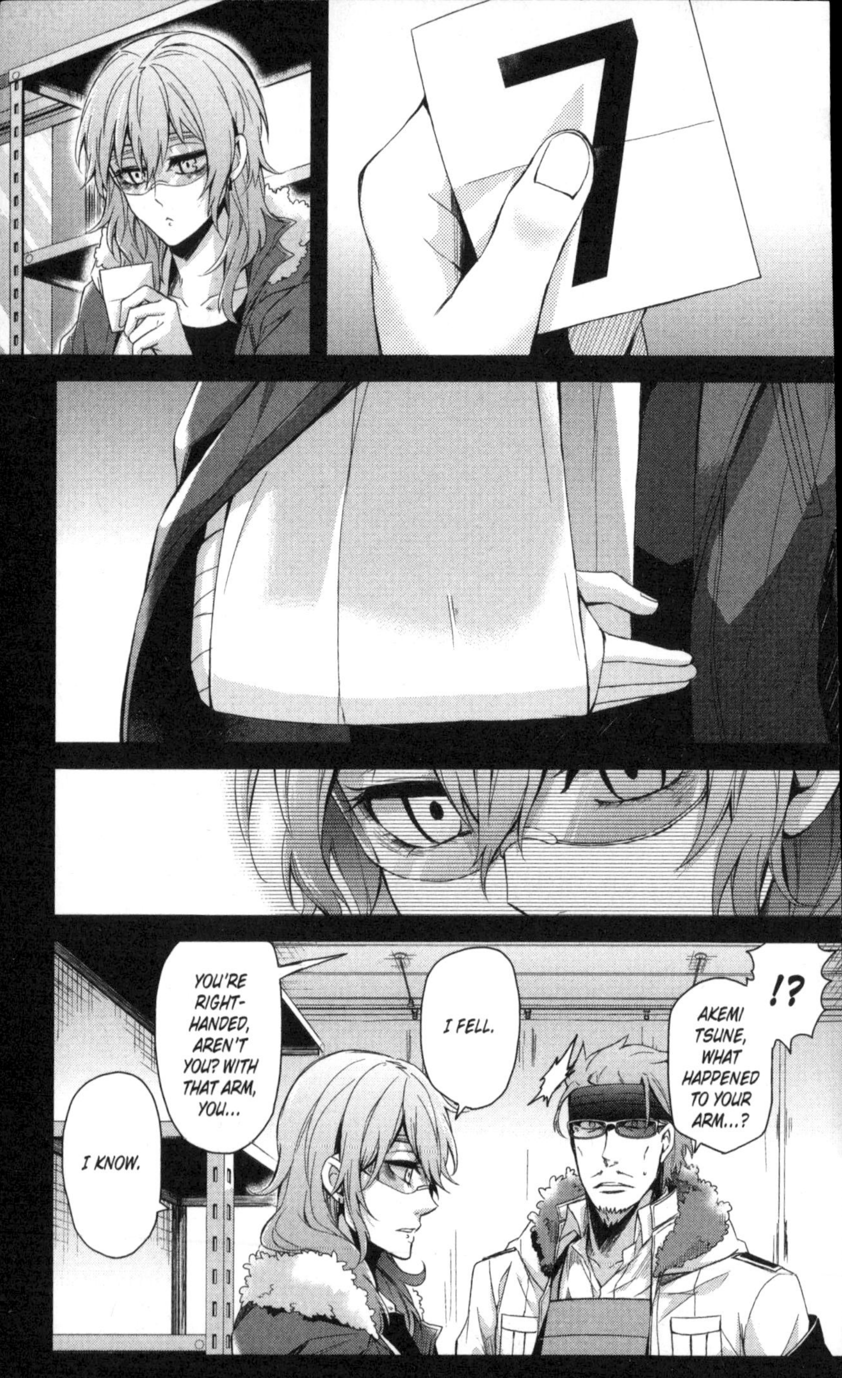
7
!?
AKEMI TSUNE, WHAT HAPPENED TO YOUR ARM...?
I FELL.
YOU'RE RIGHT-HANDED, AREN'T YOU? WITH THAT ARM, YOU...
I KNOW.

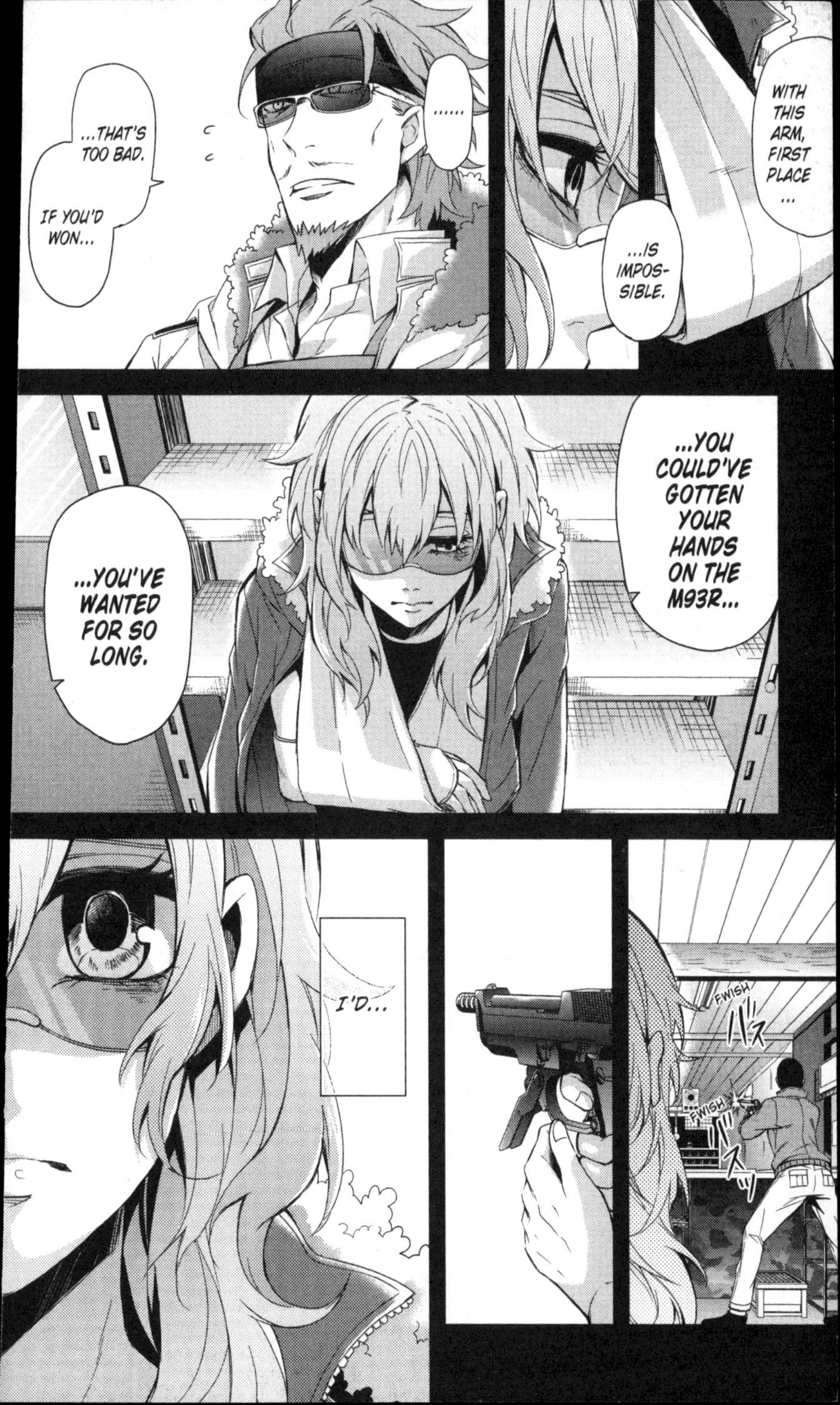
WITH THIS ARM, FIRST PLACE ...
...IS IMPOSSIBLE.
......
...THAT'S TOO BAD.
IF YOU'D WON...
...YOU COULD'VE GOTTEN YOUR HANDS ON THE M93R...
...YOU'VE WANTED FOR SO LONG.
FWISH
FWISH
I'D...

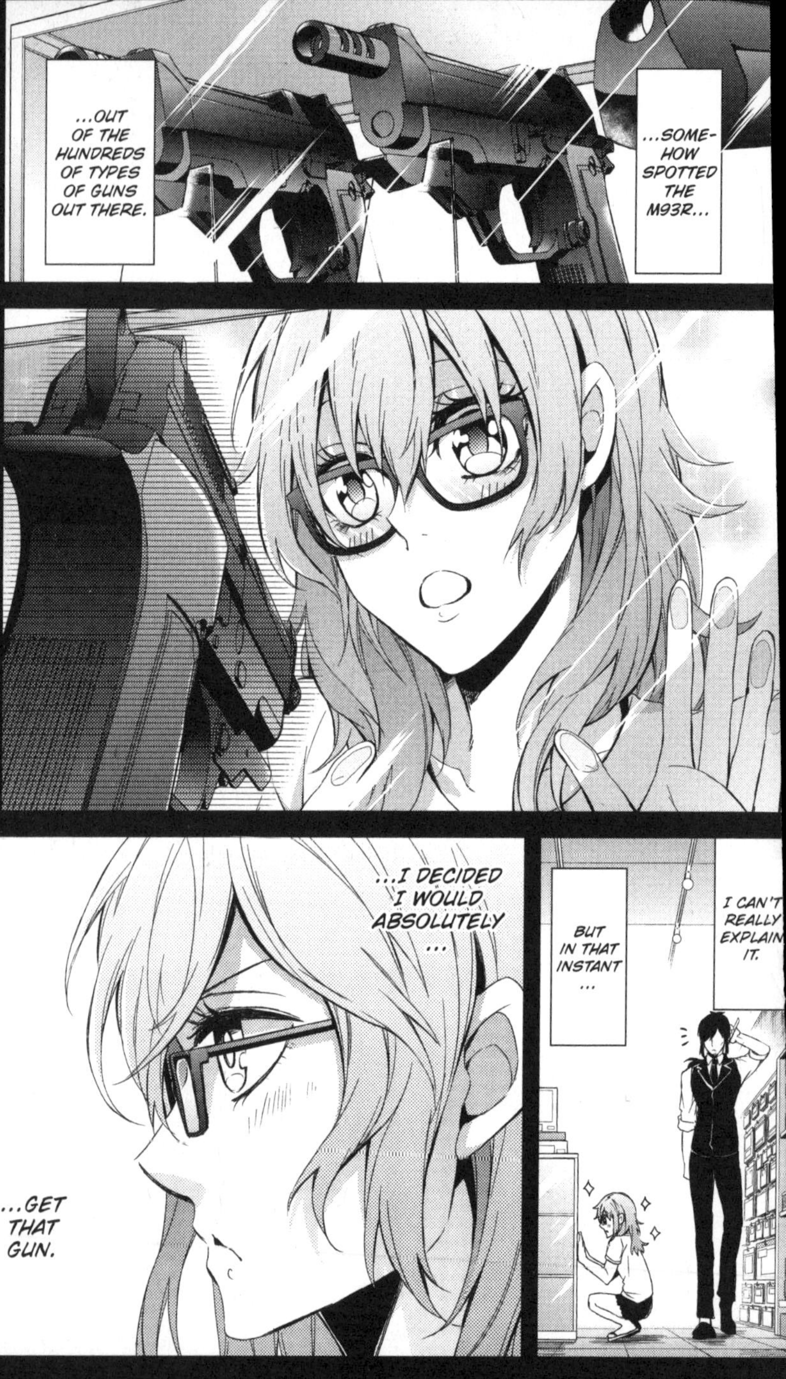
...SOME-HOW SPOTTED THE M93R...
...OUT OF THE HUNDREDS OF TYPES OF GUNS OUT THERE.
I CAN'T REALLY EXPLAIN IT.
BUT IN THAT INSTANT...
...I DECIDED I WOULD ABSOLUTELY...
...GET THAT GUN.

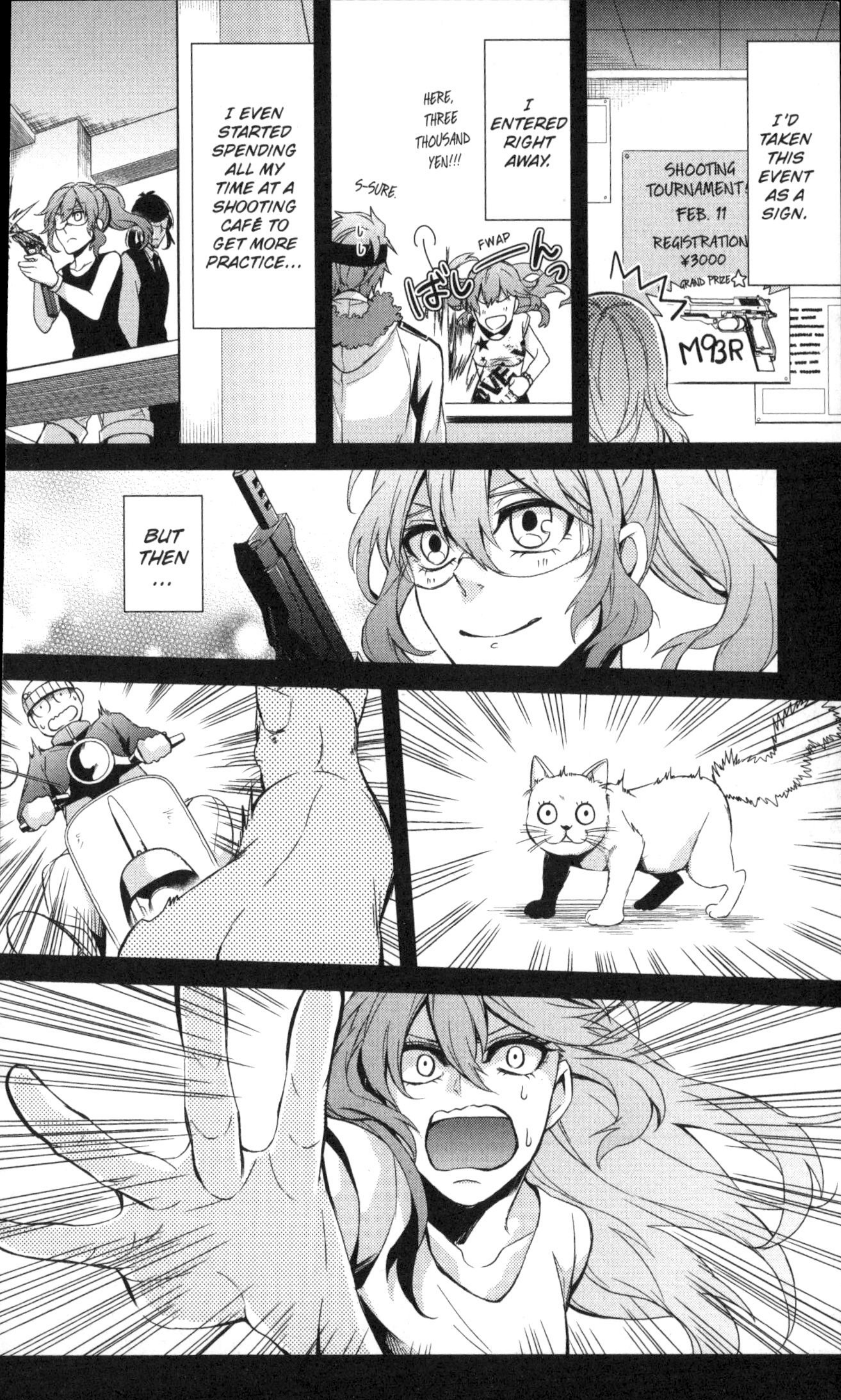
I'D TAKEN THIS EVENT AS A SIGN.
SHOOTING TOURNAMENT!
FEB. 11
REGISTRATION ¥3000
GRAND PRIZE☆
M93R
I ENTERED RIGHT AWAY.
HERE, THREE THOUSAND YEN!!!
FWAP
ばしーんっ
S-SURE.
I EVEN STARTED SPENDING ALL MY TIME AT A SHOOTING CAFÉ TO GET MORE PRACTICE...
BUT THEN ...

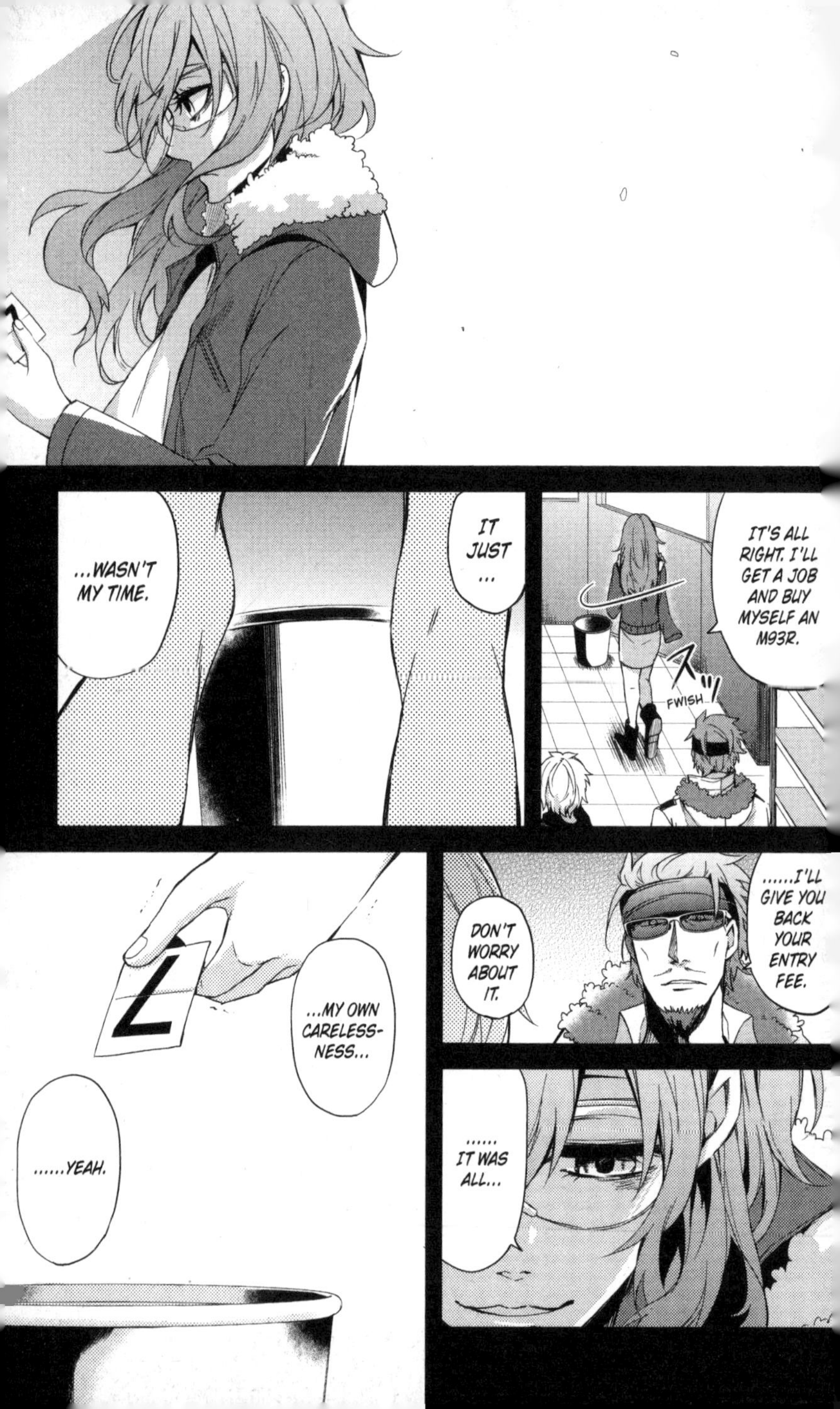
IT'S ALL RIGHT. I'LL GET A JOB AND BUY MYSELF AN M93R.
FWISH
IT JUST ...
...WASN'T MY TIME.
......I'LL GIVE YOU BACK YOUR ENTRY FEE.
DON'T WORRY ABOUT IT.
...... IT WAS ALL...
...MY OWN CARELESS-NESS...
......YEAH.

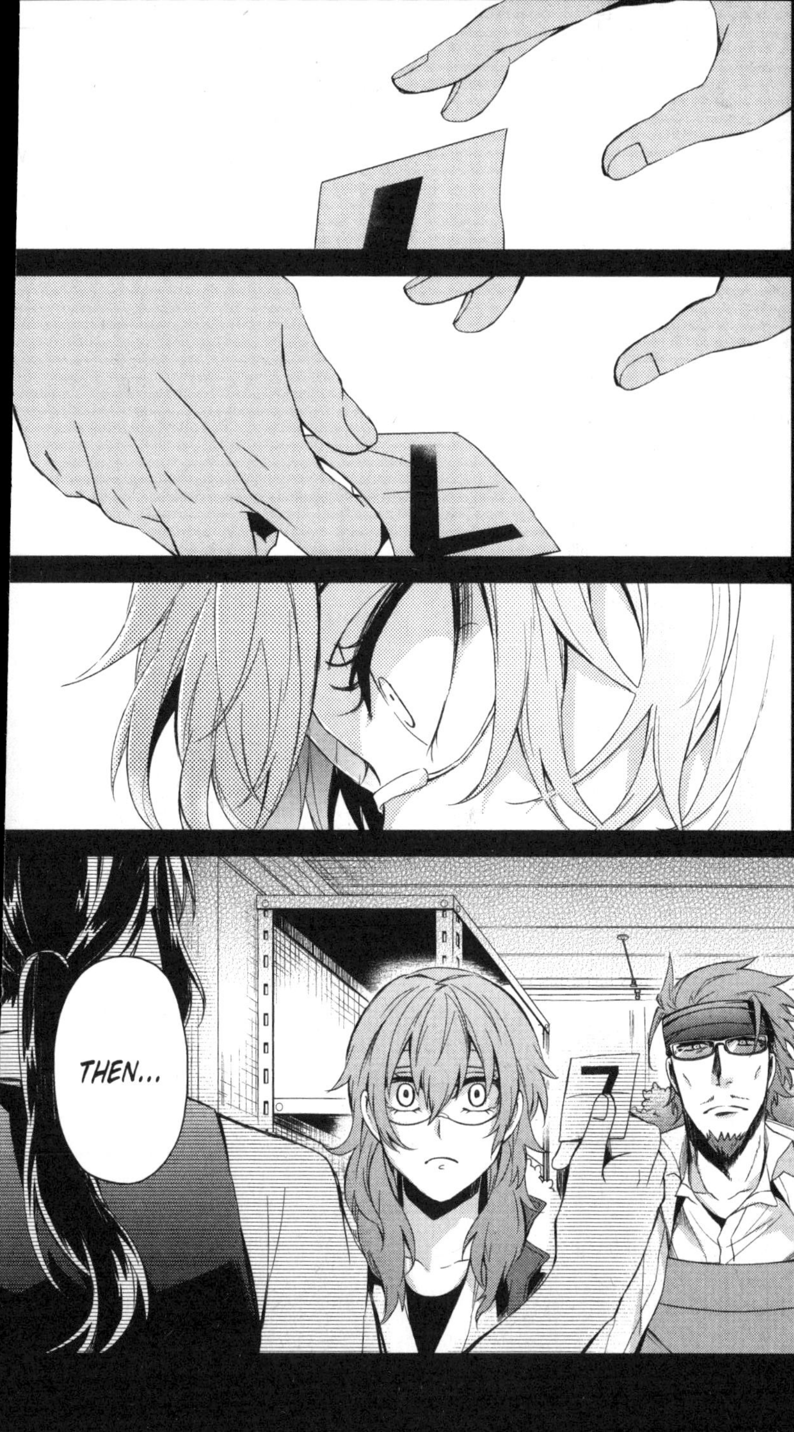
THEN...

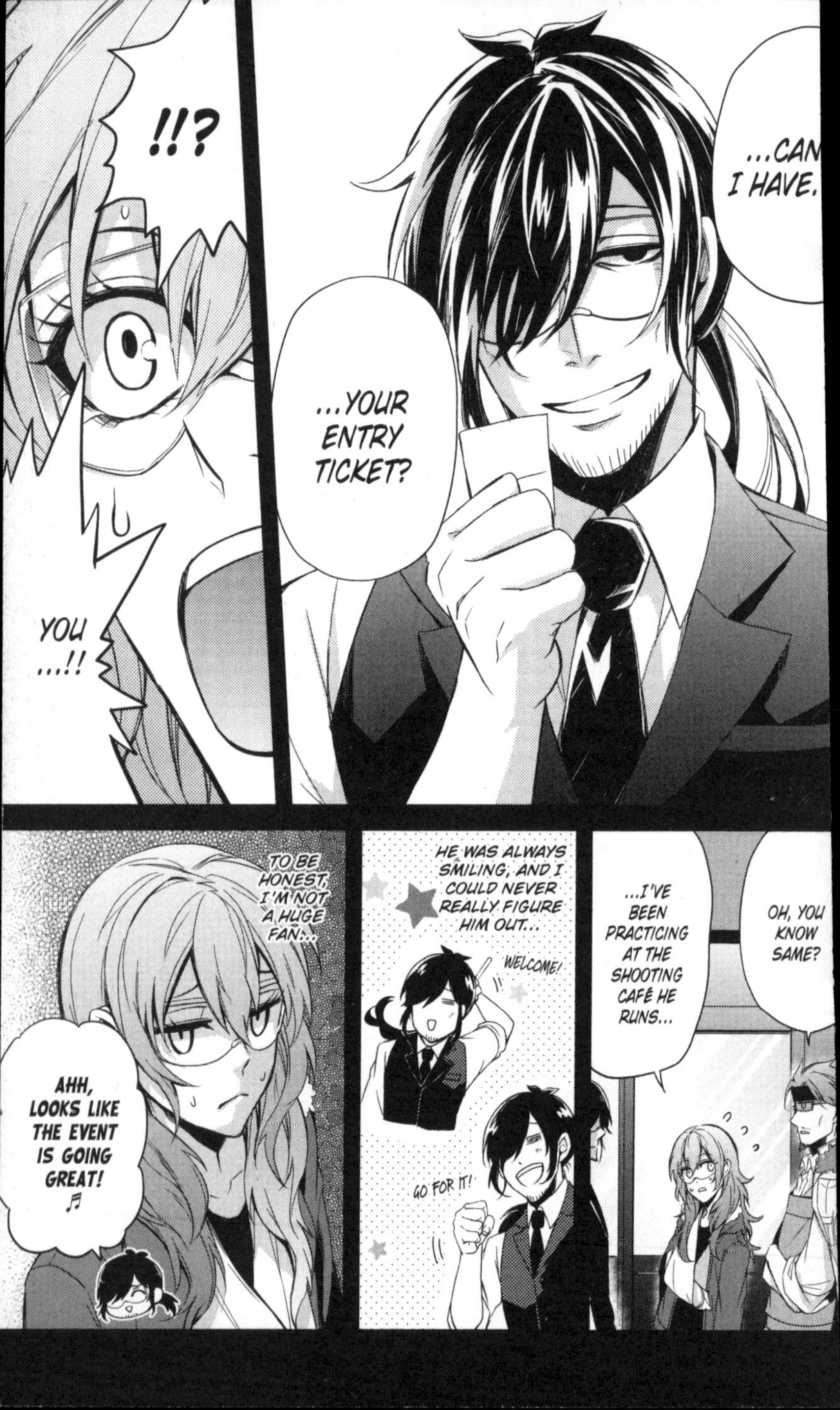
...CAN I HAVE.
...YOUR ENTRY TICKET?
!!?
YOU ...!!
OH, YOU KNOW SAME?
...I'VE BEEN PRACTICING AT THE SHOOTING CAFÉ HE RUNS...
HE WAS ALWAYS SMILING, AND I COULD NEVER REALLY FIGURE HIM OUT...
WELCOME!
GO FOR IT!
TO BE HONEST, I'M NOT A HUGE FAN...
AHH, LOOKS LIKE THE EVENT IS GOING GREAT! ♬

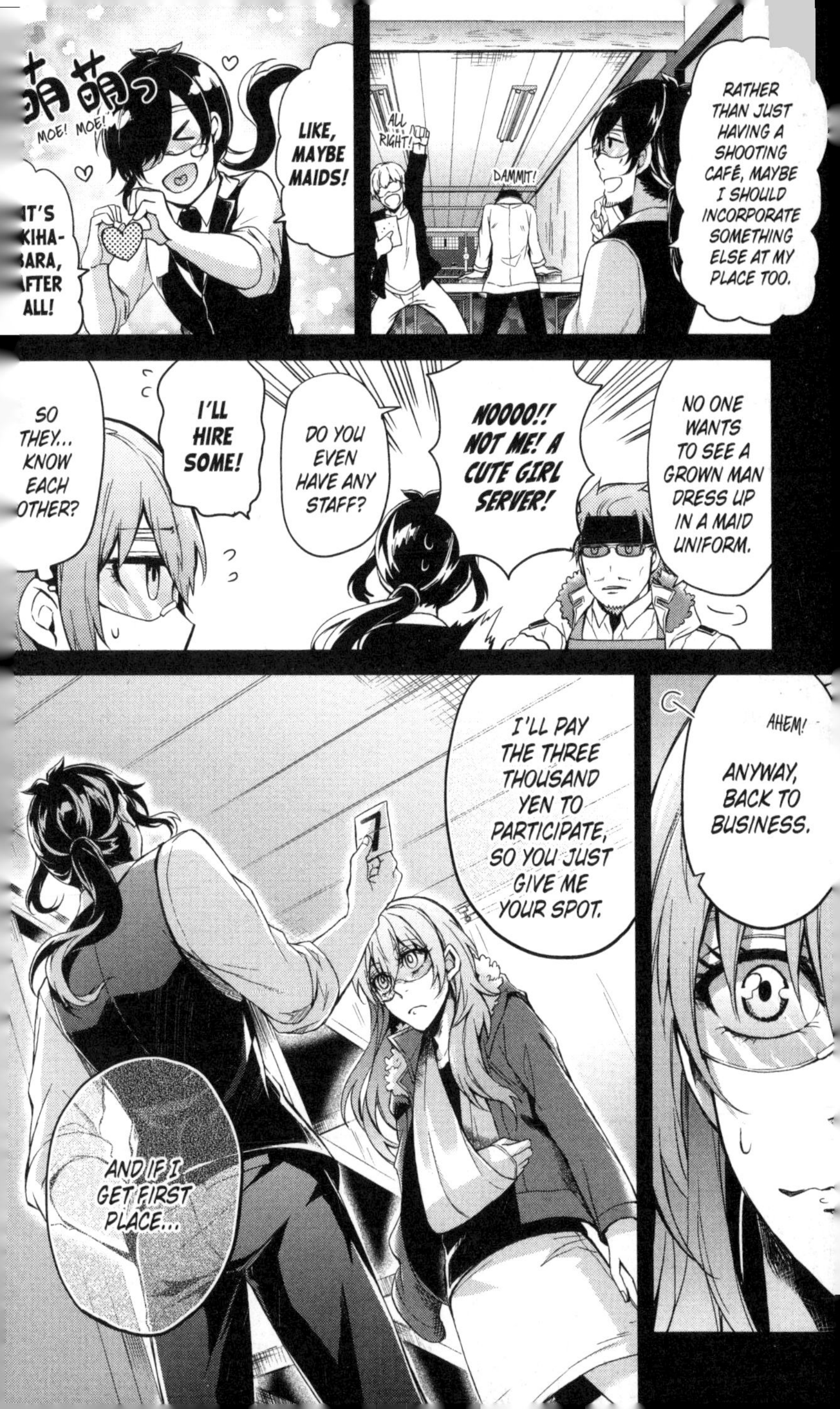
RATHER THAN JUST HAVING A SHOOTING CAFÉ, MAYBE I SHOULD INCORPORATE SOMETHING ELSE AT MY PLACE TOO.
DAMMIT!
ALL RIGHT!
LIKE, MAYBE MAIDS!
萌萌っ
MOE! MOE!
IT'S KIHA- BARA, FTER ALL!
NO ONE WANTS TO SEE A GROWN MAN DRESS UP IN A MAID UNIFORM.
NOOOO!! NOT ME! A CUTE GIRL SERVER!
DO YOU EVEN HAVE ANY STAFF?
I'LL HIRE SOME!
SO THEY... KNOW EACH OTHER?
AHEM!
ANYWAY, BACK TO BUSINESS.
I'LL PAY THE THREE THOUSAND YEN TO PARTICIPATE, SO YOU JUST GIVE ME YOUR SPOT.
AND IF I GET FIRST PLACE...

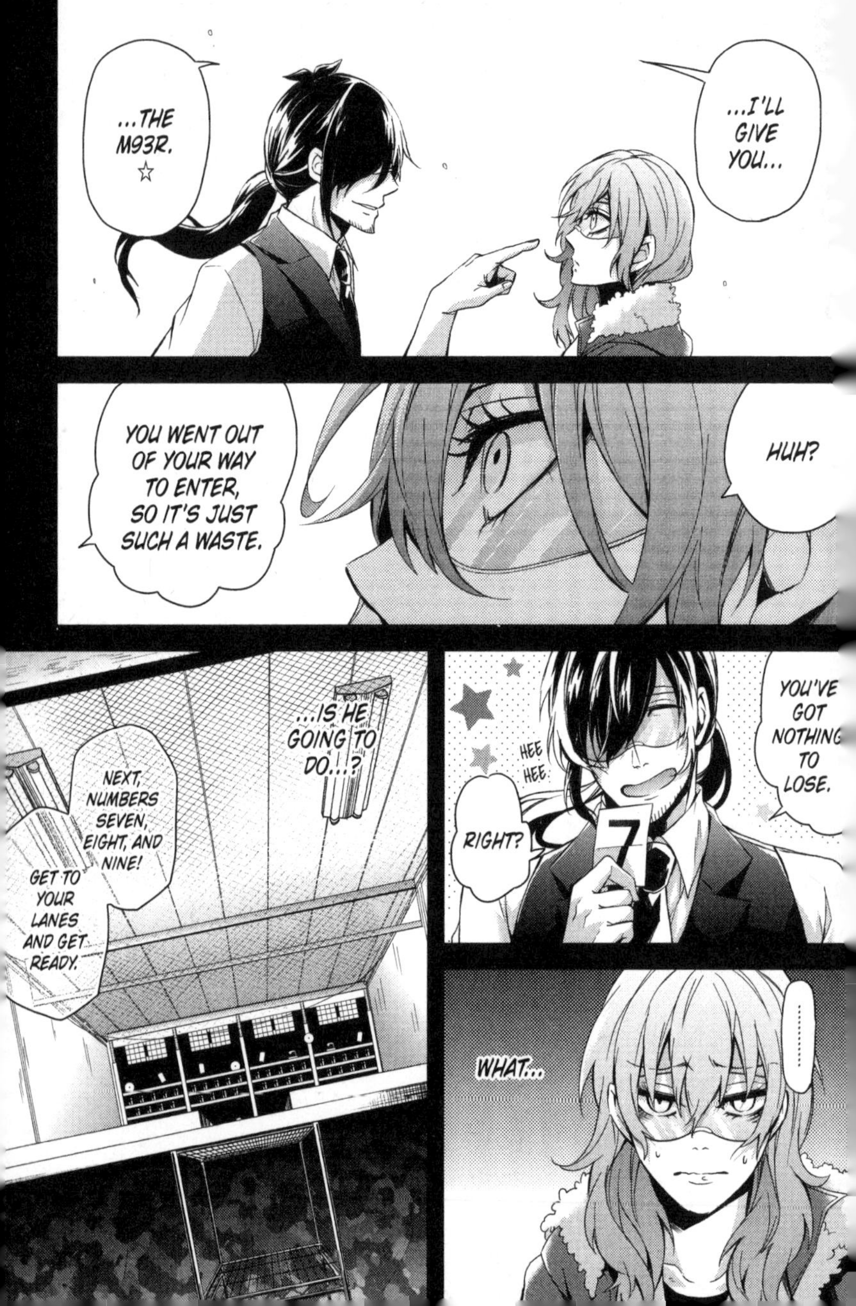
...I'LL GIVE YOU...
...THE M93R. ☆
HUH?
YOU WENT OUT OF YOUR WAY TO ENTER, SO IT'S JUST SUCH A WASTE.
YOU'VE GOT NOTHING TO LOSE.
HEE HEE
RIGHT?
......
WHAT...
...IS HE GOING TO DO...?
NEXT, NUMBERS SEVEN, EIGHT, AND NINE!
GET TO YOUR LANES AND GET READY.

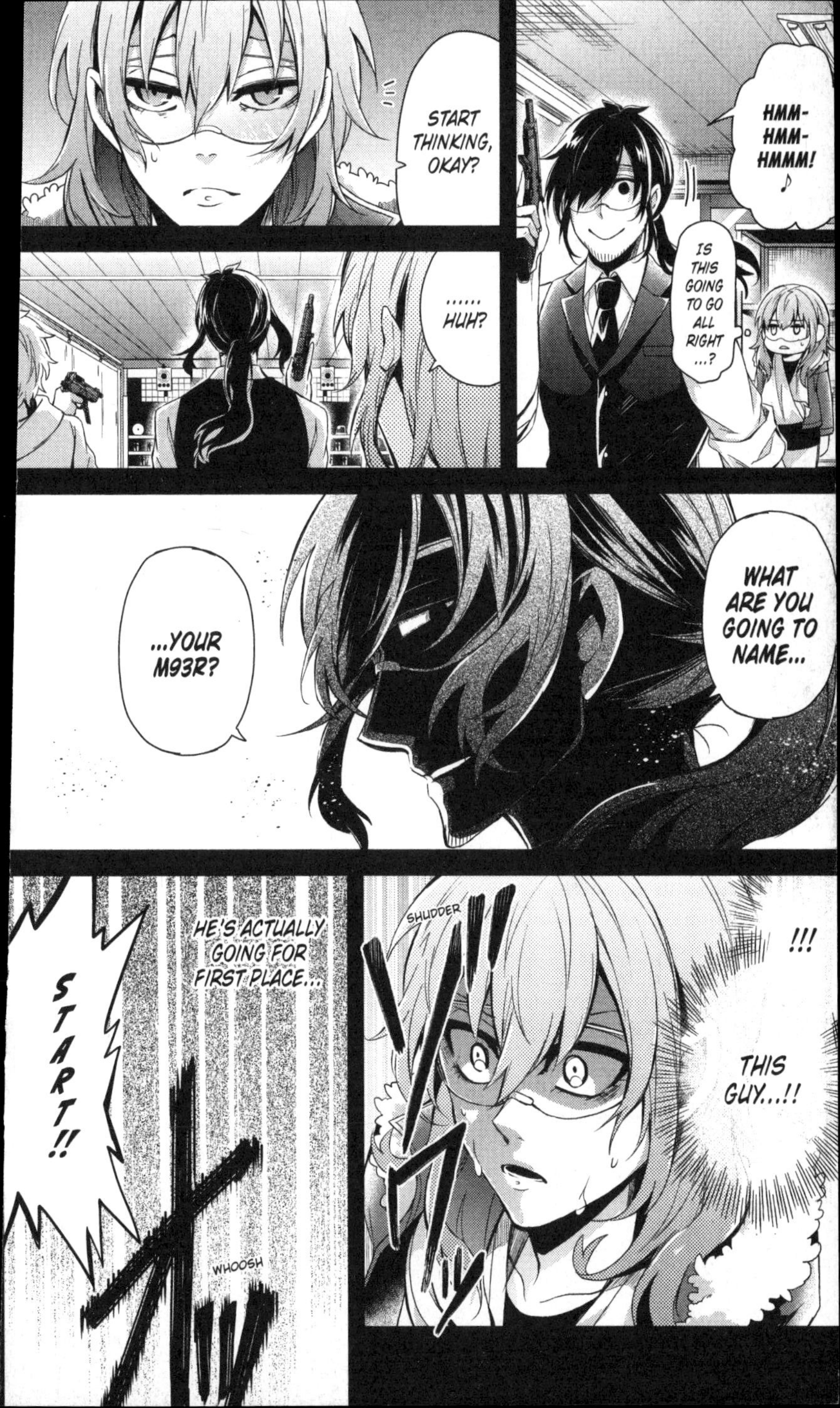
HMM-HMM-HMMM! ♪
IS THIS GOING TO GO ALL RIGHT ...?
START THINKING, OKAY?
...... HUH?
WHAT ARE YOU GOING TO NAME...
...YOUR M93R?
SHUDDER
!!!
THIS GUY...!!
HE'S ACTUALLY GOING FOR FIRST PLACE...
START!!
WHOOSH

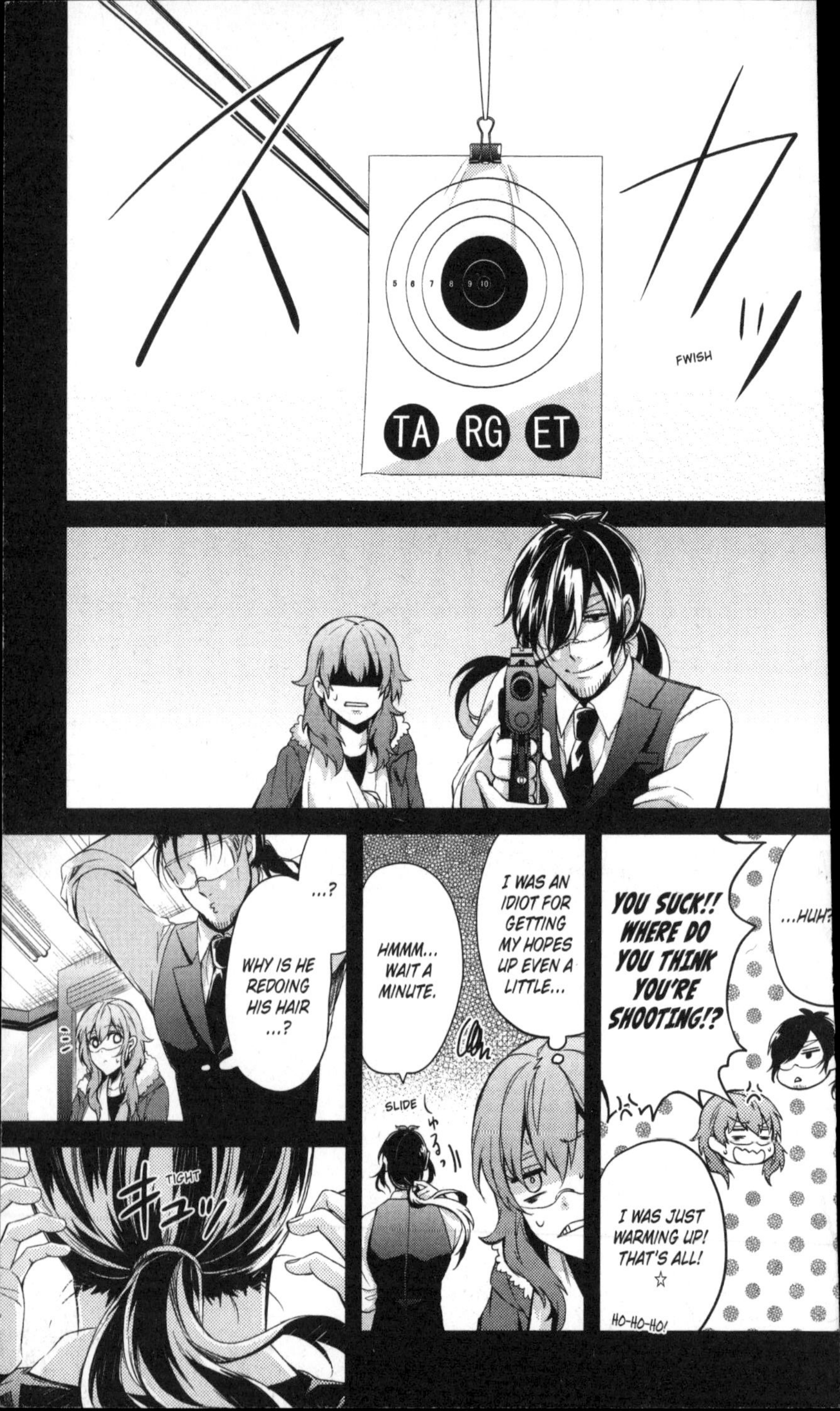
FWISH
TA RG ET
I WAS AN IDIOT FOR GETTING MY HOPES UP EVEN A LITTLE...
HMMM... WAIT A MINUTE.
SLIDE
...?
WHY IS HE REDOING HIS HAIR ...?
TIGHT
...HUH?
YOU SUCK!! WHERE DO YOU THINK YOU'RE SHOOTING!?
I WAS JUST WARMING UP! THAT'S ALL! ☆
HO-HO-HO!

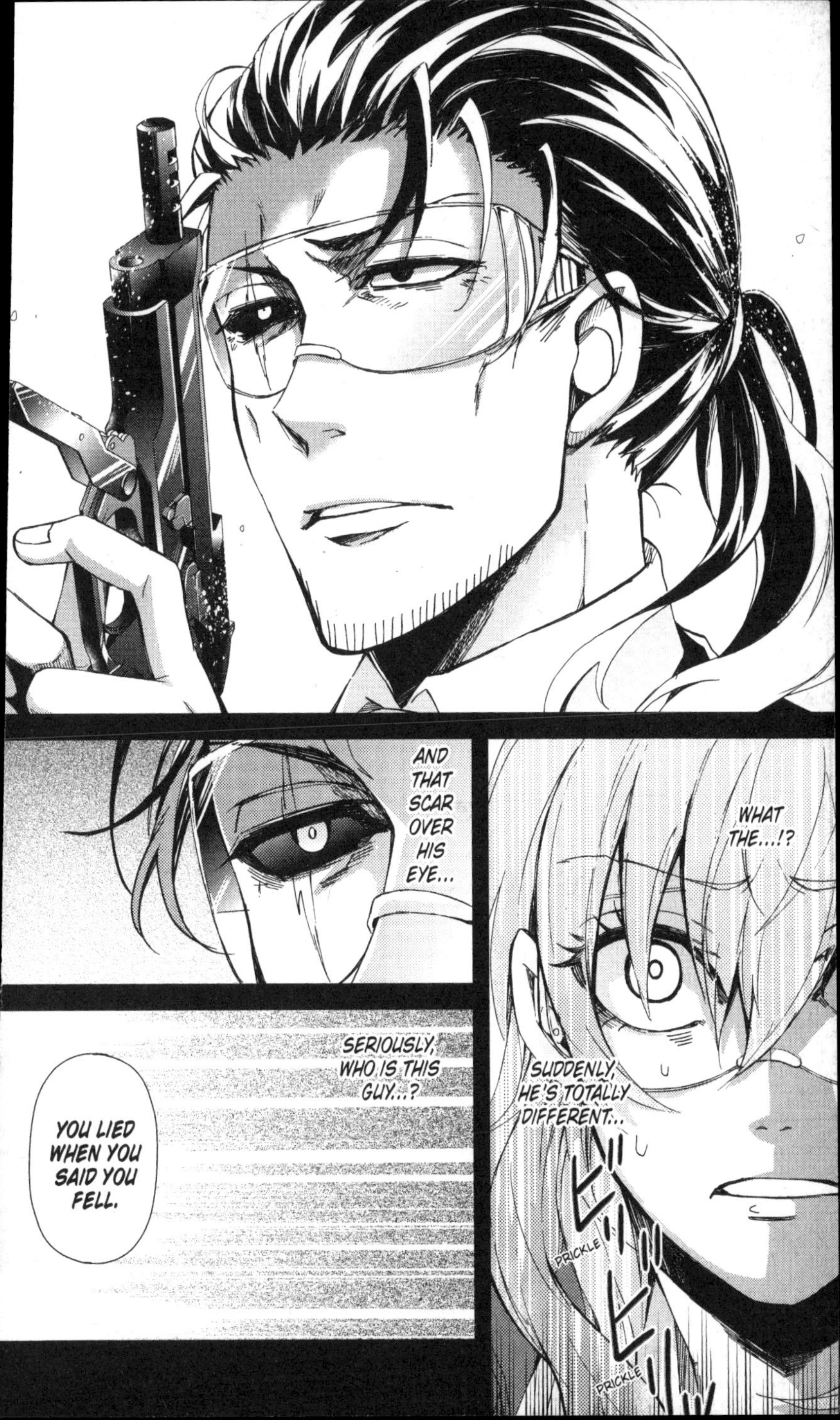
WHAT THE...!?
SUDDENLY, HE'S TOTALLY DIFFERENT...
PRICKLE
PRICKLE
AND THAT SCAR OVER HIS EYE...
SERIOUSLY, WHO IS THIS GUY...?
YOU LIED WHEN YOU SAID YOU FELL.

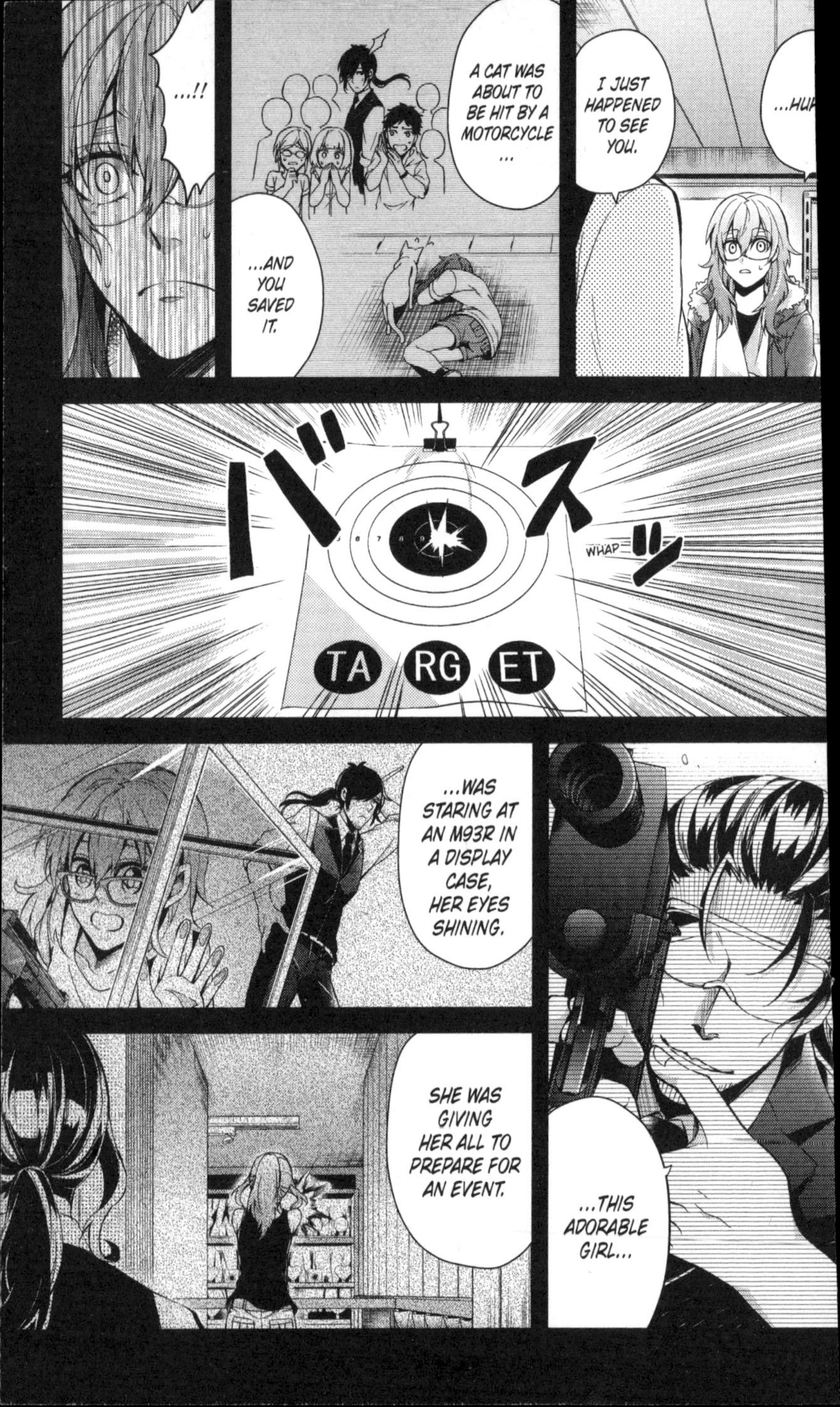
...HU
I JUST HAPPENED TO SEE YOU.
A CAT WAS ABOUT TO BE HIT BY A MOTORCYCLE ...
...AND YOU SAVED IT.
...!!
バス
ッ
WHAP
TA RG ET
...THIS ADORABLE GIRL...
...WAS STARING AT AN M93R IN A DISPLAY CASE, HER EYES SHINING.
SHE WAS GIVING HER ALL TO PREPARE FOR AN EVENT.

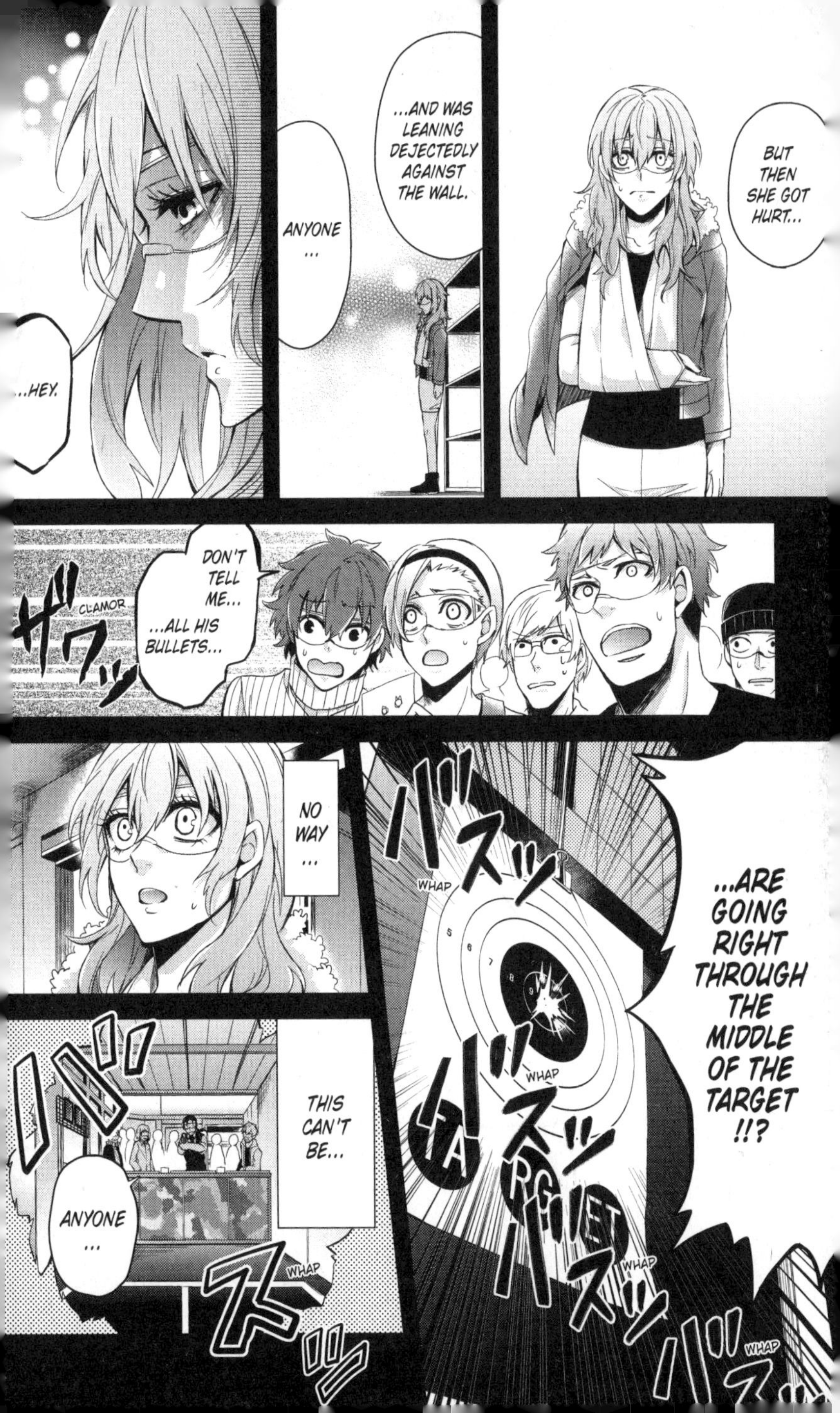
BUT THEN SHE GOT HURT...
...AND WAS LEANING DEJECTEDLY AGAINST THE WALL.
ANYONE ...
...HEY.
ザワッ
CLAMOR
DON'T TELL ME... ...ALL HIS BULLETS...
バスッ
WHAP
WHAP
TARGET
WHAP
WHAP
...ARE GOING RIGHT THROUGH THE MIDDLE OF THE TARGET!!?
NO WAY ...
THIS CAN'T BE...
ANYONE ...
WHAP

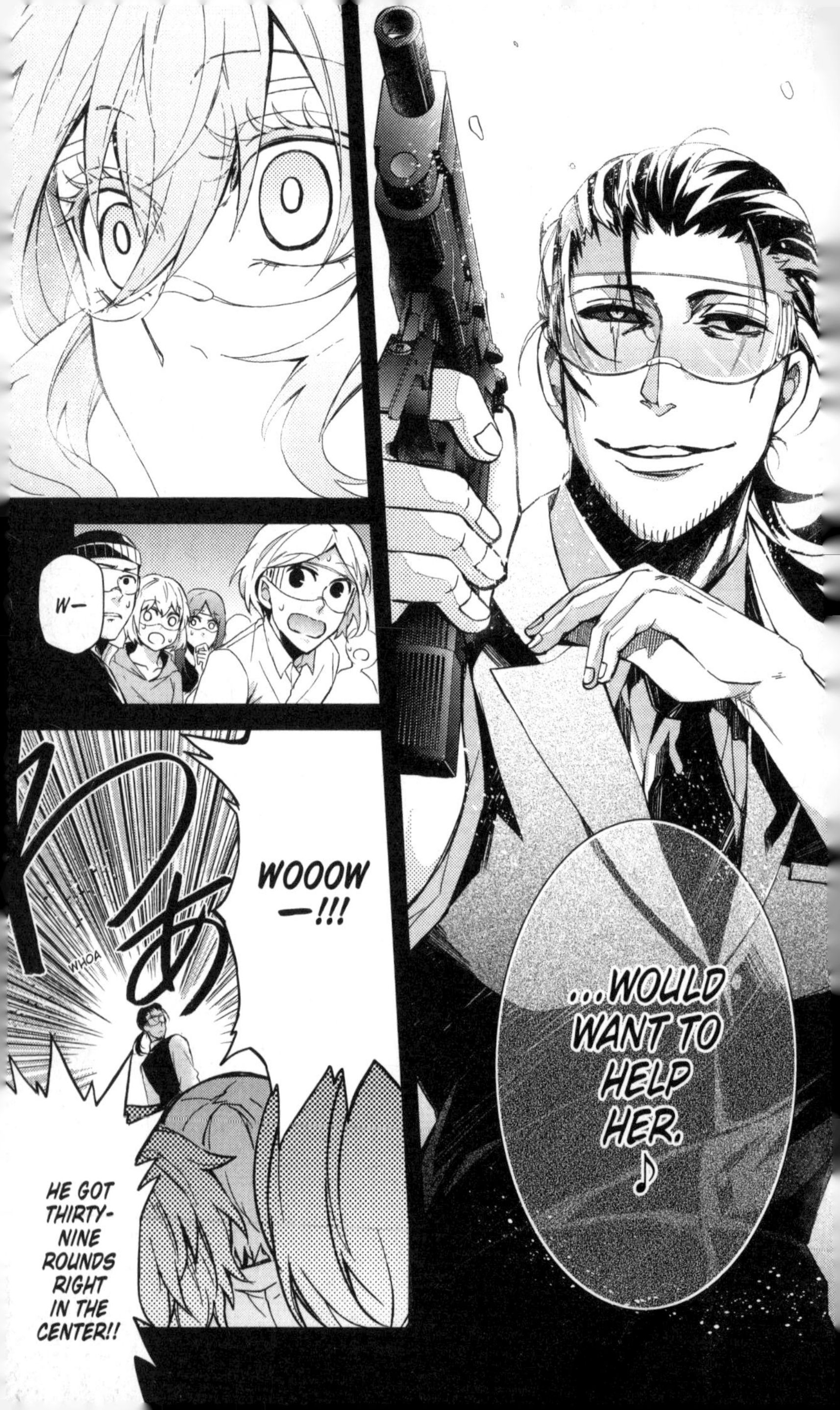
...WOULD WANT TO HELP HER. ♪
W—
WOOOW—!!!
WHOA
HE GOT THIRTY-NINE ROUNDS RIGHT IN THE CENTER!!

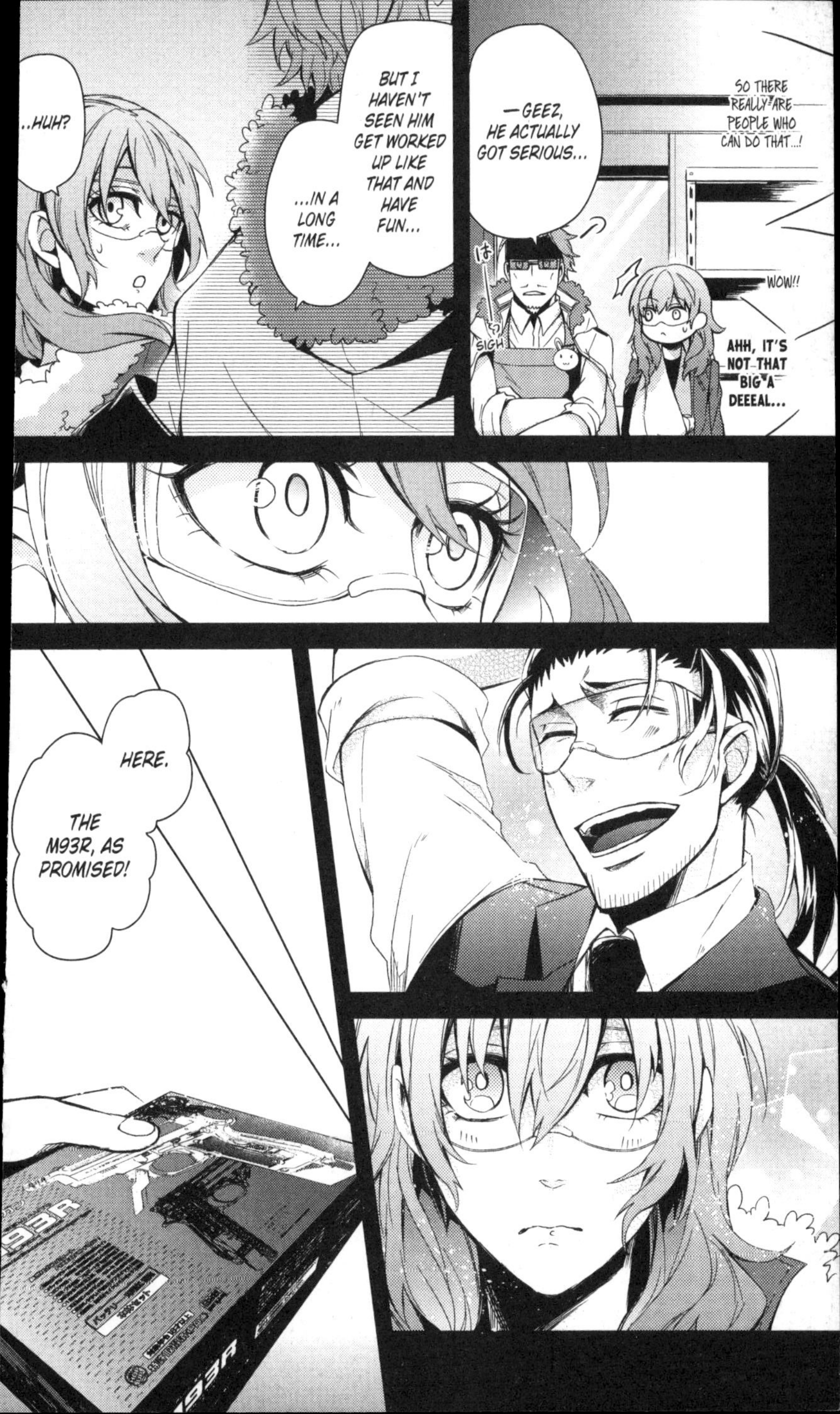
SO THERE REALLY ARE PEOPLE WHO CAN DO THAT...!
—GEEZ, HE ACTUALLY GOT SERIOUS...
WOW!!
AHH, IT'S NOT THAT BIG A DEEEAL...
SIGH
BUT I HAVEN'T SEEN HIM GET WORKED UP LIKE THAT AND HAVE FUN...
...IN A LONG TIME...
..HUH?
HERE.
THE M93R, AS PROMISED!

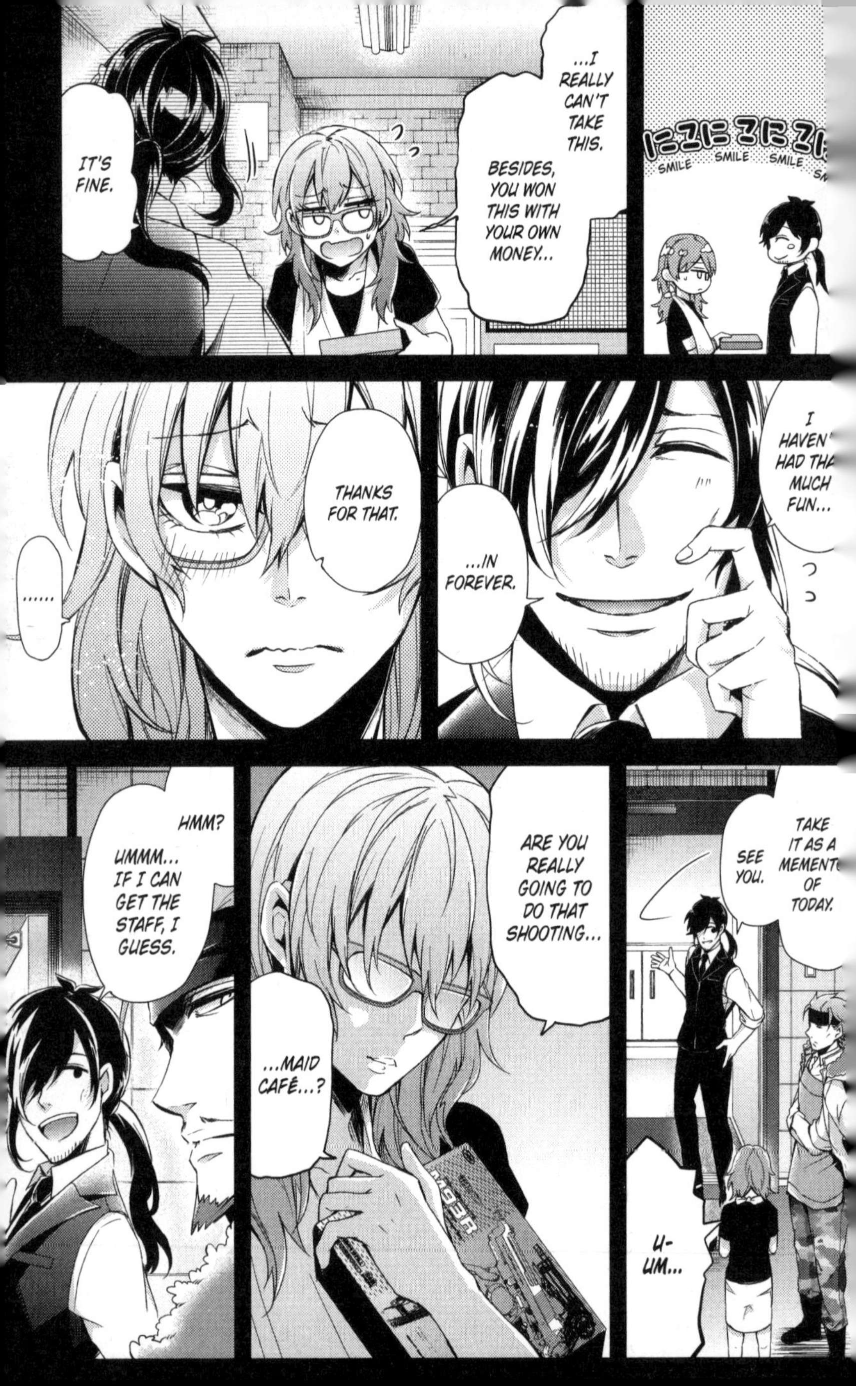
にこにこにこにこ
SMILE SMILE SMILE SM
...I REALLY CAN'T TAKE THIS.
BESIDES, YOU WON THIS WITH YOUR OWN MONEY...
IT'S FINE.
I HAVEN' HAD THA MUCH FUN...
...IN FOREVER.
THANKS FOR THAT.
......
TAKE IT AS A MEMENT OF TODAY.
SEE YOU.
U-UM...
ARE YOU REALLY GOING TO DO THAT SHOOTING...
...MAID CAFÉ...?
HMM? UMMM... IF I CAN GET THE STAFF, I GUESS.

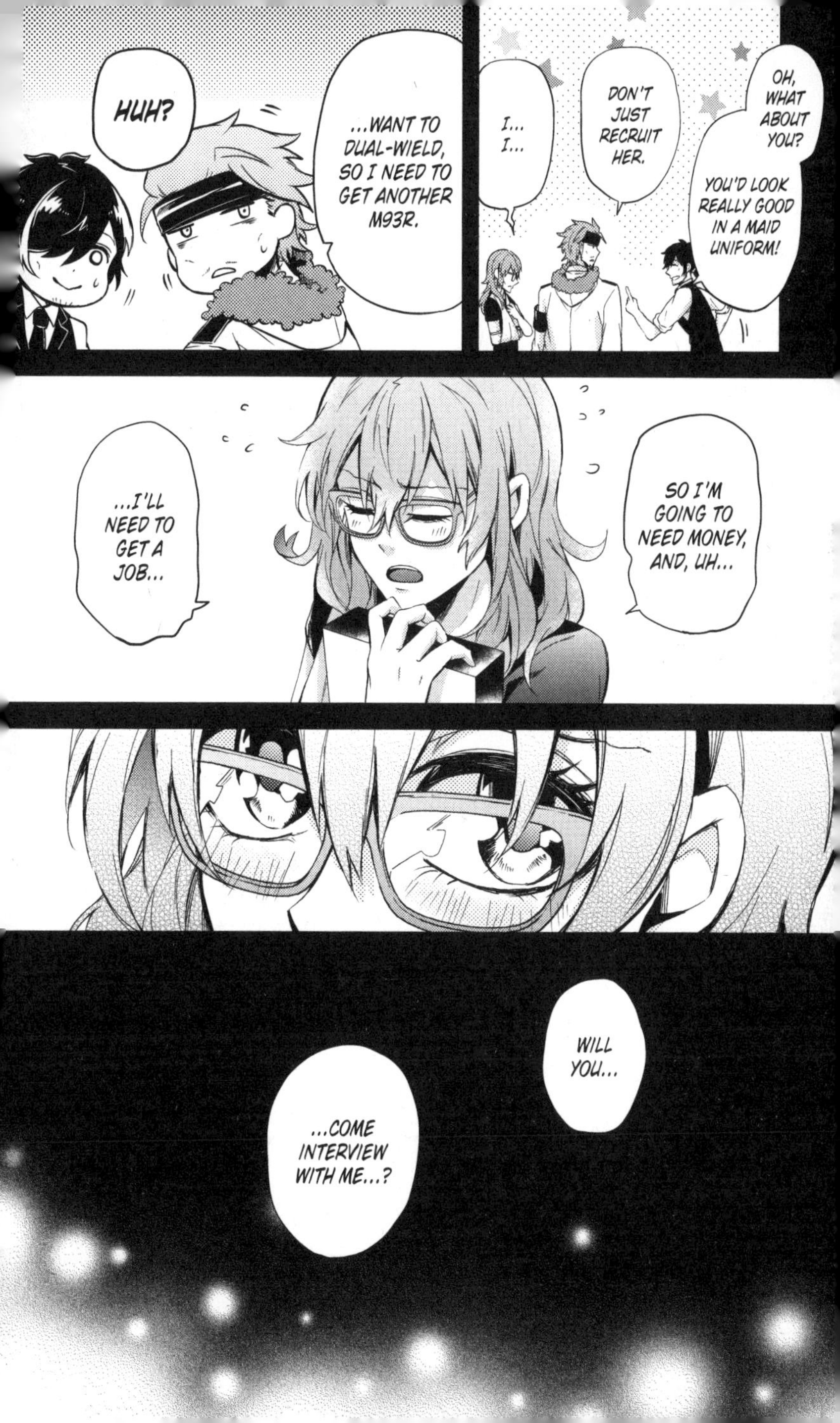
OH, WHAT ABOUT YOU?
YOU'D LOOK REALLY GOOD IN A MAID UNIFORM!
DON'T JUST RECRUIT HER.
I... I...
...WANT TO DUAL-WIELD, SO I NEED TO GET ANOTHER M93R.
HUH?
SO I'M GOING TO NEED MONEY, AND, UH...
...I'LL NEED TO GET A JOB...
WILL YOU...
...COME INTERVIEW WITH ME...?

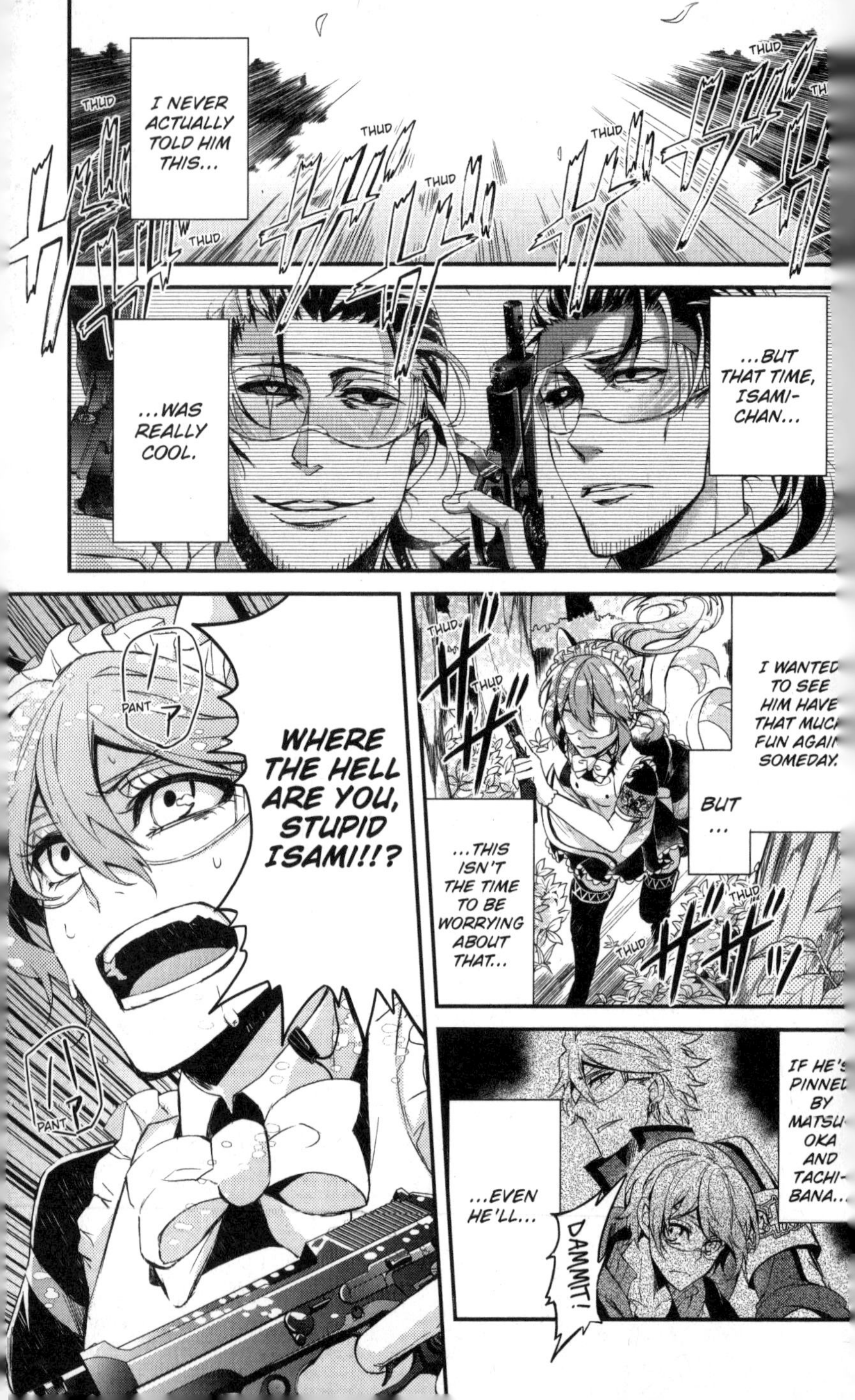
THUD
THUD
THUD
THUD
THUD
THUD
I NEVER ACTUALLY TOLD HIM THIS...
THUD
...BUT THAT TIME, ISAMI-CHAN...
...WAS REALLY COOL.
I WANTED TO SEE HIM HAVE THAT MUCH FUN AGAIN SOMEDAY.
BUT...
THUD
THUD
...THIS ISN'T THE TIME TO BE WORRYING ABOUT THAT...
THUD
THUD
IF HE'S PINNED BY MATSUOKA AND TACHIBANA...
...EVEN HE'LL...
DAMMIT!
PANT
WHERE THE HELL ARE YOU, STUPID ISAMI!!?
PANT

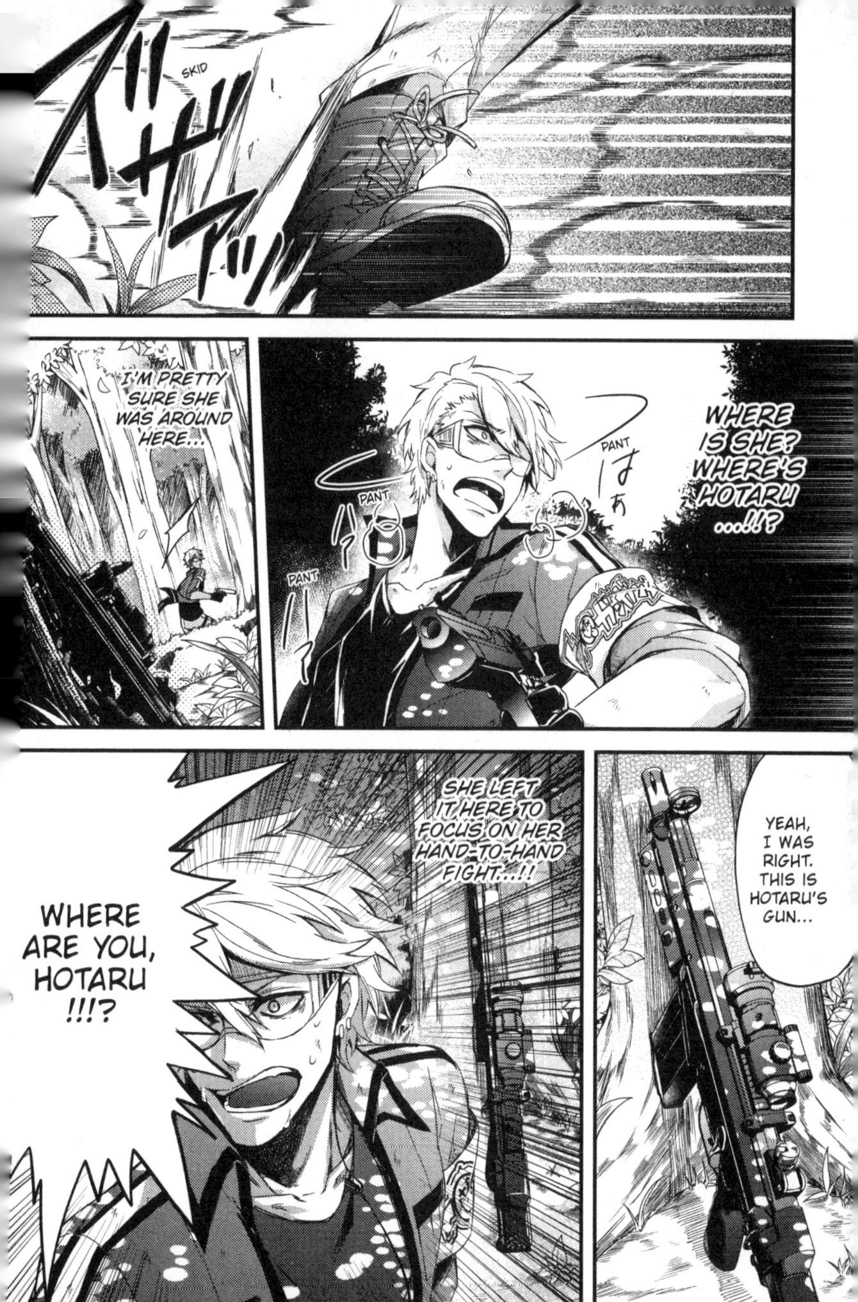
SKID
WHERE IS SHE? WHERE'S HOTARU ...!!?
PANT
PANT
PANT
I'M PRETTY SURE SHE WAS AROUND HERE...
YEAH, I WAS RIGHT. THIS IS HOTARU'S GUN...
SHE LEFT IT HERE TO FOCUS ON HER HAND-TO-HAND FIGHT...!!
WHERE ARE YOU, HOTARU !!!?

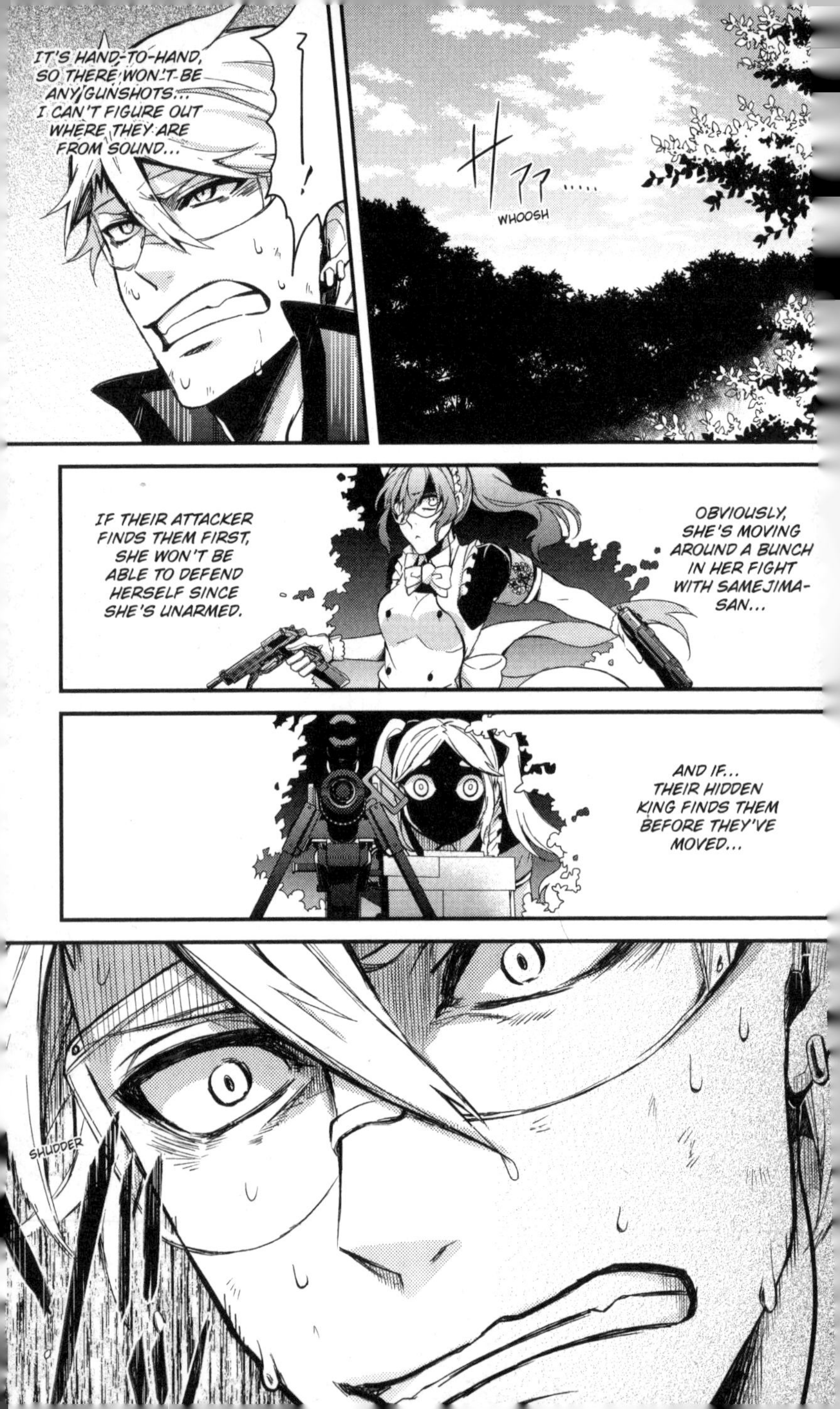
ザァァ.....
WHOOSH
IT'S HAND-TO-HAND, SO THERE WON'T BE ANY GUNSHOTS... I CAN'T FIGURE OUT WHERE THEY ARE FROM SOUND...
OBVIOUSLY, SHE'S MOVING AROUND A BUNCH IN HER FIGHT WITH SAMEJIMA-SAN...
IF THEIR ATTACKER FINDS THEM FIRST, SHE WON'T BE ABLE TO DEFEND HERSELF SINCE SHE'S UNARMED.
AND IF... THEIR HIDDEN KING FINDS THEM BEFORE THEY'VE MOVED...
SHUDDER

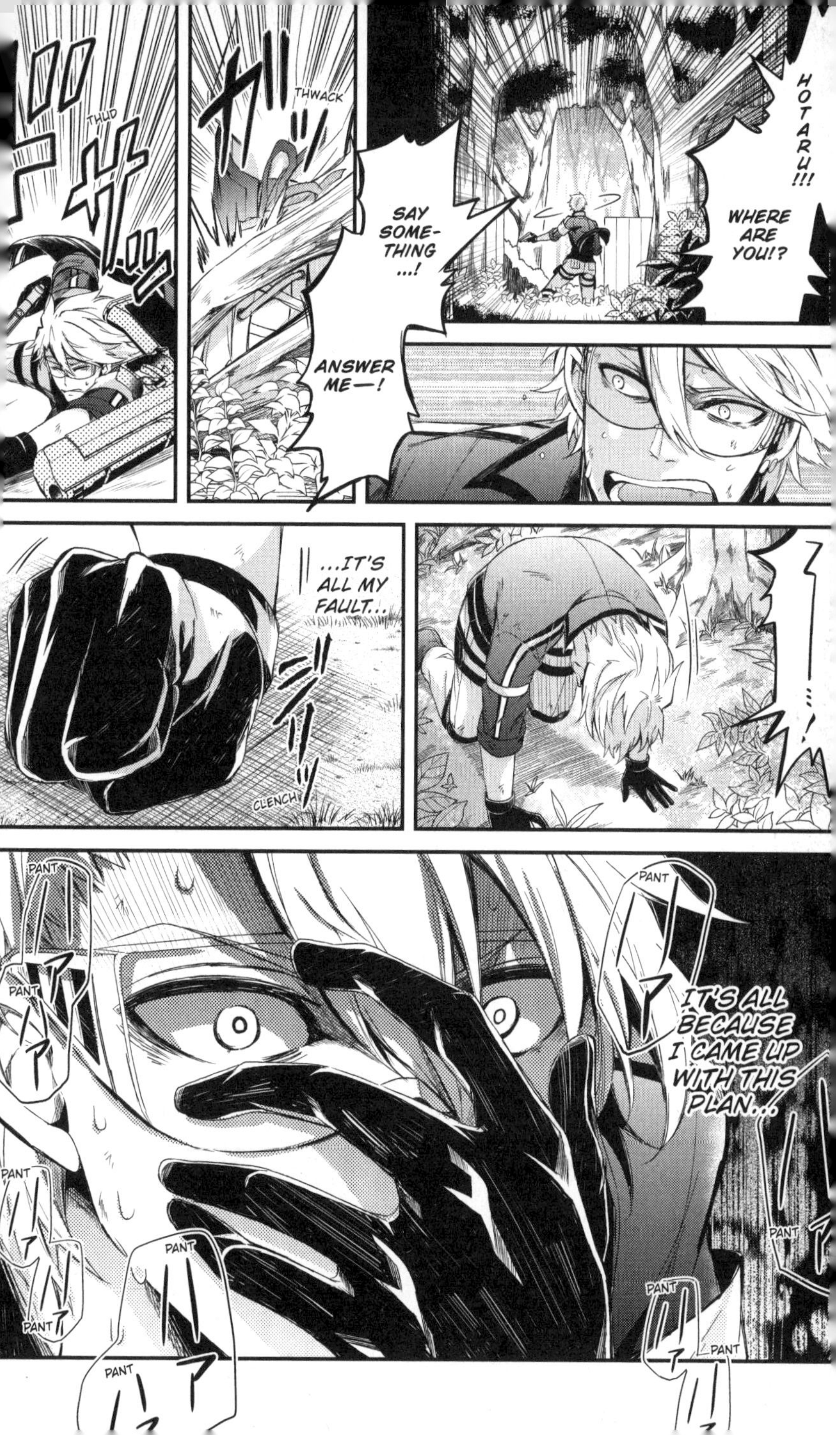
HOTARU!!!
WHERE ARE YOU!?
SAY SOME-THING ...!
ANSWER ME—!
THWACK
THUD
...!
...IT'S ALL MY FAULT...
CLENCH
PANT
PANT
IT'S ALL BECAUSE I CAME UP WITH THIS PLAN...
PANT
PANT
PANT
PANT
PANT
PANT
PANT

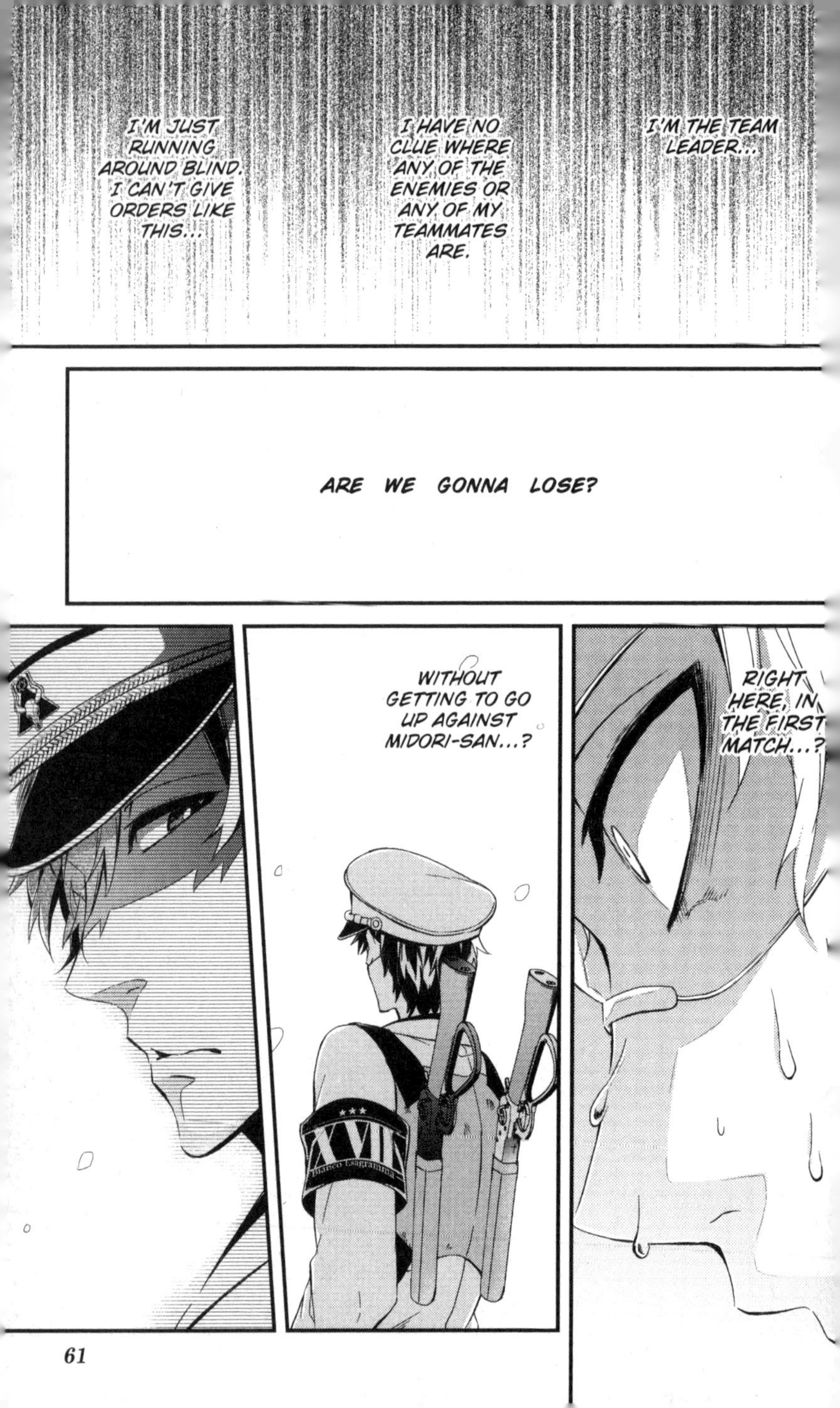
I'M THE TEAM LEADER...
I HAVE NO CLUE WHERE ANY OF THE ENEMIES OR ANY OF MY TEAMMATES ARE.
I'M JUST RUNNING AROUND BLIND. I CAN'T GIVE ORDERS LIKE THIS...
ARE WE GONNA LOSE?
RIGHT HERE, IN THE FIRST MATCH...?
WITHOUT GETTING TO GO UP AGAINST MIDORI-SAN...?

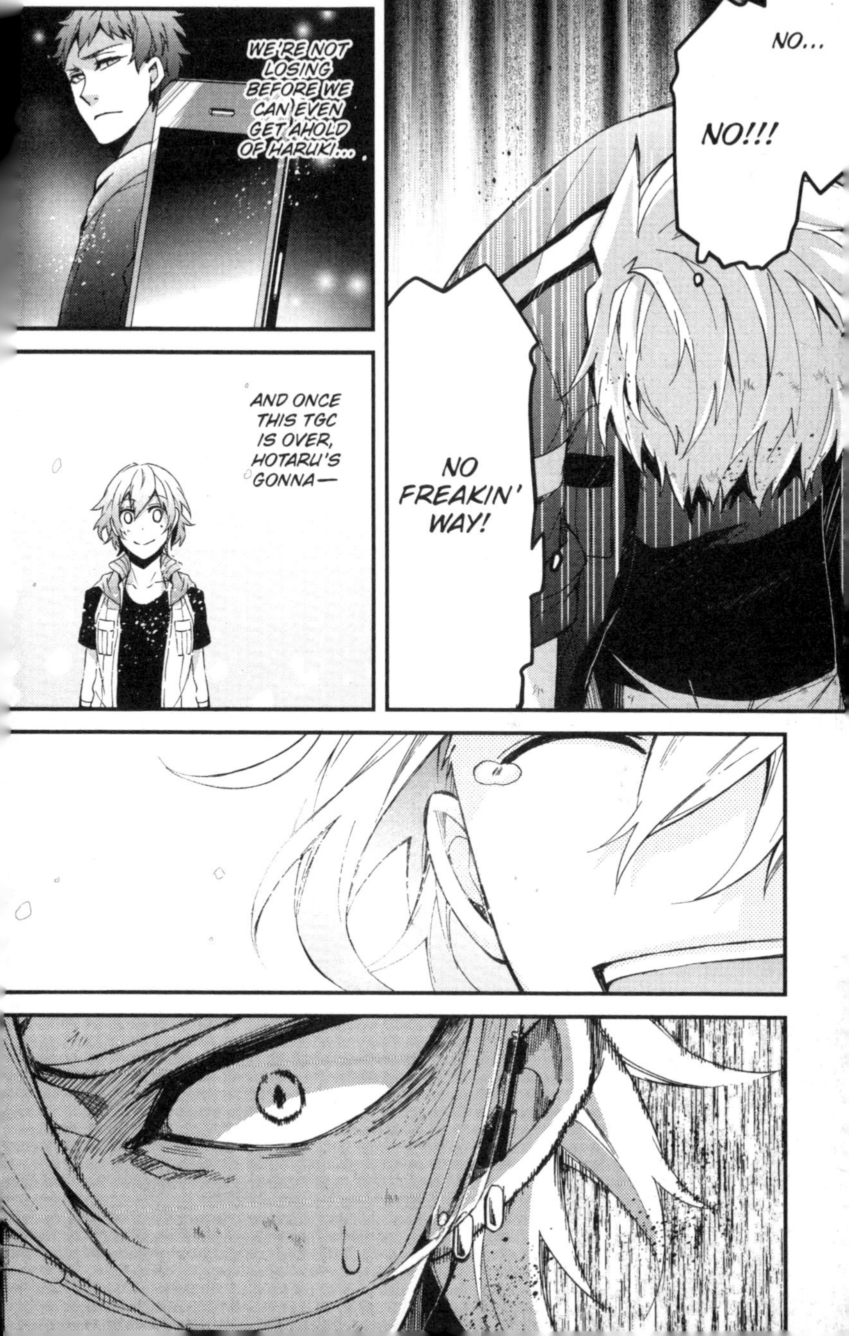
NO...
NO!!!
NO FREAKIN' WAY!
WE'RE NOT LOSING BEFORE WE CAN EVEN GET AHOLD OF HARUKI...
AND ONCE THIS TGC IS OVER, HOTARU'S GONNA—

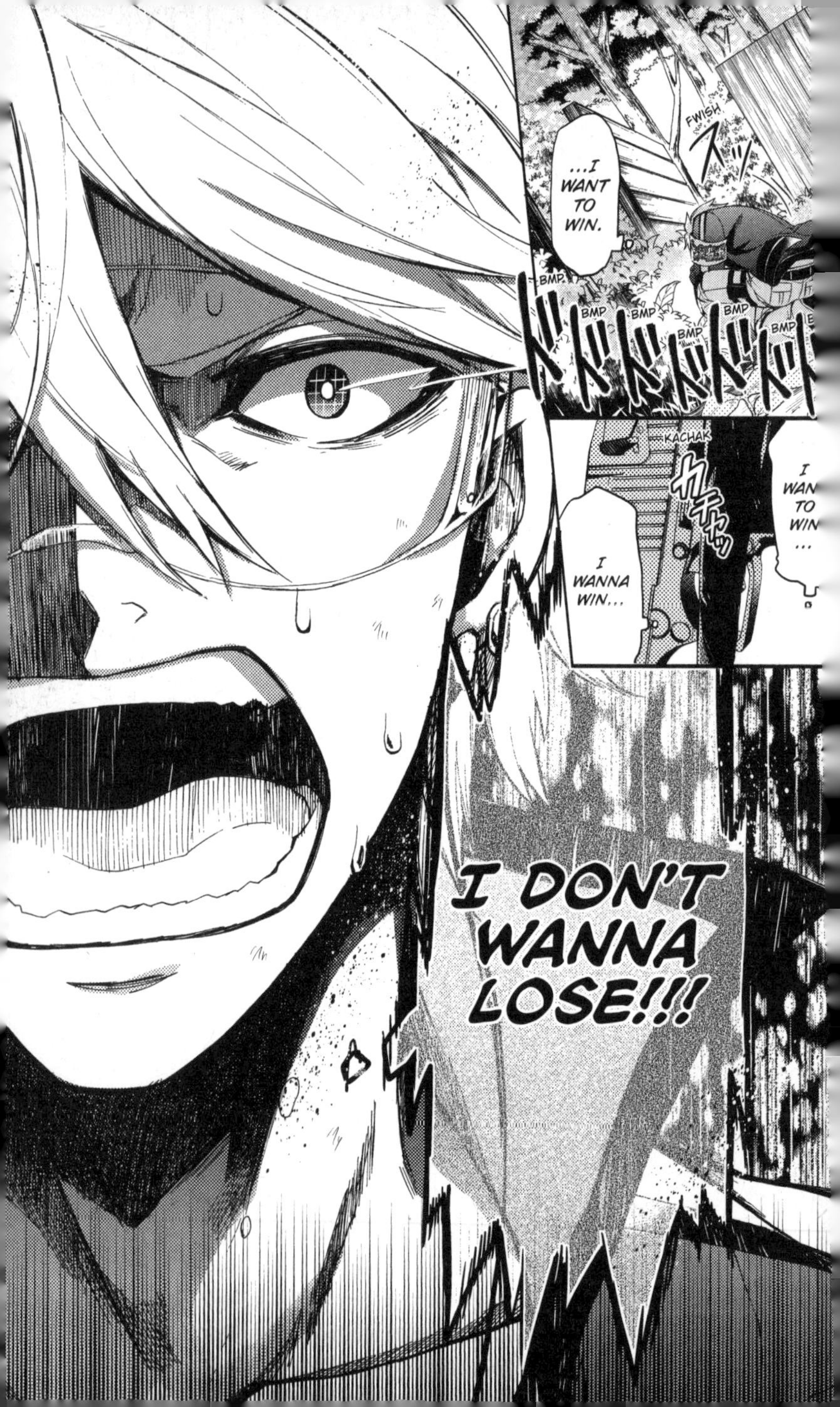
FWISH
ズッ
...I WANT TO WIN.
BMP BMP BMP BMP BMP BMP
I WAN TO WIN ...
KACHAK
カチャッ
I WANNA WIN...
I DON'T WANNA LOSE!!!

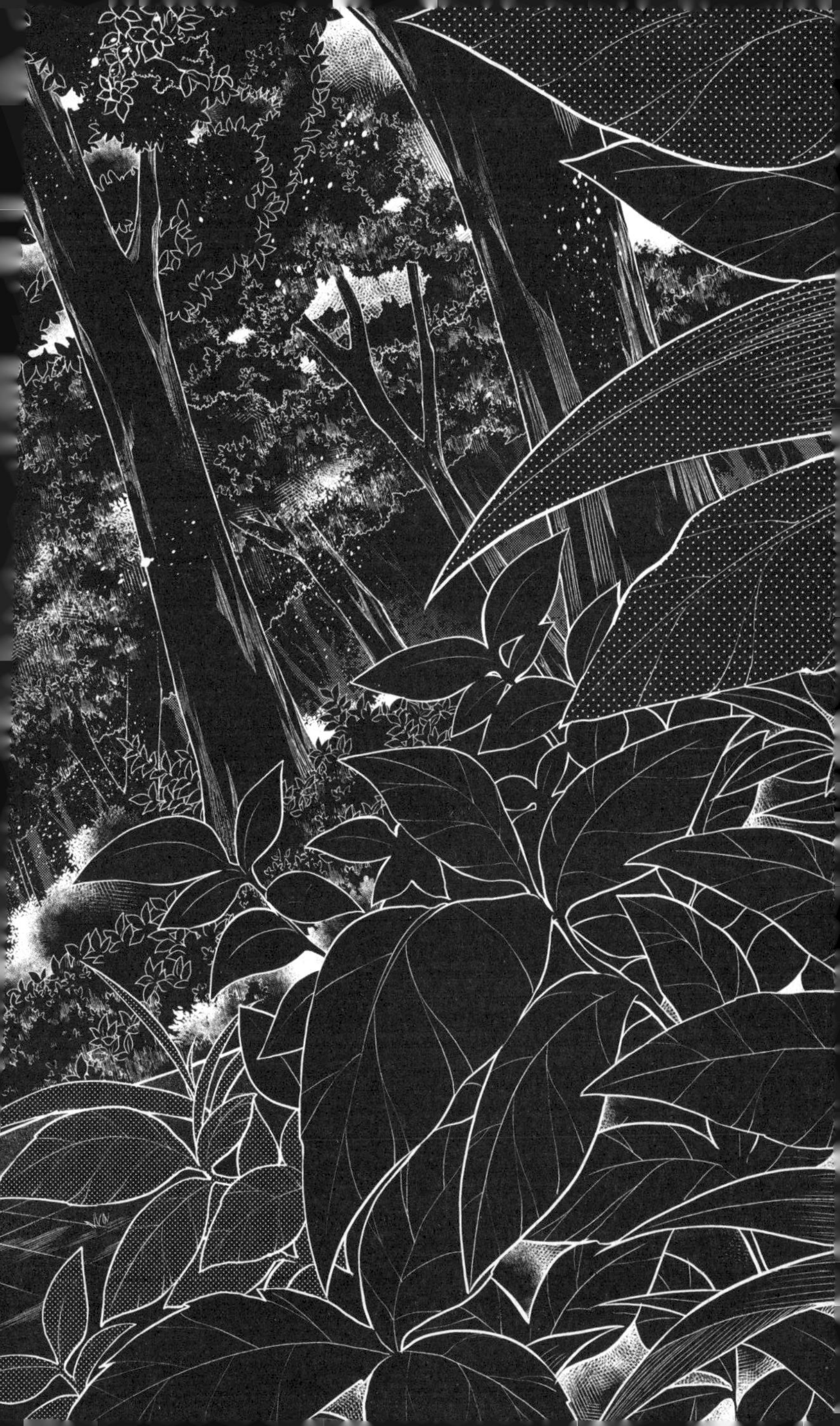

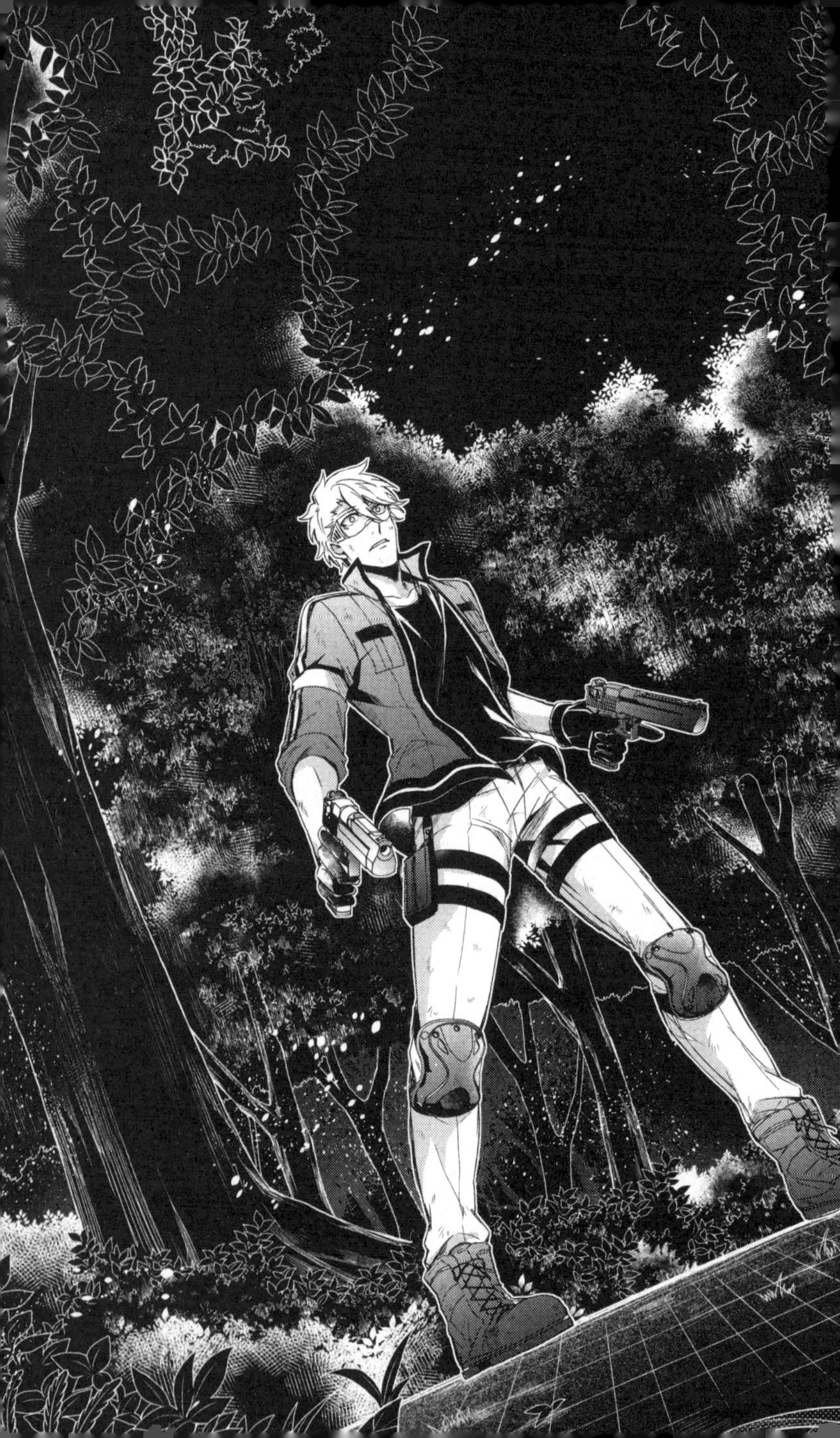

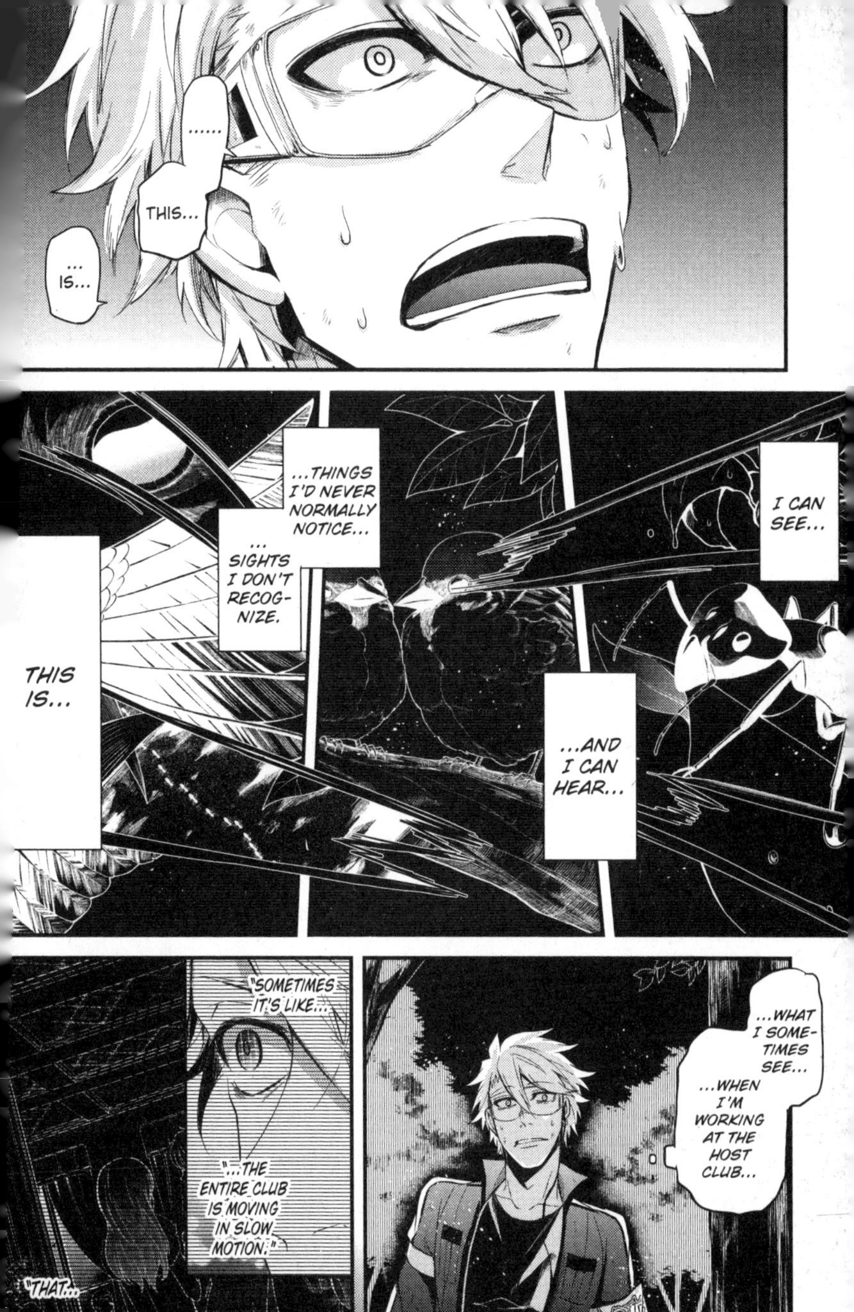
......
THIS...
... IS...
I CAN SEE...
...AND I CAN HEAR...
...THINGS I'D NEVER NORMALLY NOTICE...
... SIGHTS I DON'T RECOG-NIZE.
THIS IS...
...WHAT I SOME-TIMES SEE...
...WHEN I'M WORKING AT THE HOST CLUB...
"SOMETIMES IT'S LIKE...
"...THE ENTIRE CLUB IS MOVING IN SLOW MOTION."
"THAT...

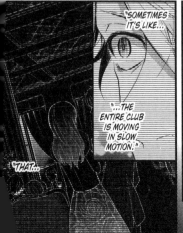

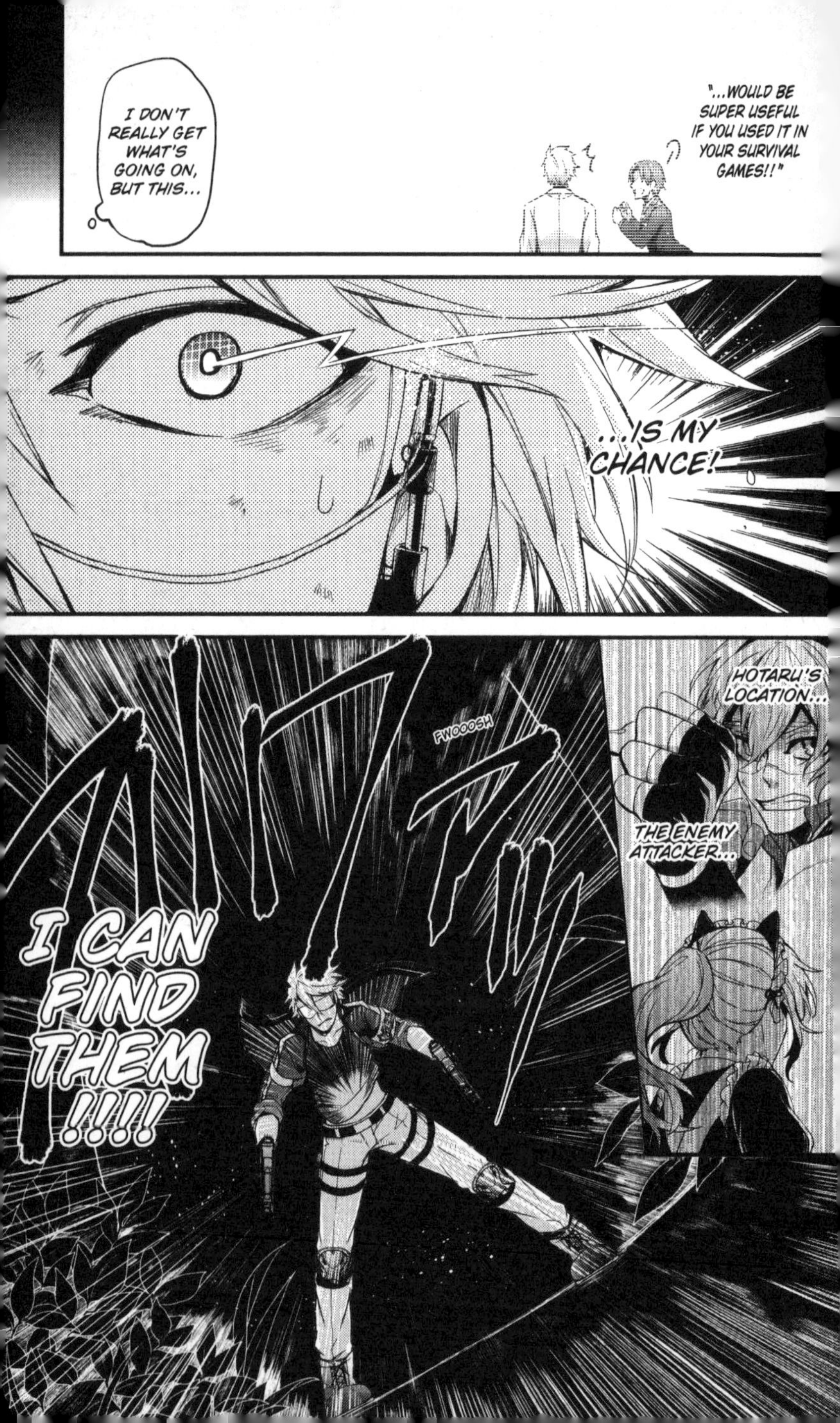
"...WOULD BE SUPER USEFUL IF YOU USED IT IN YOUR SURVIVAL GAMES!!"
I DON'T REALLY GET WHAT'S GOING ON, BUT THIS...
...IS MY CHANCE!
HOTARU'S LOCATION...
THE ENEMY ATTACKER...
FWOOOSH
I CAN FIND THEM!!!!!

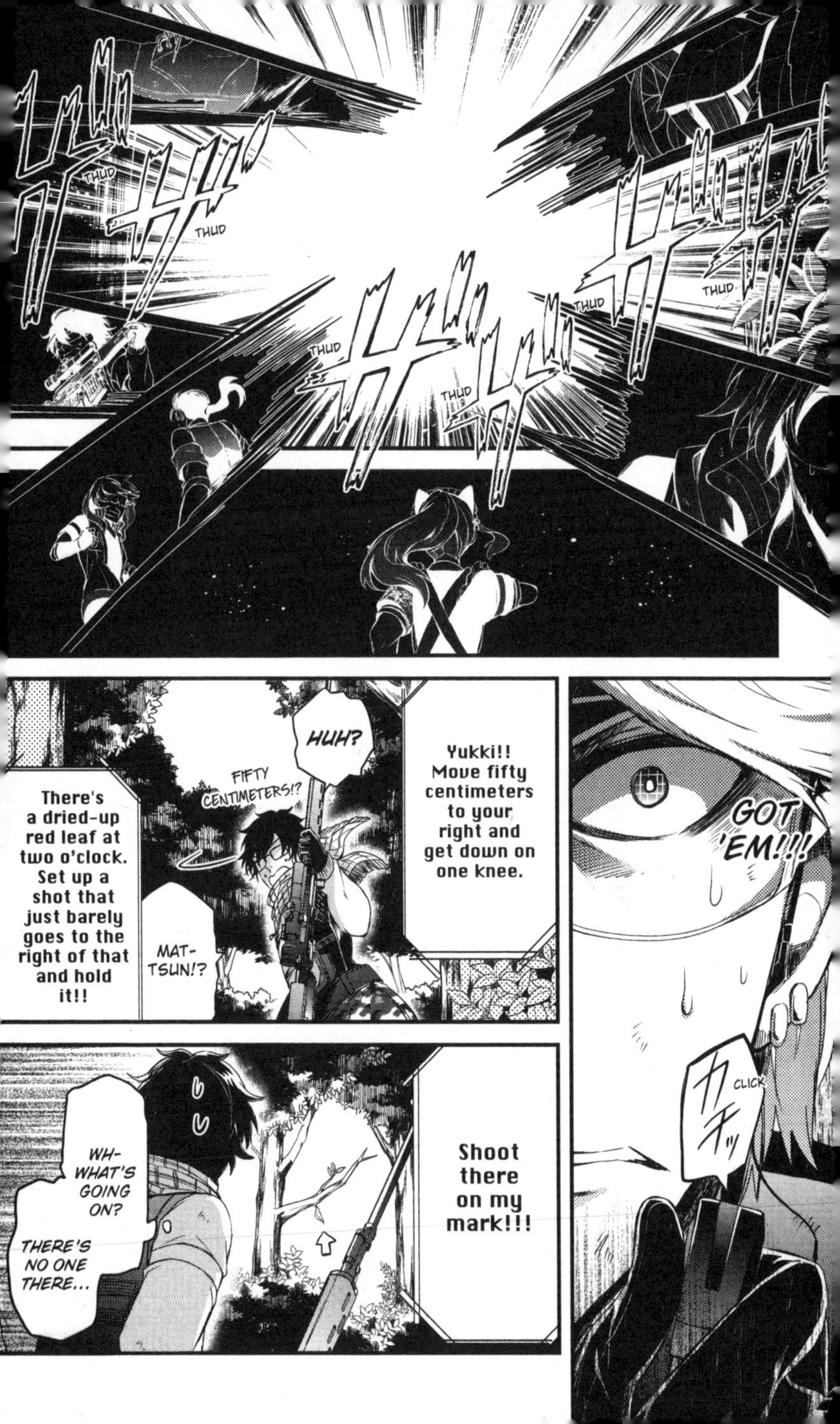
THUD
THUD
THUD
THUD
THUD
THUD
GOT 'EM!!!
CLICK
Yukki!! Move fifty centimeters to your right and get down on one knee.
HUH?
FIFTY CENTIMETERS!?
There's a dried-up red leaf at two o'clock. Set up a shot that just barely goes to the right of that and hold it!!
MAT-TSUN!?
Shoot there on my mark!!!
WH-WHAT'S GOING ON?
THERE'S NO ONE THERE...

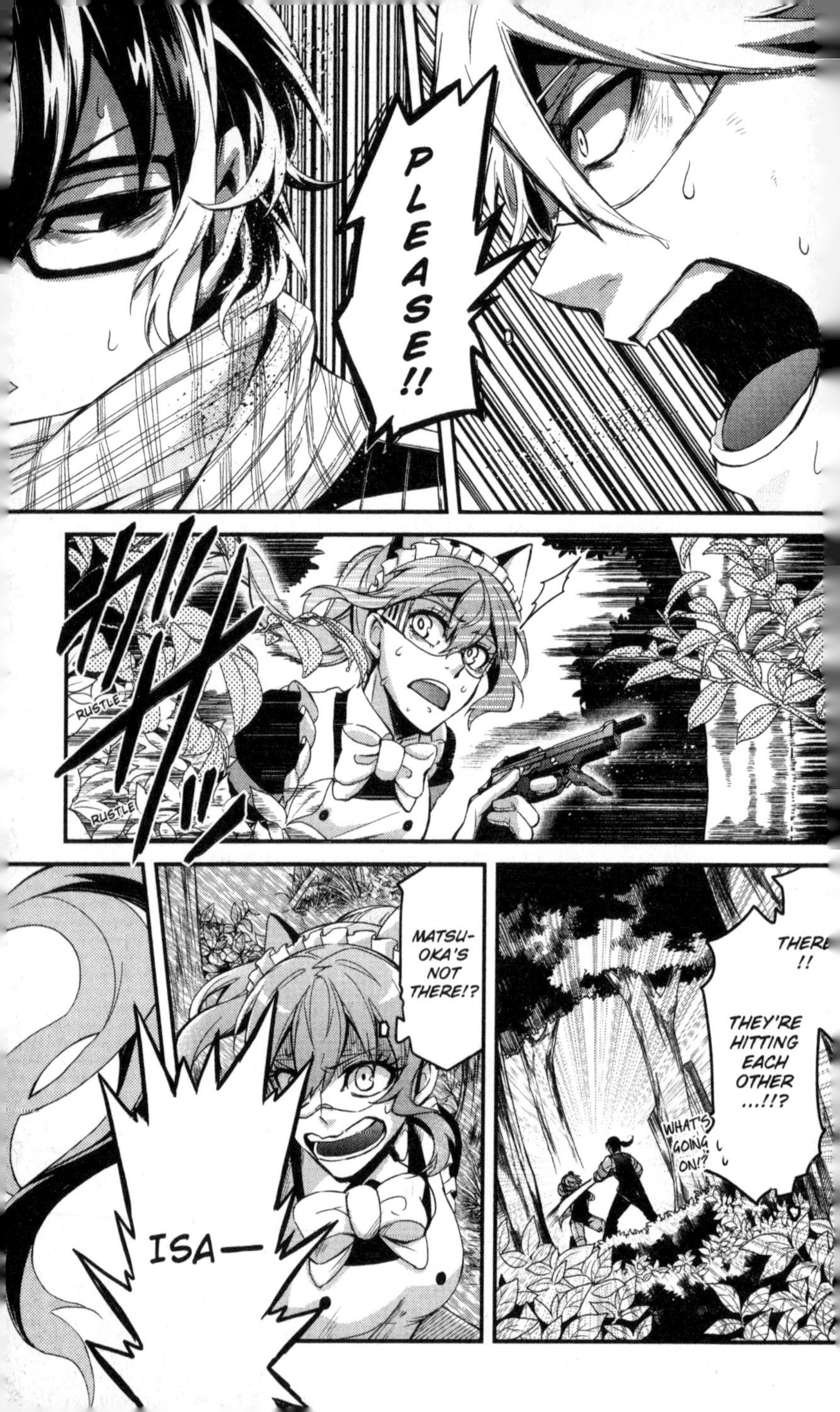
PLEASE!!
RUSTLE
RUSTLE
THERE !!
THEY'RE HITTING EACH OTHER ...!!?
WHAT'S GOING ON!?
MATSU-OKA'S NOT THERE!?
ISA—

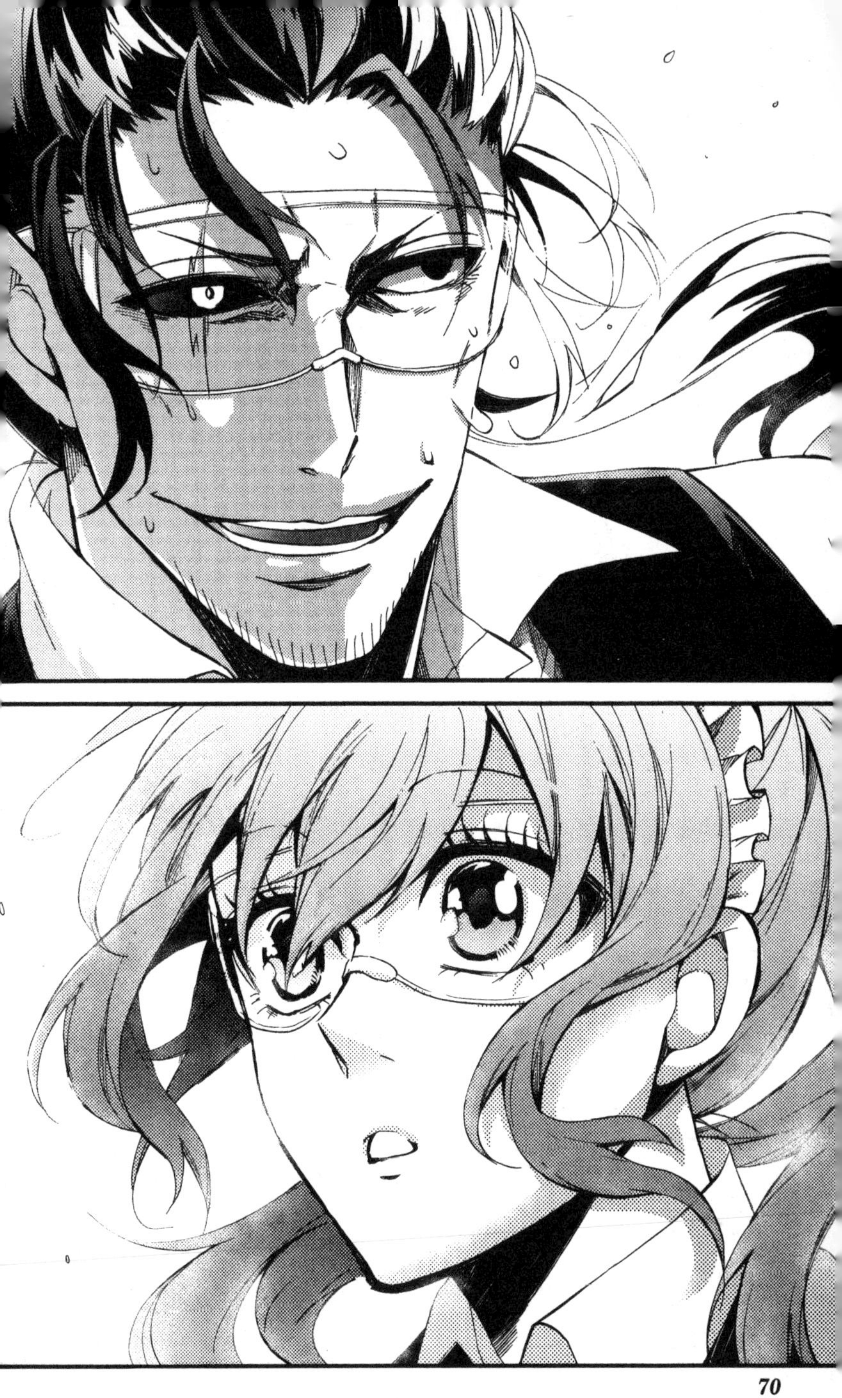

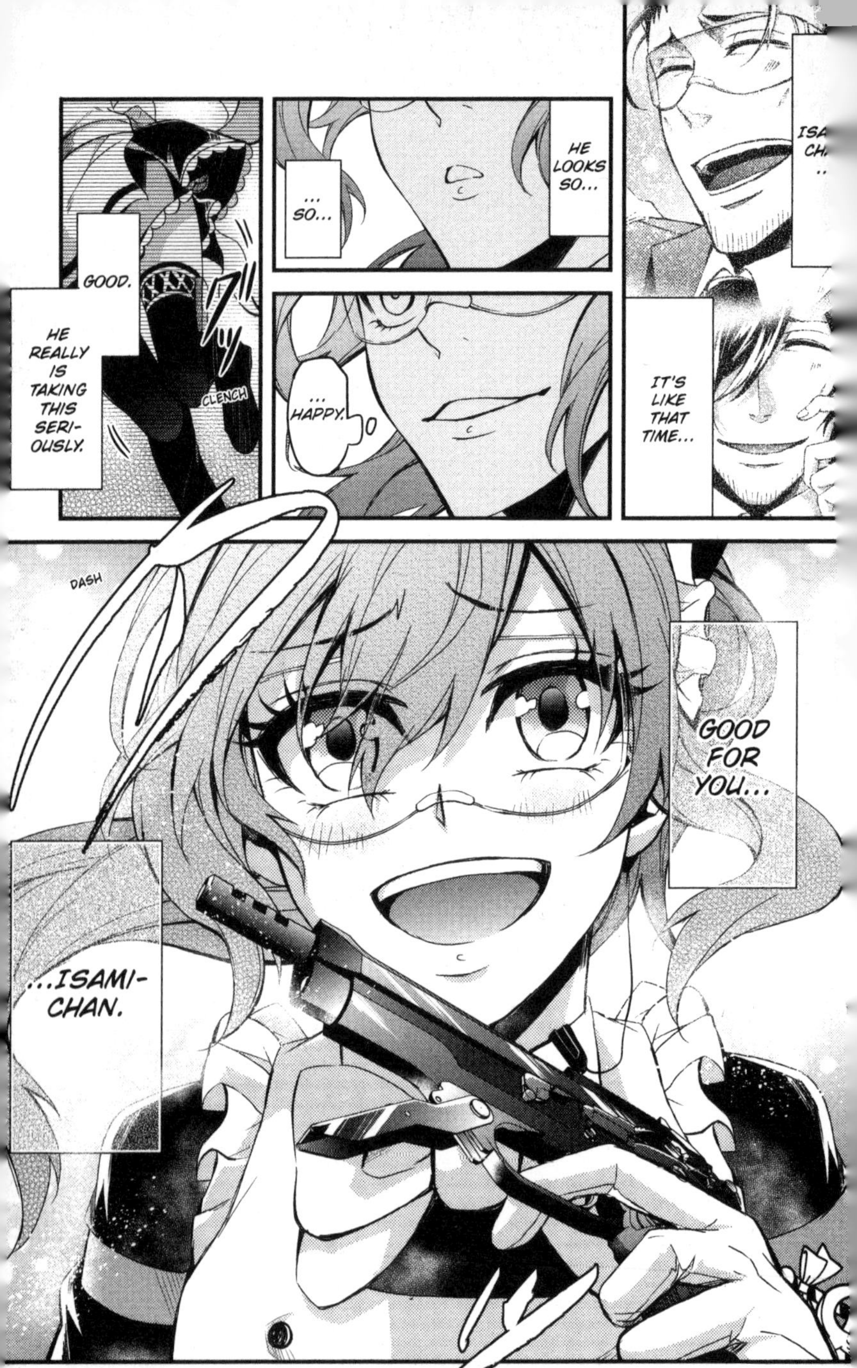

ISA CH...
IT'S LIKE THAT TIME...
HE LOOKS SO...
... SO...
... HAPPY.
GOOD.
HE REALLY IS TAKING THIS SERI-OUSLY.
CLENCH
DASH
GOOD FOR YOU...
...ISAMI-CHAN.

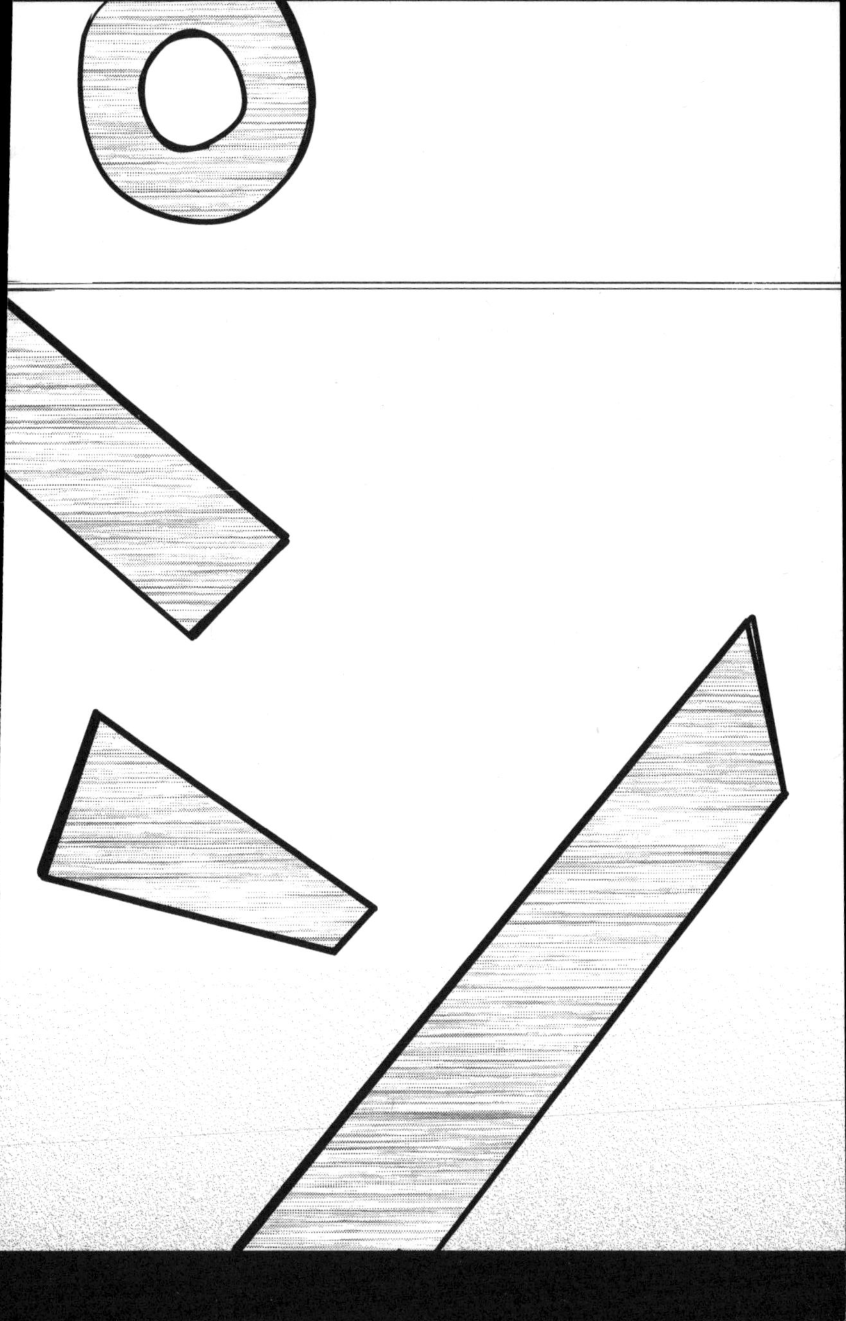

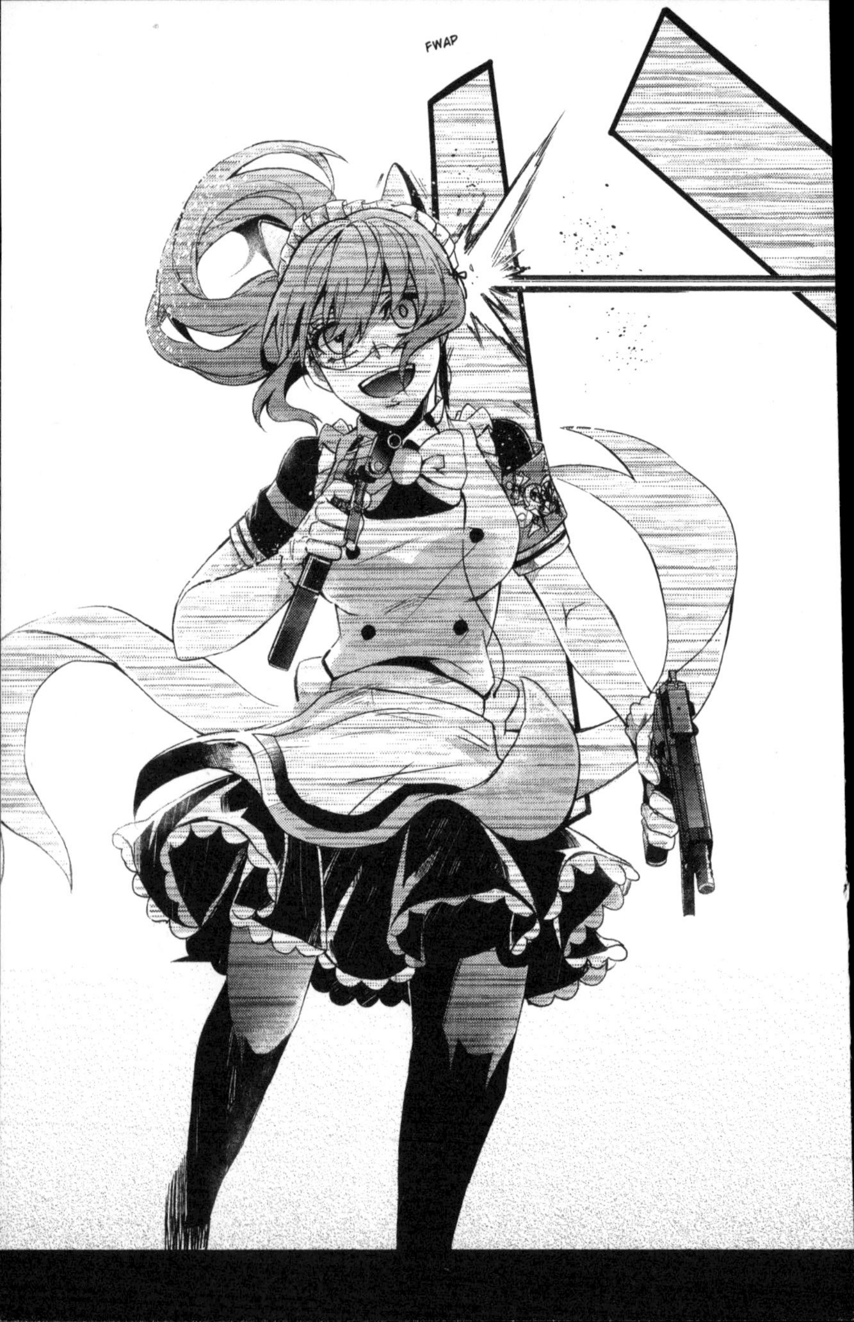
FWAP

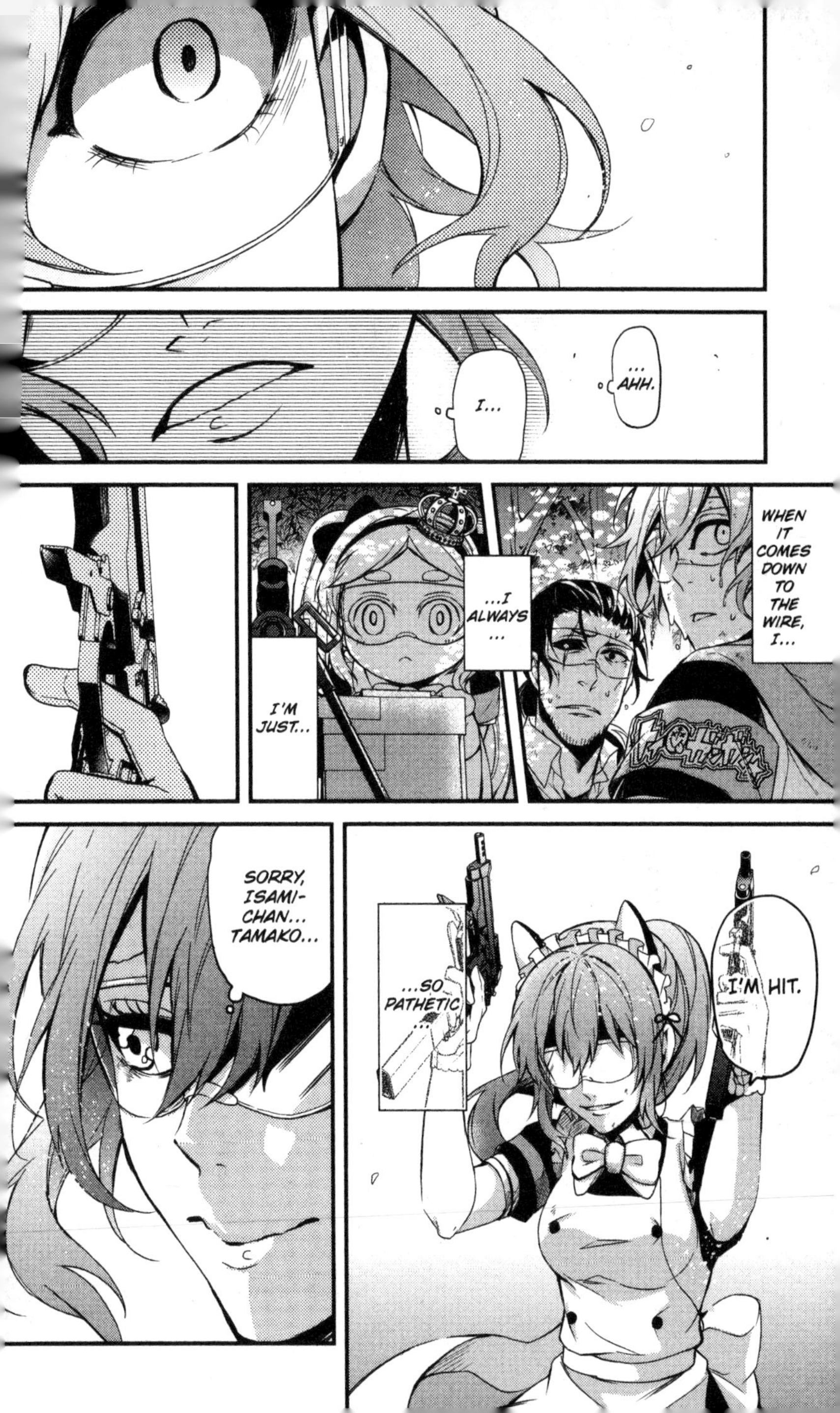
...AHH.
I...
WHEN IT COMES DOWN TO THE WIRE, I...
...I ALWAYS ...
I'M JUST...
I'M HIT.
...SO PATHETIC ...
SORRY, ISAMI-CHAN... TAMAKO...

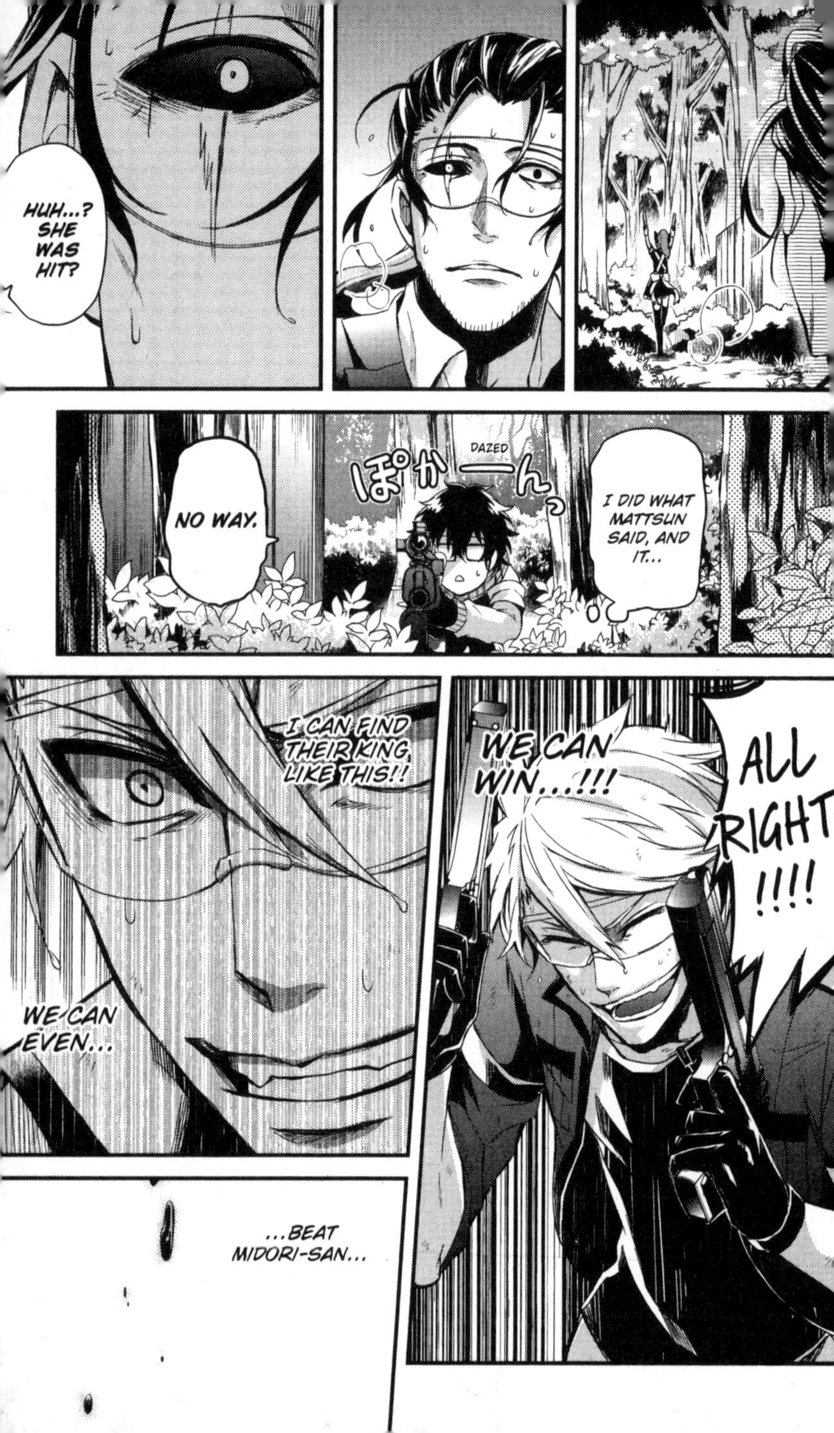
HUH...? SHE WAS HIT?
I DID WHAT MATTSUN SAID, AND IT...
DAZED
ぽかーんっ
NO WAY.
ALL RIGHT !!!!
WE CAN WIN...!!!
I CAN FIND THEIR KING LIKE THIS!!
WE CAN EVEN...
...BEAT MIDORI-SAN...

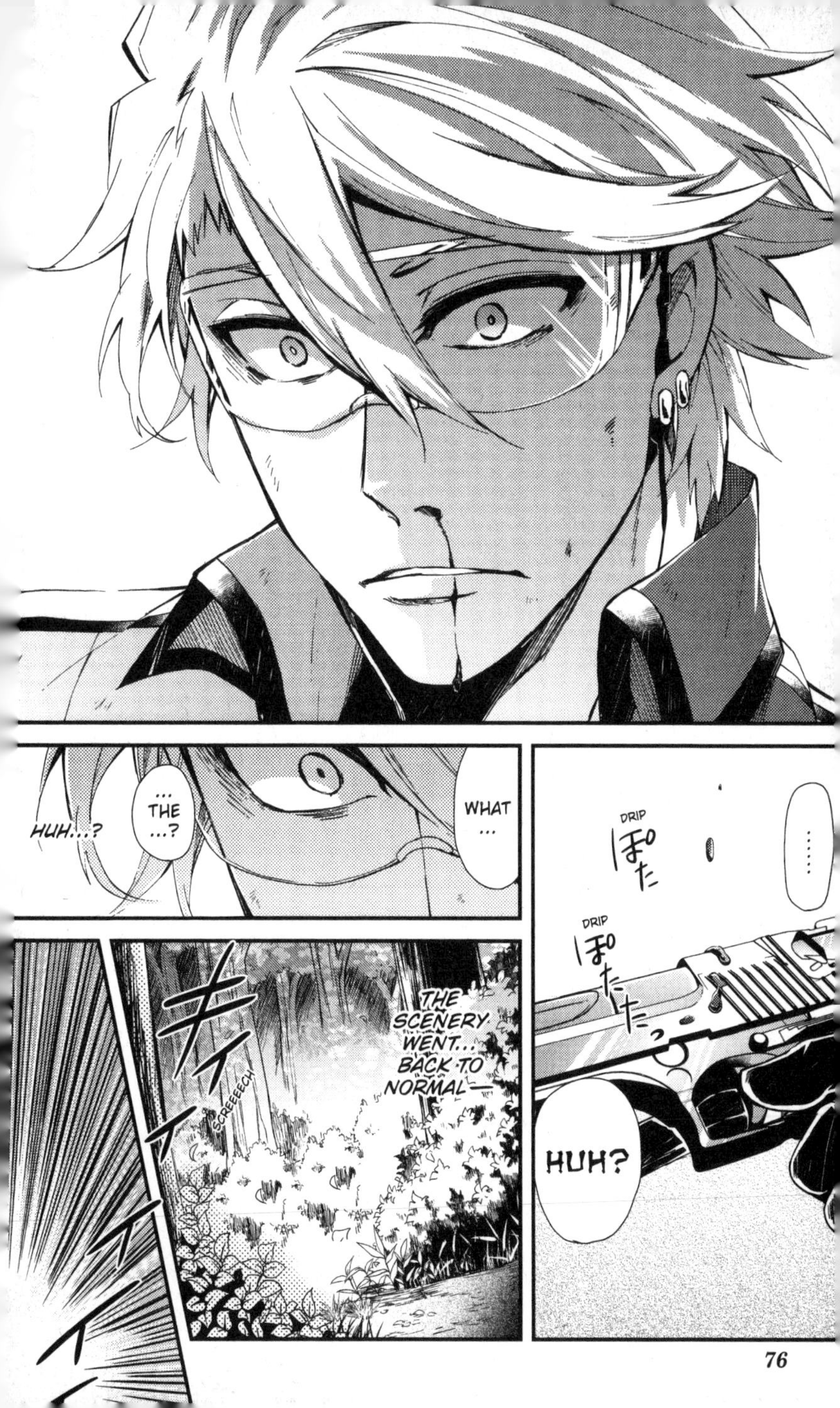
......
DRIP
ぽた
DRIP
ぽたたっ
HUH?
WHAT...
...THE...?
HUH...?
THE SCENERY WENT... BACK TO NORMAL—
SCREEEECH

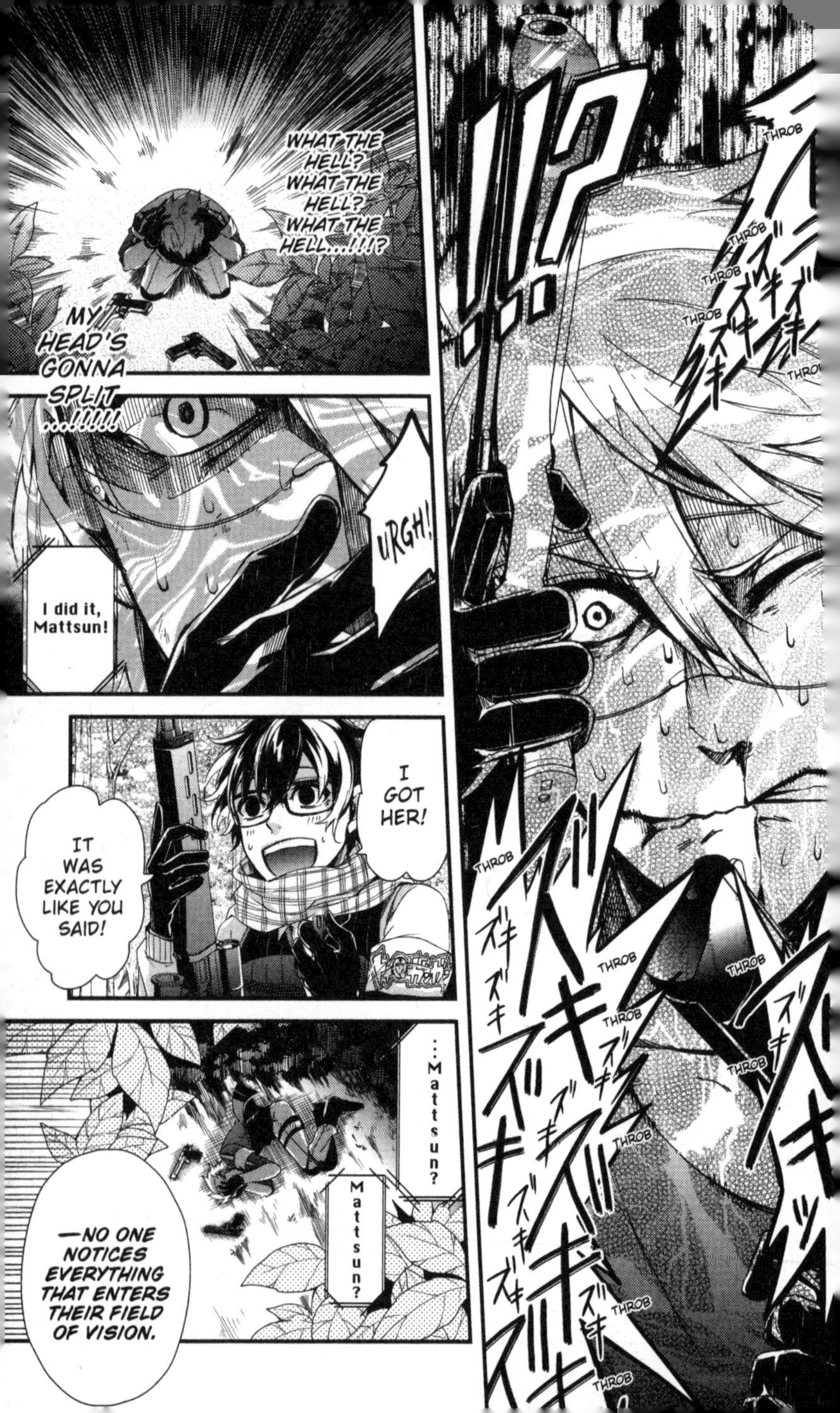

!!?
THROB
THROB
THROB
THROB
THROB
THROB
THROB
THROB
THROB
THROB
THROB
THROB
WHAT THE HELL? WHAT THE HELL? WHAT THE HELL...!!!?
MY HEAD'S GONNA SPLIT...!!!!!!
URGH!
I did it, Mattsun!
I GOT HER!
IT WAS EXACTLY LIKE YOU SAID!
...Mattsun?
Mattsun?
—NO ONE NOTICES EVERYTHING THAT ENTERS THEIR FIELD OF VISION.

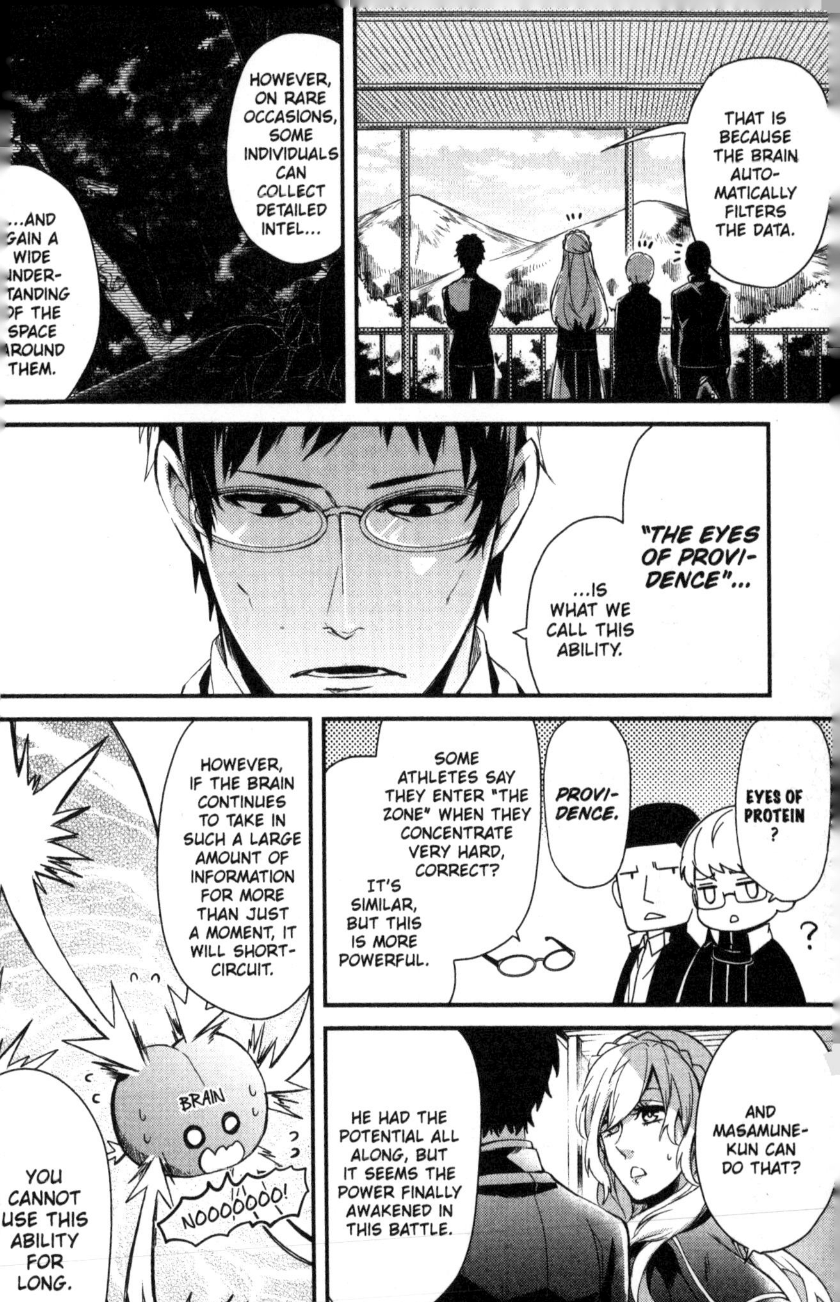
THAT IS BECAUSE THE BRAIN AUTO-MATICALLY FILTERS THE DATA.
HOWEVER, ON RARE OCCASIONS, SOME INDIVIDUALS CAN COLLECT DETAILED INTEL...
...AND GAIN A WIDE UNDER-STANDING OF THE SPACE AROUND THEM.
"THE EYES OF PROVI-DENCE"...
...IS WHAT WE CALL THIS ABILITY.
EYES OF PROTEIN?
PROVI-DENCE.
SOME ATHLETES SAY THEY ENTER "THE ZONE" WHEN THEY CONCENTRATE VERY HARD, CORRECT?
IT'S SIMILAR, BUT THIS IS MORE POWERFUL.
AND MASAMUNE-KUN CAN DO THAT?
HE HAD THE POTENTIAL ALL ALONG, BUT IT SEEMS THE POWER FINALLY AWAKENED IN THIS BATTLE.
HOWEVER, IF THE BRAIN CONTINUES TO TAKE IN SUCH A LARGE AMOUNT OF INFORMATION FOR MORE THAN JUST A MOMENT, IT WILL SHORT-CIRCUIT.
BRAIN
NOOOOOOOO!
YOU CANNOT USE THIS ABILITY FOR LONG.

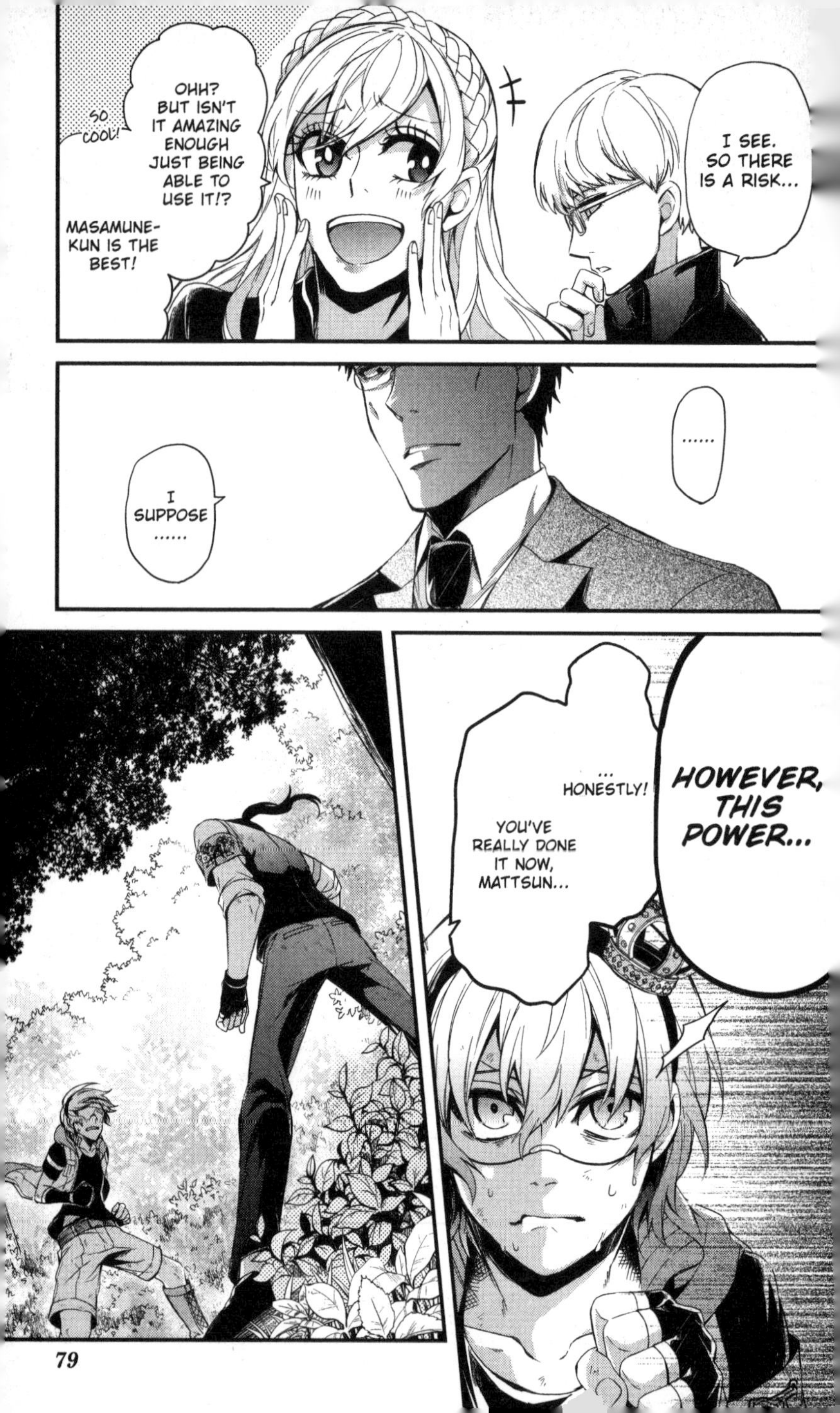
I SEE. SO THERE IS A RISK...
OHH? BUT ISN'T IT AMAZING ENOUGH JUST BEING ABLE TO USE IT!?
SO COOL!
MASAMUNE-KUN IS THE BEST!
......
I SUPPOSE ......
HOWEVER, THIS POWER...
... HONESTLY!
YOU'VE REALLY DONE IT NOW, MATTSUN...

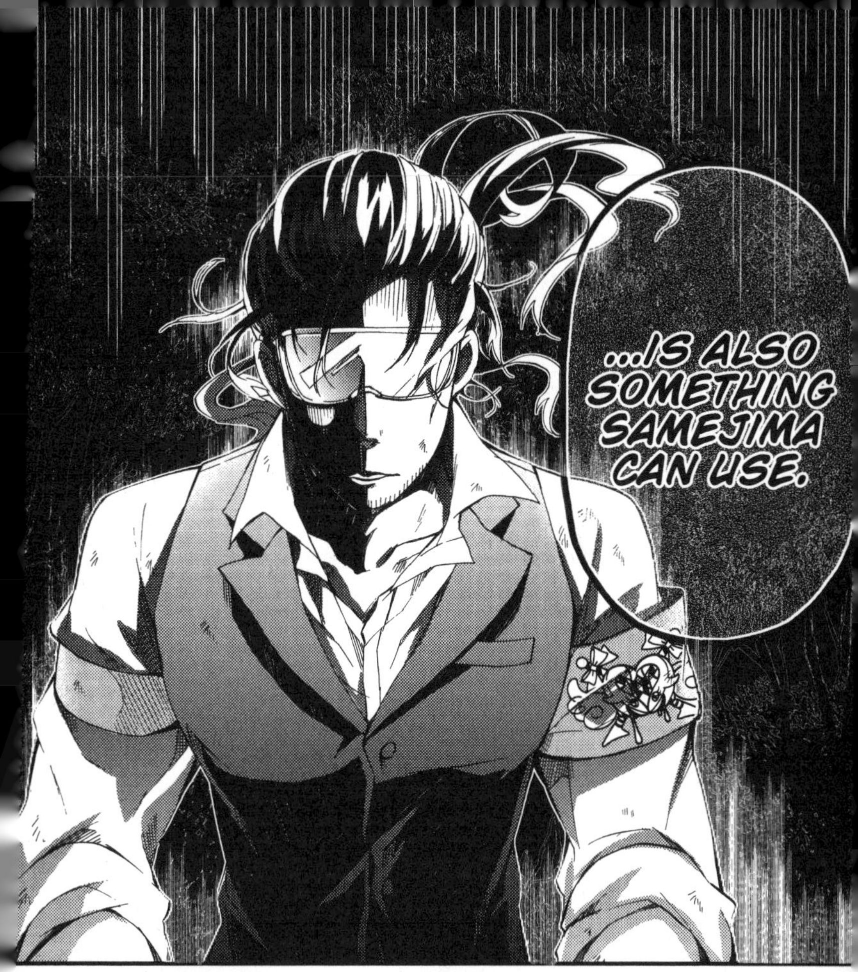
...IS ALSO SOMETHING SAMEJIMA CAN USE.
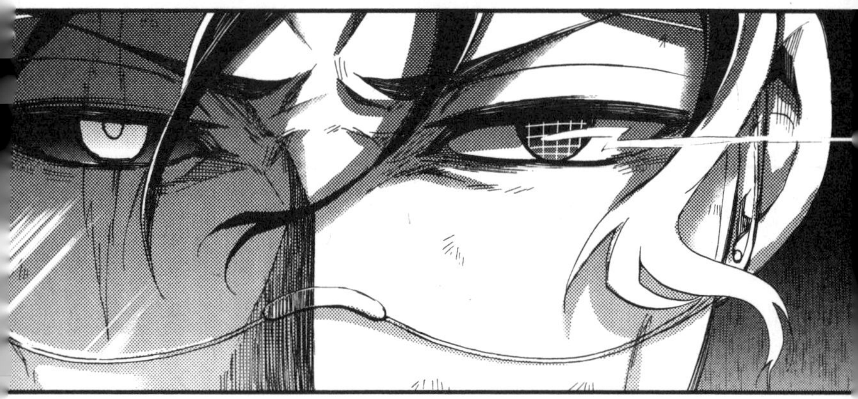

AOHARU
MACHINE
GUN

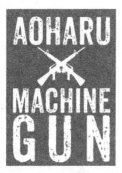

OP
ECRET ?
MEETING WITH NAOE

MAYBE WHEN THE NAME "THE EYES OF PROVIDENCE" CAME UP, YOU THOUGHT, "IS AOHARU A STORY ABOUT SUPERPOWERS?" BUT IT'S NOT A TALE OF SUPERPOWERED BATTLES. (IF YOU HAVE TO CALL IT SOMETHING, I'D SAY IT'S A STORY ABOUT SKILL AND TALENT...)

BUT THE MEETING WHEN I EXPLAINED MATSUOKA'S ABILITY WAS PRETTY MEMORABLE...

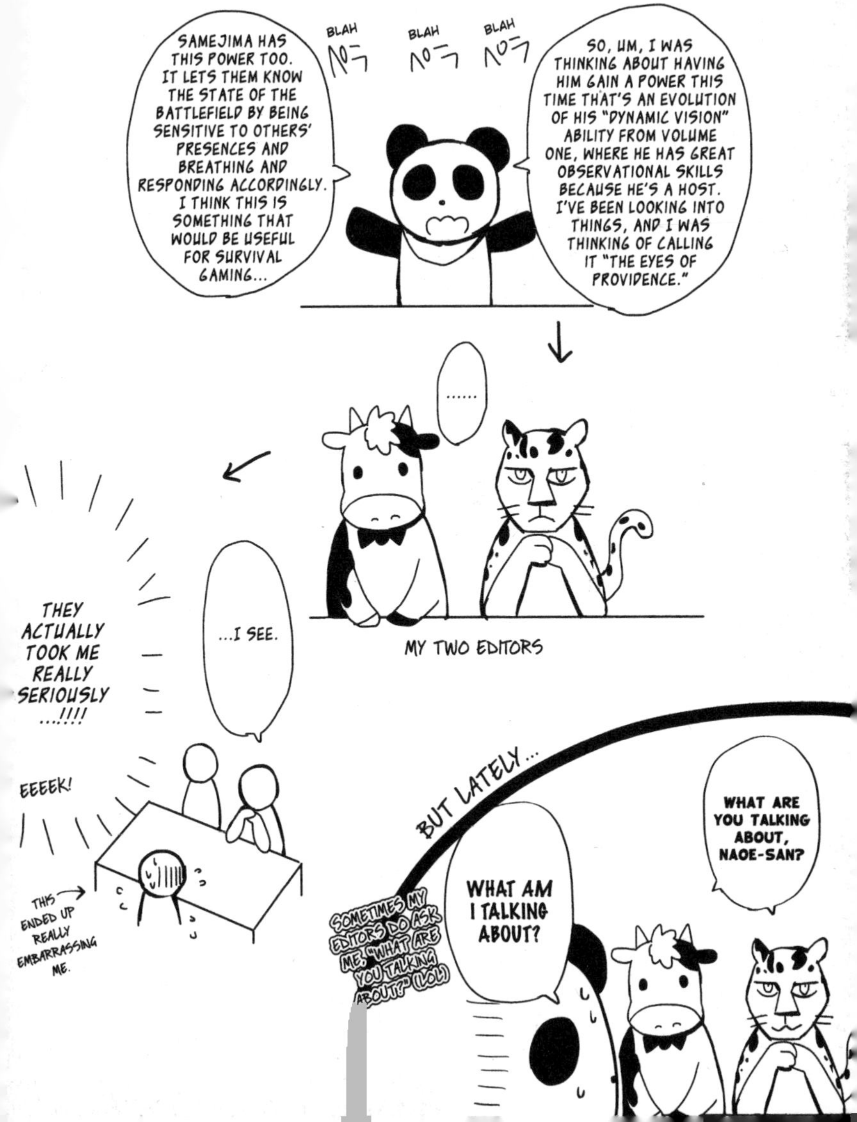
BLAH BLAH BLAH
SO, UM, I WAS THINKING ABOUT HAVING HIM GAIN A POWER THIS TIME THAT'S AN EVOLUTION OF HIS "DYNAMIC VISION" ABILITY FROM VOLUME ONE, WHERE HE HAS GREAT OBSERVATIONAL SKILLS BECAUSE HE'S A HOST. I'VE BEEN LOOKING INTO THINGS, AND I WAS THINKING OF CALLING IT "THE EYES OF PROVIDENCE."
SAMEJIMA HAS THIS POWER TOO. IT LETS THEM KNOW THE STATE OF THE BATTLEFIELD BY BEING SENSITIVE TO OTHERS' PRESENCES AND BREATHING AND RESPONDING ACCORDINGLY. I THINK THIS IS SOMETHING THAT WOULD BE USEFUL FOR SURVIVAL GAMING...
......
MY TWO EDITORS
...I SEE.
THEY ACTUALLY TOOK ME REALLY SERIOUSLY ....!!!!
EEEEK!
THIS ENDED UP REALLY EMBARRASSING ME.
BUT LATELY...
WHAT ARE YOU TALKING ABOUT, NAOE-SAN?
WHAT AM I TALKING ABOUT?
SOMETIMES MY EDITORS DO ASK ME, "WHAT ARE YOU TALKING ABOUT?" (LOL)

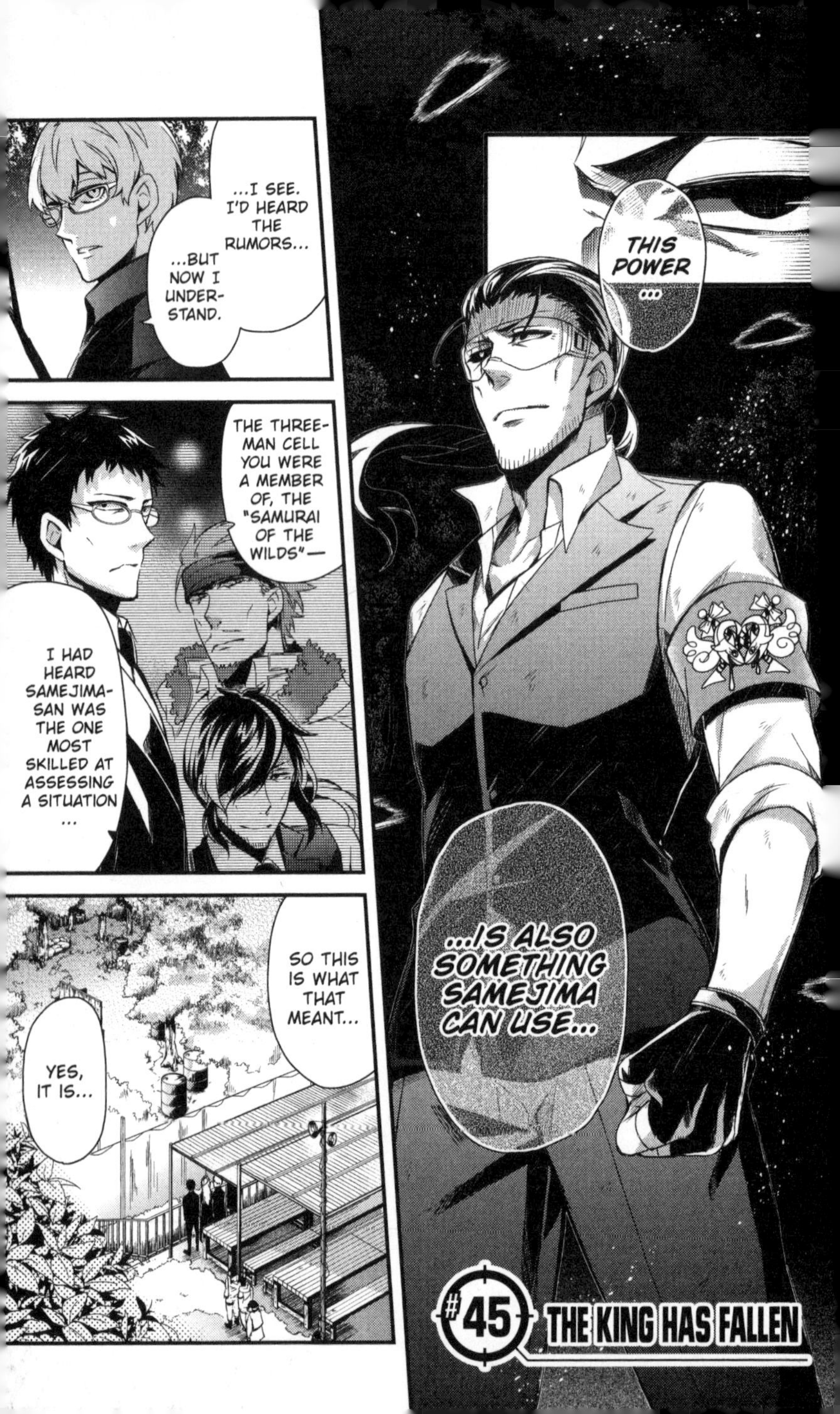
THIS POWER ...
...IS ALSO SOMETHING SAMEJIMA CAN USE...
#45 THE KING HAS FALLEN
...I SEE. I'D HEARD THE RUMORS...
...BUT NOW I UNDER-STAND.
THE THREE-MAN CELL YOU WERE A MEMBER OF, THE "SAMURAI OF THE WILDS"—
I HAD HEARD SAMEJIMA-SAN WAS THE ONE MOST SKILLED AT ASSESSING A SITUATION ...
SO THIS IS WHAT THAT MEANT...
YES, IT IS...

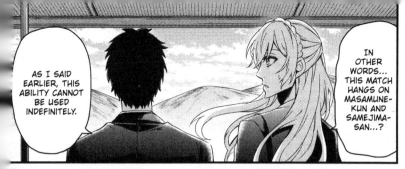

IN OTHER WORDS... THIS MATCH HANGS ON MASAMUNE-KUN AND SAMEJIMA-SAN...?
AS I SAID EARLIER, THIS ABILITY CANNOT BE USED INDEFINITELY.
MATSUOKA DID NOT UNDERSTAND THE RISKS AND PUSHED HIS BODY TOO HARD.
I'M SURE HE'LL BE USELESS FOR THE REST OF THE MATCH.
THROB
THROB
THROB
HOW-EVER...
......
INCH...
... WHAT?

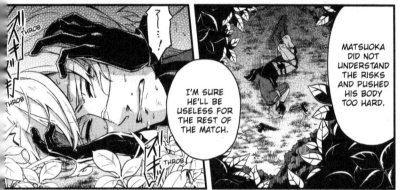

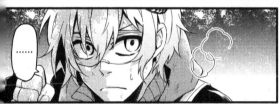

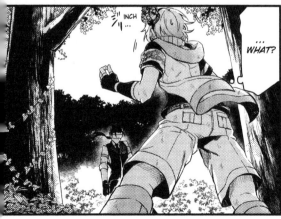

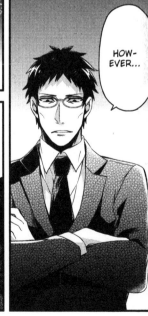

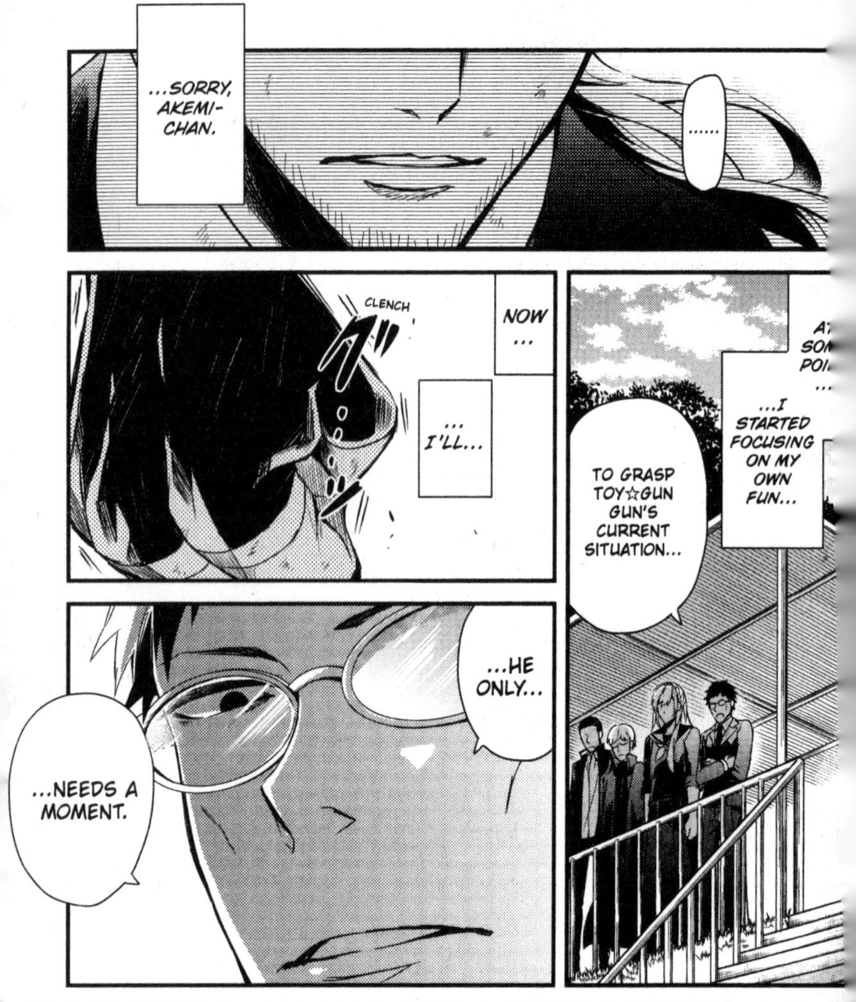
......
...SORRY, AKEMI-CHAN.
...I STARTED FOCUSING ON MY OWN FUN...
TO GRASP TOY☆GUN GUN'S CURRENT SITUATION...
NOW ...
... I'LL...
CLENCH
...HE ONLY...
...NEEDS A MOMENT.

...END IT...

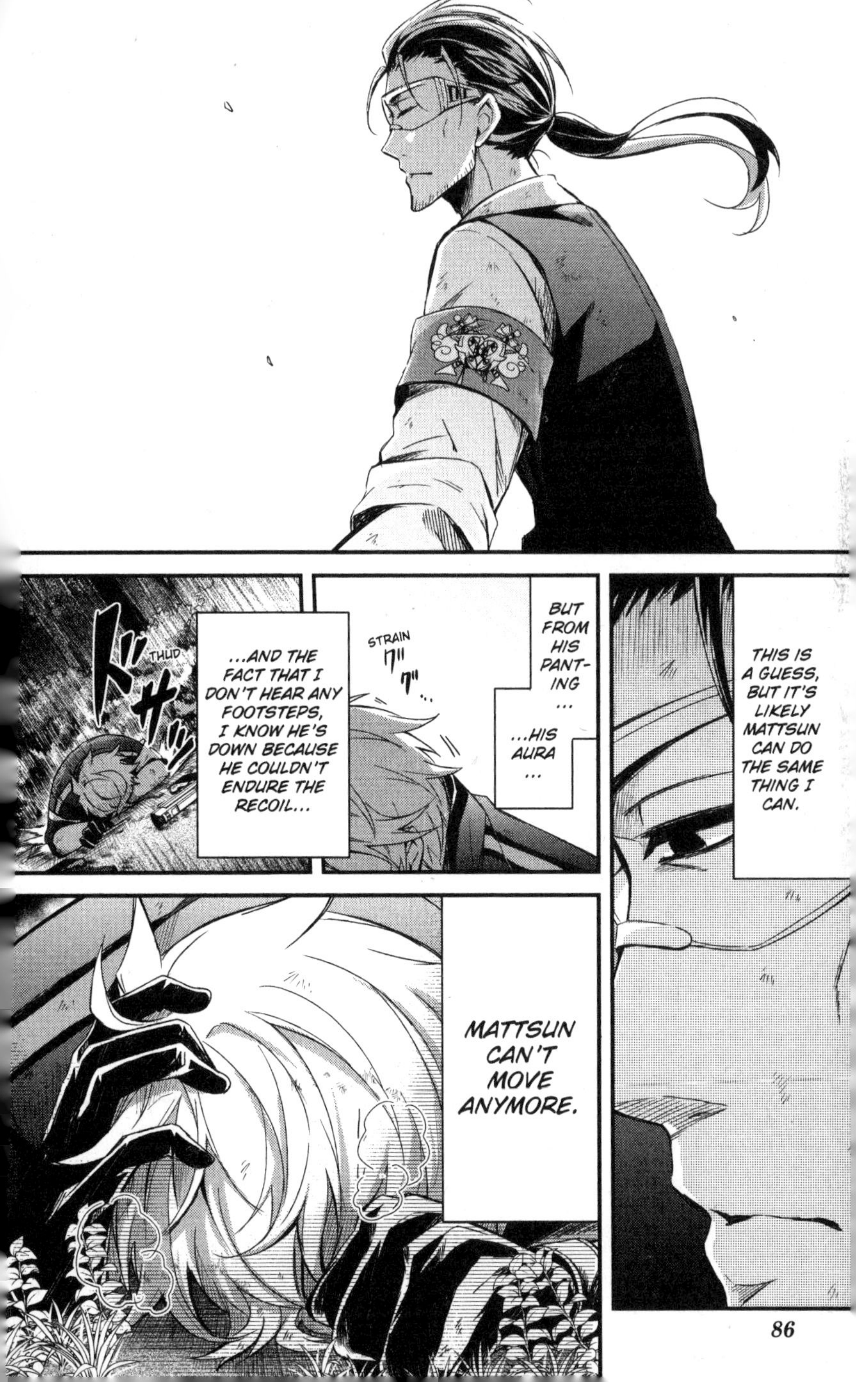
THIS IS A GUESS, BUT IT'S LIKELY MATTSUN CAN DO THE SAME THING I CAN.
BUT FROM HIS PANTING...
...HIS AURA...
STRAIN
...AND THE FACT THAT I DON'T HEAR ANY FOOTSTEPS, I KNOW HE'S DOWN BECAUSE HE COULDN'T ENDURE THE RECOIL...
THUD
MATTSUN CAN'T MOVE ANYMORE.

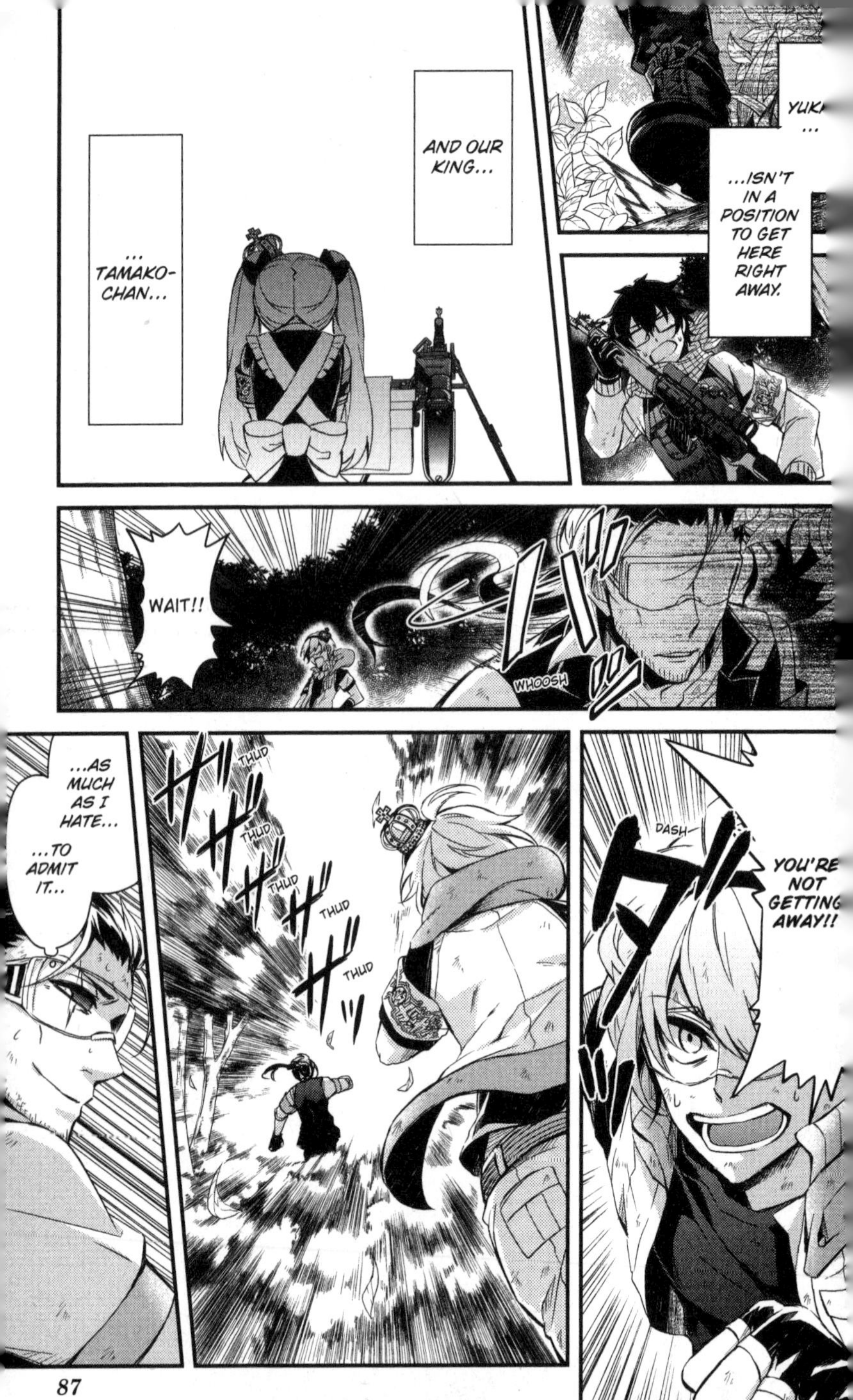
YUK
...
...ISN'T IN A POSITION TO GET HERE RIGHT AWAY.
AND OUR KING...
...TAMAKO-CHAN...
WAIT!!
WHOOSH
DASH
YOU'RE NOT GETTING AWAY!!
THUD
THUD
THUD
THUD
THUD
...AS MUCH AS I HATE...
...TO ADMIT IT...

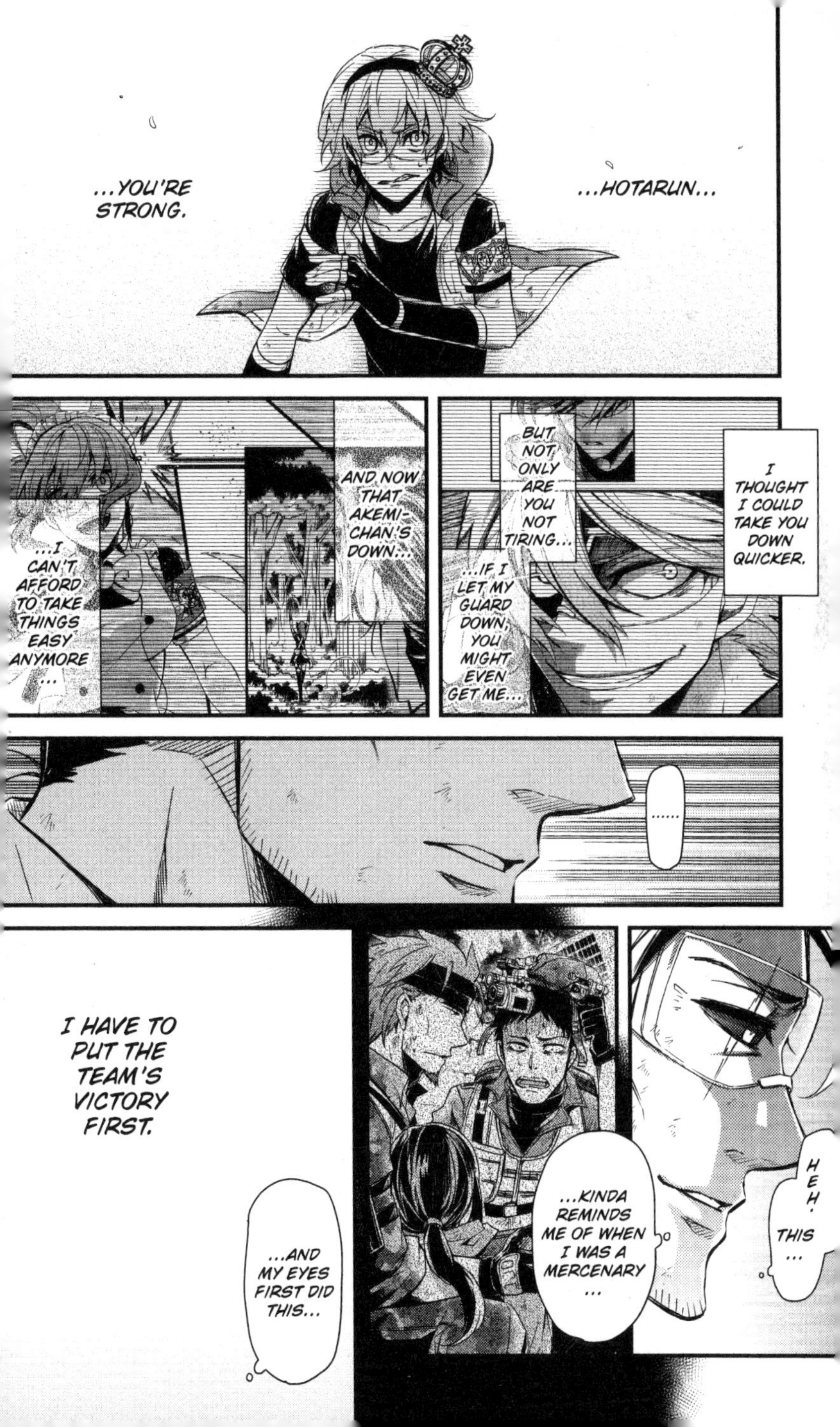
...HOTARUN...
...YOU'RE STRONG.
I THOUGHT I COULD TAKE YOU DOWN QUICKER.
BUT NOT ONLY ARE YOU NOT TIRING...
...IF I LET MY GUARD DOWN, YOU MIGHT EVEN GET ME...
AND NOW THAT AKEMI-CHAN'S DOWN...
...I CAN'T AFFORD TO TAKE THINGS EASY ANYMORE...
......
HEH. THIS...
...KINDA REMINDS ME OF WHEN I WAS A MERCENARY...
...AND MY EYES FIRST DID THIS...
I HAVE TO PUT THE TEAM'S VICTORY FIRST.

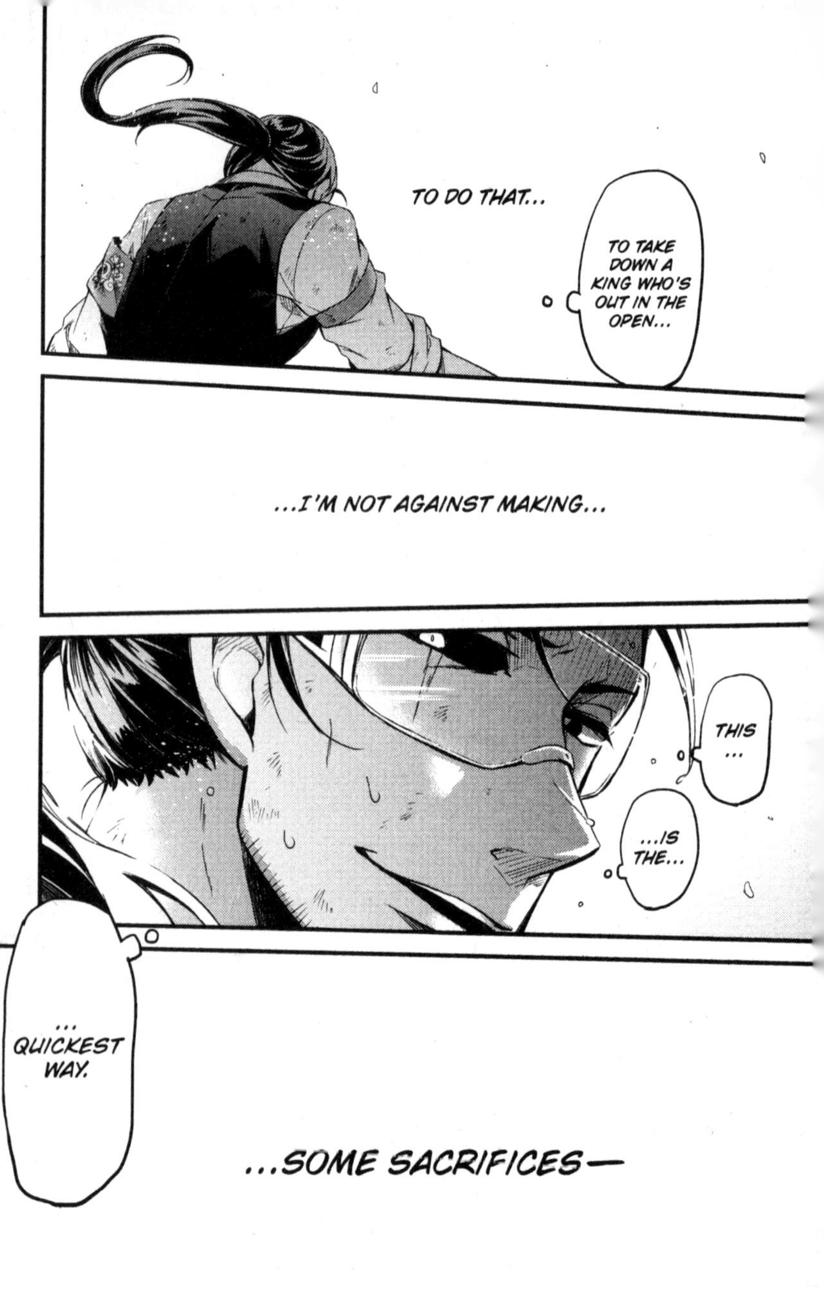
TO TAKE DOWN A KING WHO'S OUT IN THE OPEN...
TO DO THAT...
...I'M NOT AGAINST MAKING...
THIS...
...IS THE...
...SOME SACRIFICES—
...QUICKEST WAY.

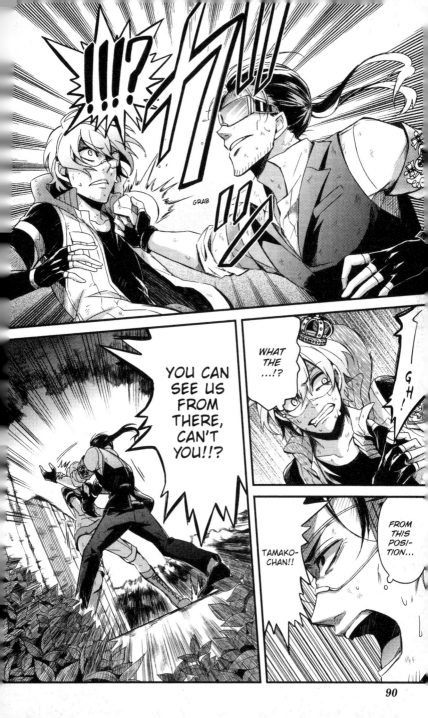

!!!?
GRAB
GH!
WHAT THE ...!?
FROM THIS POSITION...
TAMAKO-CHAN!!
YOU CAN SEE US FROM THERE, CAN'T YOU!!?

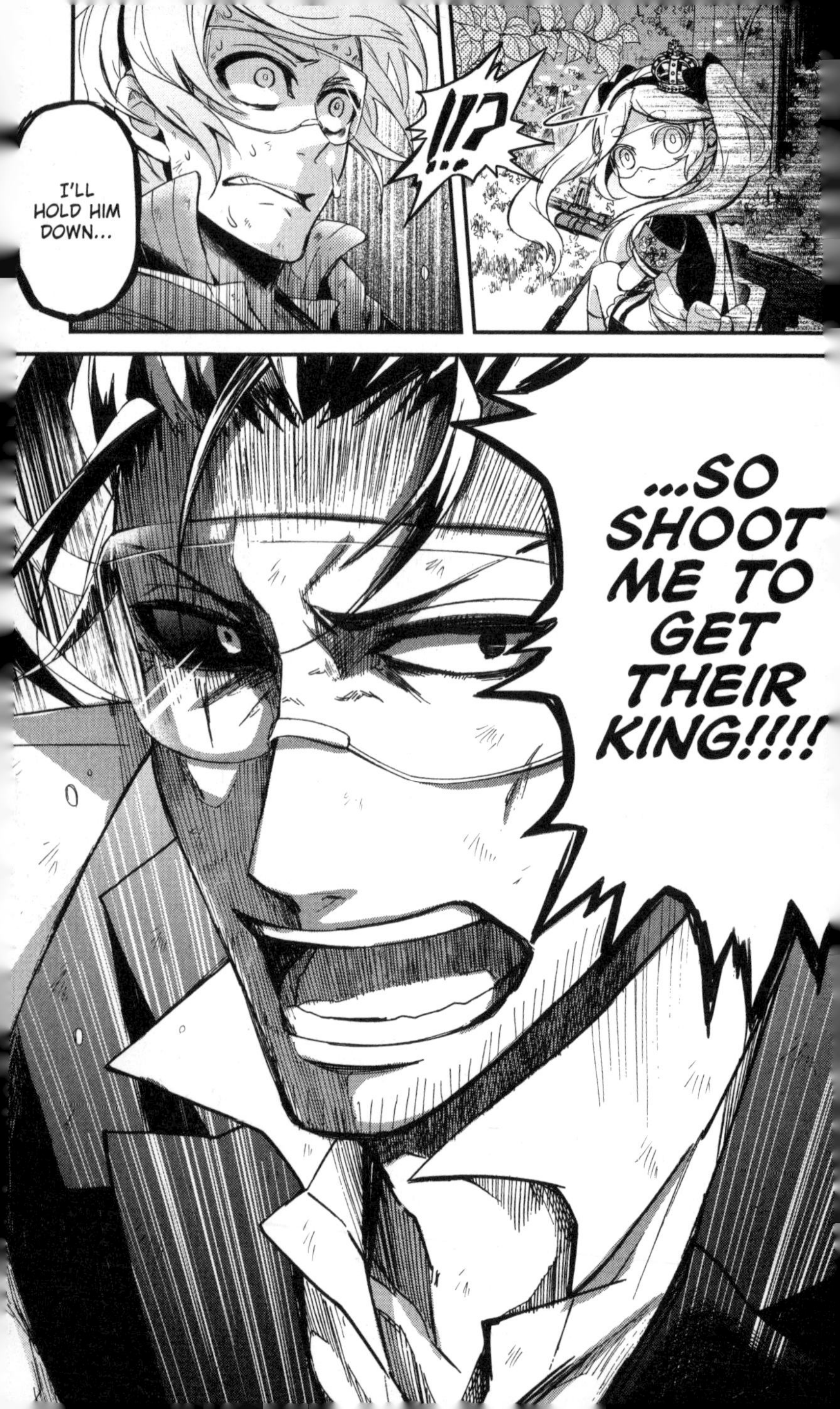
!!?
I'LL HOLD HIM DOWN...
...SO SHOOT ME TO GET THEIR KING!!!!

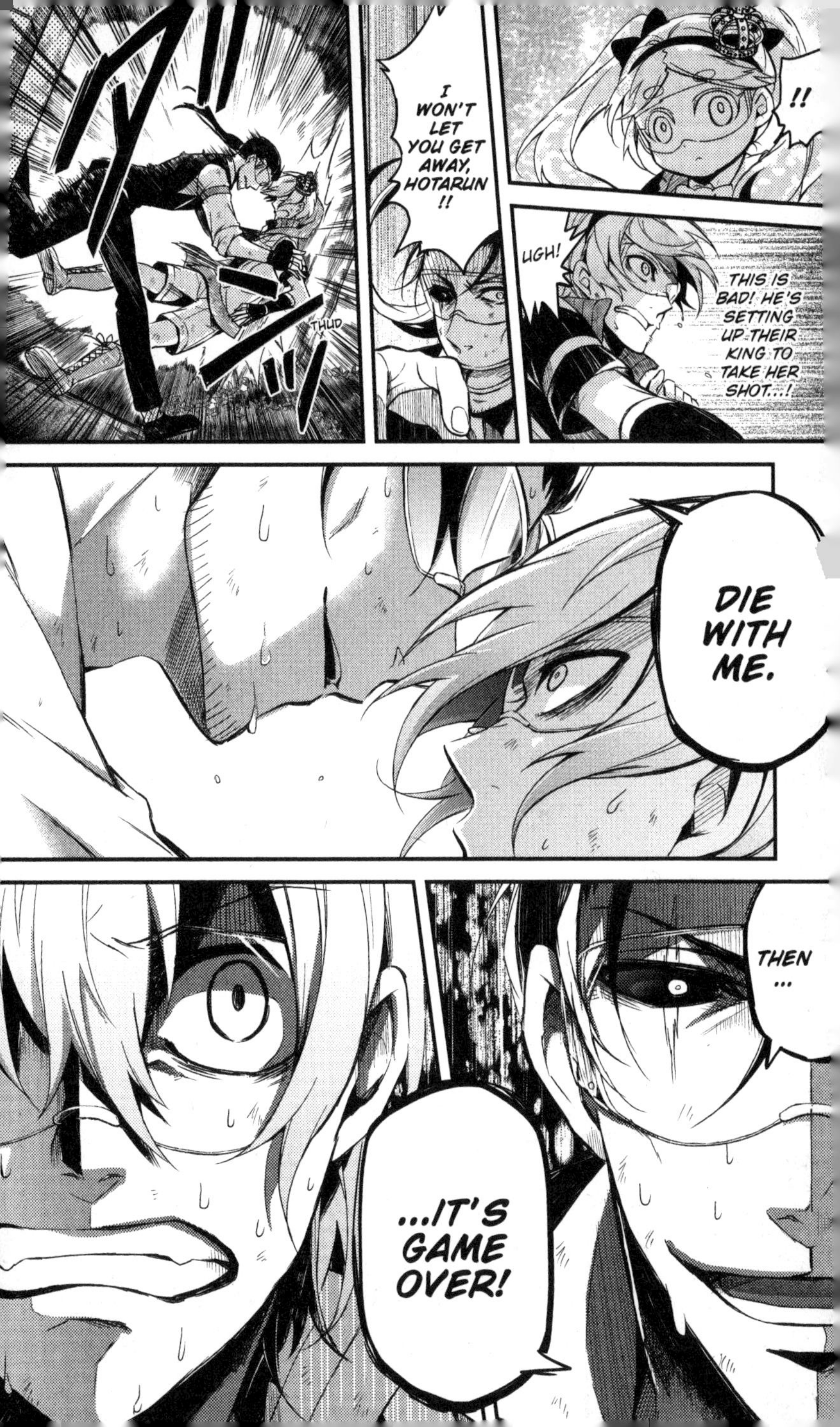
!!
UGH!
THIS IS BAD! HE'S SETTING UP THEIR KING TO TAKE HER SHOT...!
I WON'T LET YOU GET AWAY, HOTARUN!!
THUD
DIE WITH ME.
THEN...
...IT'S GAME OVER!

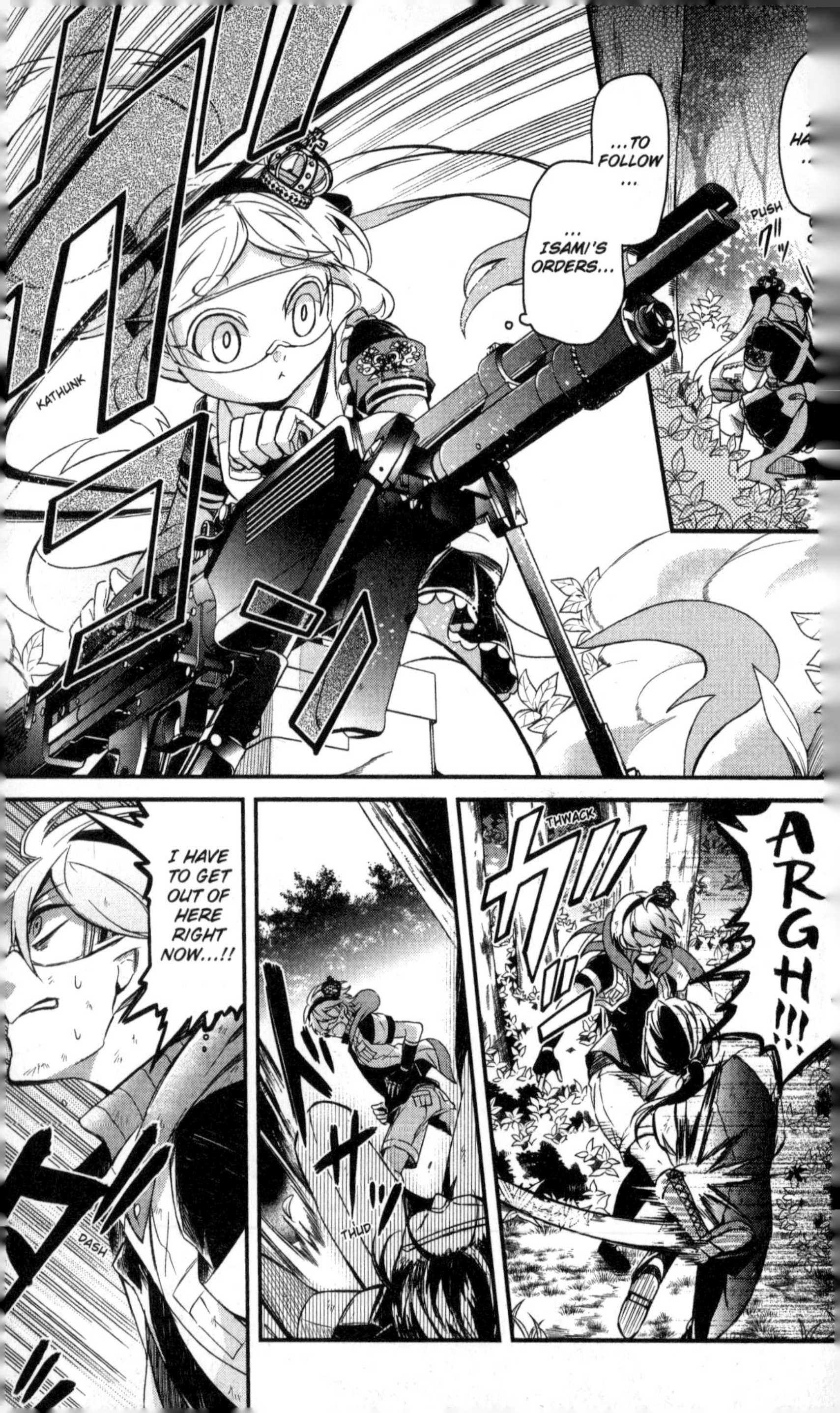
PUSH
...TO FOLLOW ...
... ISAMI'S ORDERS...
KATHUNK
THWACK
ARGH!!!
THUD
I HAVE TO GET OUT OF HERE RIGHT NOW...!!
DASH

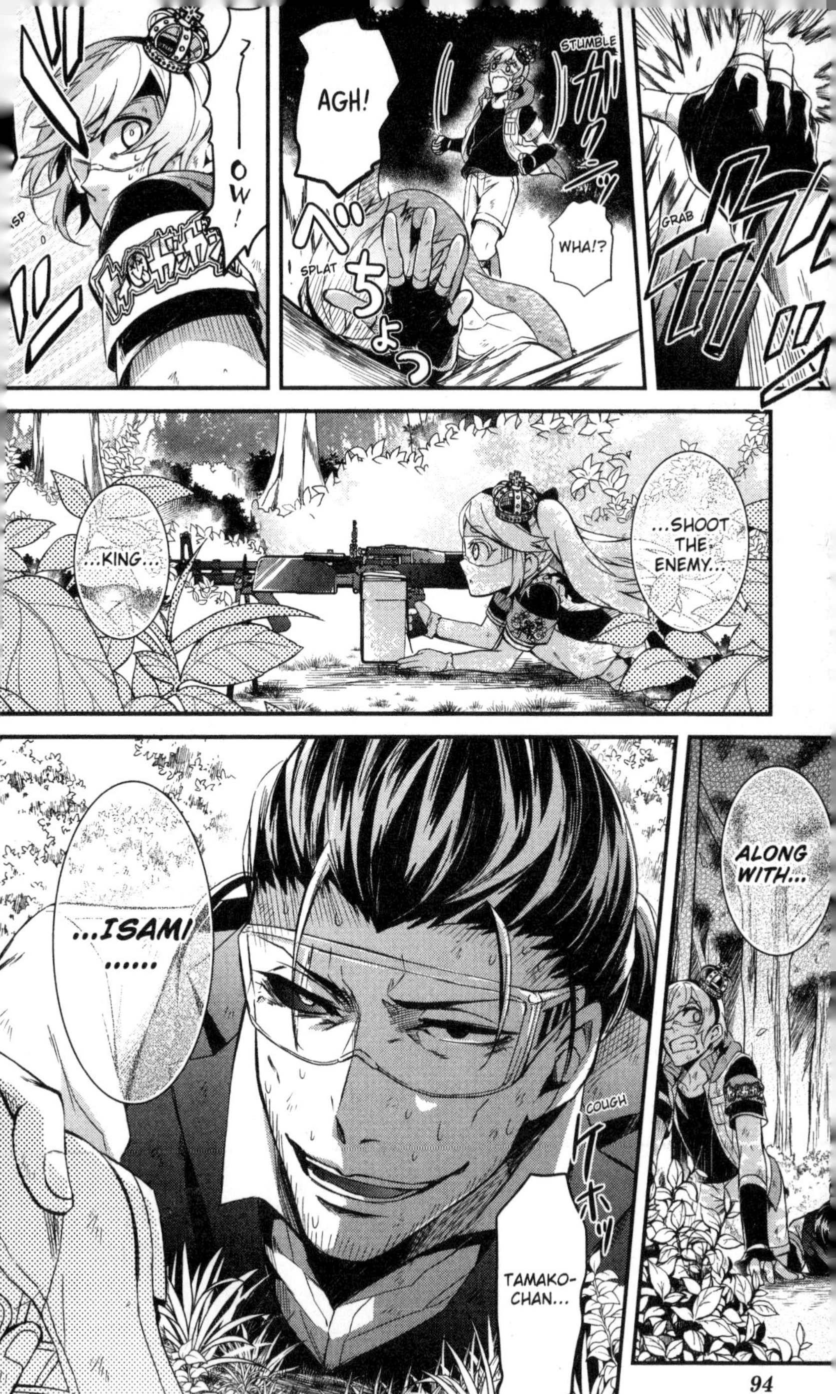
GRAB
STUMBLE
AGH!
WHA!?
SPLAT
OW!
...SHOOT THE ENEMY...
...KING...
ALONG WITH...
...ISAMI ......
COUGH
TAMAKO-CHAN...

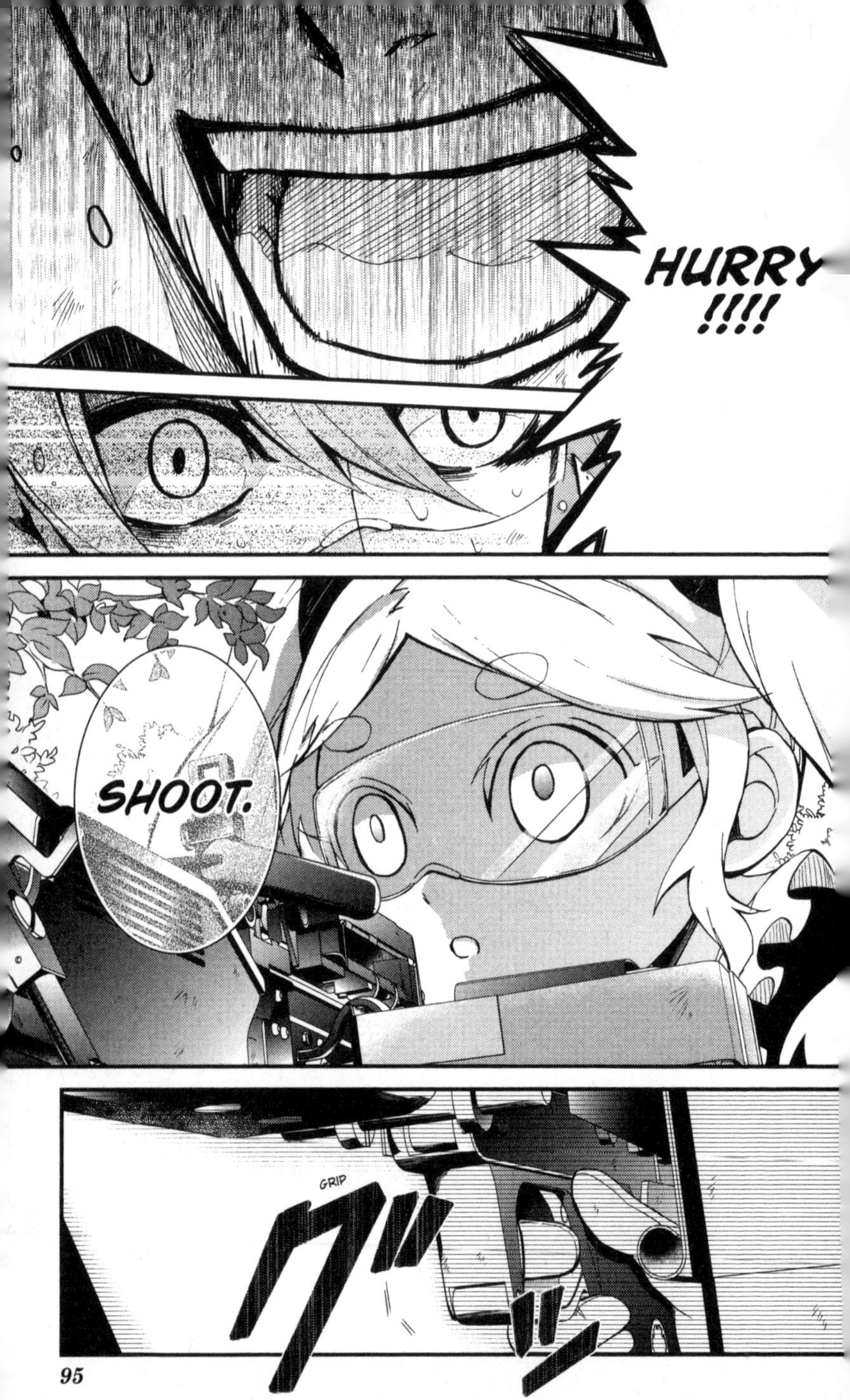
HURRY
!!!!
SHOOT.
GRIP
グッ

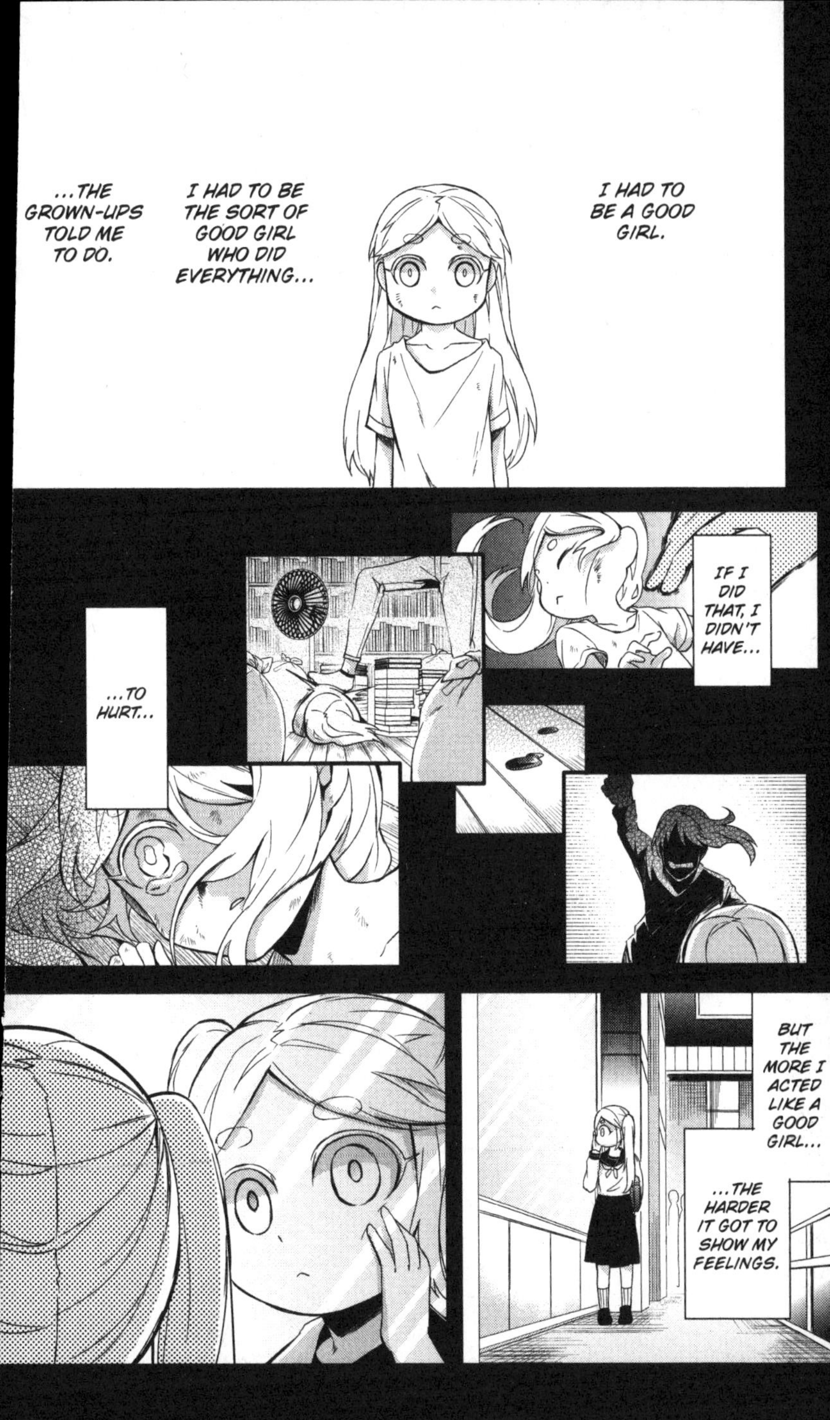
I HAD TO BE A GOOD GIRL.
I HAD TO BE THE SORT OF GOOD GIRL WHO DID EVERYTHING...
...THE GROWN-UPS TOLD ME TO DO.
IF I DID THAT, I DIDN'T HAVE...
...TO HURT...
BUT THE MORE I ACTED LIKE A GOOD GIRL...
...THE HARDER IT GOT TO SHOW MY FEELINGS.

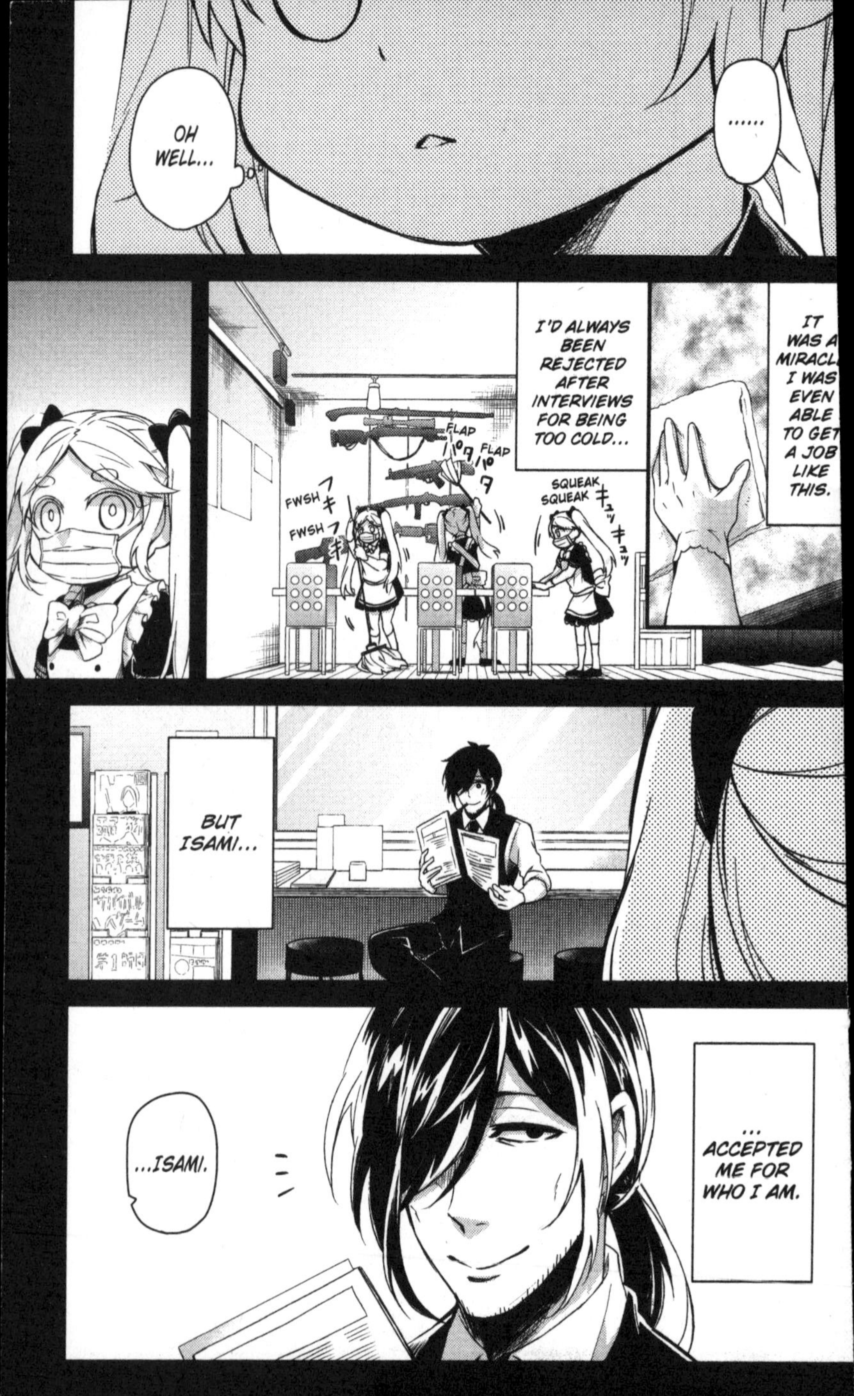
......
OH WELL...
IT WAS A MIRACL I WAS EVEN ABLE TO GET A JOB LIKE THIS.
I'D ALWAYS BEEN REJECTED AFTER INTERVIEWS FOR BEING TOO COLD...
FLAP パタ
FLAP パタ
SQUEAK SQUEAK キュッキュッ
FWSH フキ
FWSH フキ
BUT ISAMI...
... ACCEPTED ME FOR WHO I AM.
...ISAMI.

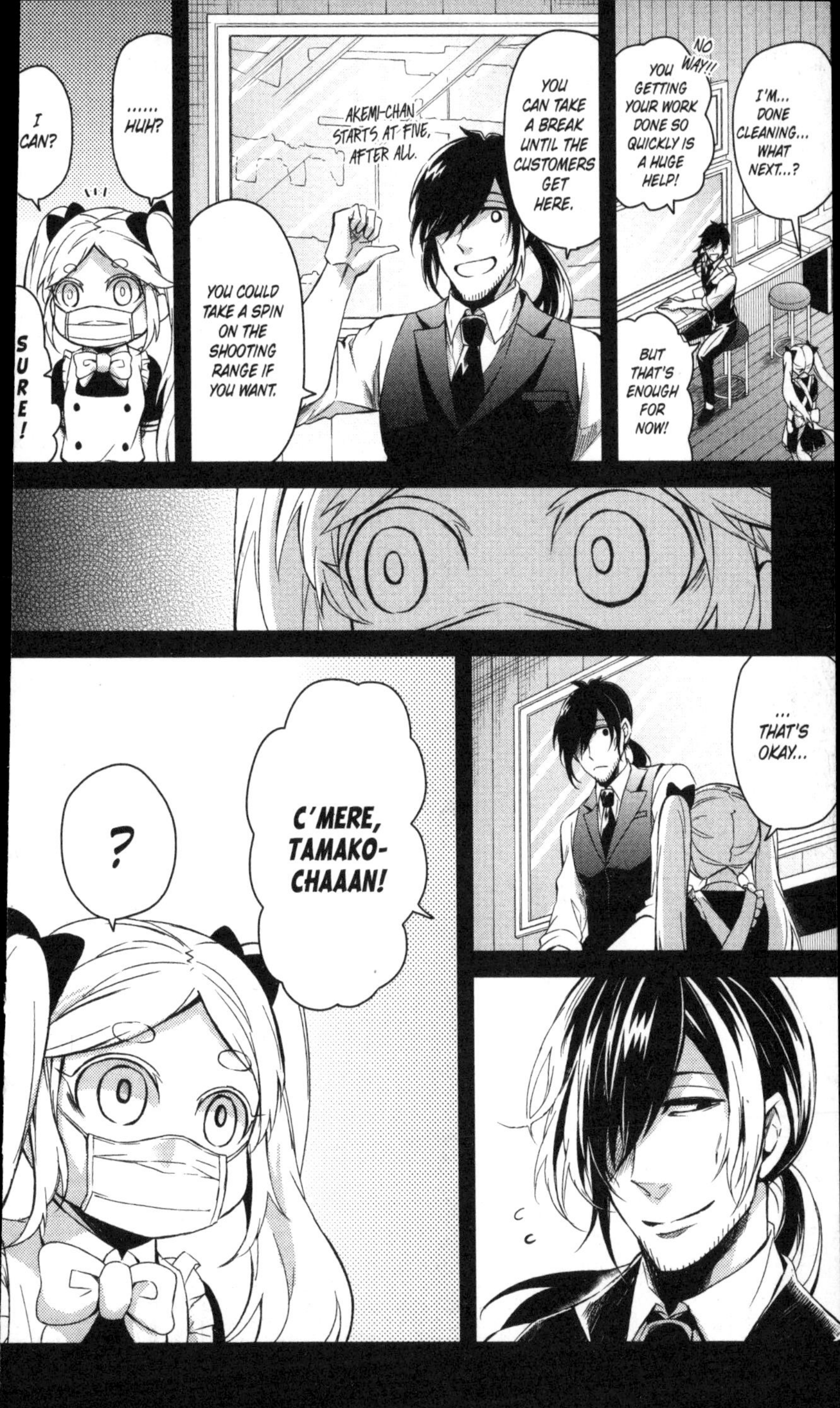
I'M... DONE CLEANING... WHAT NEXT...?
NO WAY!!
YOU GETTING YOUR WORK DONE SO QUICKLY IS A HUGE HELP!
BUT THAT'S ENOUGH FOR NOW!
YOU CAN TAKE A BREAK UNTIL THE CUSTOMERS GET HERE.
AKEMI-CHAN STARTS AT FIVE, AFTER ALL.
YOU COULD TAKE A SPIN ON THE SHOOTING RANGE IF YOU WANT.
...... HUH?
I CAN?
SURE!
... THAT'S OKAY...
C'MERE, TAMAKO-CHAAAN!
?

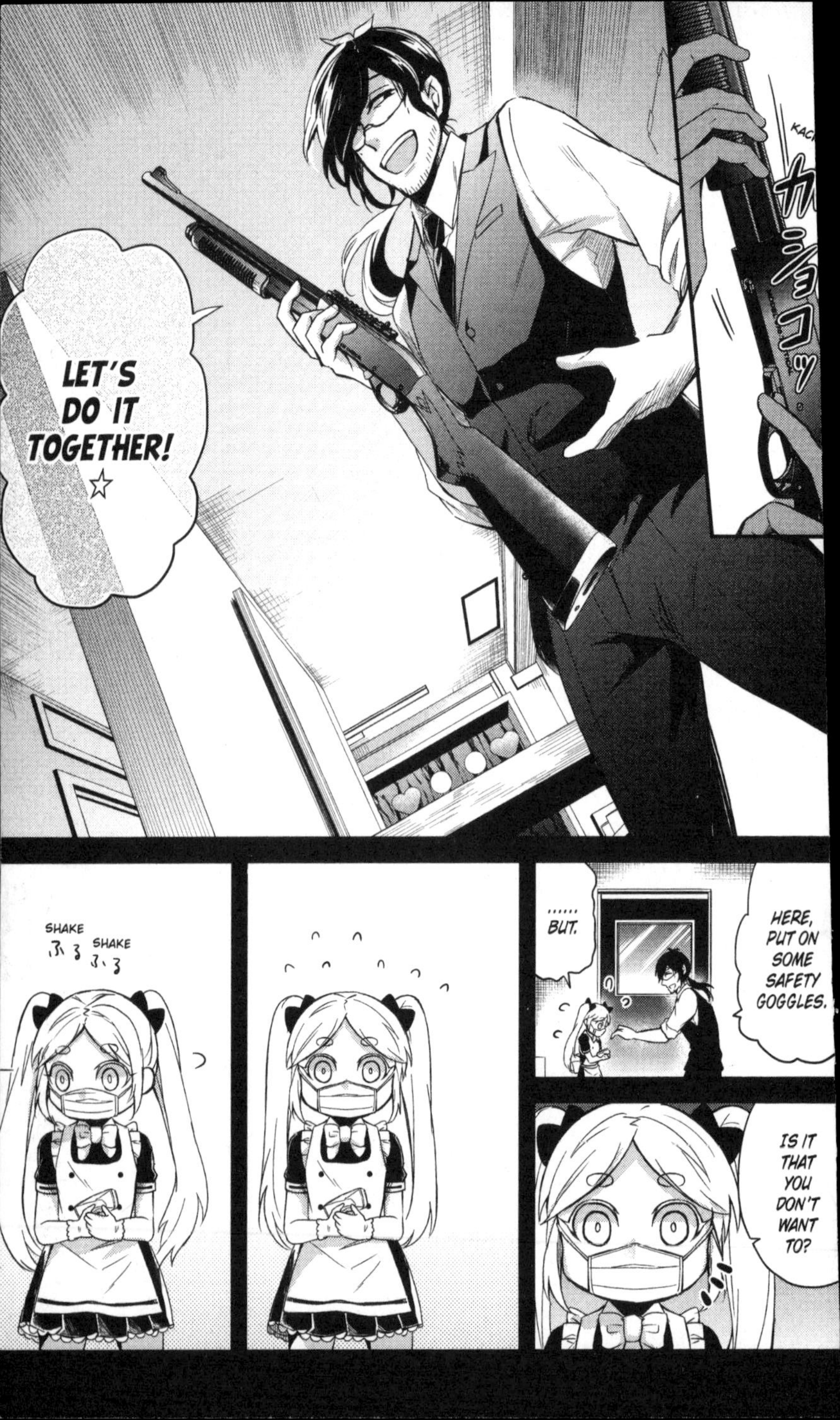
KACH
カシャコッ
LET'S DO IT TOGETHER! ☆
HERE, PUT ON SOME SAFETY GOGGLES.
...... BUT.
IS IT THAT YOU DON'T WANT TO?
SHAKE ふる SHAKE ふる

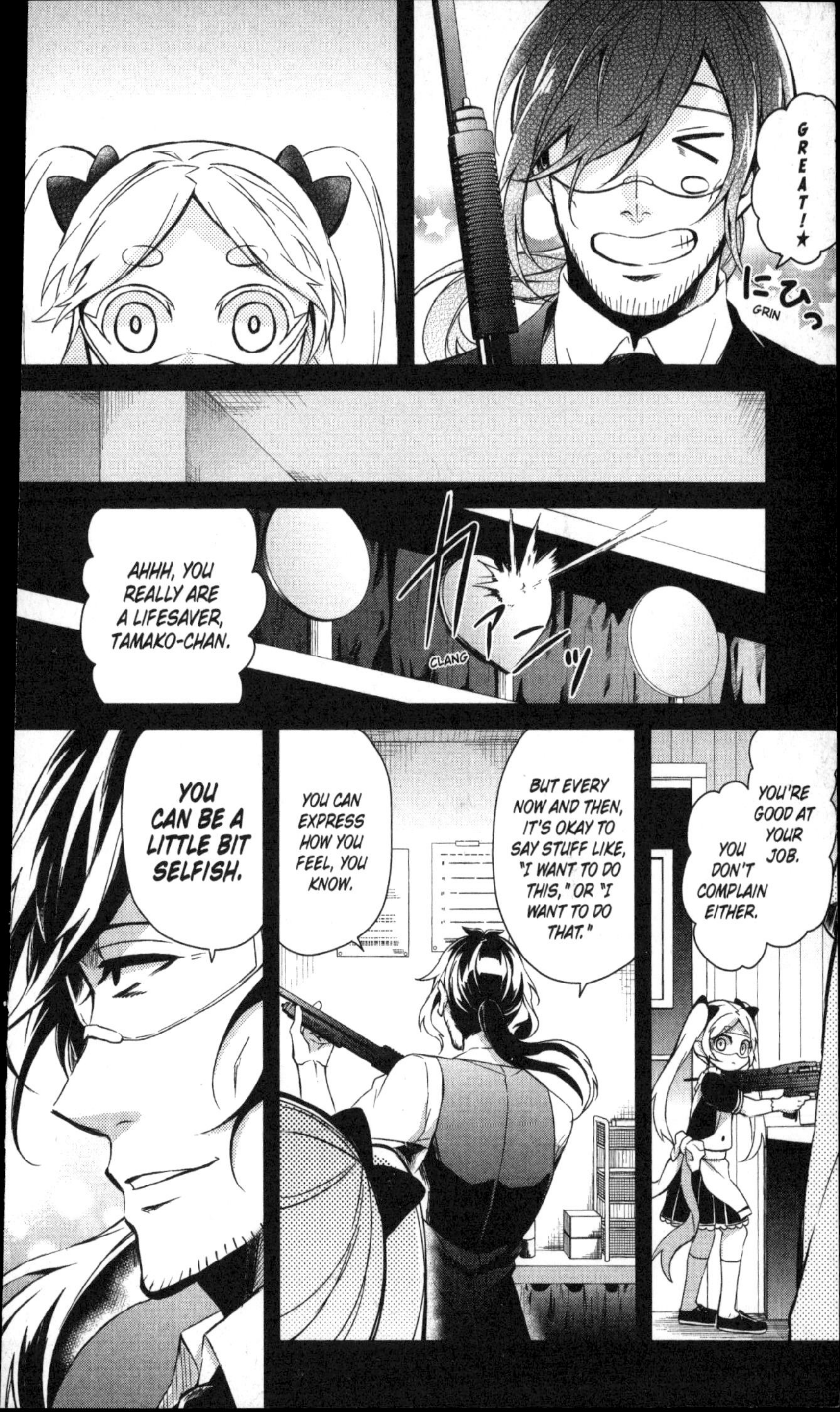
GREAT!★
にひっ
GRIN
カァーンッ
CLANG
AHHH, YOU REALLY ARE A LIFESAVER, TAMAKO-CHAN.
YOU'RE GOOD AT YOUR JOB.
YOU DON'T COMPLAIN EITHER.
BUT EVERY NOW AND THEN, IT'S OKAY TO SAY STUFF LIKE, "I WANT TO DO THIS," OR "I WANT TO DO THAT."
YOU CAN EXPRESS HOW YOU FEEL, YOU KNOW.
YOU CAN BE A LITTLE BIT SELFISH.

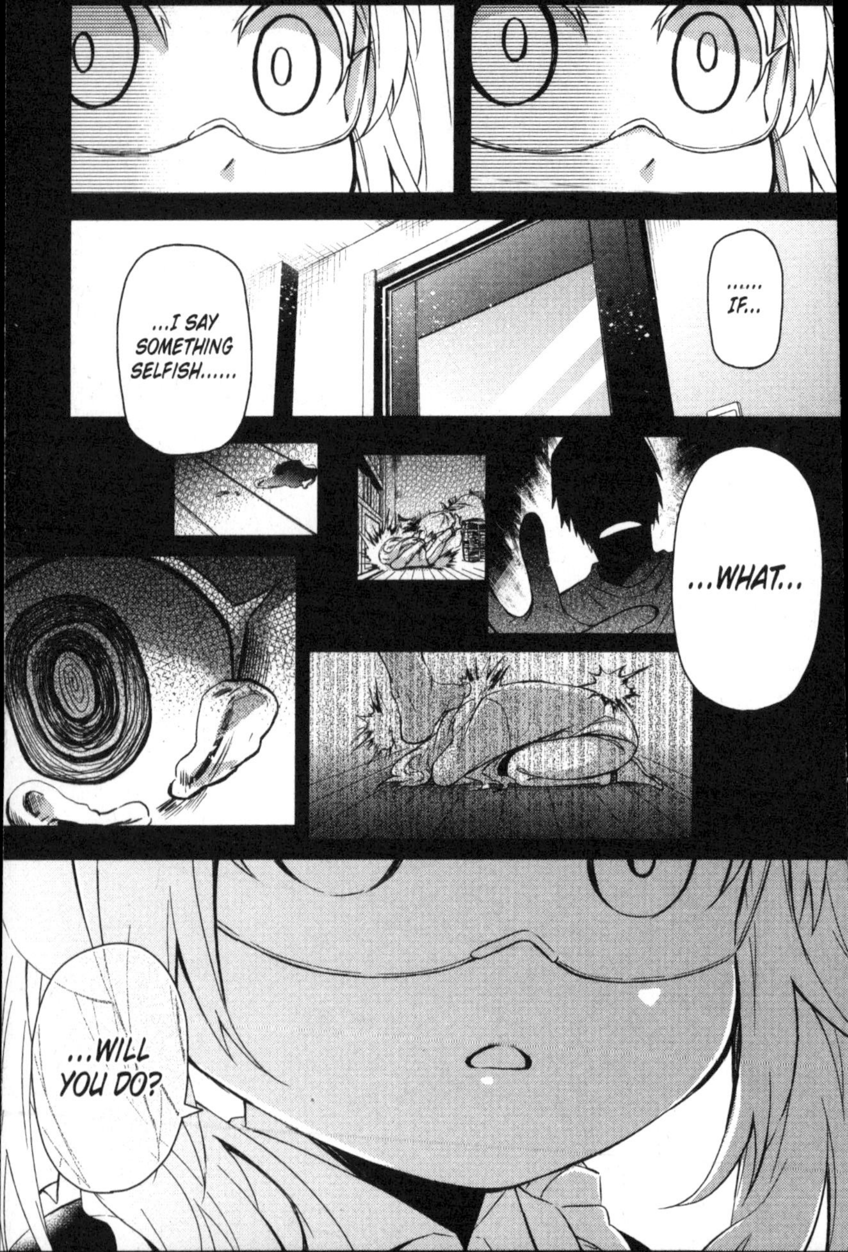
...... IF...
...I SAY SOMETHING SELFISH......
...WHAT...
...WILL YOU DO?

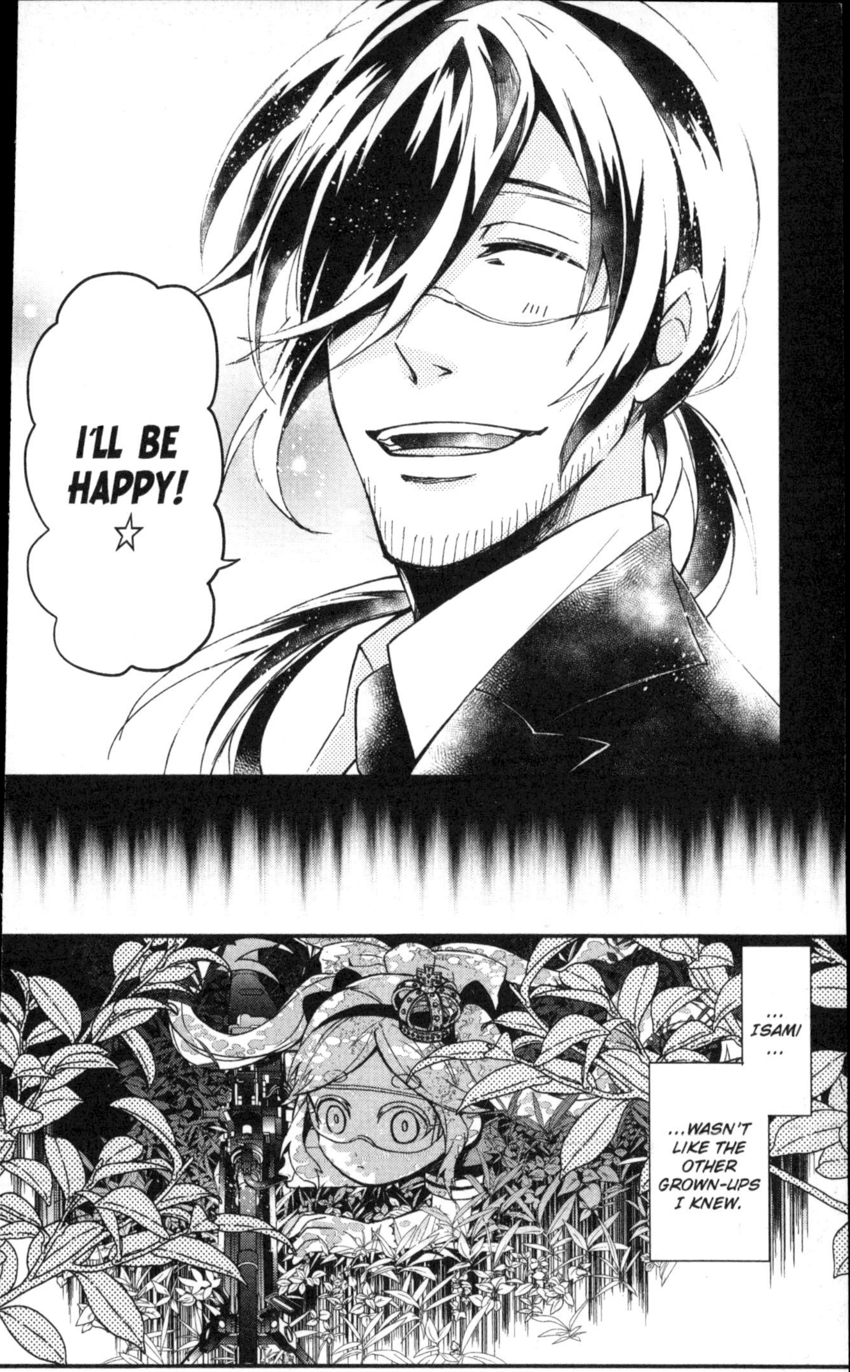
I'LL BE HAPPY! ☆
... ISAMI ...
...WASN'T LIKE THE OTHER GROWN-UPS I KNEW.

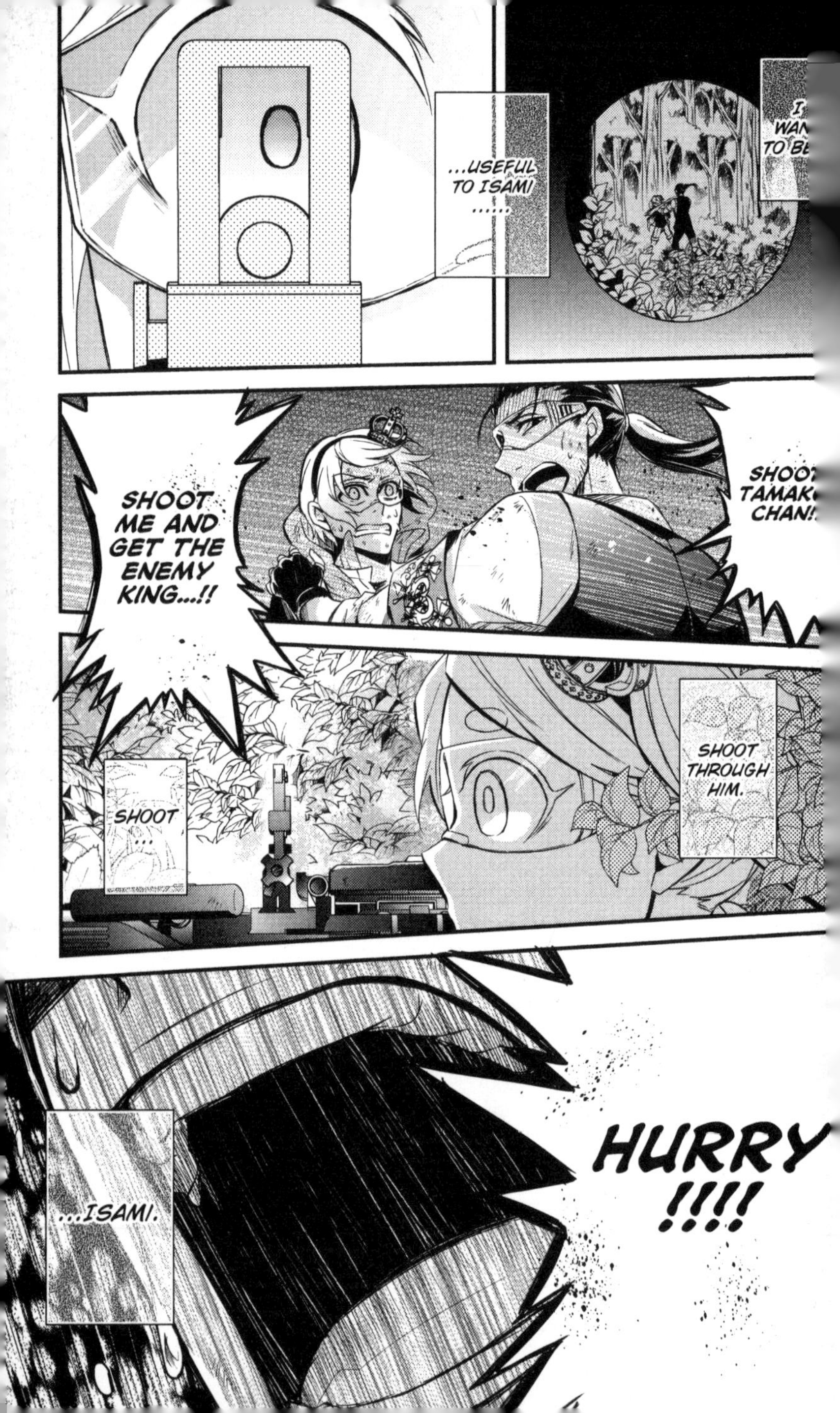
I WAN TO BE
...USEFUL TO ISAMI ......
SHOOT TAMAK CHAN!!
SHOOT ME AND GET THE ENEMY KING...!!
SHOOT THROUGH HIM.
SHOOT ...
HURRY !!!!
...ISAMI.

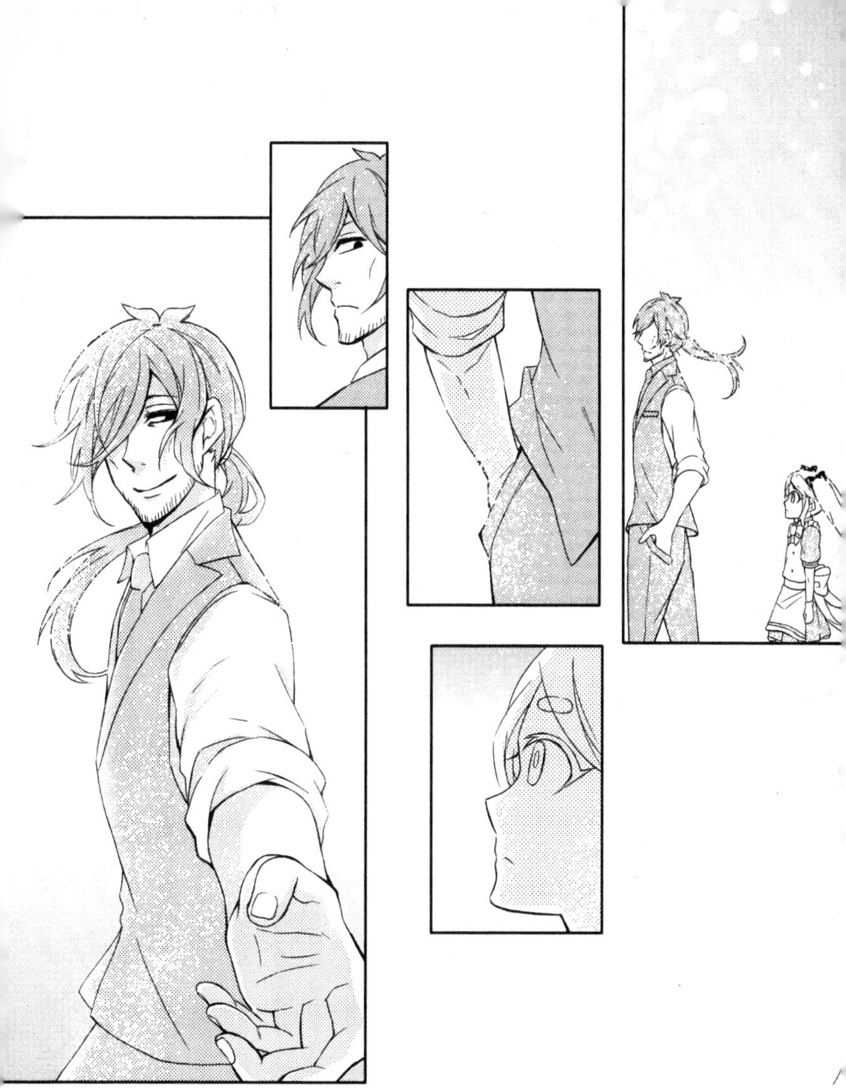

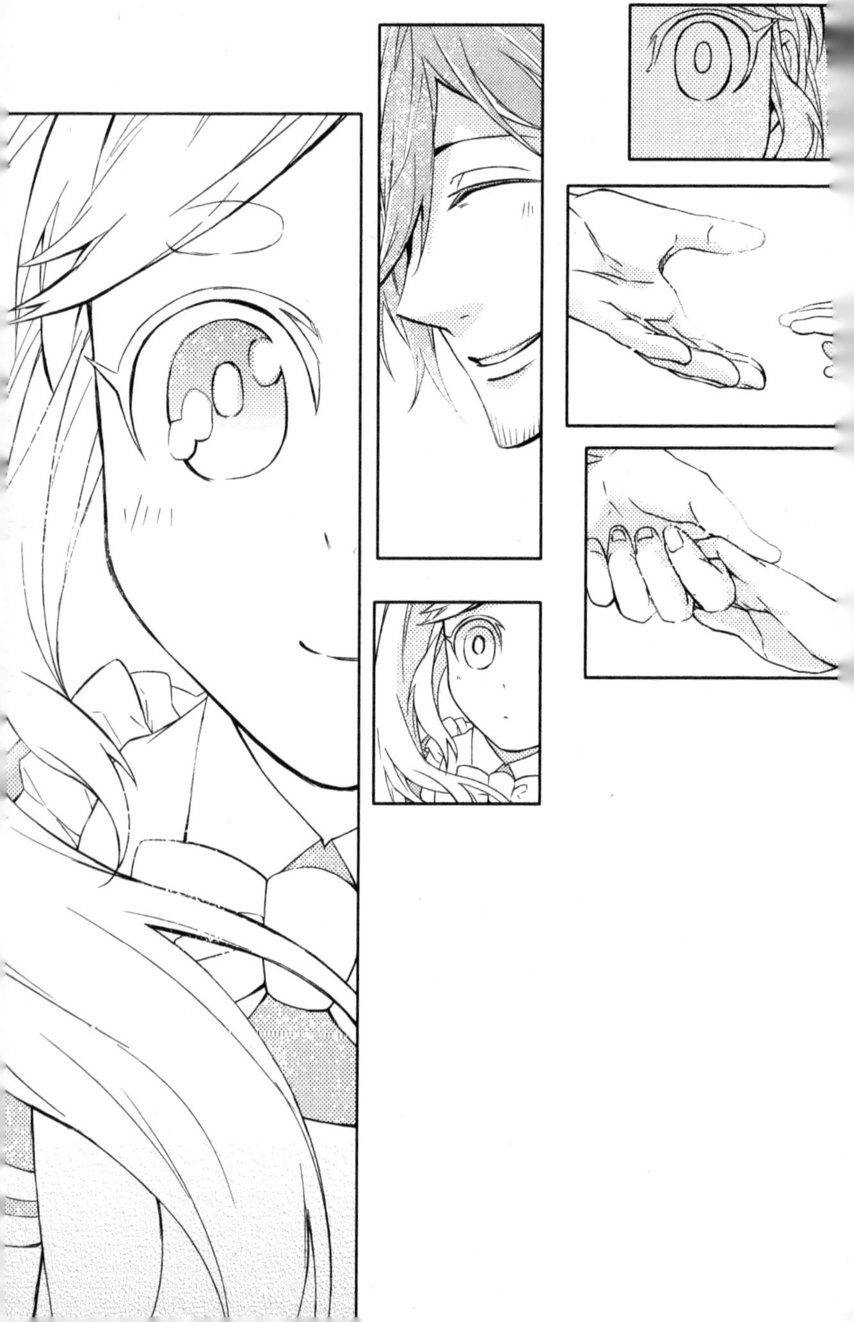

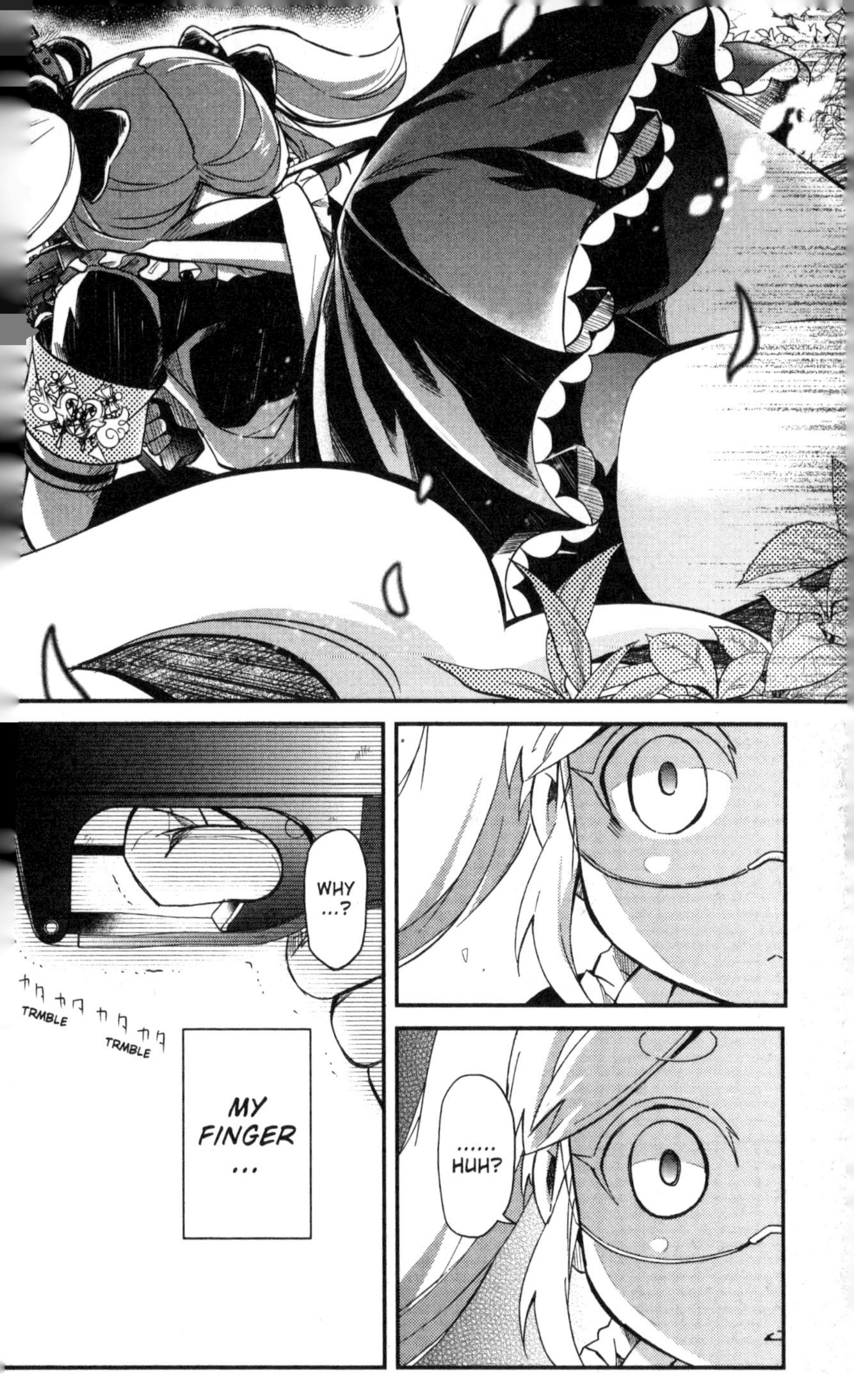

......
HUH?
WHY
...?
カタカタ
TRMBLE
カタカタ
TRMBLE
MY
FINGER
...

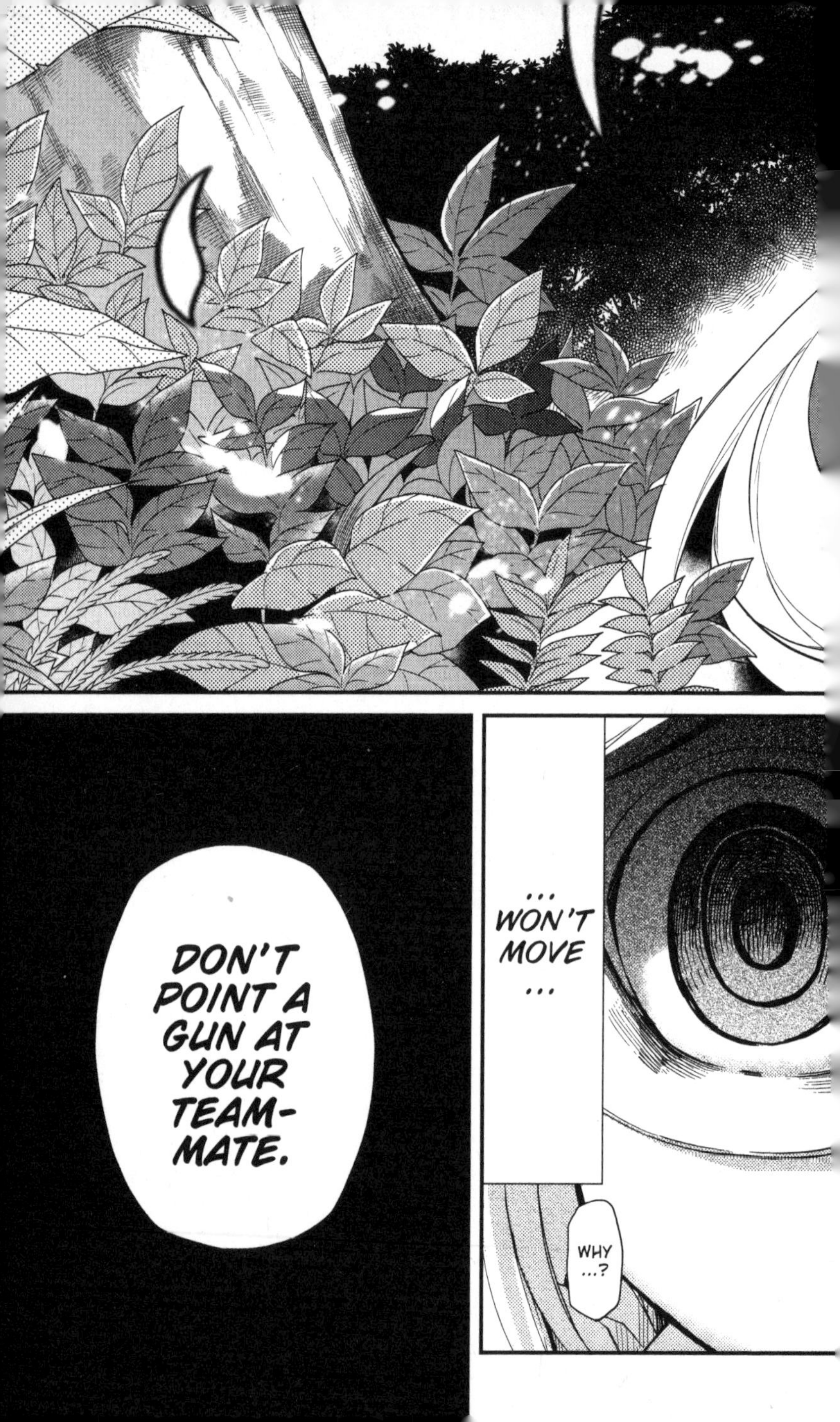

... WON'T MOVE ...
WHY ...?
DON'T POINT A GUN AT YOUR TEAM-MATE.

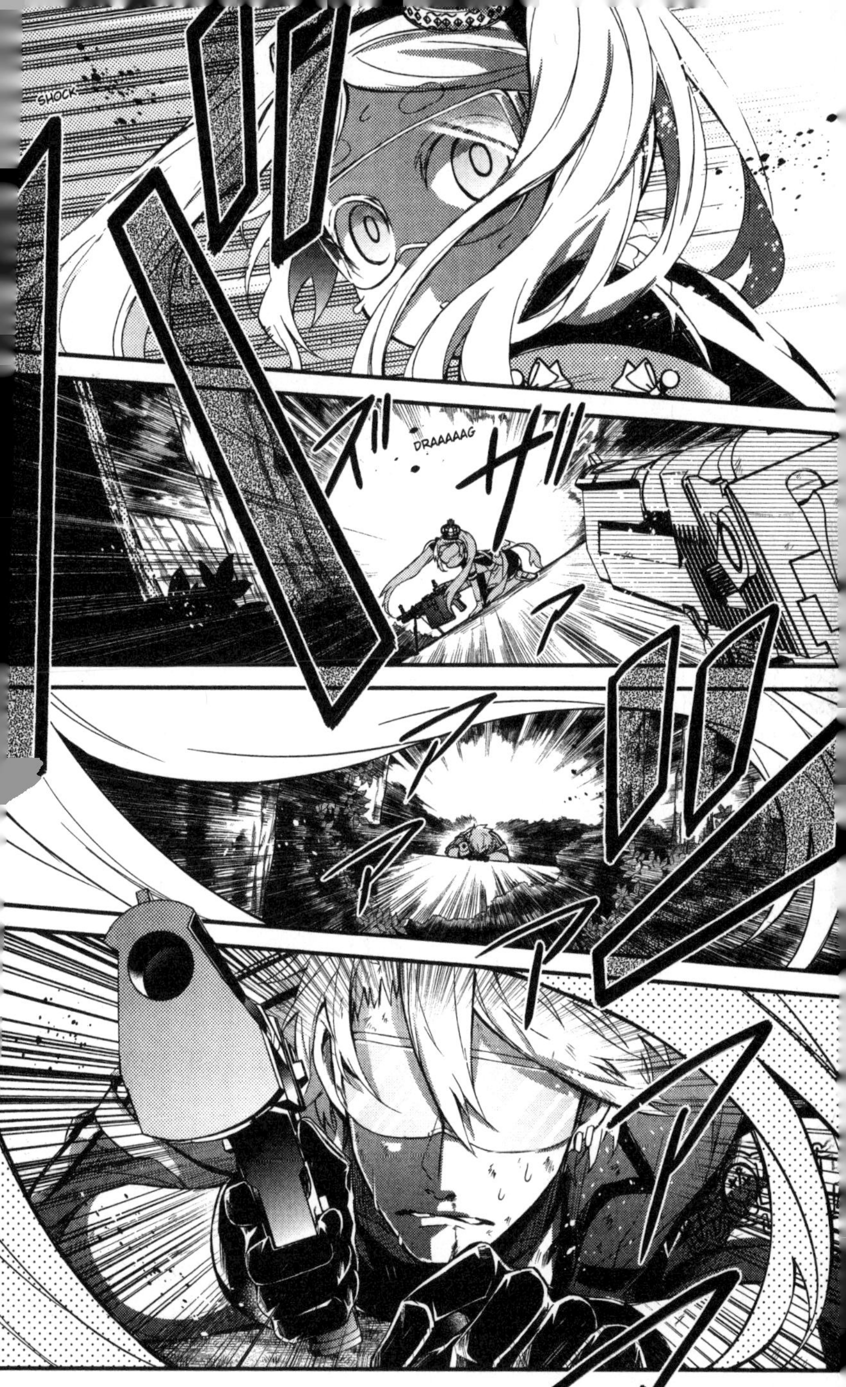
SHOCK
DRAAAAAG

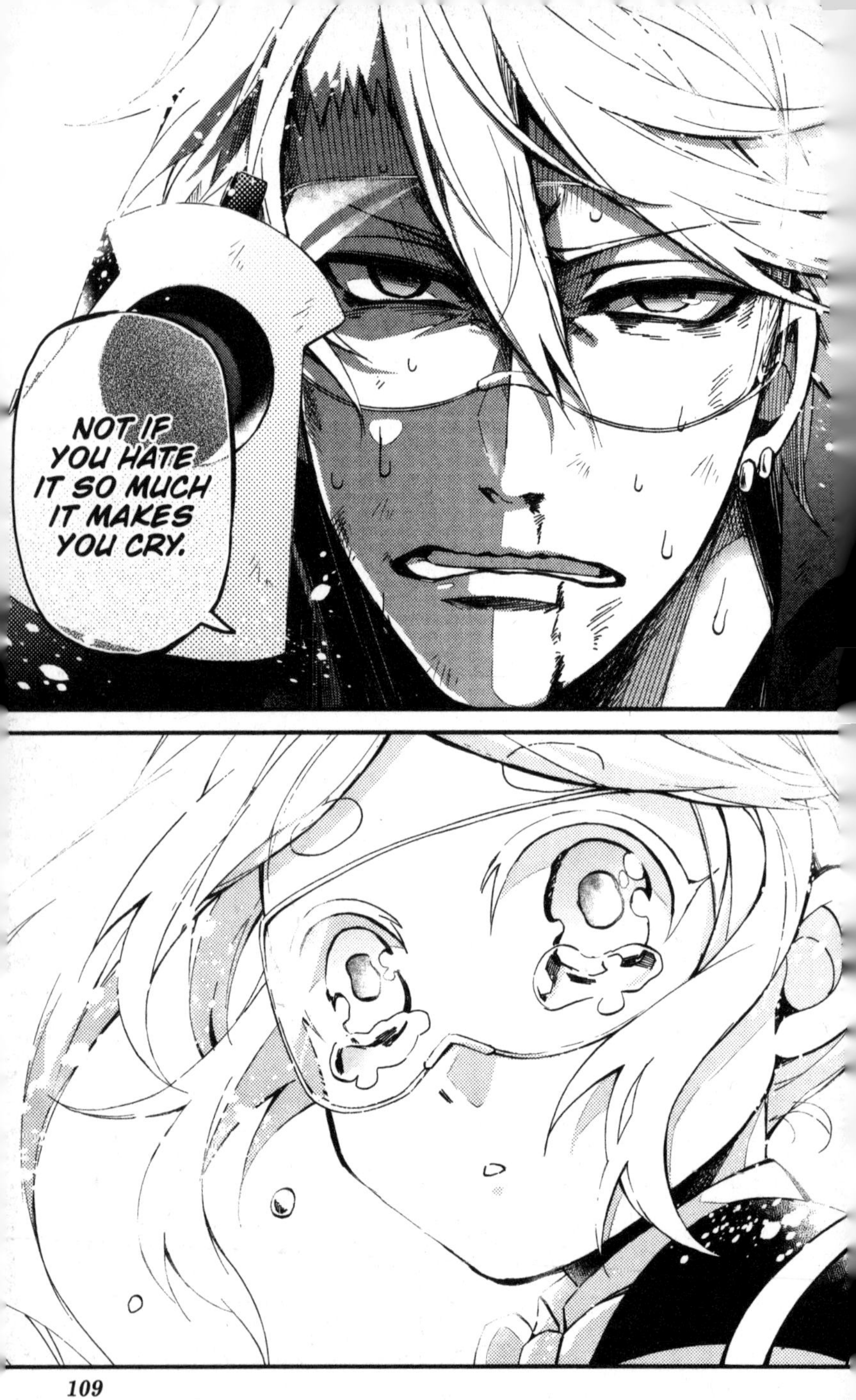
NOT IF YOU HATE IT SO MUCH IT MAKES YOU CRY.

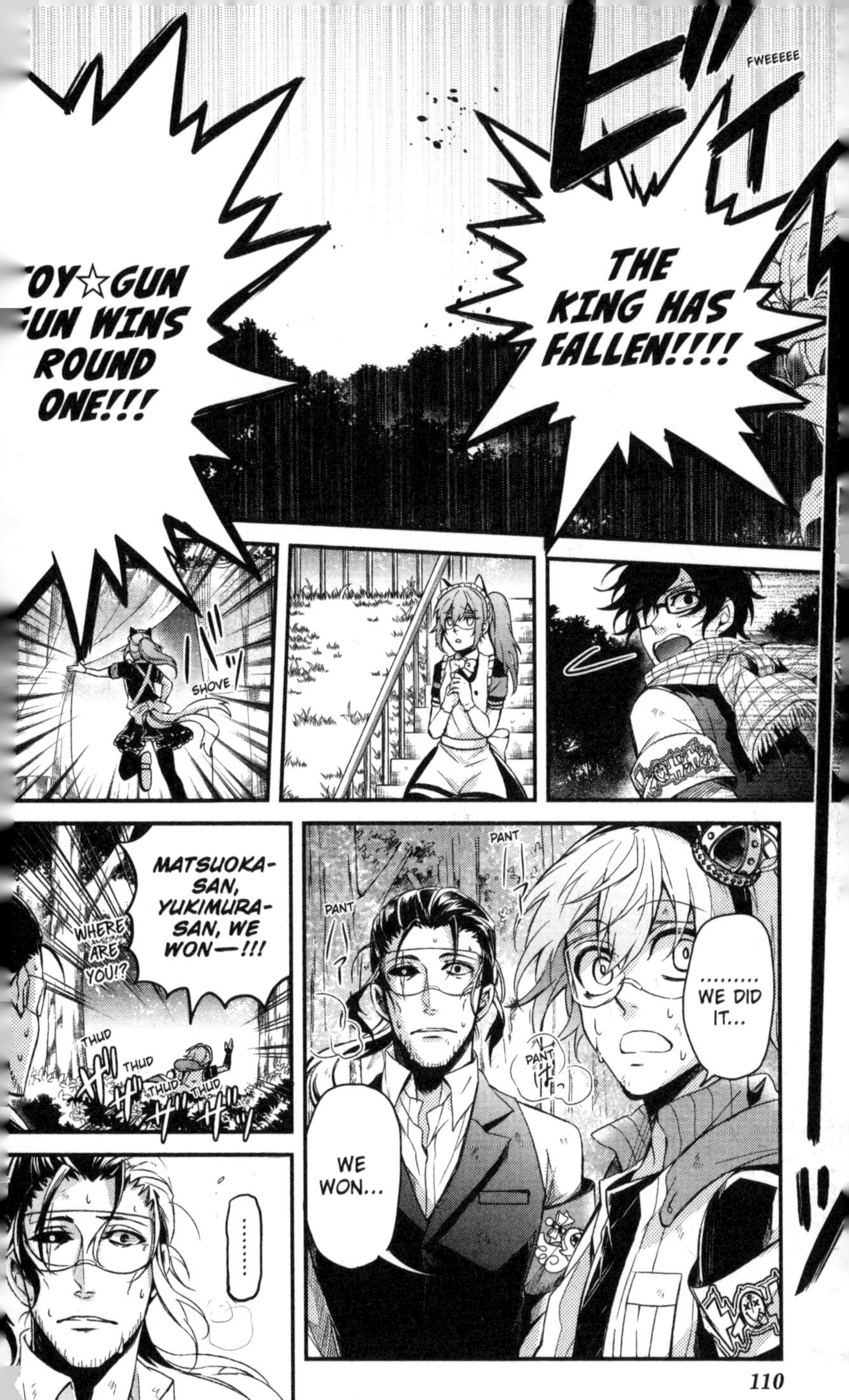
FWEEEEE
THE KING HAS FALLEN!!!!
OY☆GUN
UN WINS ROUND ONE!!!
SHOVE
PANT
PANT
.........WE DID IT...
PANT
WE WON...
MATSUOKA-SAN, YUKIMURA-SAN, WE WON—!!!
WHERE ARE YOU!?
THUD
THUD
THUD
THUD
....

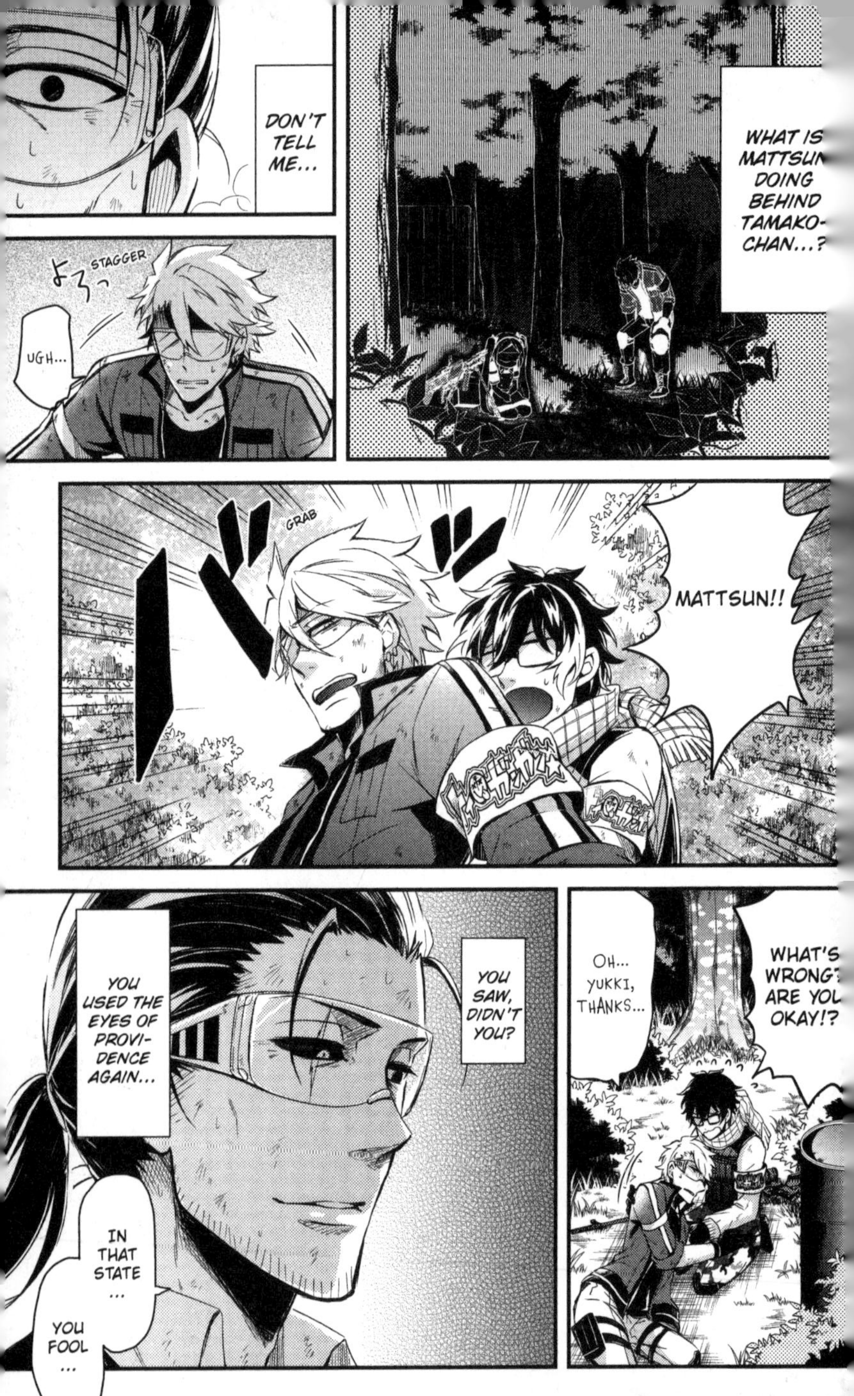
WHAT IS MATTSUN DOING BEHIND TAMAKO-CHAN...?
DON'T TELL ME...
よろっ STAGGER
UGH...
GRAB
MATTSUN!!
WHAT'S WRONG!? ARE YOU OKAY!?
OH... YUKKI, THANKS...
YOU SAW, DIDN'T YOU?
YOU USED THE EYES OF PROVIDENCE AGAIN...
IN THAT STATE ...
YOU FOOL ...

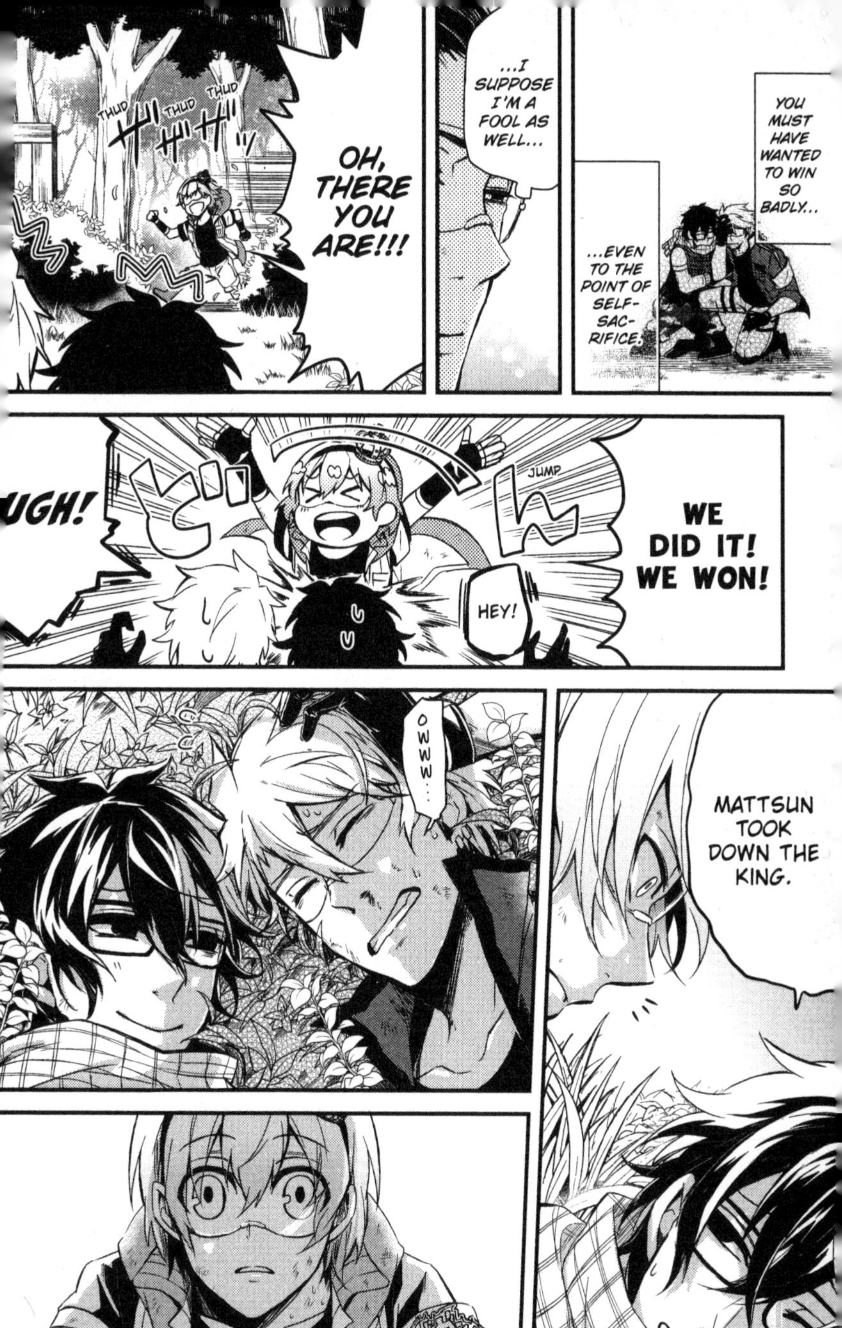
YOU MUST HAVE WANTED TO WIN SO BADLY...
...EVEN TO THE POINT OF SELF-SACRIFICE.
...I SUPPOSE I'M A FOOL AS WELL...
THUD THUD THUD
OH, THERE YOU ARE!!!
WE DID IT! WE WON!
HEY!
JUMP
UGH!
MATTSUN TOOK DOWN THE KING.
OWWW...

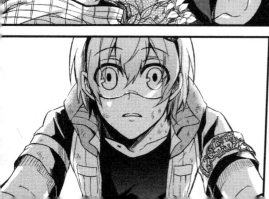

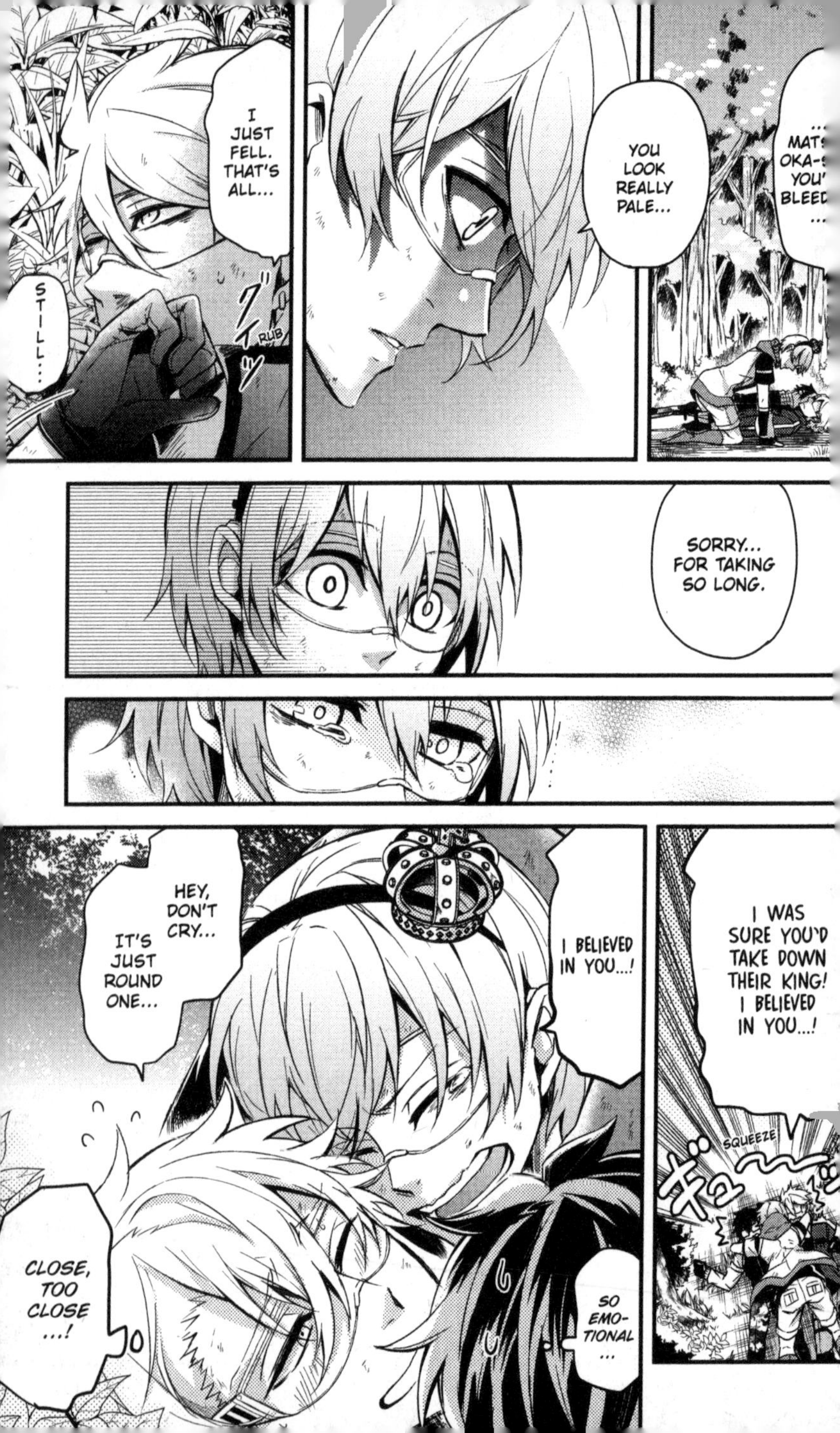

... MATS OKA-S YOU' BLEED ...
YOU LOOK REALLY PALE...
I JUST FELL. THAT'S ALL...
RUB
STILL...
SORRY... FOR TAKING SO LONG.
I WAS SURE YOU'D TAKE DOWN THEIR KING! I BELIEVED IN YOU...!
SQUEEZE
I BELIEVED IN YOU...!
HEY, DON'T CRY...
IT'S JUST ROUND ONE...
CLOSE, TOO CLOSE ...!
SO EMOTIONAL ...

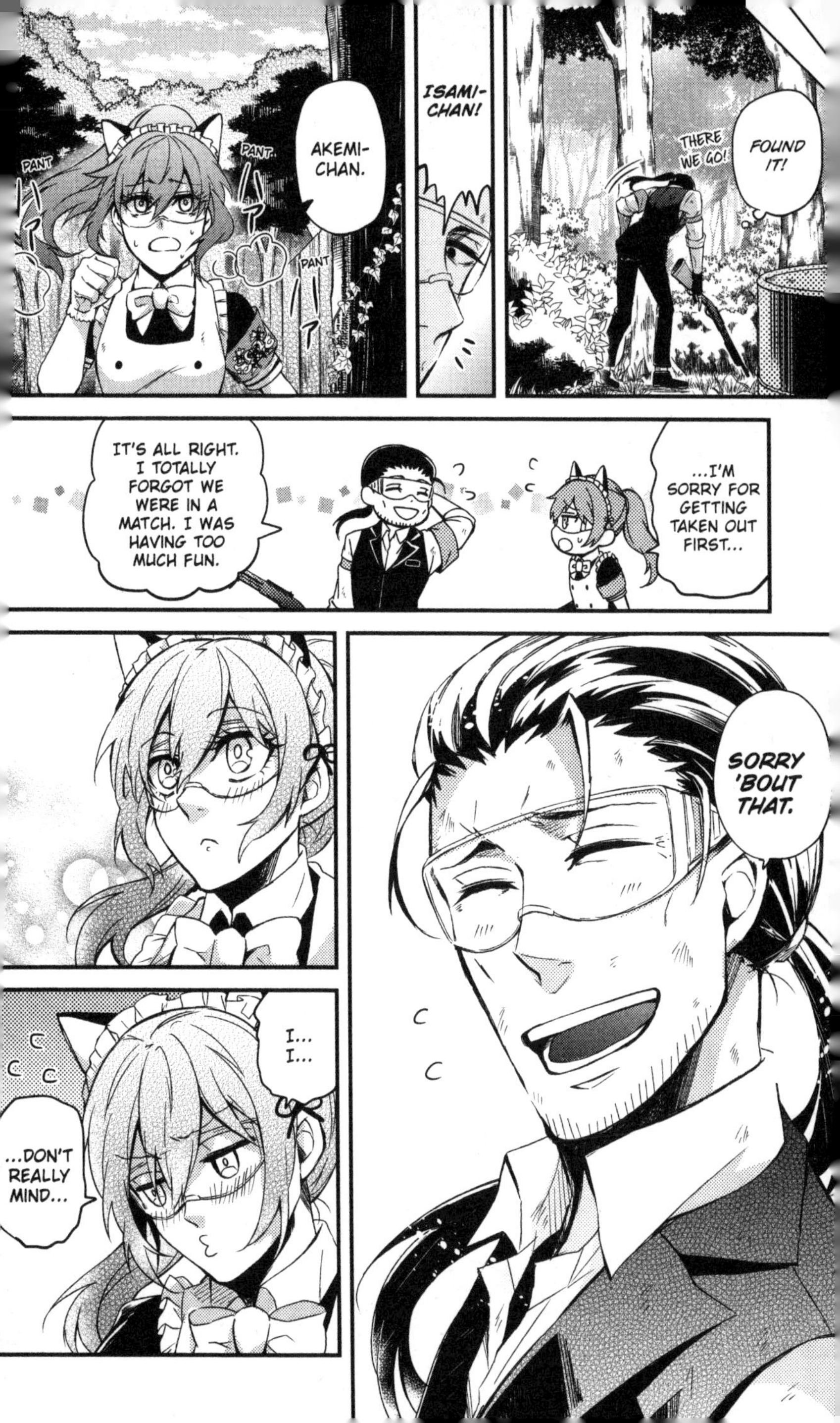
FOUND IT!
THERE WE GO!
ISAMI-CHAN!
AKEMI-CHAN.
PANT.
PANT
PANT
...I'M SORRY FOR GETTING TAKEN OUT FIRST...
IT'S ALL RIGHT. I TOTALLY FORGOT WE WERE IN A MATCH. I WAS HAVING TOO MUCH FUN.
SORRY 'BOUT THAT.
I... I...
...DON'T REALLY MIND...

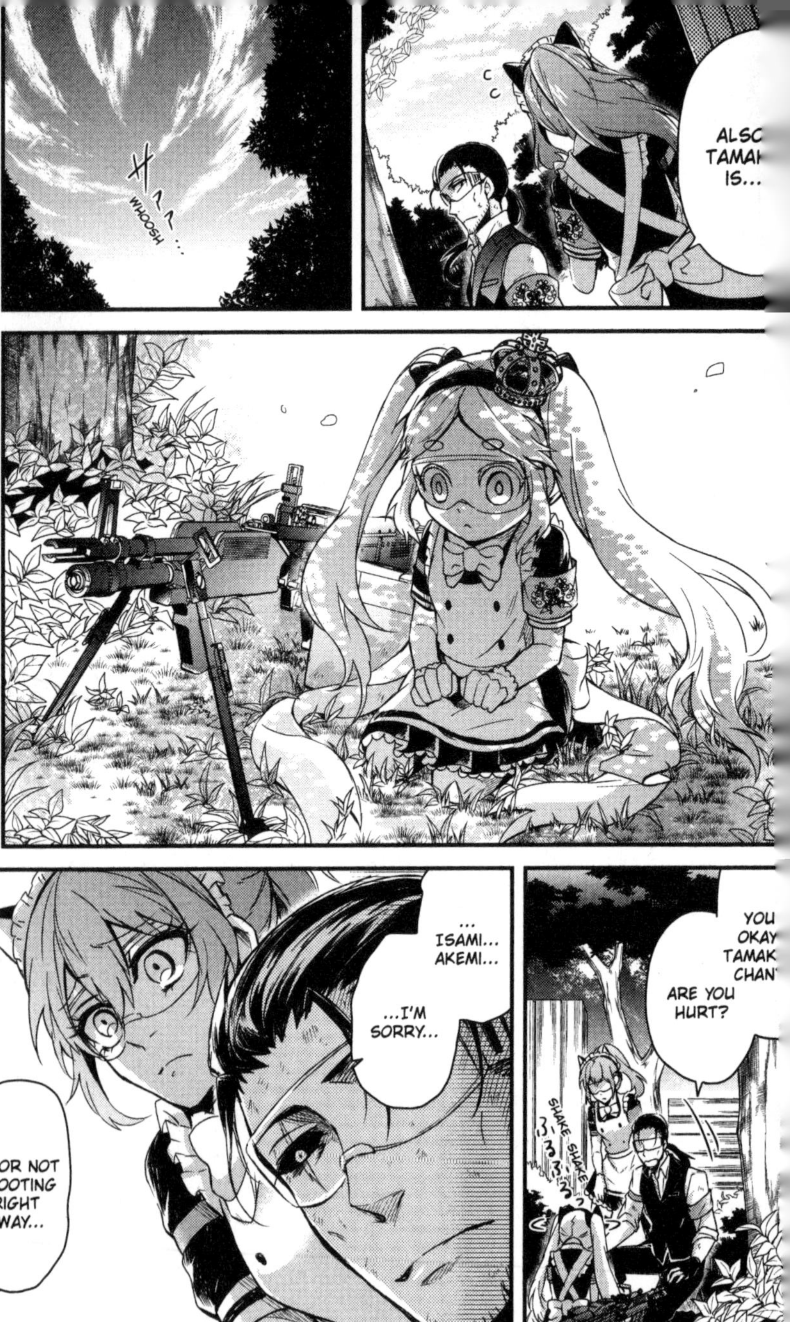
ALSO TAMAKI IS...
WHOOSH
YOU OKAY TAMAKI CHAN?
ARE YOU HURT?
SHAKE SHAKE
... ISAMI... AKEMI...
...I'M SORRY...
...FOR NOT SHOOTING RIGHT AWAY...

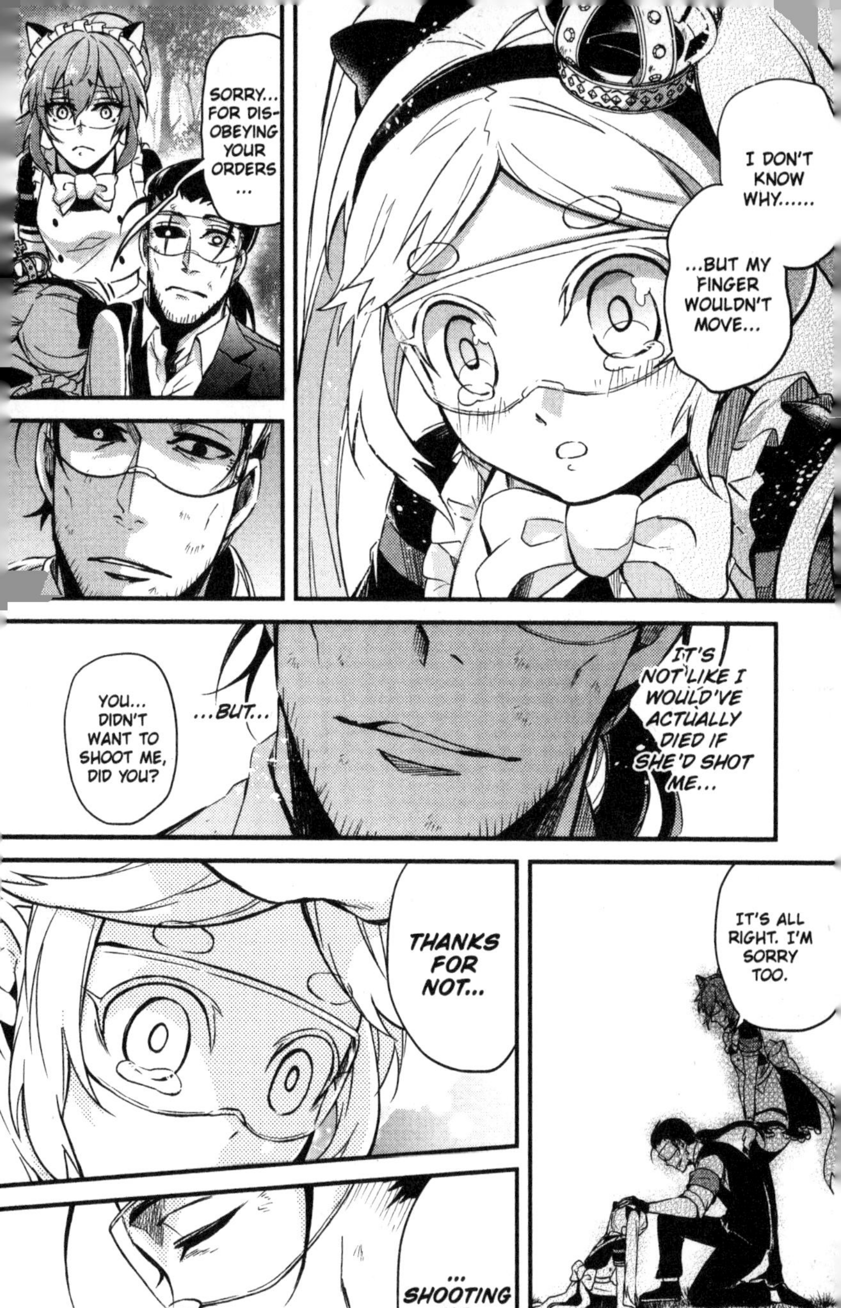
I DON'T KNOW WHY......
...BUT MY FINGER WOULDN'T MOVE...
SORRY... FOR DIS-OBEYING YOUR ORDERS ...
IT'S NOT LIKE I WOULD'VE ACTUALLY DIED IF SHE'D SHOT ME...
...BUT...
YOU... DIDN'T WANT TO SHOOT ME, DID YOU?
IT'S ALL RIGHT. I'M SORRY TOO.
THANKS FOR NOT...
...SHOOTING ME.

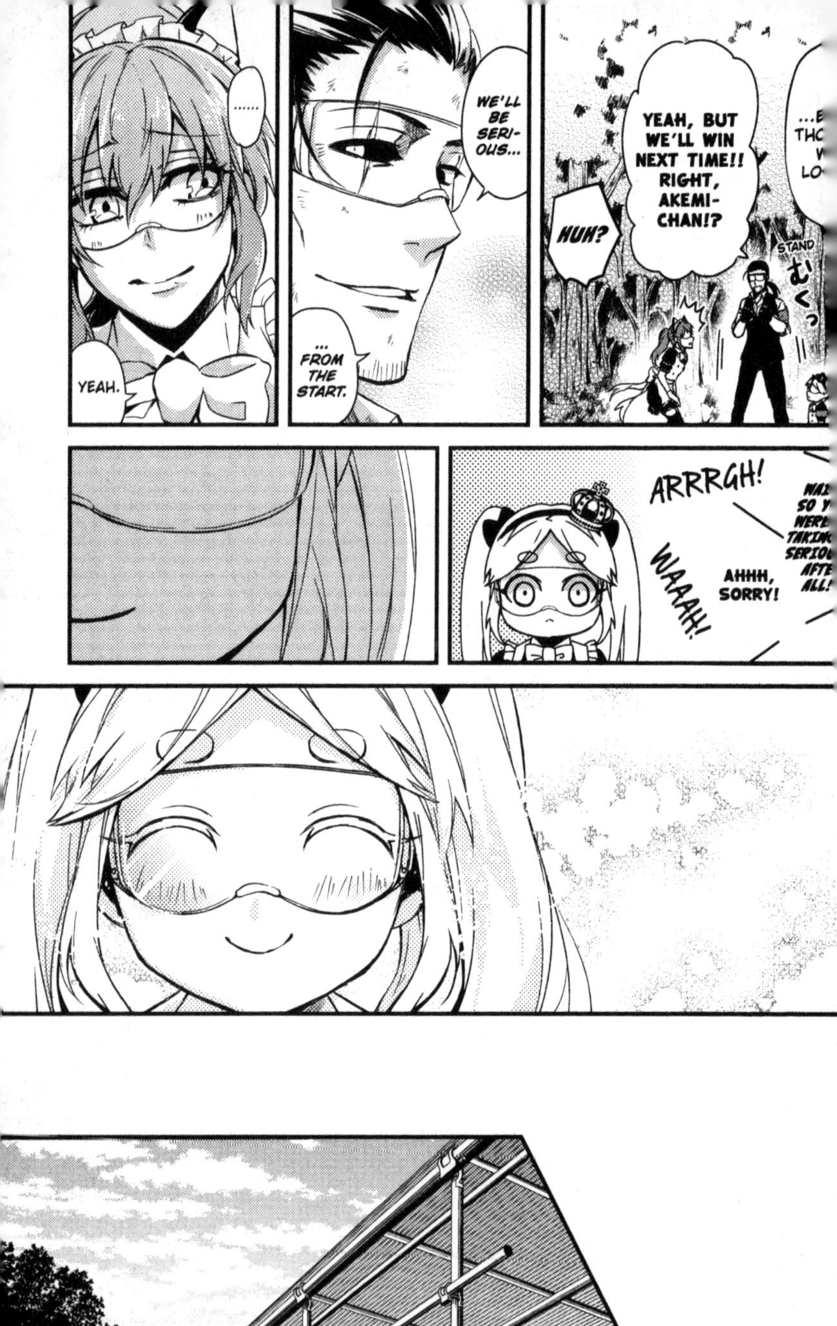
YEAH, BUT WE'LL WIN NEXT TIME!! RIGHT, AKEMI-CHAN!?
HUH?
STAND むくっ
WE'LL BE SERI-OUS...
...FROM THE START.
......
YEAH.
ARRRGH!
AHHH, SORRY!
WAAAH!

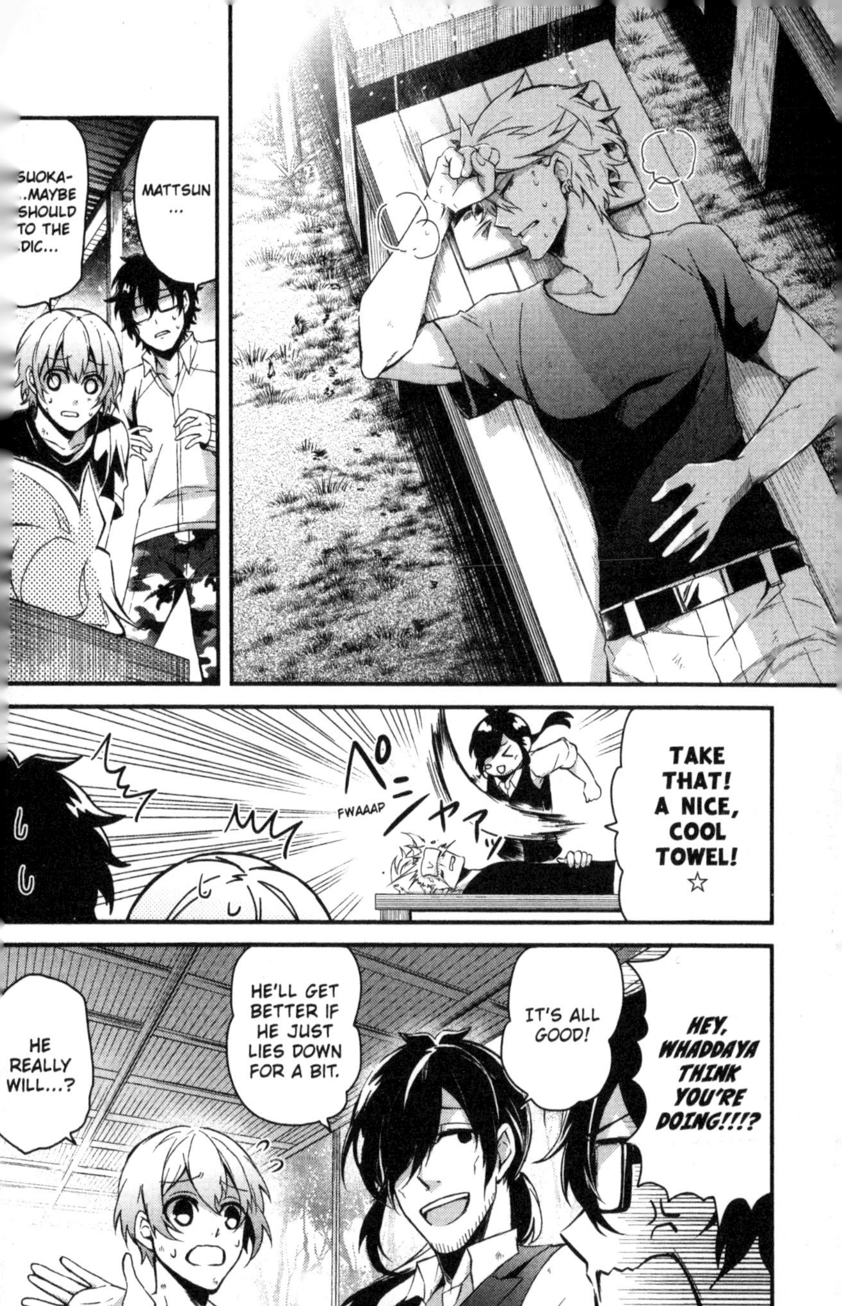
MATTSUN ...
SUOKA- ..MAYBE SHOULD TO THE DIC...
TAKE THAT! A NICE, COOL TOWEL! ☆
FWAAAP
HEY, WHADDAYA THINK YOU'RE DOING!!!?
IT'S ALL GOOD!
HE'LL GET BETTER IF HE JUST LIES DOWN FOR A BIT.
HE REALLY WILL...?

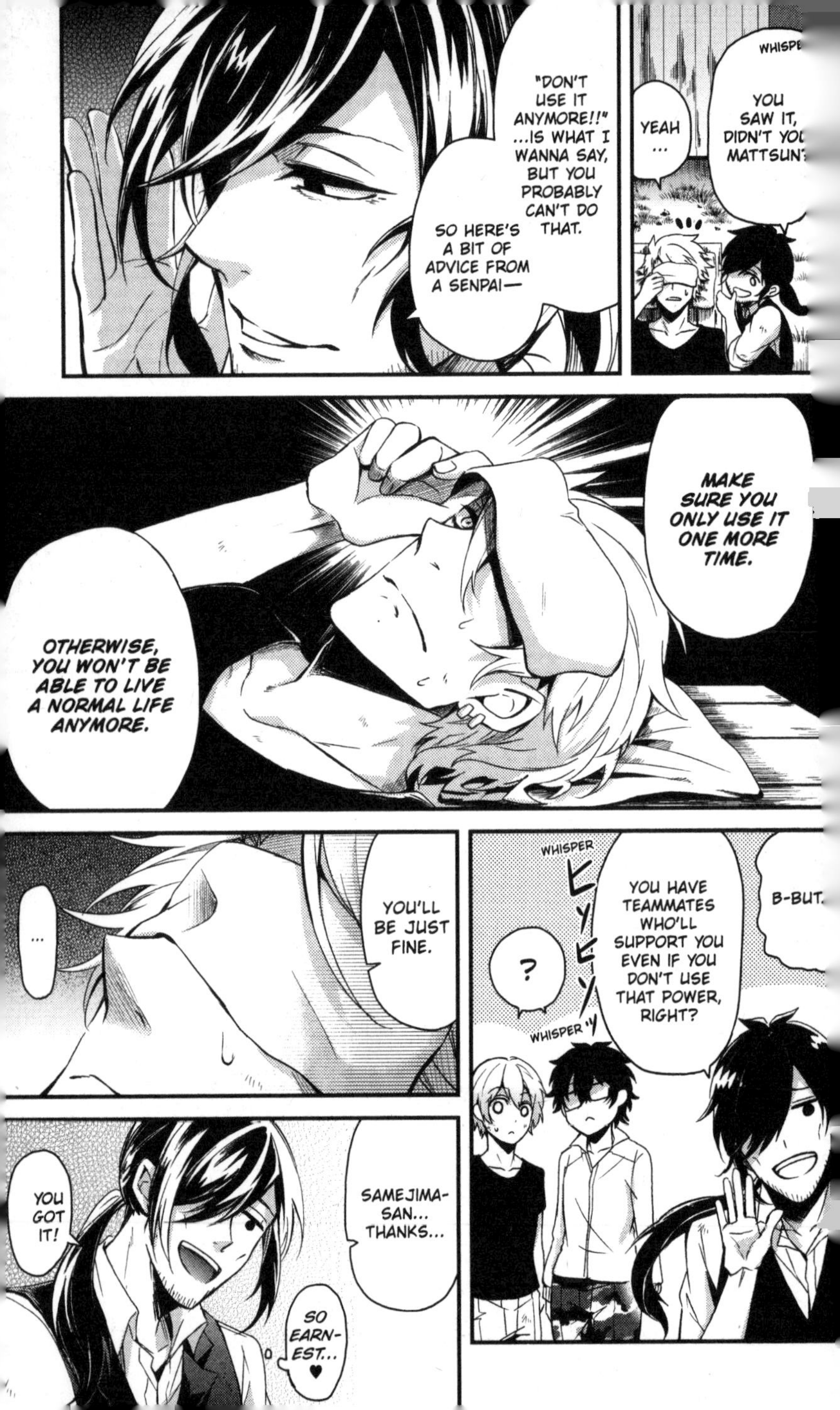
WHISPE
YOU SAW IT, DIDN'T YO MATTSUN
YEAH ...
"DON'T USE IT ANYMORE!!" ...IS WHAT I WANNA SAY, BUT YOU PROBABLY CAN'T DO THAT.
SO HERE'S A BIT OF ADVICE FROM A SENPAI—
MAKE SURE YOU ONLY USE IT ONE MORE TIME.
OTHERWISE, YOU WON'T BE ABLE TO LIVE A NORMAL LIFE ANYMORE.
B-BUT.
WHISPER
YOU HAVE TEAMMATES WHO'LL SUPPORT YOU EVEN IF YOU DON'T USE THAT POWER, RIGHT?
?
WHISPER
YOU'LL BE JUST FINE.
...
SAMEJIMA-SAN... THANKS...
YOU GOT IT!
SO EARN-EST... ♥

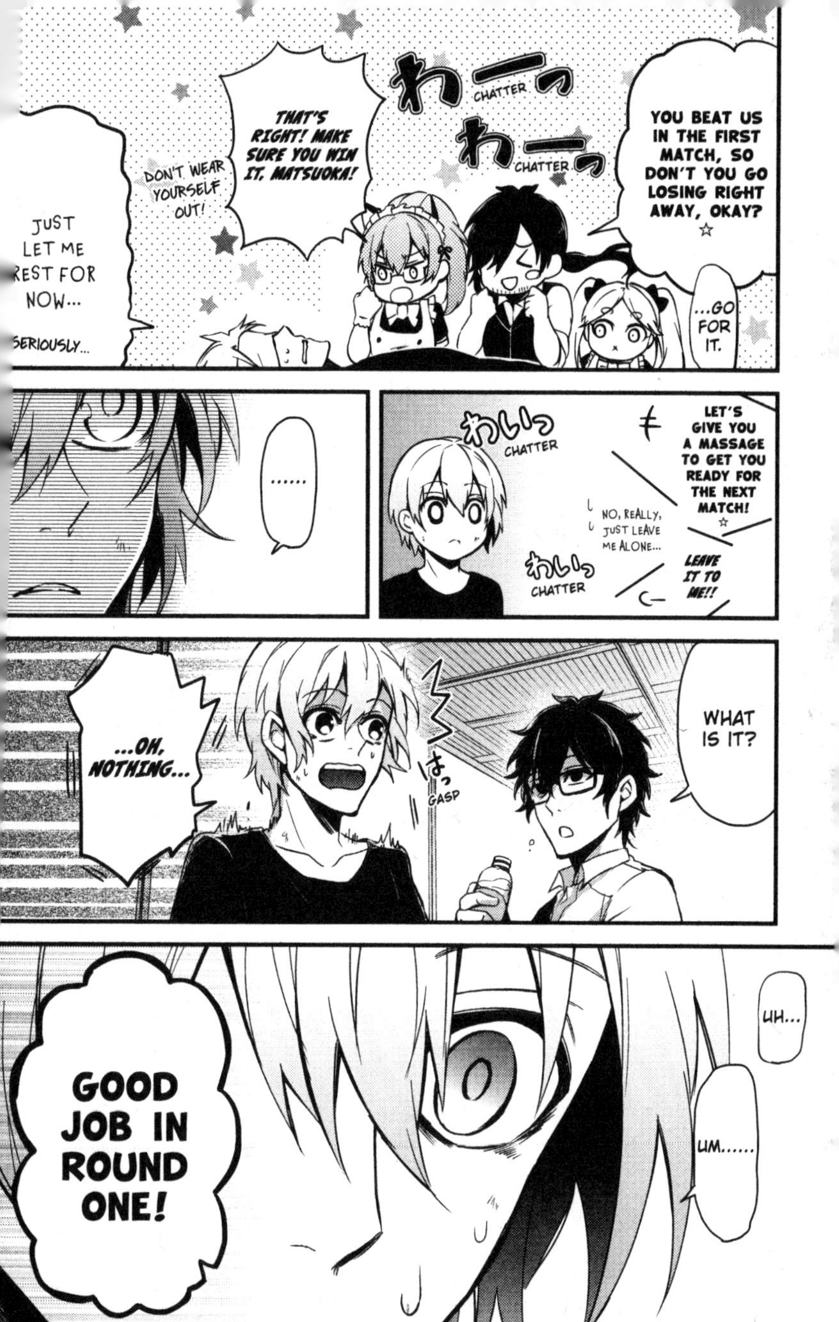
YOU BEAT US IN THE FIRST MATCH, SO DON'T YOU GO LOSING RIGHT AWAY, OKAY? ☆
わーっ CHATTER
わーっ CHATTER
THAT'S RIGHT! MAKE SURE YOU WIN IT, MATSUOKA!
DON'T WEAR YOURSELF OUT!
...GO FOR IT.
JUST LET ME REST FOR NOW...
SERIOUSLY...
わしっ CHATTER
LET'S GIVE YOU A MASSAGE TO GET YOU READY FOR THE NEXT MATCH! ☆
NO, REALLY, JUST LEAVE ME ALONE...
LEAVE IT TO ME!!
わしっ CHATTER
......
WHAT IS IT?
はっ GASP
...OH, NOTHING...
UH...
UM......
GOOD JOB IN ROUND ONE!

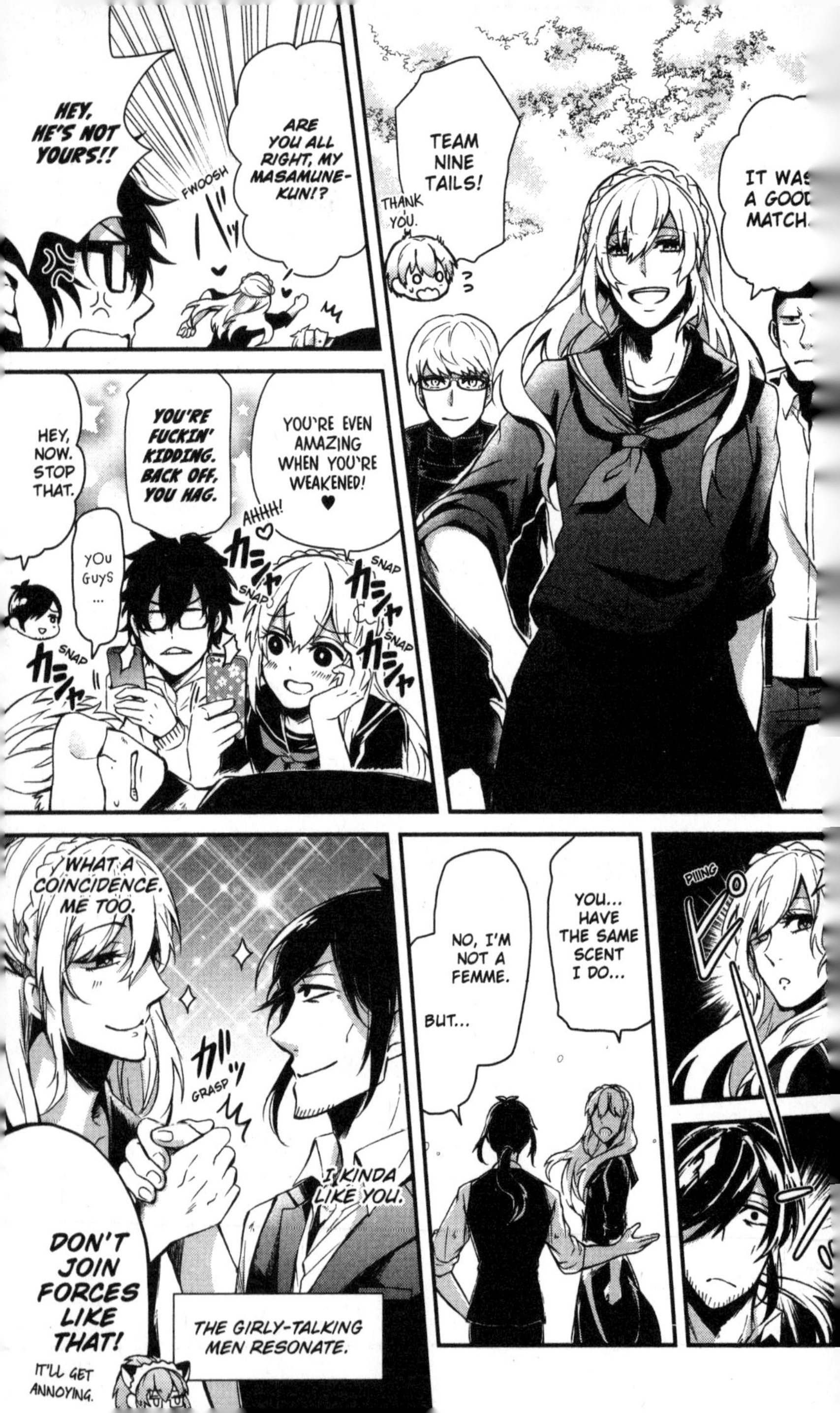
IT WAS A GOOD MATCH.
TEAM NINE TAILS!
THANK YOU.
ARE YOU ALL RIGHT, MY MASAMUNE-KUN!?
FWOOSH
HEY, HE'S NOT YOURS!!
YOU'RE EVEN AMAZING WHEN YOU'RE WEAKENED! ♥
AHHH! ♡
SNAP
SNAP
SNAP
YOU'RE FUCKIN' KIDDING. BACK OFF, YOU HAG.
HEY, NOW. STOP THAT.
YOU GUYS ...
SNAP
PIING
YOU... HAVE THE SAME SCENT I DO...
NO, I'M NOT A FEMME.
BUT...
I KINDA LIKE YOU.
WHAT A COINCIDENCE. ME TOO.
GRASP
THE GIRLY-TALKING MEN RESONATE.
DON'T JOIN FORCES LIKE THAT!
IT'LL GET ANNOYING.

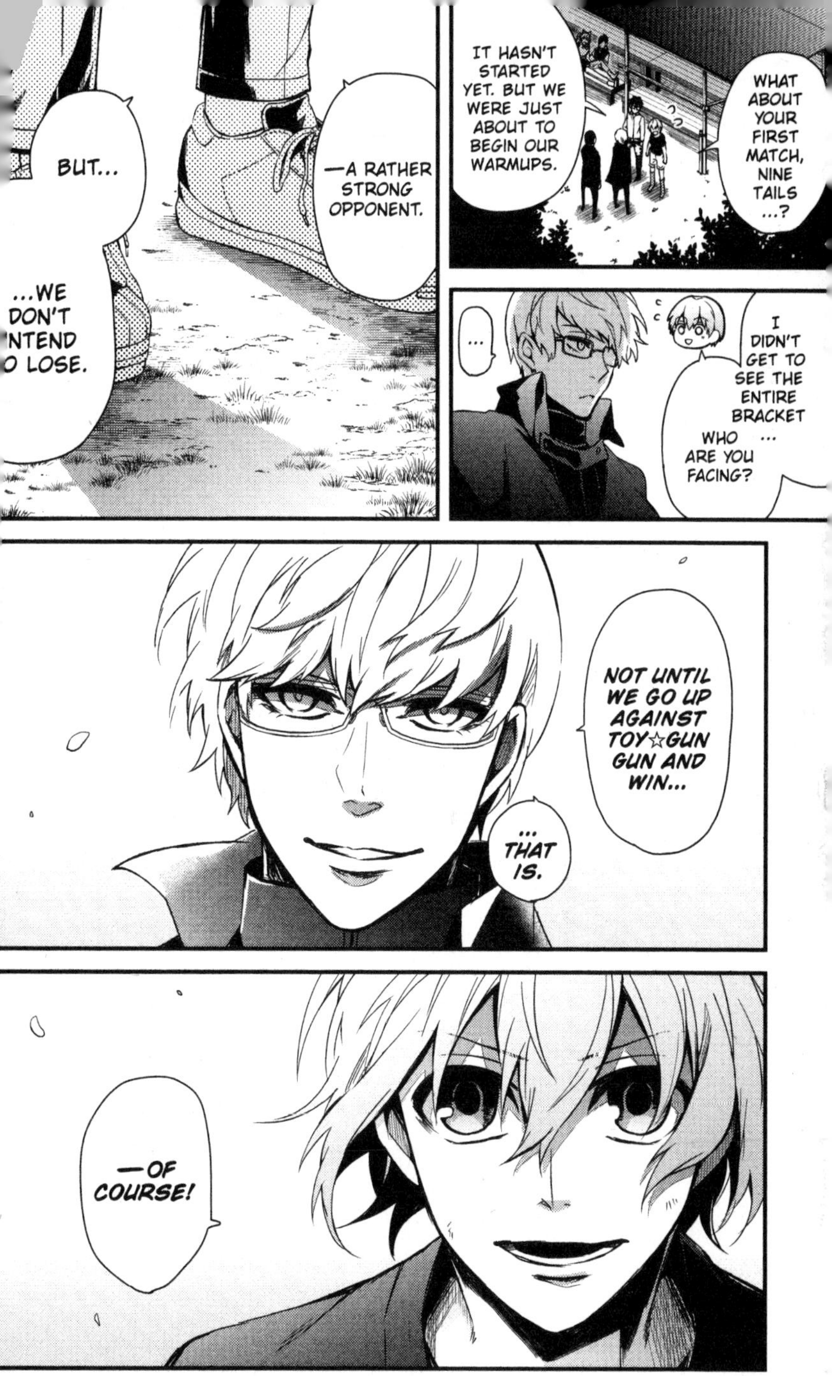
WHAT ABOUT YOUR FIRST MATCH, NINE TAILS ...?
IT HASN'T STARTED YET. BUT WE WERE JUST ABOUT TO BEGIN OUR WARMUPS.
I DIDN'T GET TO SEE THE ENTIRE BRACKET ... WHO ARE YOU FACING?
...
—A RATHER STRONG OPPONENT.
BUT...
...WE DON'T 'NTEND 'O LOSE.
NOT UNTIL WE GO UP AGAINST TOY☆GUN GUN AND WIN...
...THAT IS.
—OF COURSE!

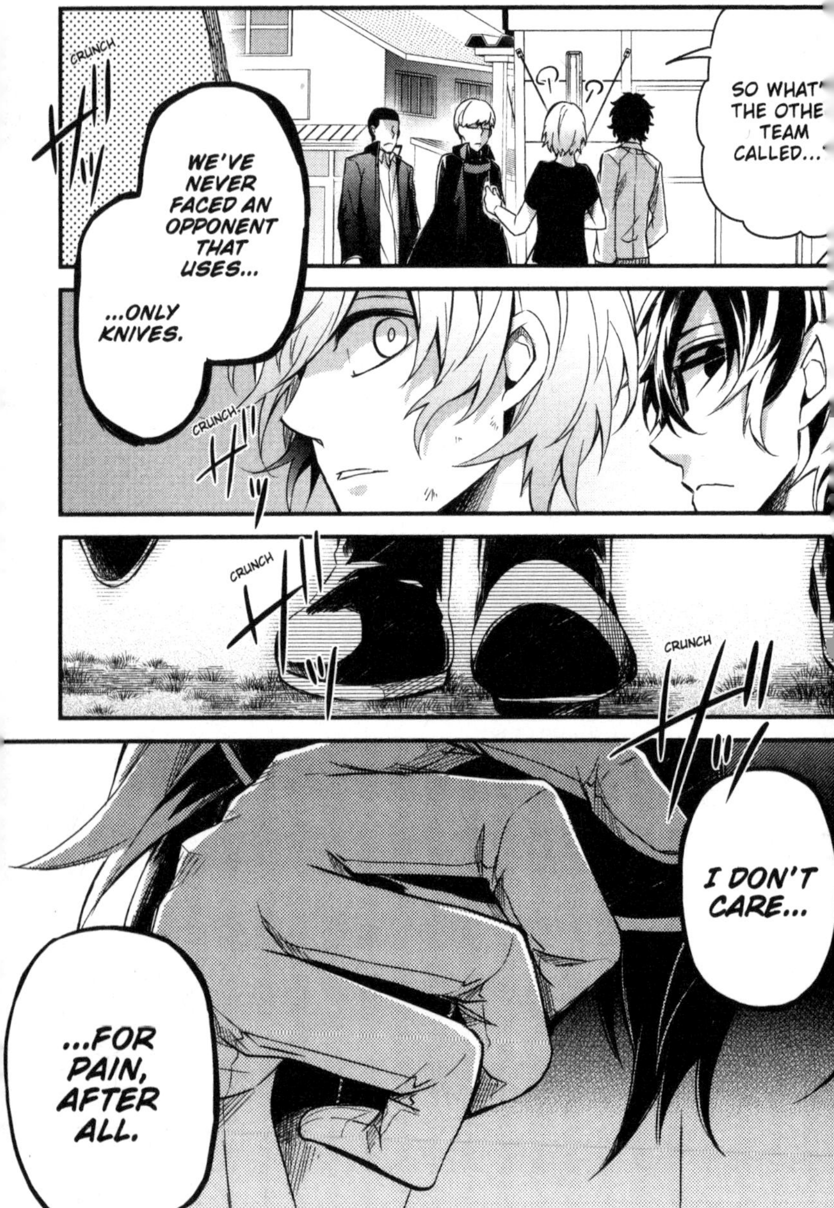
SO WHAT' THE OTHE TEAM CALLED...
CRUNCH
WE'VE NEVER FACED AN OPPONENT THAT USES...
...ONLY KNIVES.
CRUNCH
CRUNCH
CRUNCH
I DON'T CARE...
...FOR PAIN, AFTER ALL.

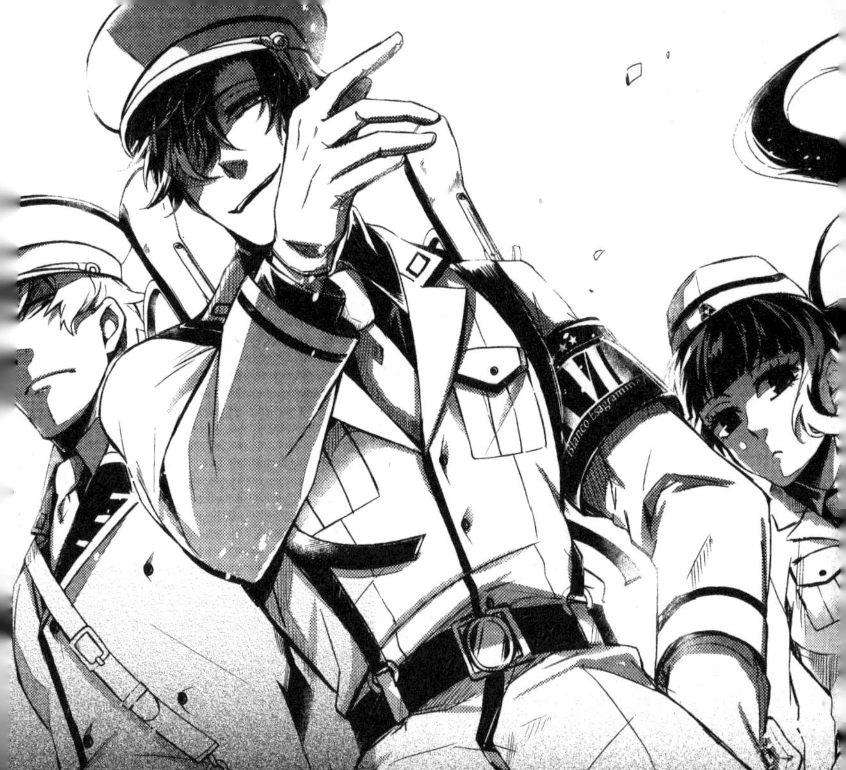

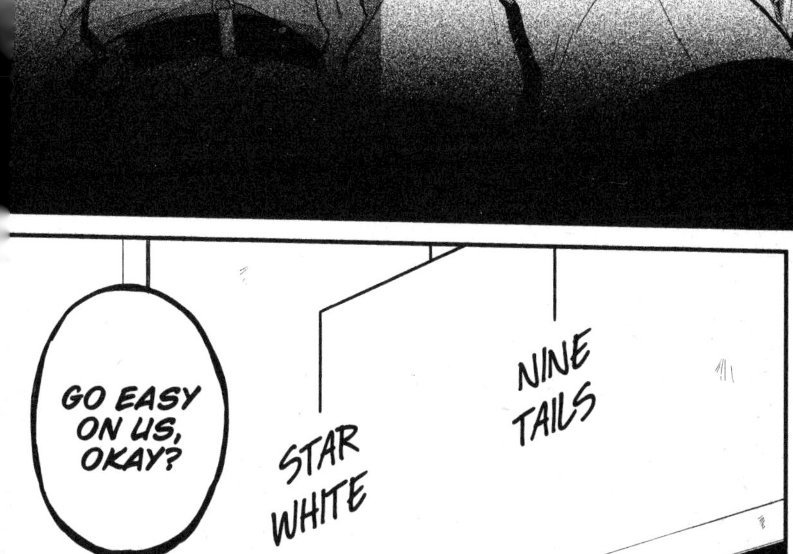
NINE TAILS
STAR WHITE
GO EASY ON US, OKAY?

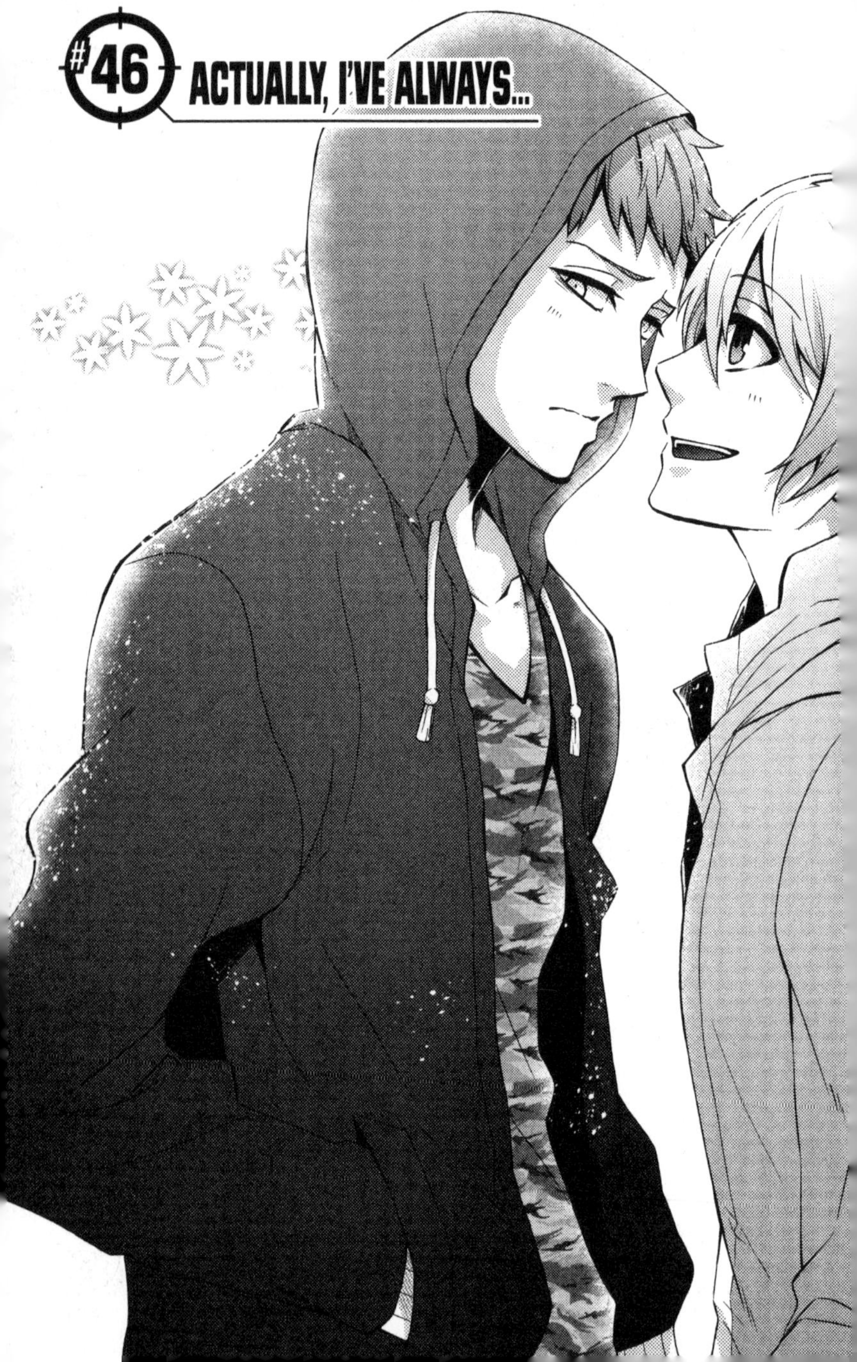
#46
ACTUALLY, I'VE ALWAYS...

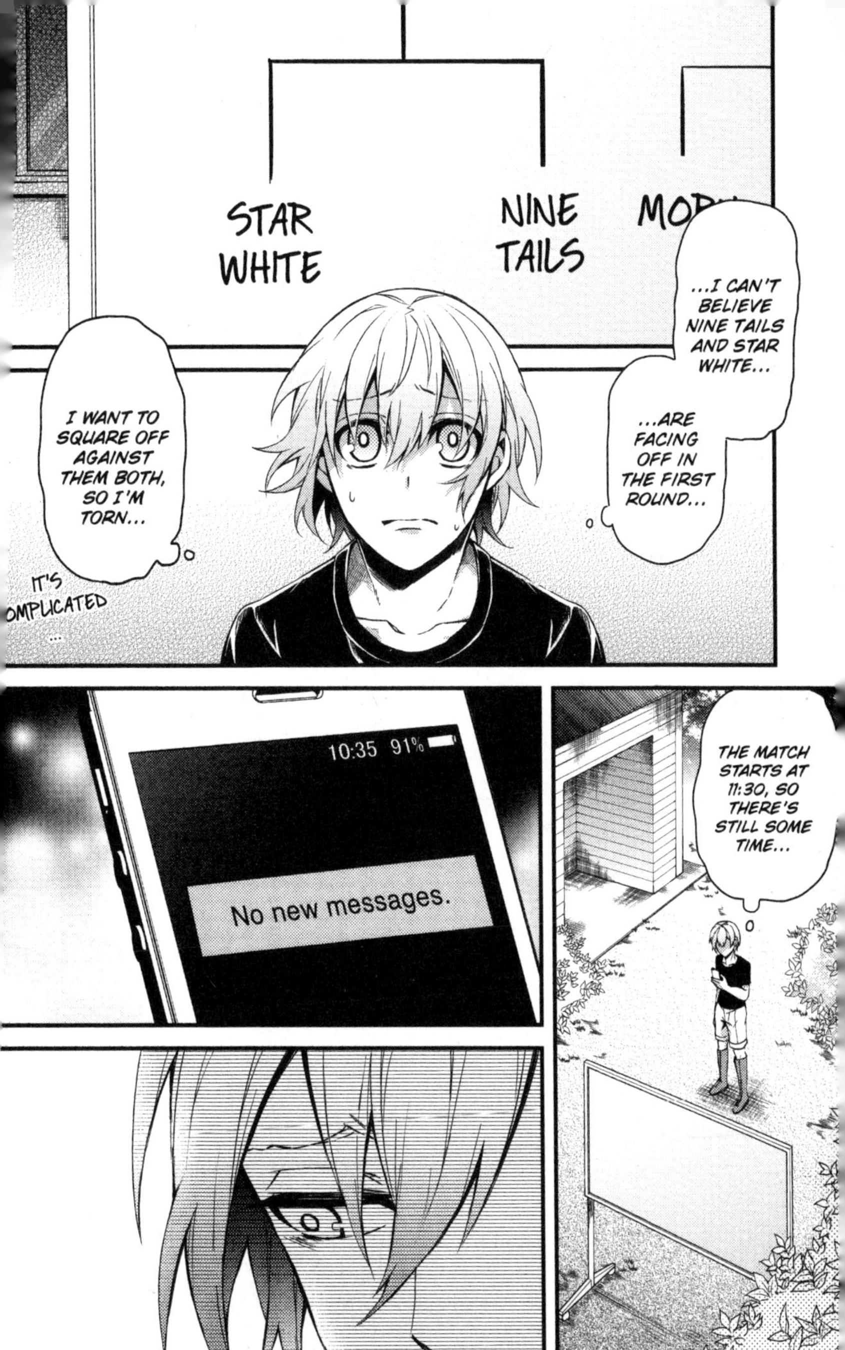
NINE TAILS
STAR WHITE
...I CAN'T BELIEVE NINE TAILS AND STAR WHITE...
...ARE FACING OFF IN THE FIRST ROUND...
I WANT TO SQUARE OFF AGAINST THEM BOTH, SO I'M TORN...
IT'S OMPLICATED ...
THE MATCH STARTS AT 11:30, SO THERE'S STILL SOME TIME...
10:35 91%
No new messages.

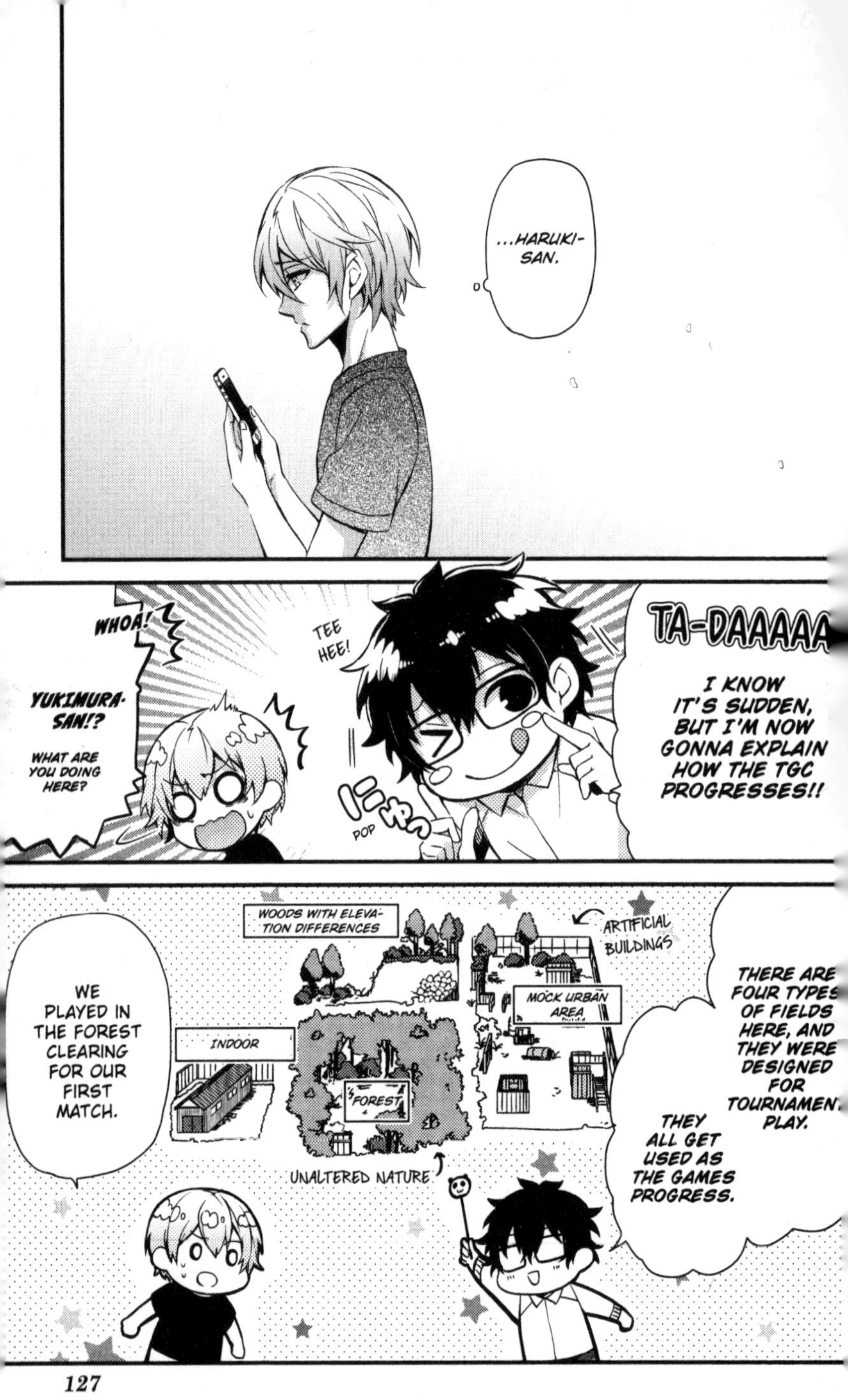
...HARUKI-SAN.
TA-DAAAAA
I KNOW IT'S SUDDEN, BUT I'M NOW GONNA EXPLAIN HOW THE TGC PROGRESSES!!
TEE HEE!
POP
WHOA!
YUKIMURA-SAN!?
WHAT ARE YOU DOING HERE?
THERE ARE FOUR TYPES OF FIELDS HERE, AND THEY WERE DESIGNED FOR TOURNAMENT PLAY.
THEY ALL GET USED AS THE GAMES PROGRESS.
ARTIFICIAL BUILDINGS
MOCK URBAN AREA
WOODS WITH ELEVATION DIFFERENCES
FOREST
UNALTERED NATURE
INDOOR
WE PLAYED IN THE FOREST CLEARING FOR OUR FIRST MATCH.

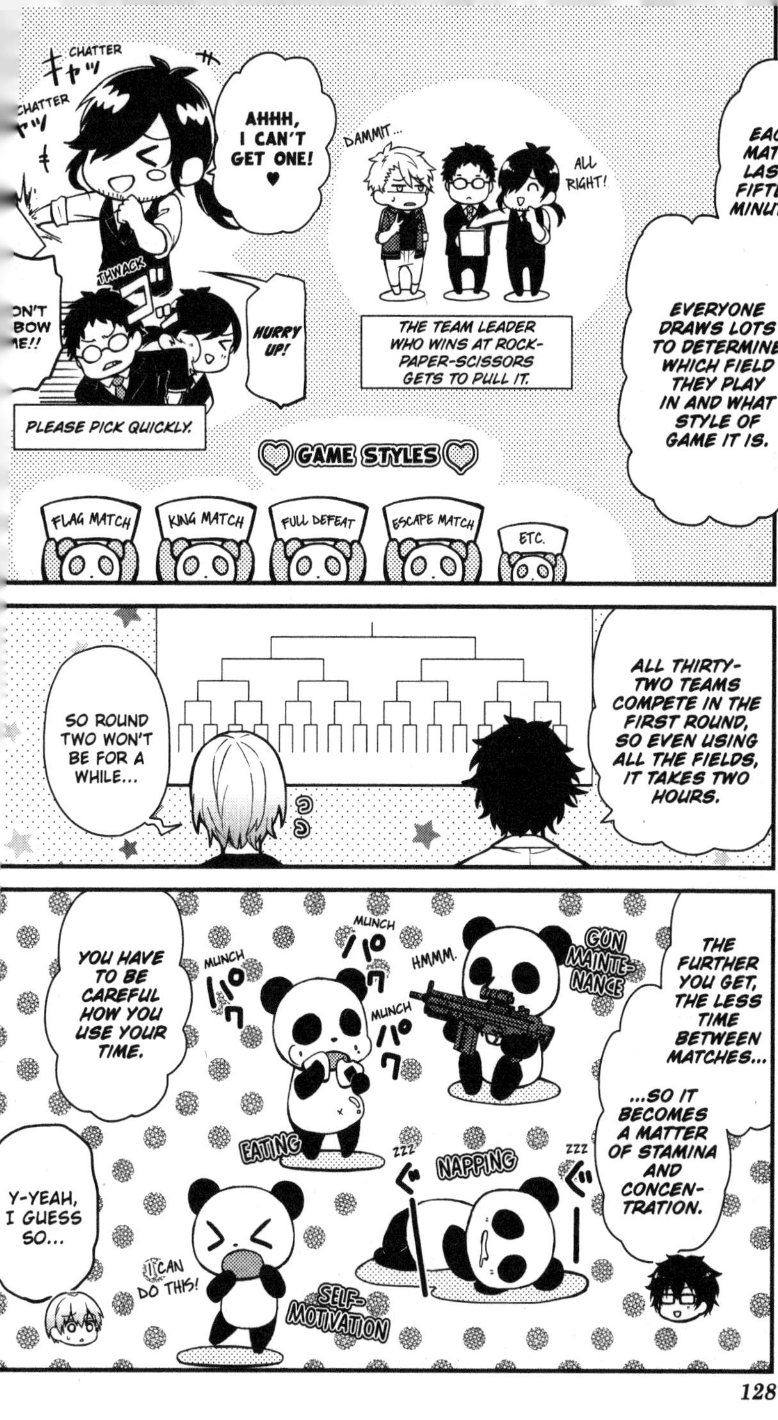
EACH MATCH LASTS FIFTEEN MINUTES.
EVERYONE DRAWS LOTS TO DETERMINE WHICH FIELD THEY PLAY IN AND WHAT STYLE OF GAME IT IS.
ALL RIGHT!
DAMMIT...
THE TEAM LEADER WHO WINS AT ROCK-PAPER-SCISSORS GETS TO PULL IT.
CHATTER
CHATTER
AHHH, I CAN'T GET ONE! ♥
HURRY UP!
THWACK
PLEASE PICK QUICKLY.
GAME STYLES
FLAG MATCH
KING MATCH
FULL DEFEAT
ESCAPE MATCH
ETC.
ALL THIRTY-TWO TEAMS COMPETE IN THE FIRST ROUND, SO EVEN USING ALL THE FIELDS, IT TAKES TWO HOURS.
SO ROUND TWO WON'T BE FOR A WHILE...
THE FURTHER YOU GET, THE LESS TIME BETWEEN MATCHES...
...SO IT BECOMES A MATTER OF STAMINA AND CONCENTRATION.
GUN MAINTENANCE
HMMM.
MUNCH
MUNCH
MUNCH
EATING
YOU HAVE TO BE CAREFUL HOW YOU USE YOUR TIME.
ZZZ
ZZZ
NAPPING
I CAN DO THIS!
SELF-MOTIVATION
Y-YEAH, I GUESS SO...

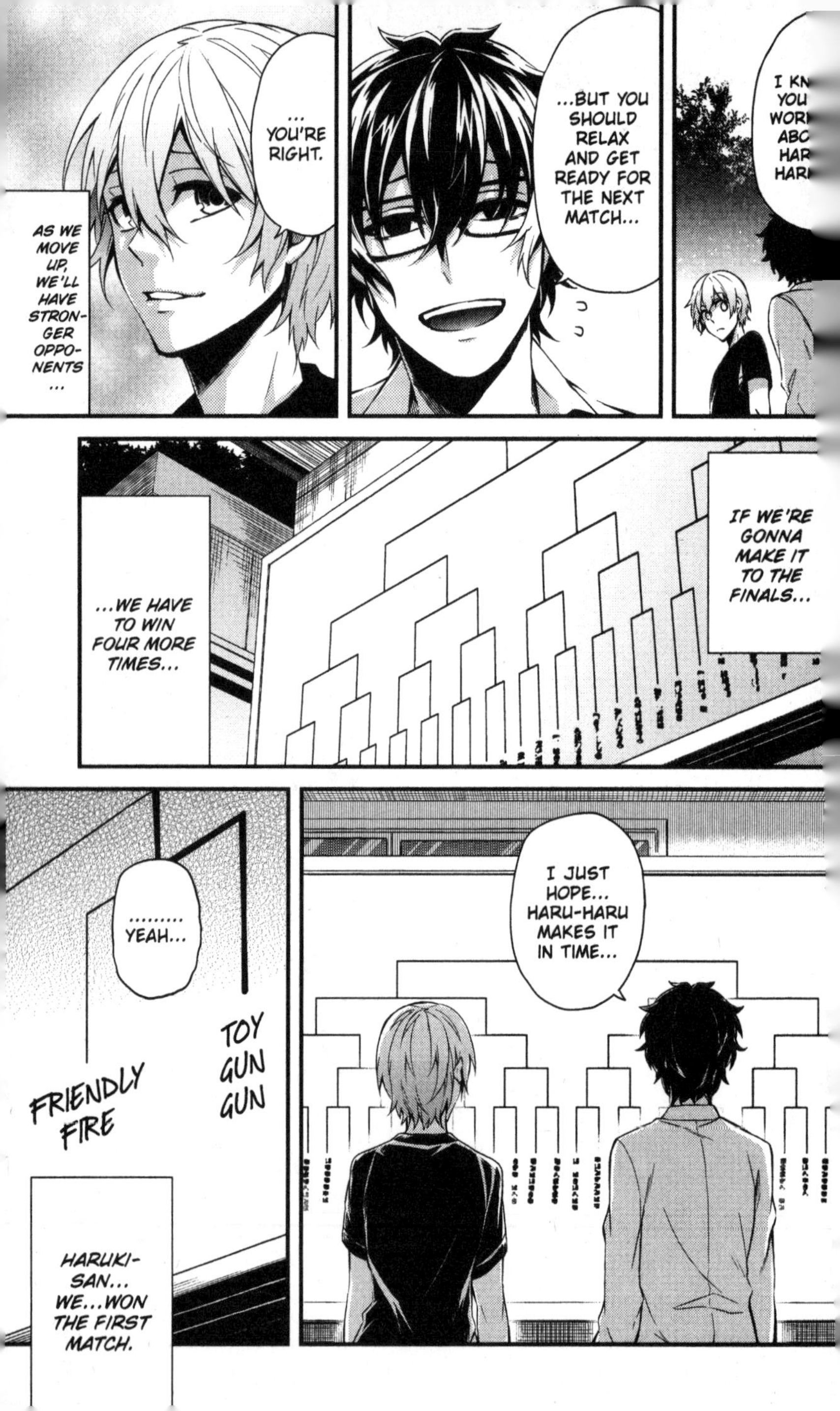
I KN YOU WOR ABO HAR HAR
...BUT YOU SHOULD RELAX AND GET READY FOR THE NEXT MATCH...
... YOU'RE RIGHT.
AS WE MOVE UP, WE'LL HAVE STRONGER OPPONENTS ...
IF WE'RE GONNA MAKE IT TO THE FINALS...
...WE HAVE TO WIN FOUR MORE TIMES...
I JUST HOPE... HARU-HARU MAKES IT IN TIME...
.... YEAH...
TOY GUN GUN
FRIENDLY FIRE
HARUKI-SAN... WE...WON THE FIRST MATCH.

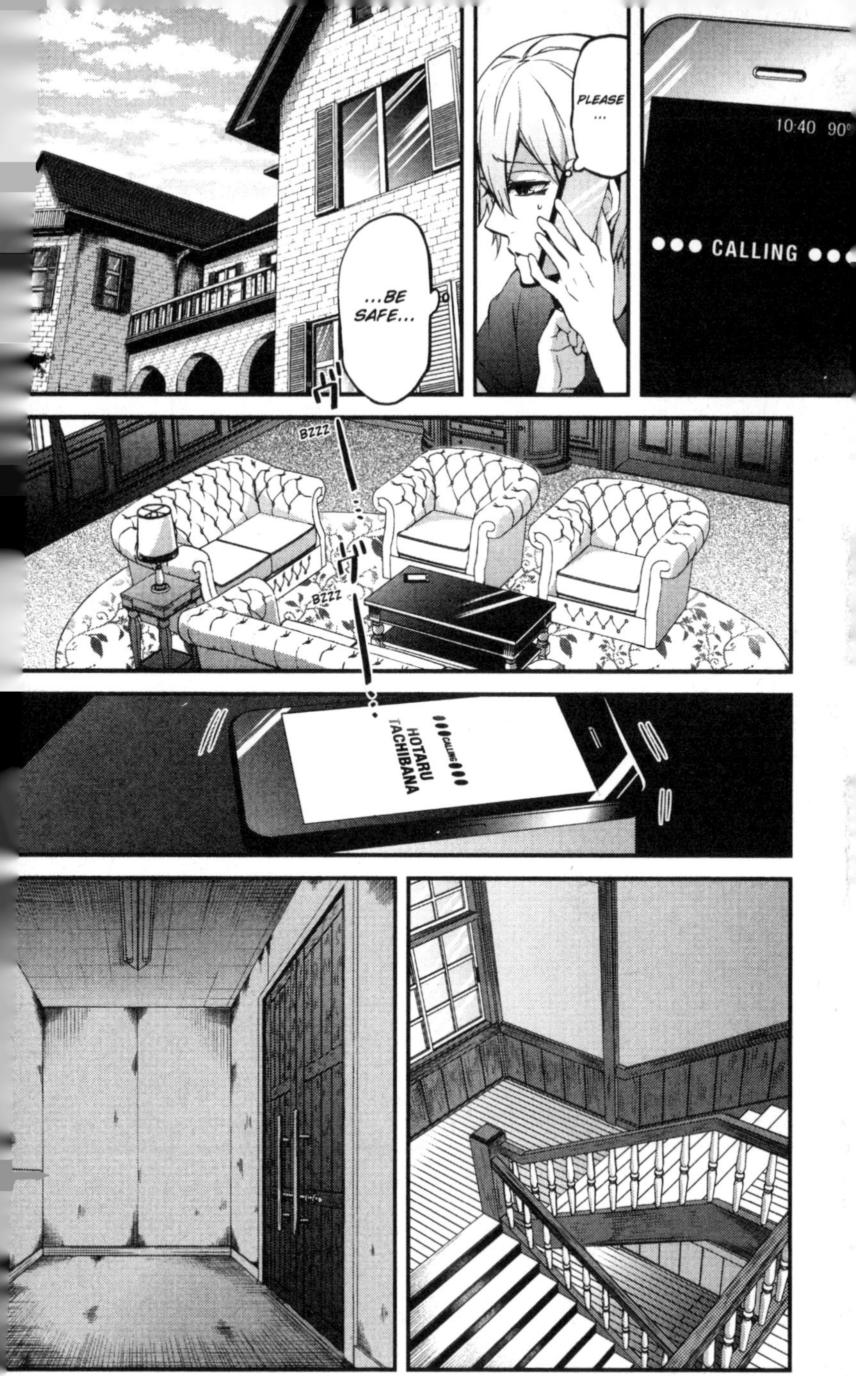
10:40 90
CALLING
PLEASE ...
...BE SAFE...
ヴ
BZZZ
ヴ
BZZZ
CALLING
HOTARU TACHIBANA

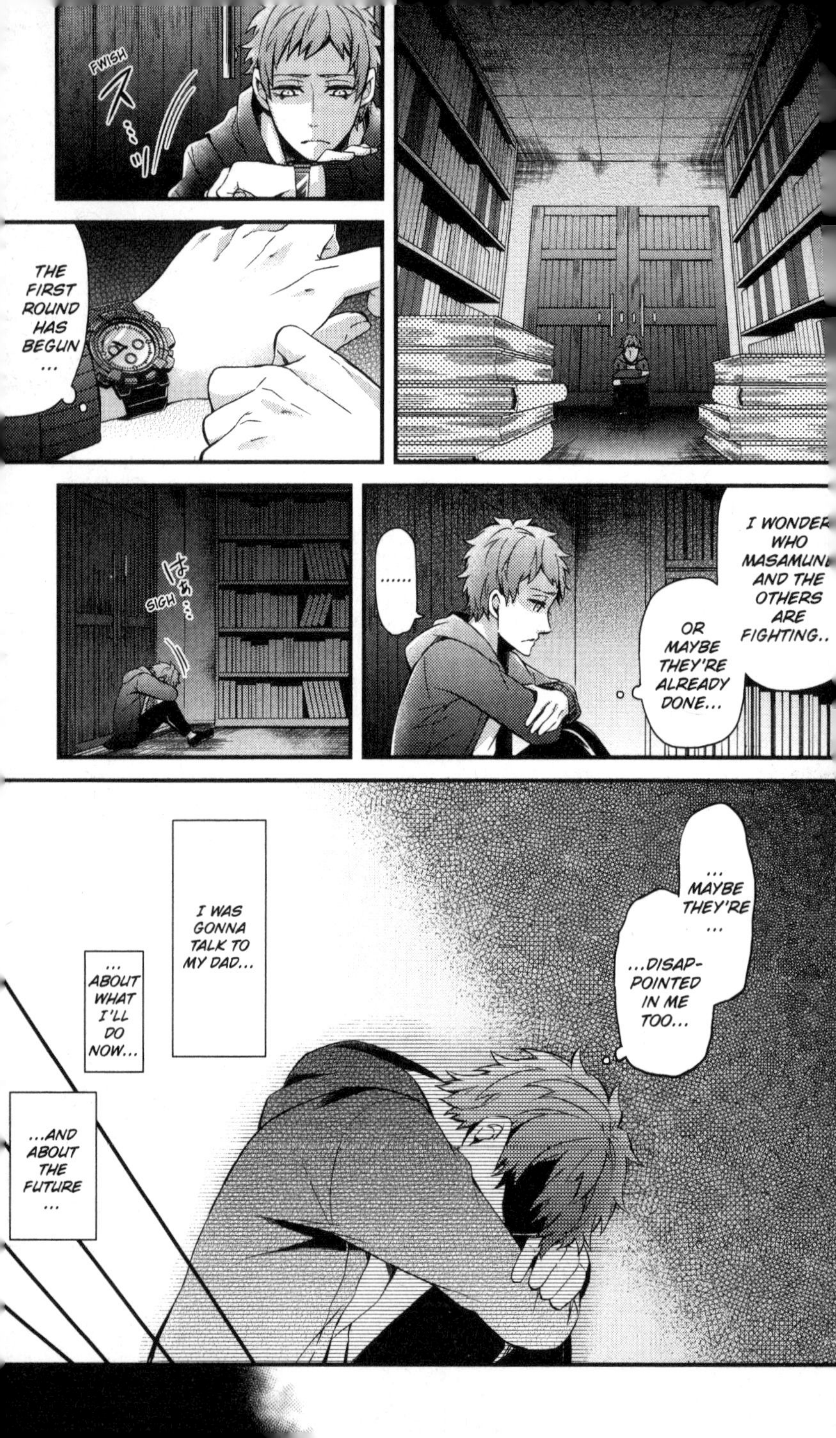
FWISH
スッ…ッ
THE FIRST ROUND HAS BEGUN...
I WONDER WHO MASAMUNE AND THE OTHERS ARE FIGHTING..
OR MAYBE THEY'RE ALREADY DONE...
......
はぁ…
SIGH
...MAYBE THEY'RE ...
...DISAP-POINTED IN ME TOO...
I WAS GONNA TALK TO MY DAD...
...ABOUT WHAT I'LL DO NOW...
...AND ABOUT THE FUTURE...

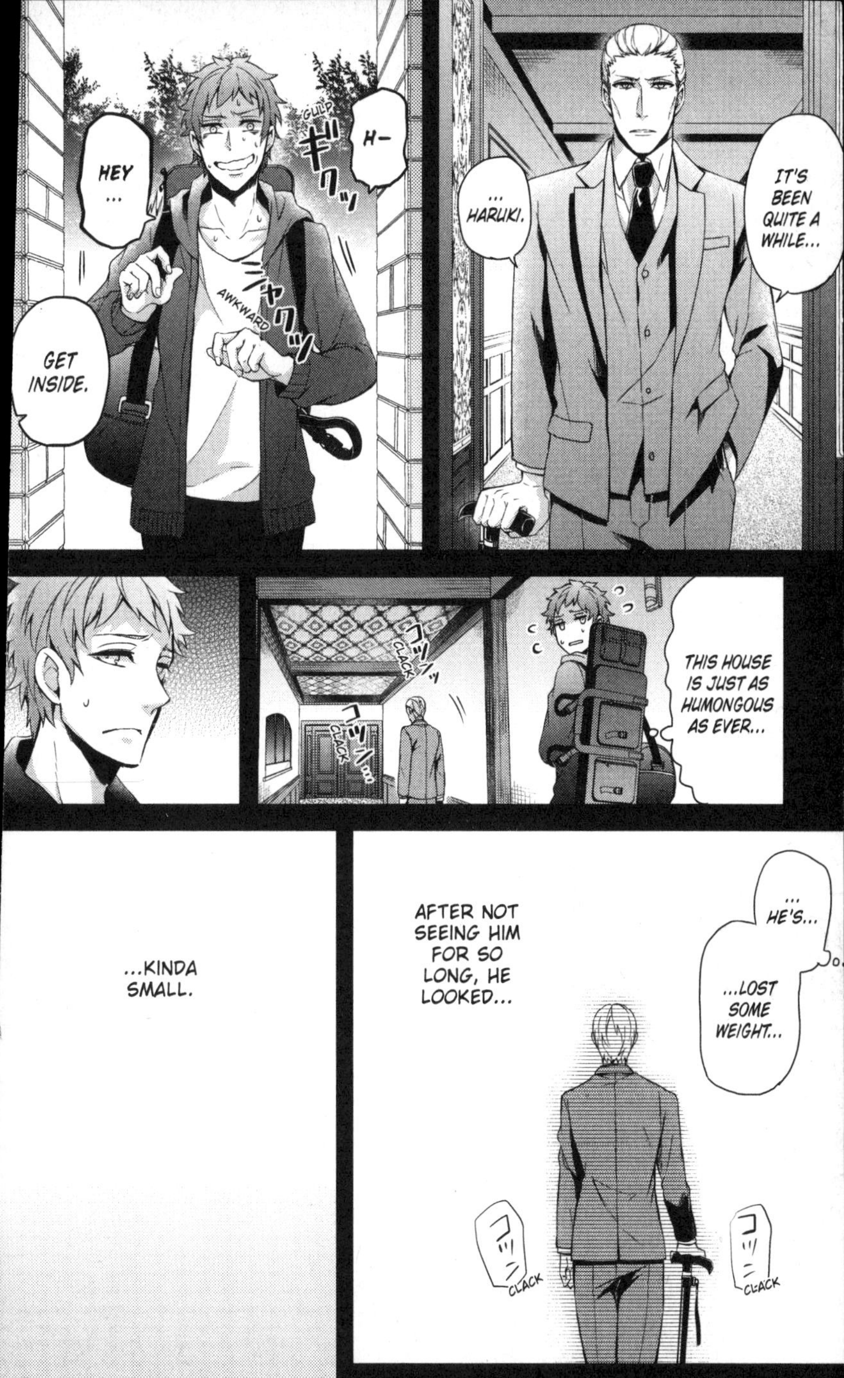
IT'S BEEN QUITE A WHILE...
... HARUKI.
H-
GULP
HEY ...
AWKWARD
GET INSIDE.
THIS HOUSE IS JUST AS HUMONGOUS AS EVER...
CLACK
CLACK
... HE'S...
...LOST SOME WEIGHT...
AFTER NOT SEEING HIM FOR SO LONG, HE LOOKED...
CLACK
CLACK
...KINDA SMALL.

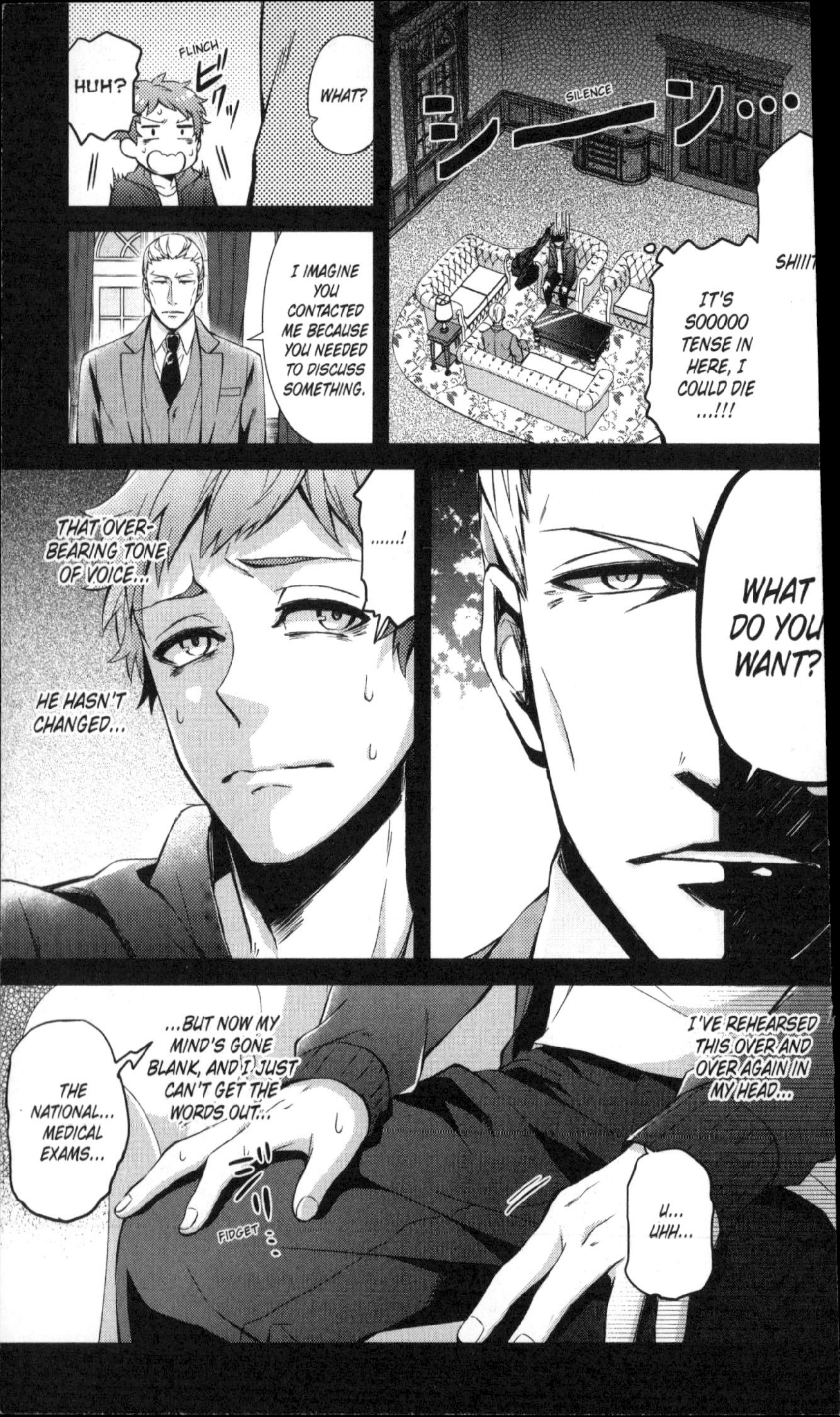
SILENCE
SHIIIT
IT'S SOOOOO TENSE IN HERE, I COULD DIE ...!!!
WHAT?
HUH?
FLINCH
I IMAGINE YOU CONTACTED ME BECAUSE YOU NEEDED TO DISCUSS SOMETHING.
WHAT DO YOU WANT?
......!
THAT OVER-BEARING TONE OF VOICE...!
HE HASN'T CHANGED...
I'VE REHEARSED THIS OVER AND OVER AGAIN IN MY HEAD...
U... UHH...
...BUT NOW MY MIND'S GONE BLANK, AND I JUST CAN'T GET THE WORDS OUT...
THE NATIONAL... MEDICAL EXAMS...
FIDGET

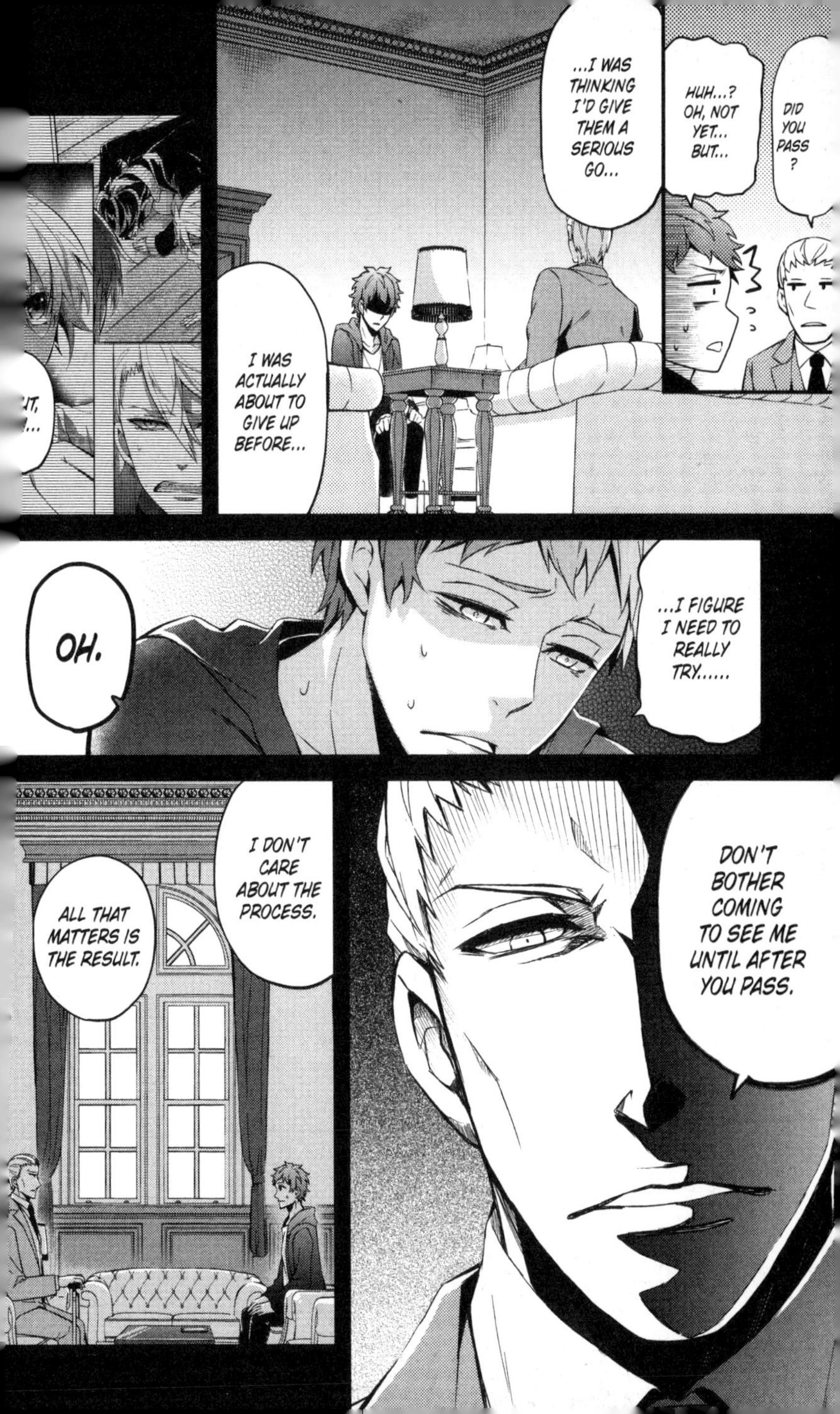
DID YOU PASS?
HUH...? OH, NOT YET... BUT...
...I WAS THINKING I'D GIVE THEM A SERIOUS GO...
I WAS ACTUALLY ABOUT TO GIVE UP BEFORE...
...I FIGURE I NEED TO REALLY TRY......
OH.
DON'T BOTHER COMING TO SEE ME UNTIL AFTER YOU PASS.
I DON'T CARE ABOUT THE PROCESS.
ALL THAT MATTERS IS THE RESULT.

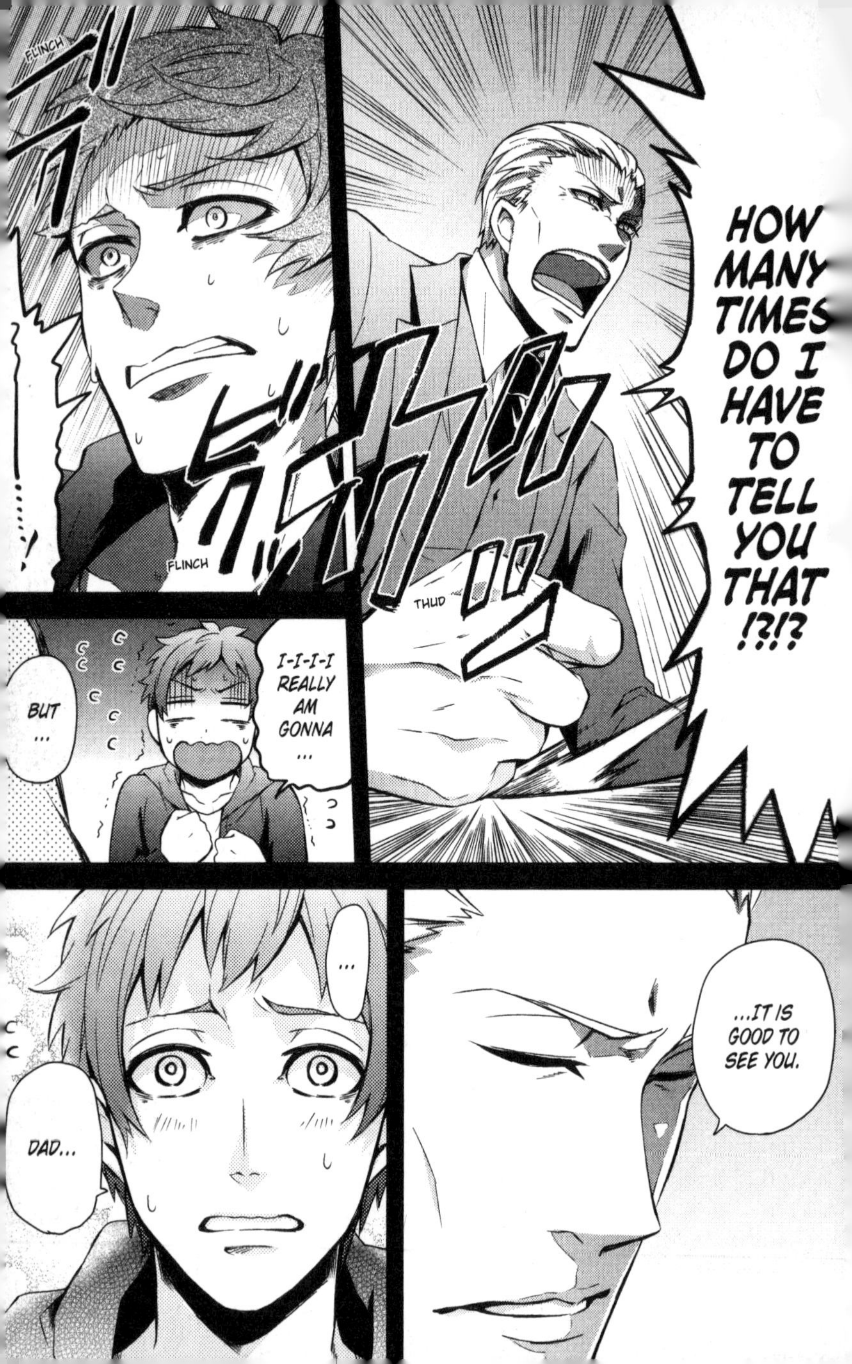
HOW MANY TIMES DO I HAVE TO TELL YOU THAT!?!?
THUD
FLINCH
FLINCH
......!
I-I-I-I REALLY AM GONNA ...
BUT ...
...IT IS GOOD TO SEE YOU.
...
DAD...

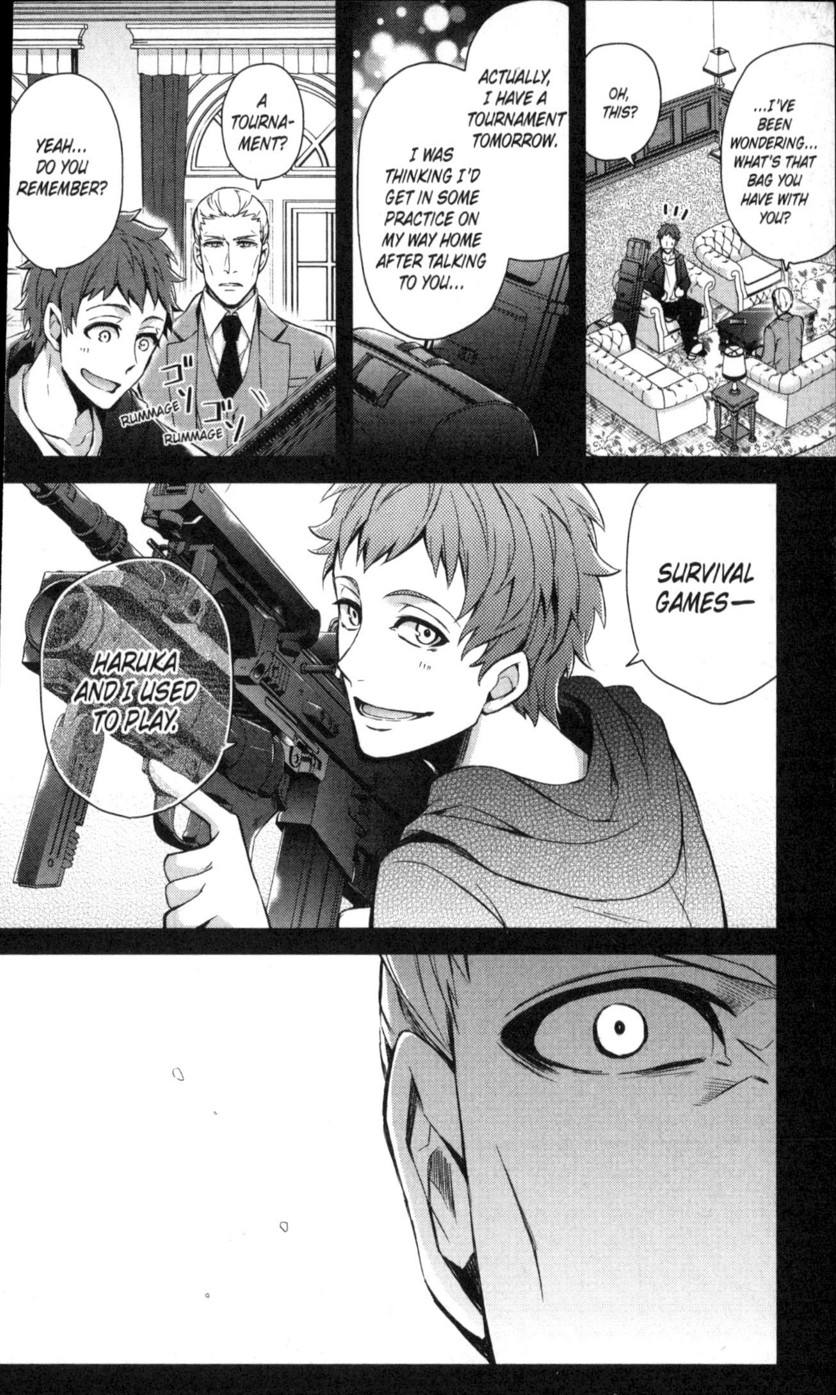
...I'VE BEEN WONDERING... WHAT'S THAT BAG YOU HAVE WITH YOU?
OH, THIS?
ACTUALLY, I HAVE A TOURNAMENT TOMORROW.
I WAS THINKING I'D GET IN SOME PRACTICE ON MY WAY HOME AFTER TALKING TO YOU...
A TOURNAMENT?
YEAH... DO YOU REMEMBER?
ゴソ RUMMAGE
ゴソ RUMMAGE
SURVIVAL GAMES—
HARUKA AND I USED TO PLAY.

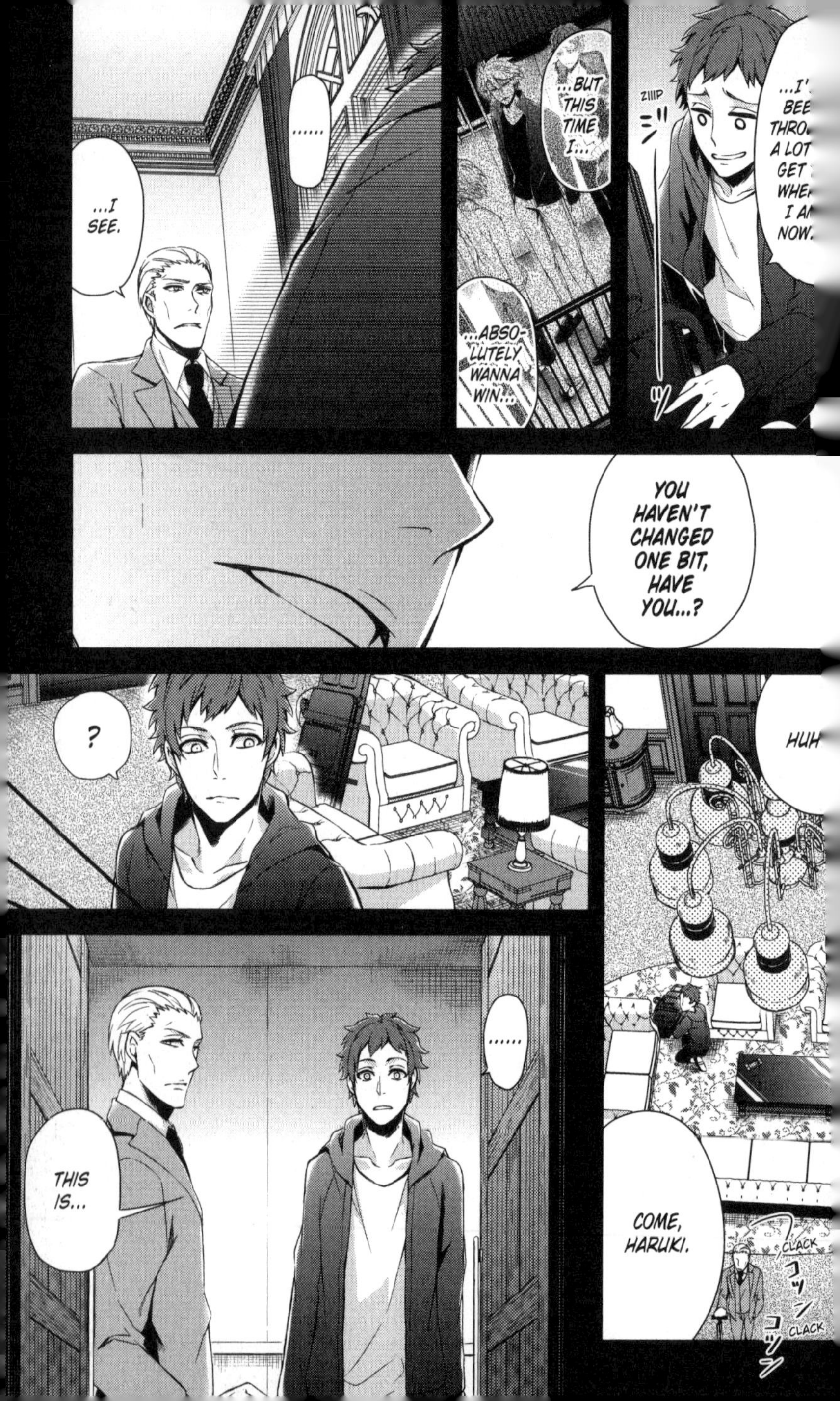
...I' BEE THRO A LOT GET WHEF I AN NOW.
ZIIIP
...BUT THIS TIME I...
...ABSO-LUTELY WANNA WIN...
......
...I SEE.
YOU HAVEN'T CHANGED ONE BIT, HAVE YOU...?
HUH
COME, HARUKI.
CLACK
CLACK
?
......
THIS IS...

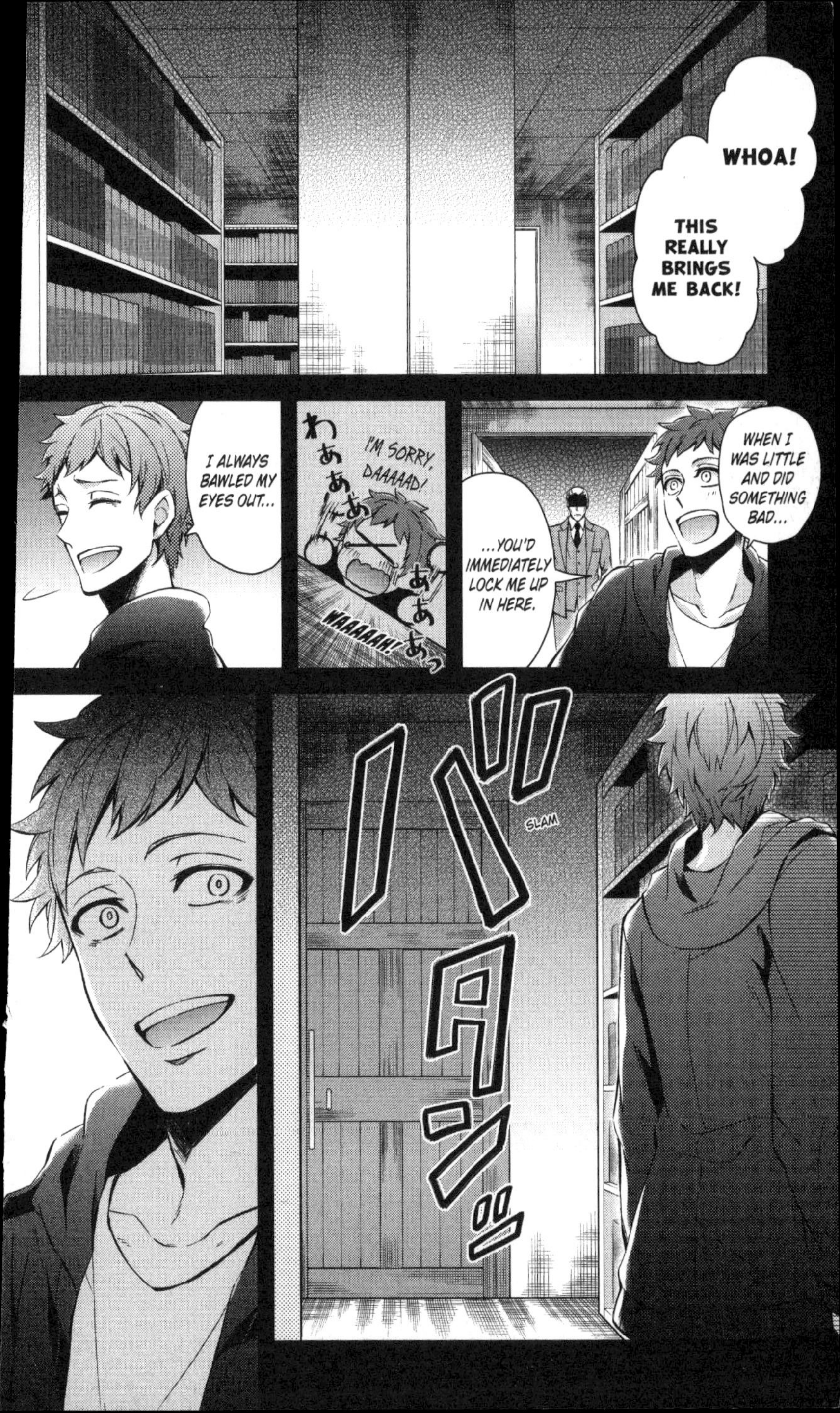
WHOA!
THIS REALLY BRINGS ME BACK!
WHEN I WAS LITTLE AND DID SOMETHING BAD...
...YOU'D IMMEDIATELY LOCK ME UP IN HERE.
I'M SORRY, DAAAAAD!
WAAAAAH!
I ALWAYS BAWLED MY EYES OUT...
バタン
SLAM

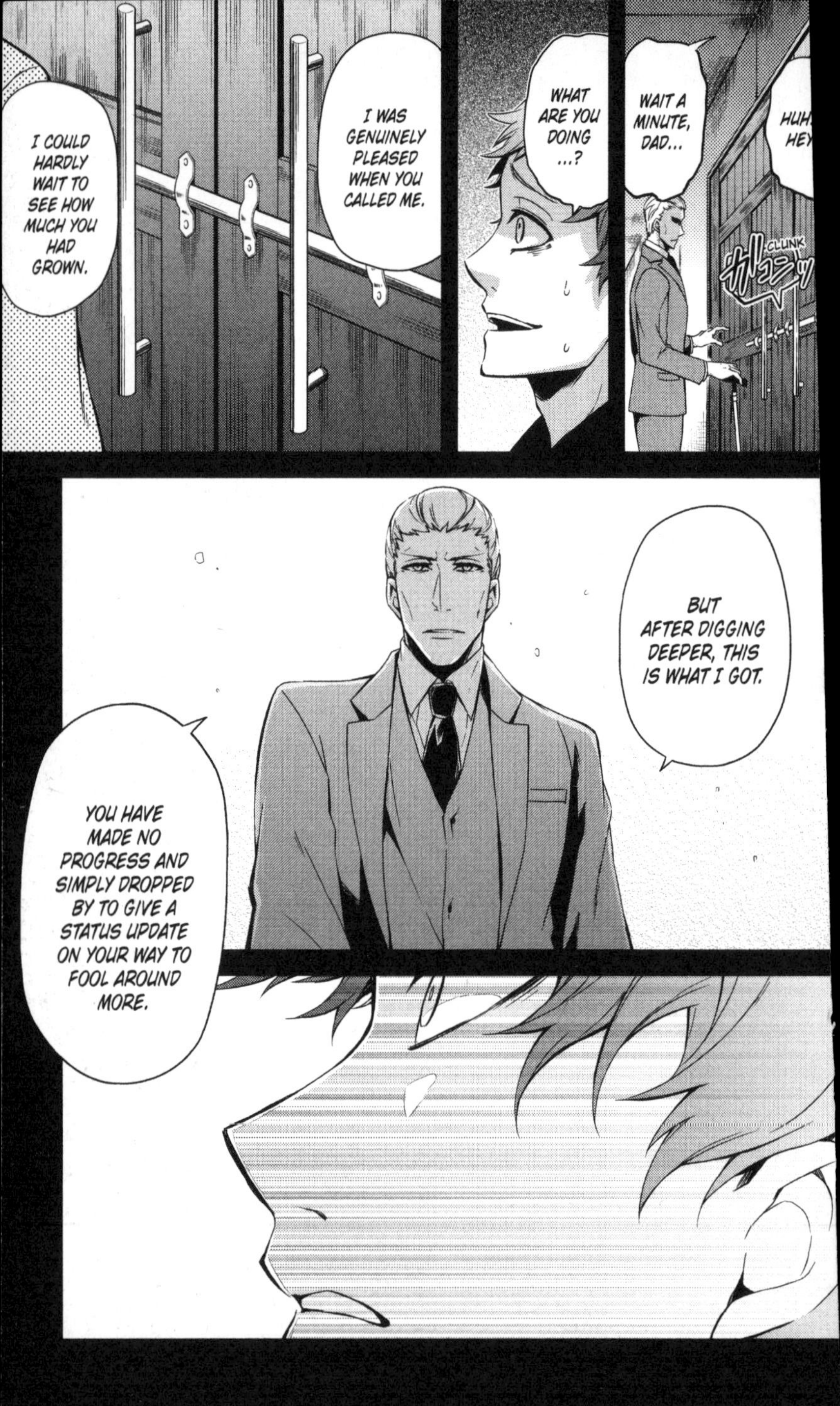
HUH! HEY
WAIT A MINUTE, DAD...
CLUNK
WHAT ARE YOU DOING ...?
I WAS GENUINELY PLEASED WHEN YOU CALLED ME.
I COULD HARDLY WAIT TO SEE HOW MUCH YOU HAD GROWN.
BUT AFTER DIGGING DEEPER, THIS IS WHAT I GOT.
YOU HAVE MADE NO PROGRESS AND SIMPLY DROPPED BY TO GIVE A STATUS UPDATE ON YOUR WAY TO FOOL AROUND MORE.

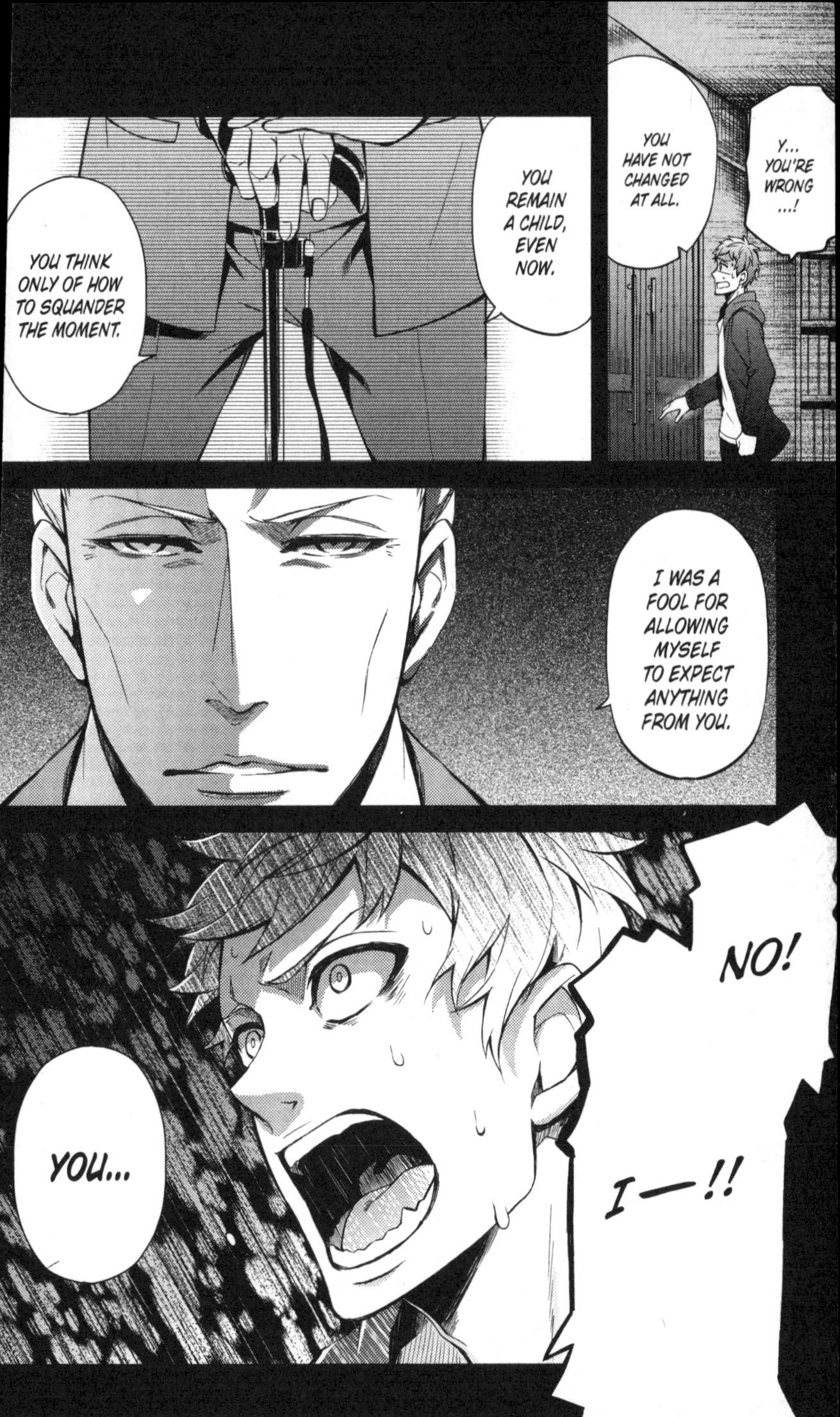
Y... YOU'RE WRONG ...!
YOU HAVE NOT CHANGED AT ALL.
YOU REMAIN A CHILD, EVEN NOW.
YOU THINK ONLY OF HOW TO SQUANDER THE MOMENT.
I WAS A FOOL FOR ALLOWING MYSELF TO EXPECT ANYTHING FROM YOU.
NO!
I—!!
YOU...

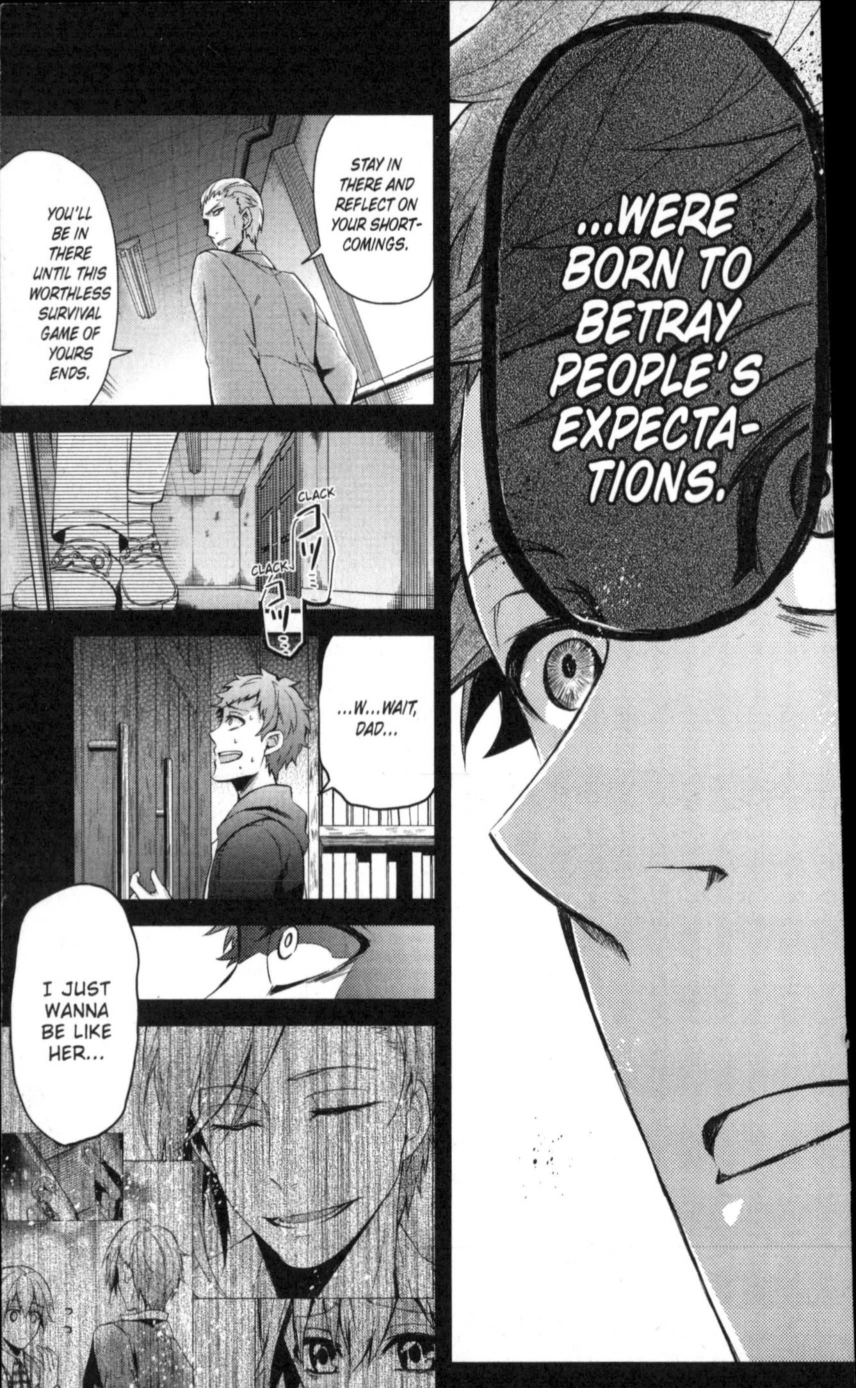
...WERE BORN TO BETRAY PEOPLE'S EXPECTATIONS.
STAY IN THERE AND REFLECT ON YOUR SHORT-COMINGS.
YOU'LL BE IN THERE UNTIL THIS WORTHLESS SURVIVAL GAME OF YOURS ENDS.
CLACK
CLACK
...W...WAIT, DAD...
I JUST WANNA BE LIKE HER...

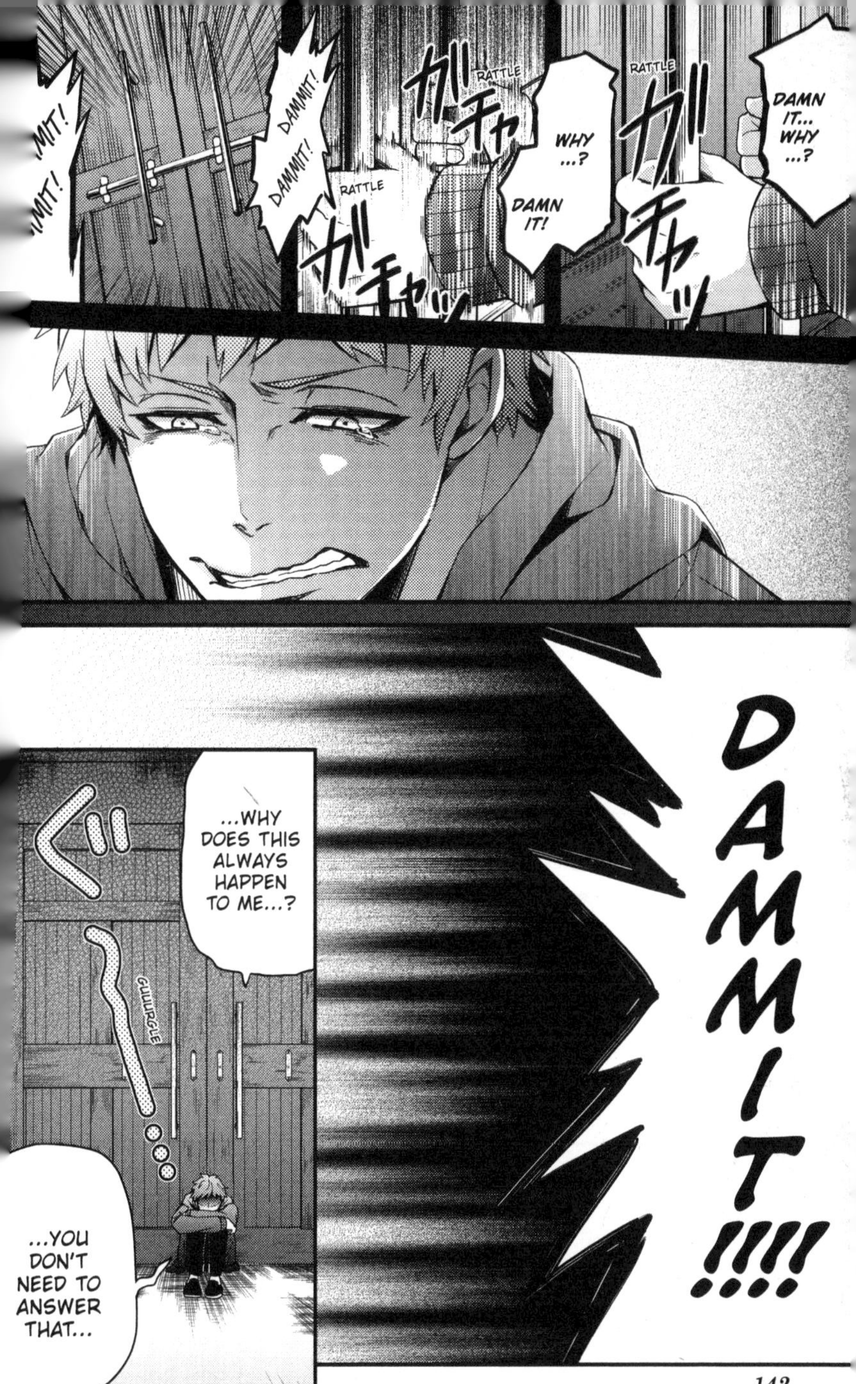
DAMN IT... WHY...?
RATTLE
ガチャ
WHY...?
DAMN IT!
RATTLE
ガチャ
RATTLE
ガチャッ
DAMMIT! DAMMIT!
DAMMIT!!!!
...WHY DOES THIS ALWAYS HAPPEN TO ME...?
ぐ〜〜…
GULURGLE
...YOU DON'T NEED TO ANSWER THAT...

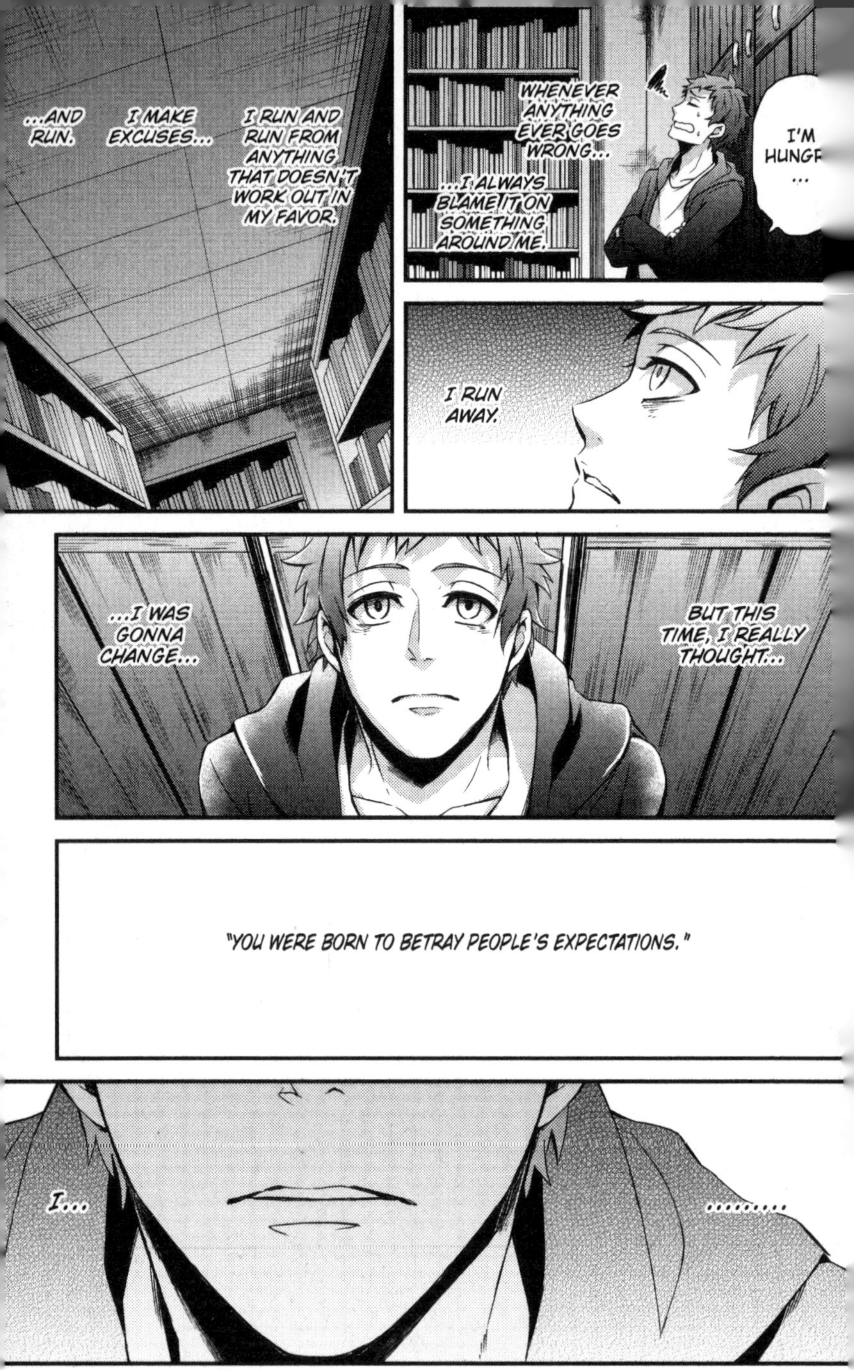
I'M HUNGR
...
WHENEVER ANYTHING EVER GOES WRONG...
...I ALWAYS BLAME IT ON SOMETHING AROUND ME.
I RUN AWAY.
I RUN AND RUN FROM ANYTHING THAT DOESN'T WORK OUT IN MY FAVOR.
I MAKE EXCUSES...
...AND RUN.
BUT THIS TIME, I REALLY THOUGHT...
...I WAS GONNA CHANGE...
"YOU WERE BORN TO BETRAY PEOPLE'S EXPECTATIONS."
....
I...

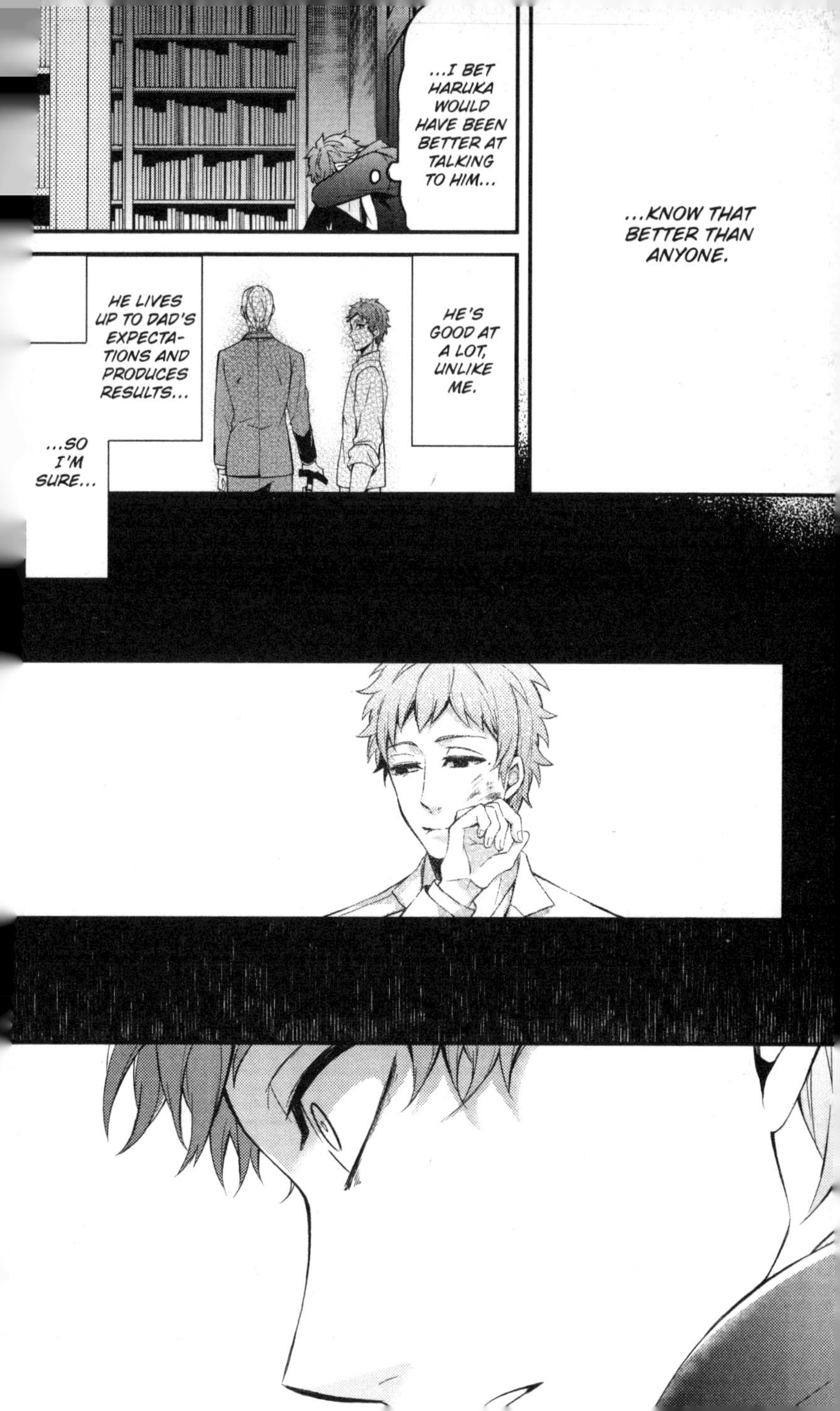
...I BET HARUKA WOULD HAVE BEEN BETTER AT TALKING TO HIM...
HE'S GOOD AT A LOT, UNLIKE ME.
HE LIVES UP TO DAD'S EXPECTATIONS AND PRODUCES RESULTS...
...SO I'M SURE...
...KNOW THAT BETTER THAN ANYONE.

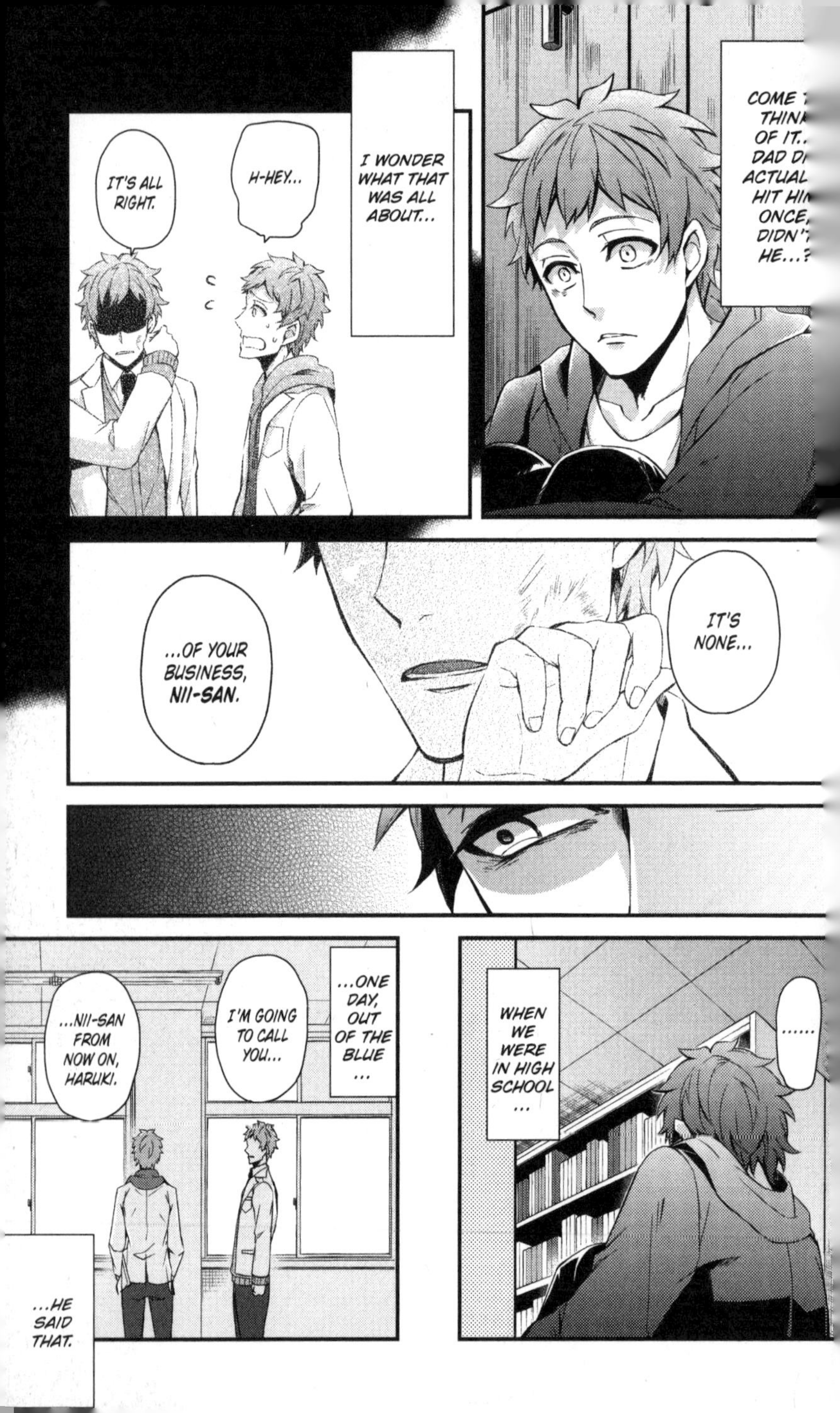
COME T
THINK
OF IT..
DAD DI
ACTUAL
HIT HI
ONCE,
DIDN'T
HE...?
I WONDER WHAT THAT WAS ALL ABOUT...
H-HEY...
IT'S ALL RIGHT.
IT'S NONE...
...OF YOUR BUSINESS, NII-SAN.
......
WHEN WE WERE IN HIGH SCHOOL...
...ONE DAY, OUT OF THE BLUE...
I'M GOING TO CALL YOU...
...NII-SAN FROM NOW ON, HARUKI.
...HE SAID THAT.

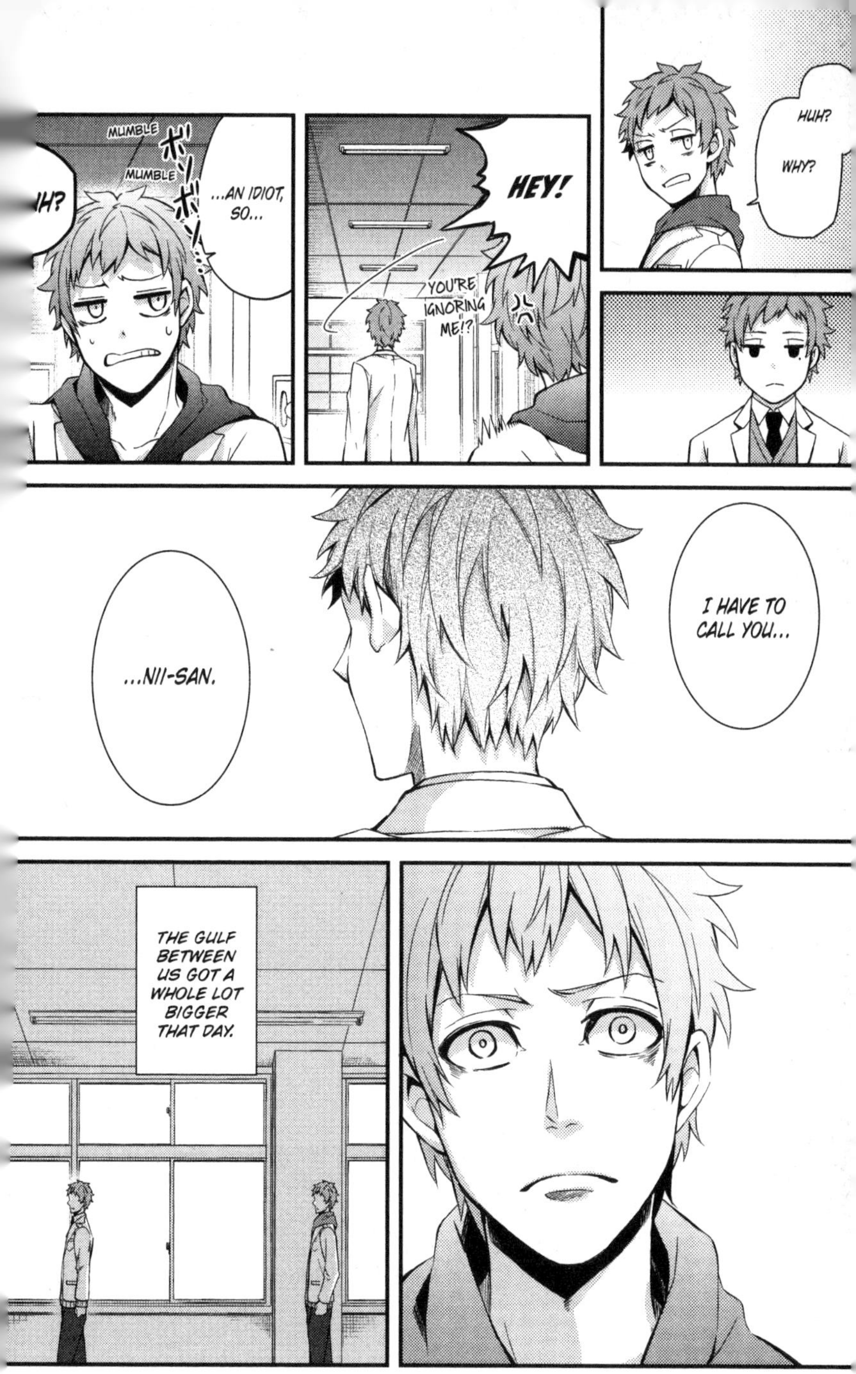
HUH?
WHY?
HEY!
YOU'RE IGNORING ME!?
...AN IDIOT, SO...
ボソボソ…
MUMBLE
MUMBLE
I HAVE TO CALL YOU...
...NII-SAN.
THE GULF BETWEEN US GOT A WHOLE LOT BIGGER THAT DAY.

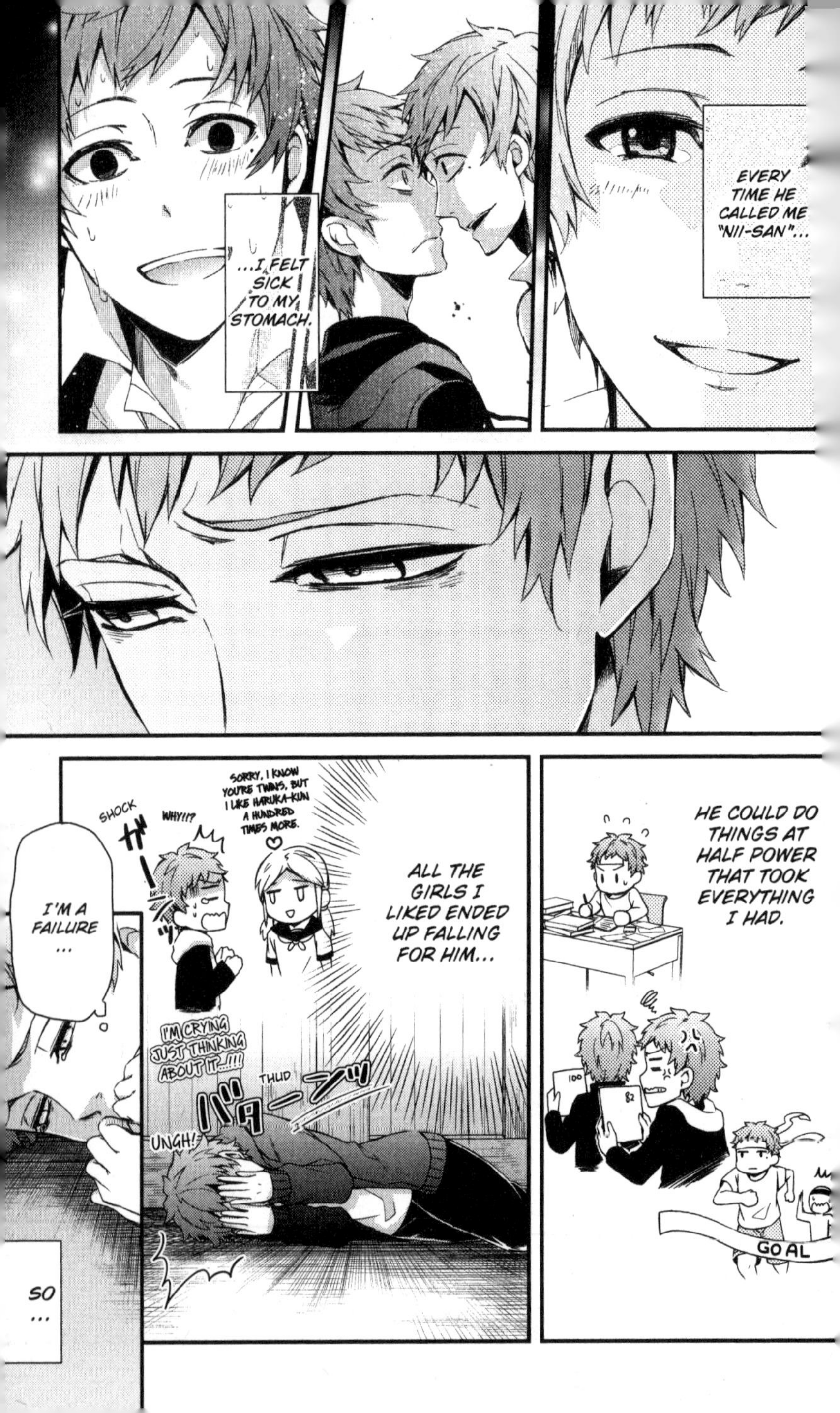
EVERY TIME HE CALLED ME "NII-SAN"...
...I FELT SICK TO MY STOMACH.
HE COULD DO THINGS AT HALF POWER THAT TOOK EVERYTHING I HAD.
100
82
GOAL
ALL THE GIRLS I LIKED ENDED UP FALLING FOR HIM...
SORRY, I KNOW YOU'RE TWINS, BUT I LIKE HARUKA-KUN A HUNDRED TIMES MORE.
WHY!!?
SHOCK
I'M CRYING JUST THINKING ABOUT IT...!!!!
THUD
UNGH!
I'M A FAILURE ...
SO ...

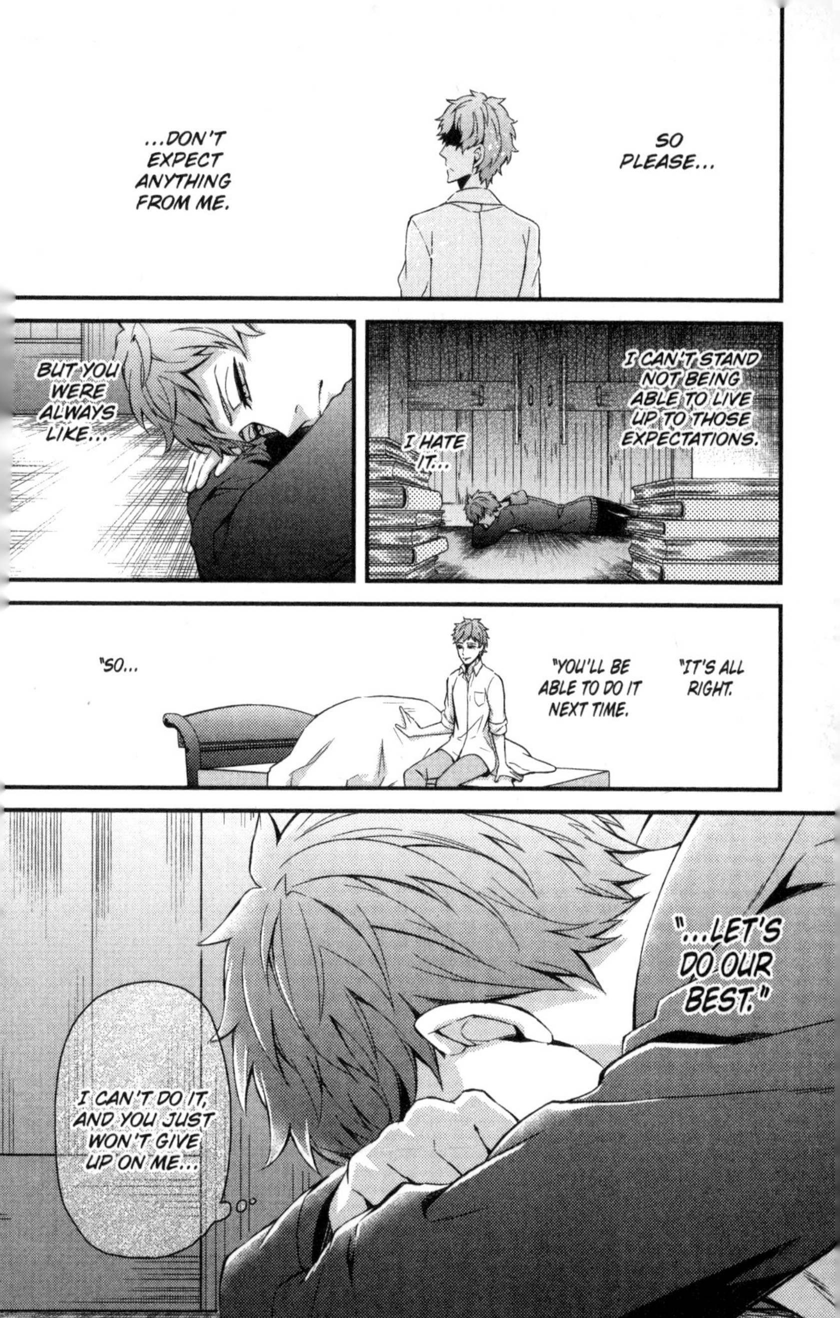
SO PLEASE...
...DON'T EXPECT ANYTHING FROM ME.
I CAN'T STAND NOT BEING ABLE TO LIVE UP TO THOSE EXPECTATIONS.
I HATE IT...
BUT YOU WERE ALWAYS LIKE...
"IT'S ALL RIGHT.
"YOU'LL BE ABLE TO DO IT NEXT TIME.
"SO...
"...LET'S DO OUR BEST."
I CAN'T DO IT, AND YOU JUST WON'T GIVE UP ON ME...

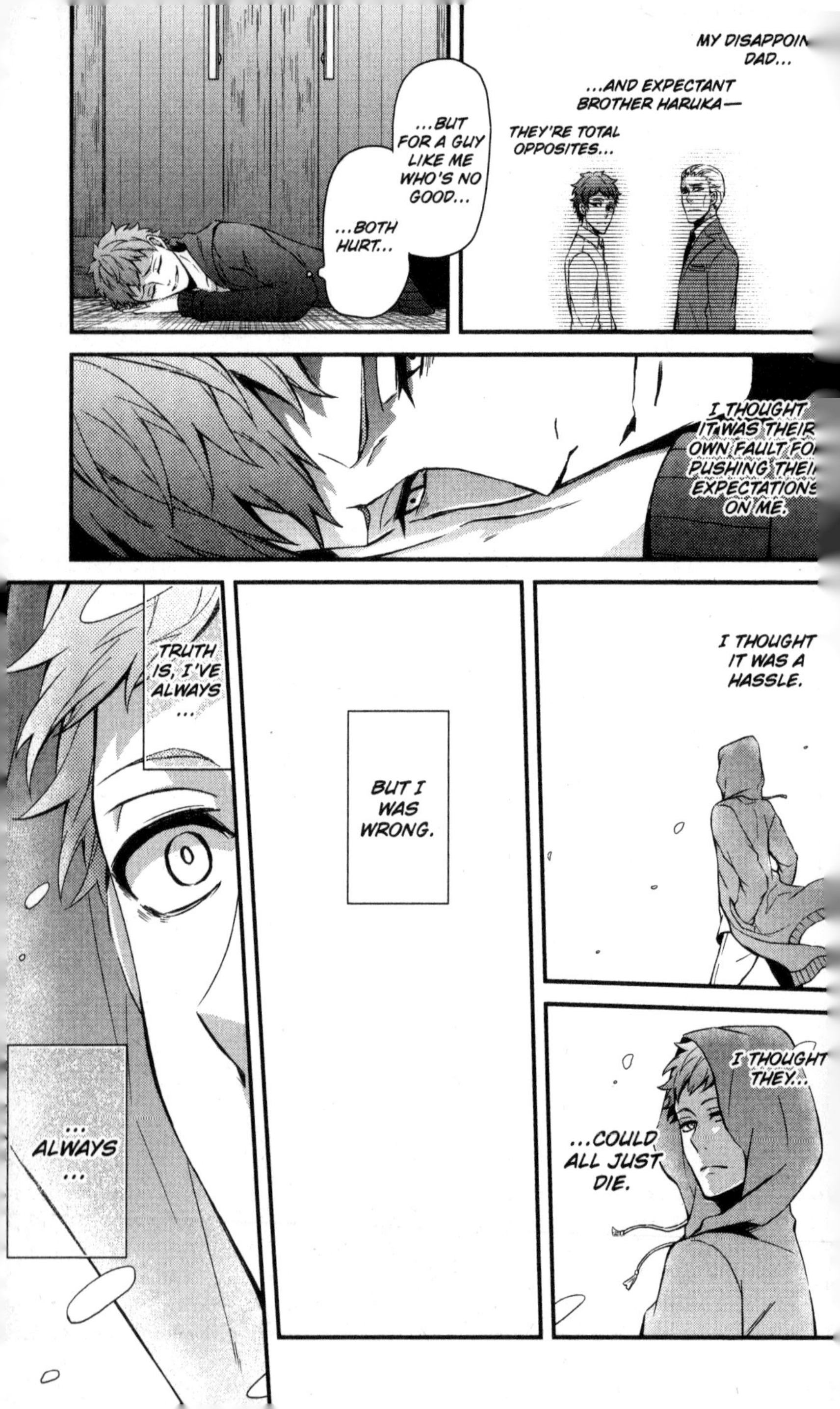
MY DISAPPOIN DAD...
...AND EXPECTANT BROTHER HARUKA—
THEY'RE TOTAL OPPOSITES...
...BUT FOR A GUY LIKE ME WHO'S NO GOOD...
...BOTH HURT...
I THOUGHT IT WAS THEIR OWN FAULT FO PUSHING THEI EXPECTATIONS ON ME.
I THOUGHT IT WAS A HASSLE.
I THOUGHT THEY...
...COULD ALL JUST DIE.
BUT I WAS WRONG.
TRUTH IS, I'VE ALWAYS ...
... ALWAYS ...

...TO...

...WANTED...

...MAKE THEM PROUD...

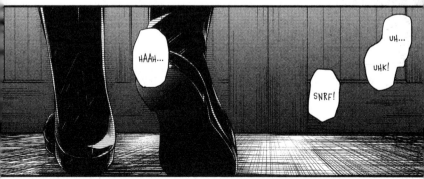

HAAH...

UH...

UHK!

SNRF!

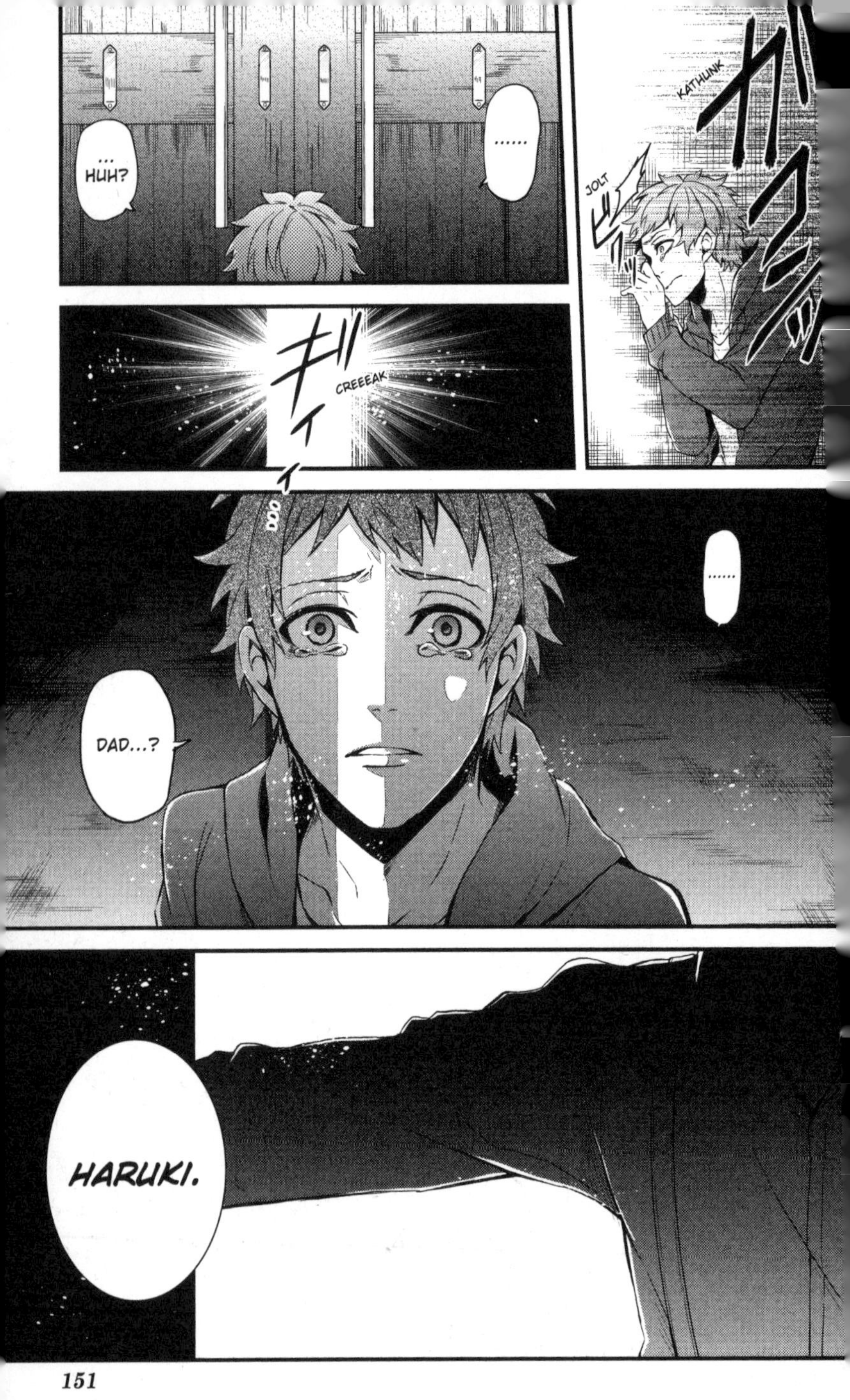
KATHUNK
JOLT
......
... HUH?
CREEEAK
......
DAD...?
HARUKI.

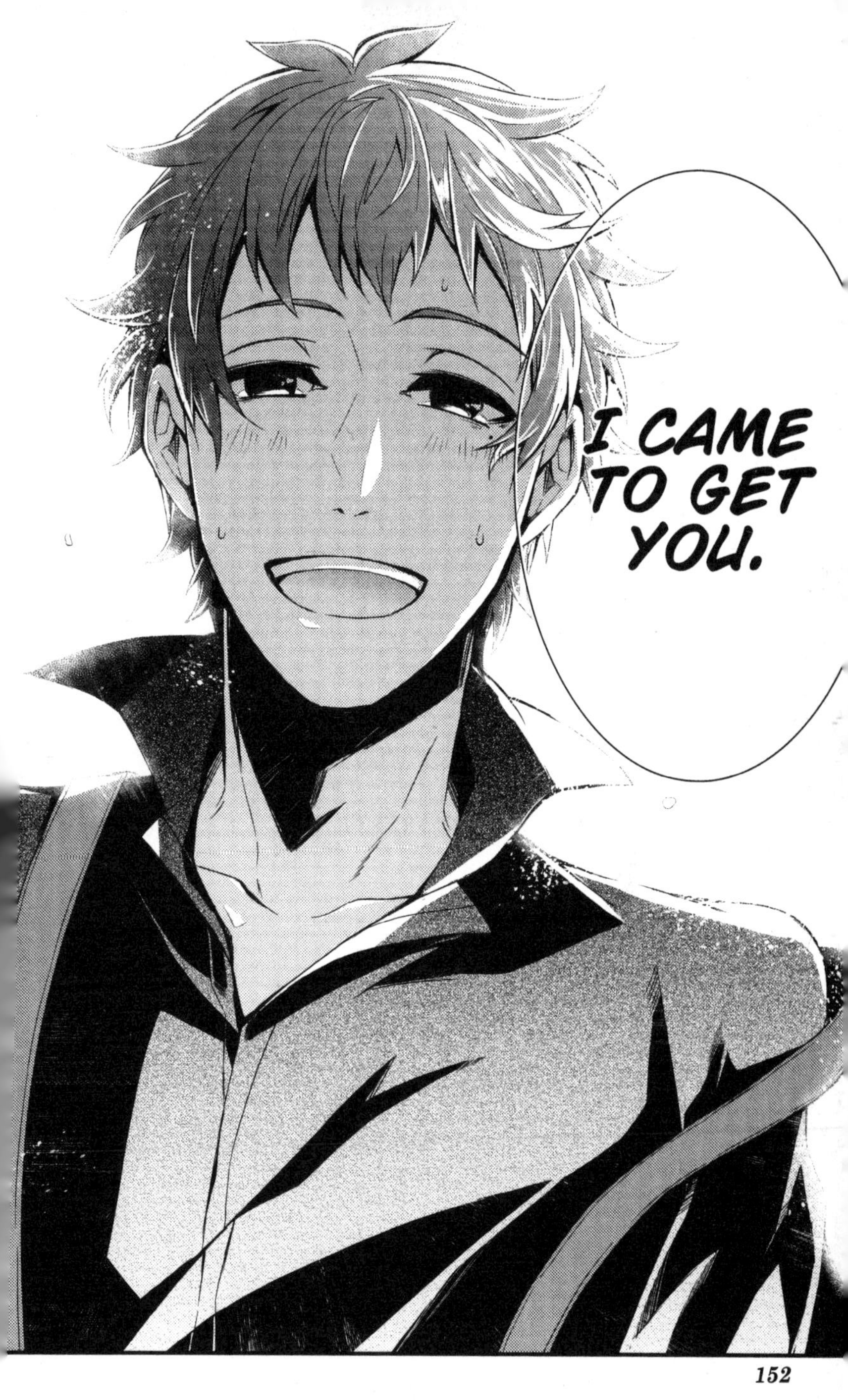
I CAME TO GET YOU.

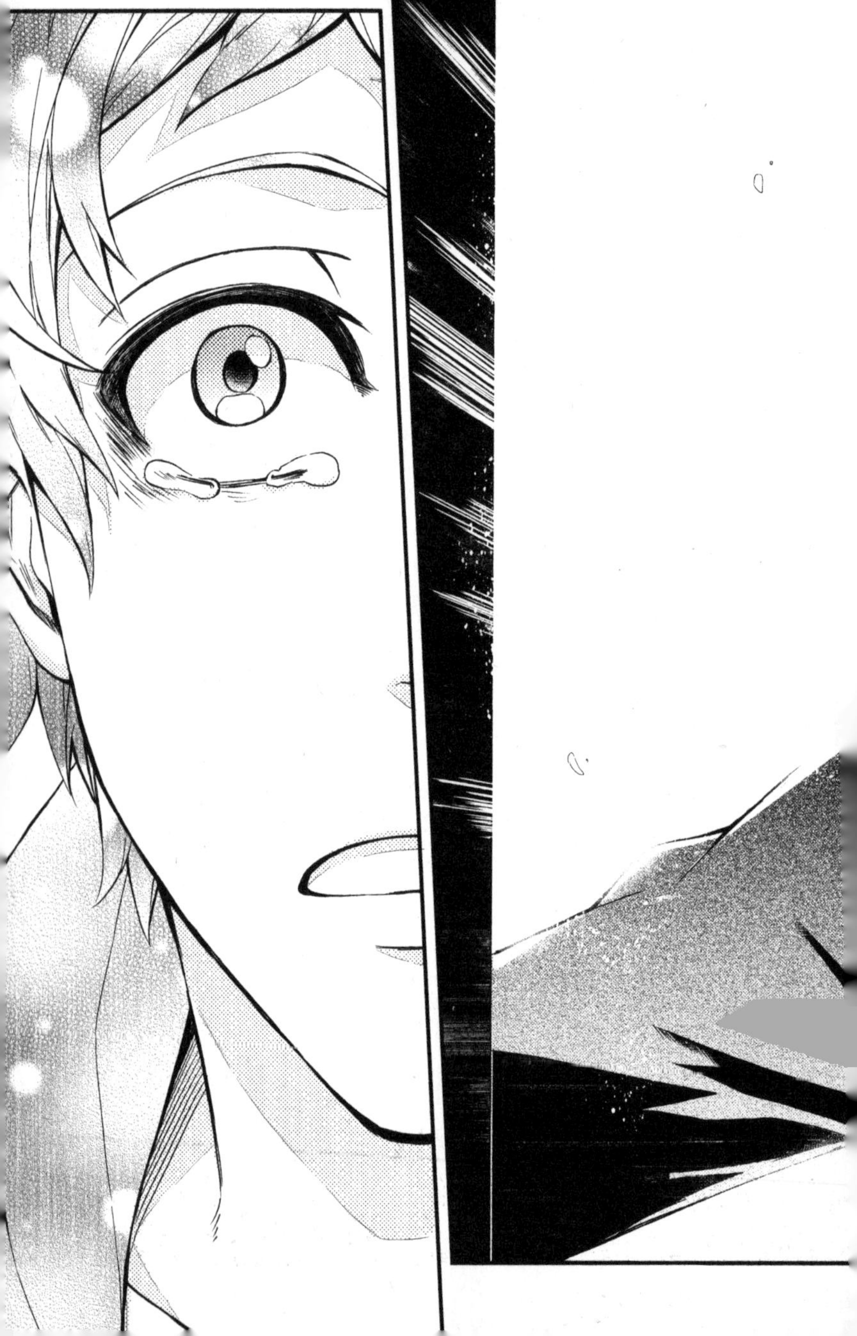

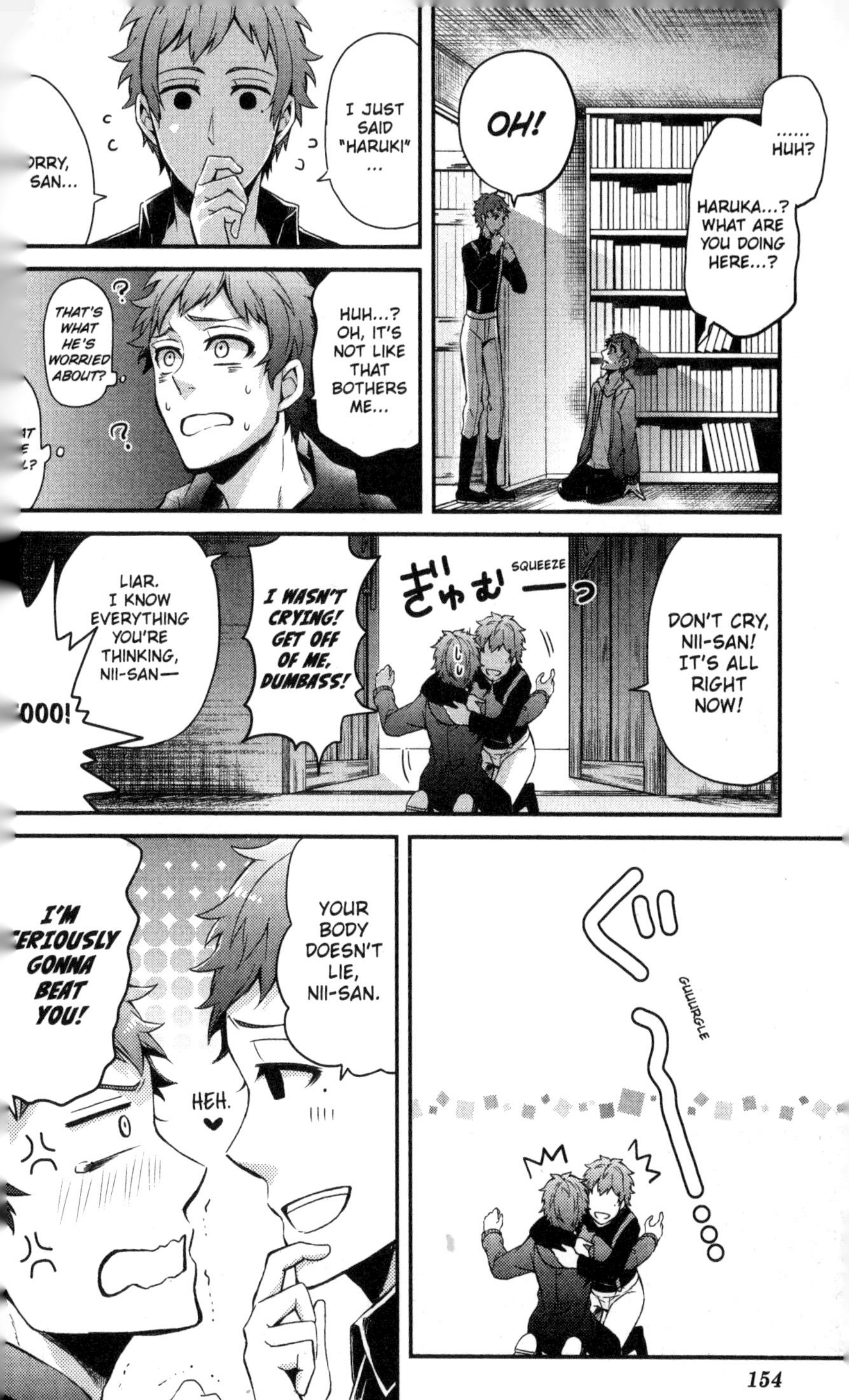
......
HUH?
HARUKA...? WHAT ARE YOU DOING HERE...?
OH!
I JUST SAID "HARUKI" ...
ORRY, SAN...
HUH...? OH, IT'S NOT LIKE THAT BOTHERS ME...
THAT'S WHAT HE'S WORRIED ABOUT?
DON'T CRY, NII-SAN! IT'S ALL RIGHT NOW!
ぎゅむーっ
SQUEEZE
I WASN'T CRYING! GET OFF OF ME, DUMBASS!
LIAR. I KNOW EVERYTHING YOU'RE THINKING, NII-SAN—
OOO!
ぐ
GUURGLE
YOUR BODY DOESN'T LIE, NII-SAN.
HEH.
I'M ERIOUSLY GONNA BEAT YOU!

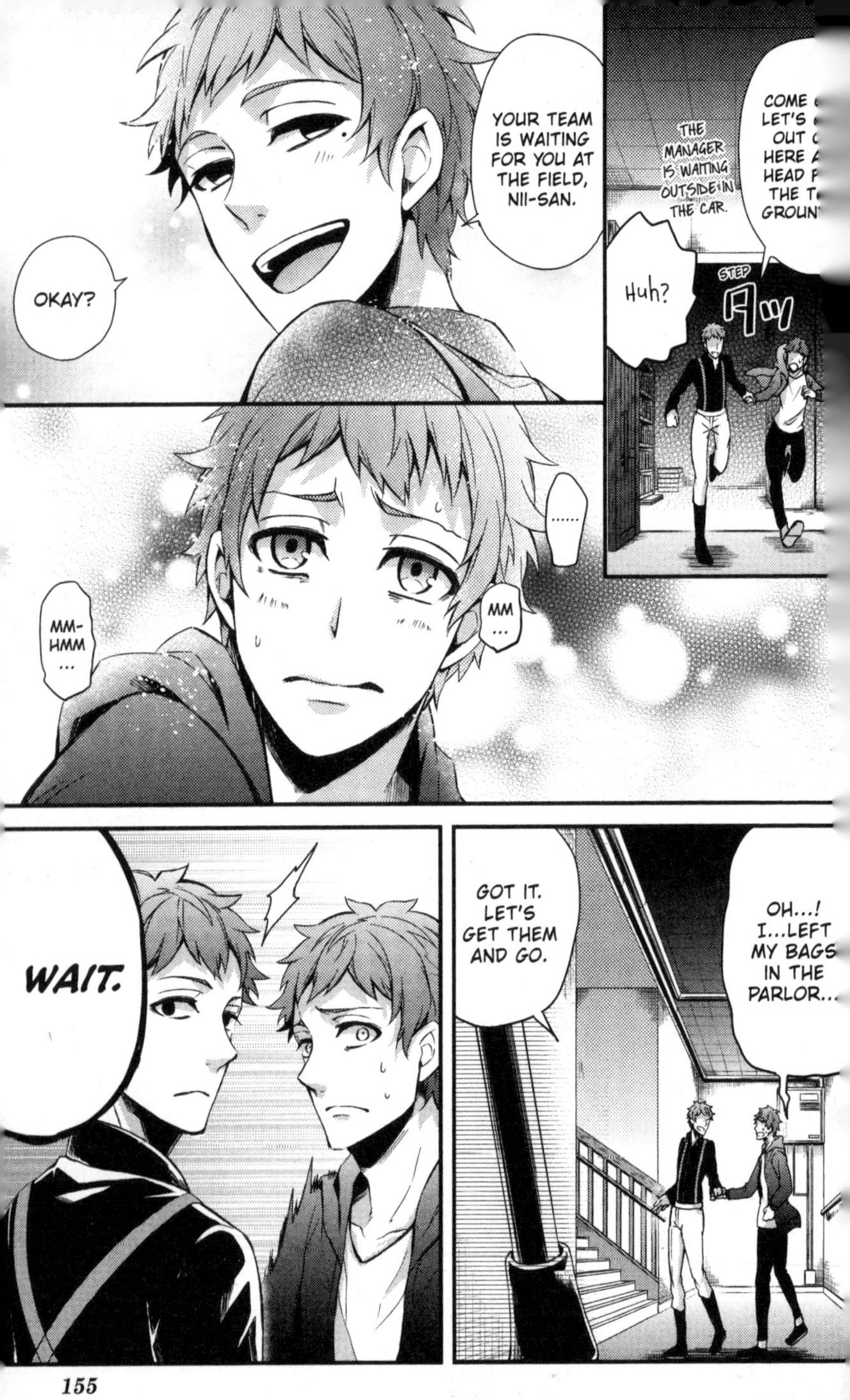
COME
LET'S
OUT
HERE A
HEAD F
THE T
GROUN
THE MANAGER IS WAITING OUTSIDE IN THE CAR.
Huh?
STEP
タッ
YOUR TEAM IS WAITING FOR YOU AT THE FIELD, NII-SAN.
OKAY?
......
MM ...
MM-HMM ...
OH...! I...LEFT MY BAGS IN THE PARLOR...
GOT IT. LET'S GET THEM AND GO.
WAIT.

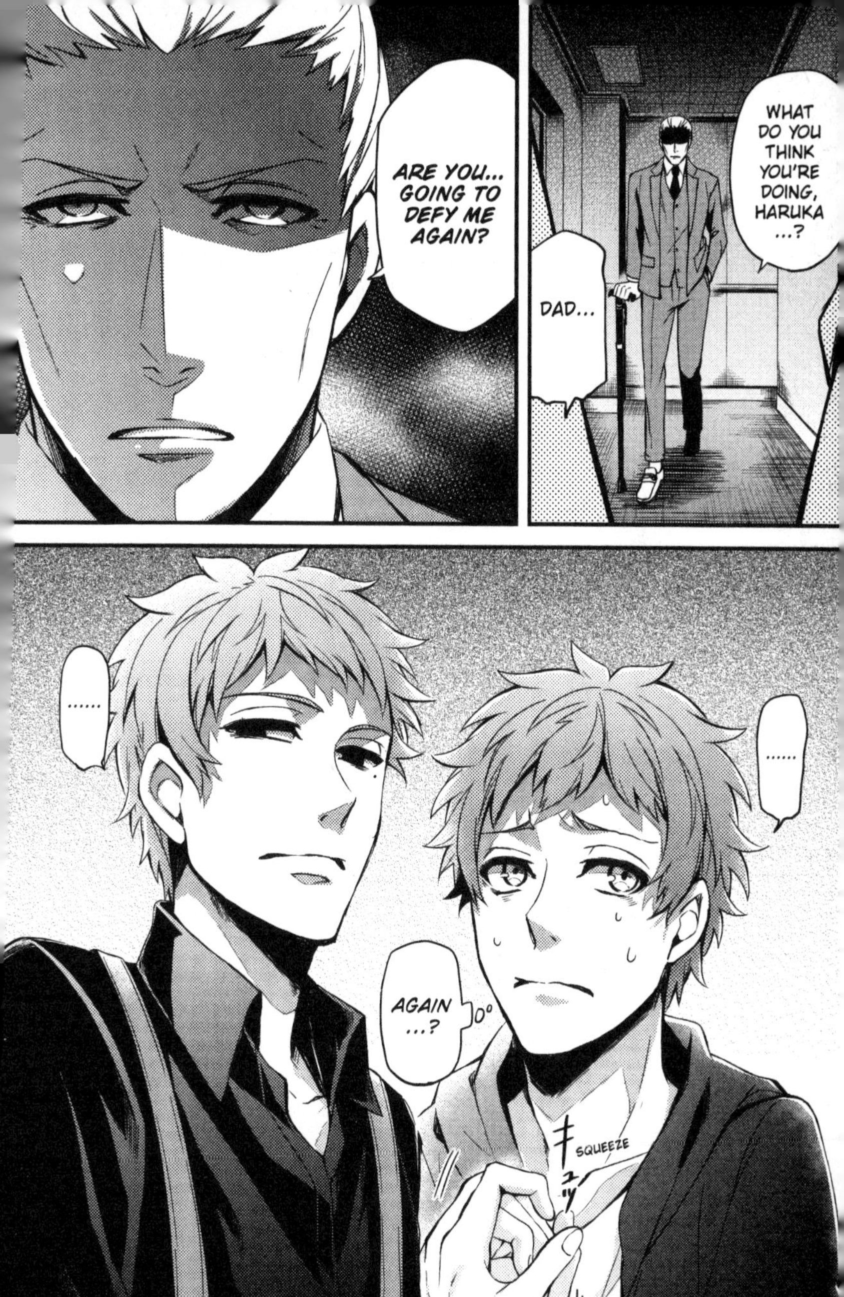
WHAT DO YOU THINK YOU'RE DOING, HARUKA ...?
DAD...
ARE YOU... GOING TO DEFY ME AGAIN?
......
......
AGAIN ...?
SQUEEZE

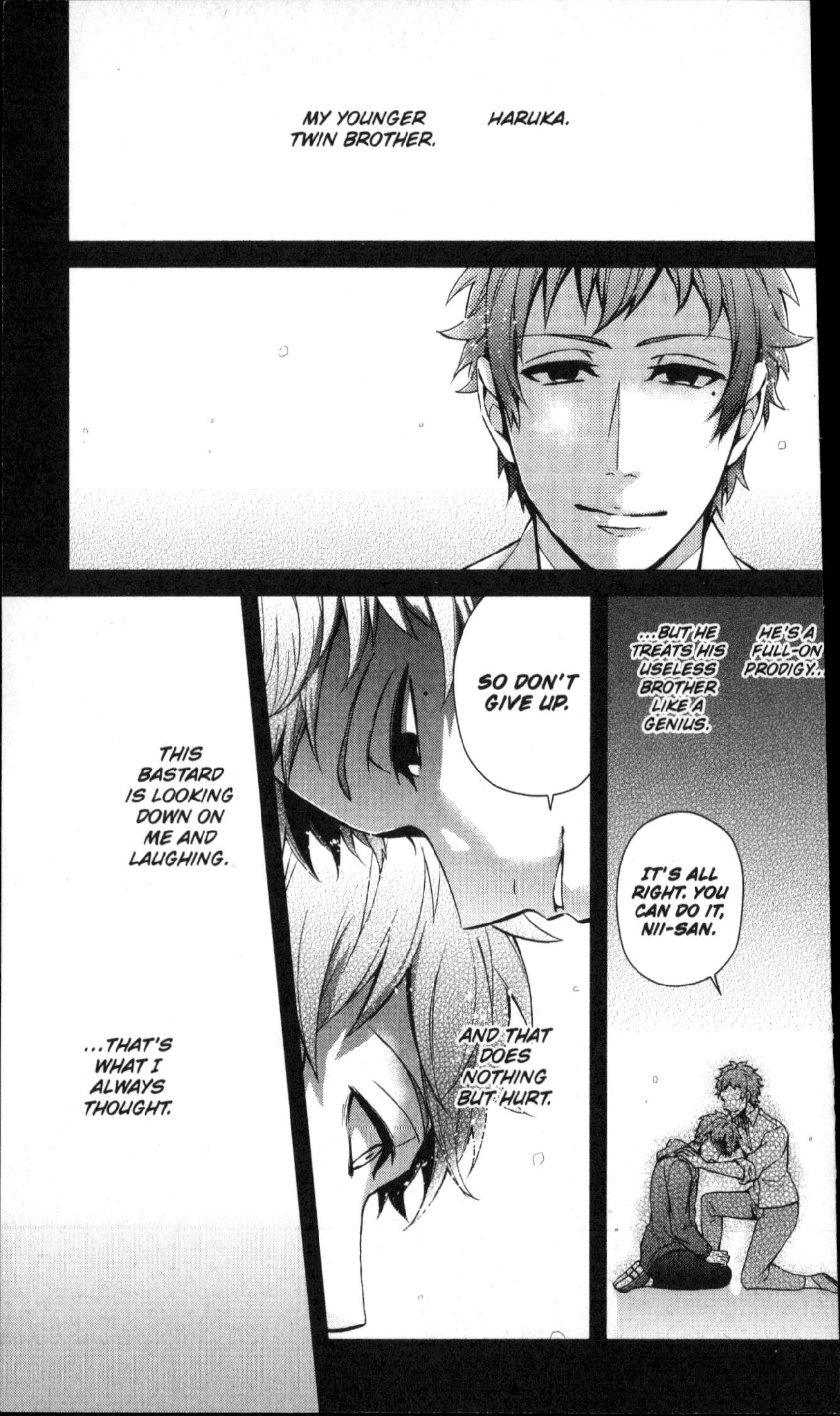
HARUKA.
MY YOUNGER TWIN BROTHER.
HE'S A FULL-ON PRODIGY...
...BUT HE TREATS HIS USELESS BROTHER LIKE A GENIUS.
IT'S ALL RIGHT. YOU CAN DO IT, NII-SAN.
SO DON'T GIVE UP.
AND THAT DOES NOTHING BUT HURT.
THIS BASTARD IS LOOKING DOWN ON ME AND LAUGHING.
...THAT'S WHAT I ALWAYS THOUGHT.

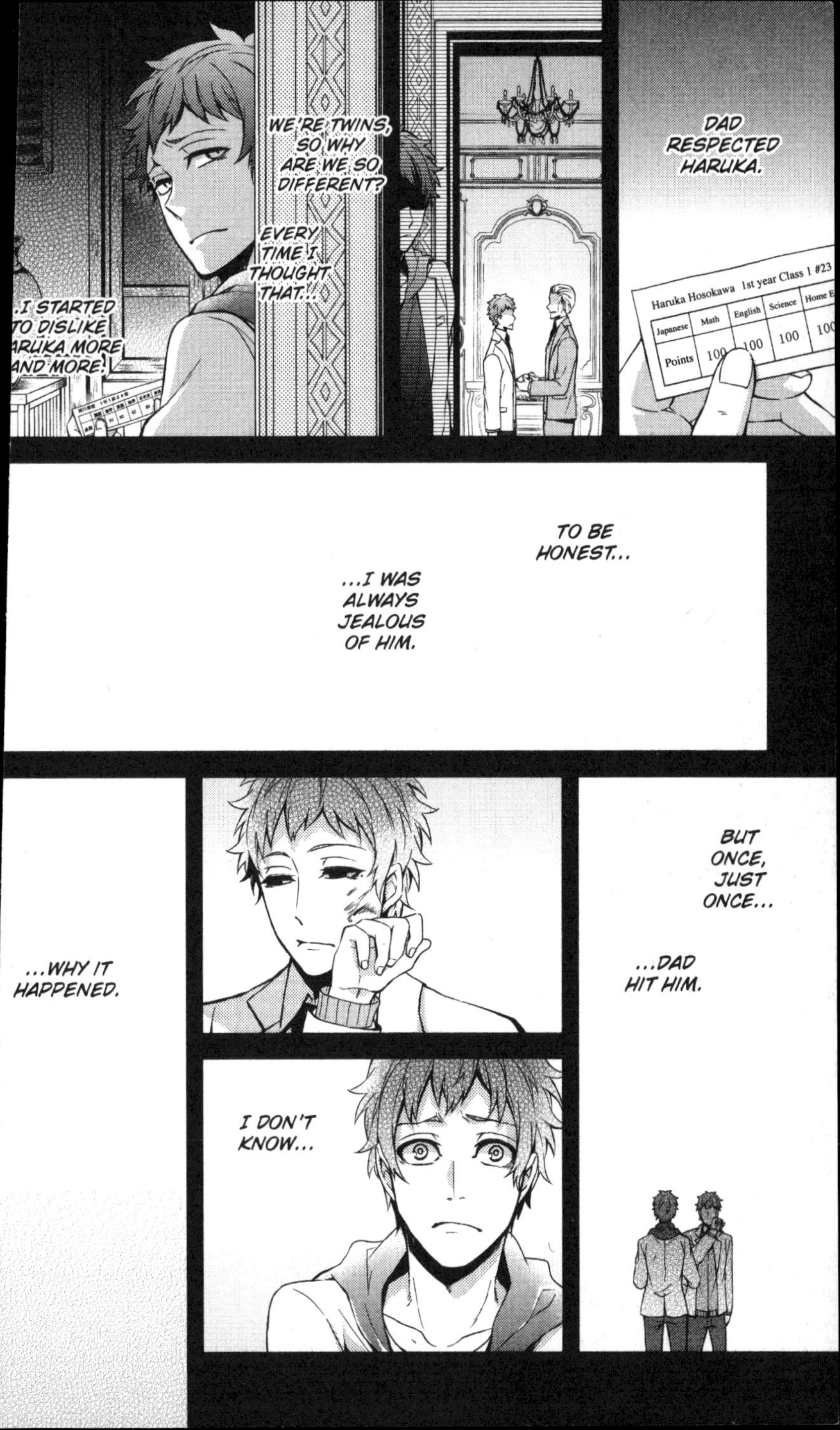
DAD RESPECTED HARUKA.
Haruka Hosokawa 1st year Class 1 #23
Japanese Math English Science Home E
Points 100 100 100 100
WE'RE TWINS, SO WHY ARE WE SO DIFFERENT?
EVERY TIME I THOUGHT THAT...
.I STARTED TO DISLIKE ARUKA MORE AND MORE.
TO BE HONEST...
...I WAS ALWAYS JEALOUS OF HIM.
BUT ONCE, JUST ONCE...
...DAD HIT HIM.
I DON'T KNOW...
...WHY IT HAPPENED.

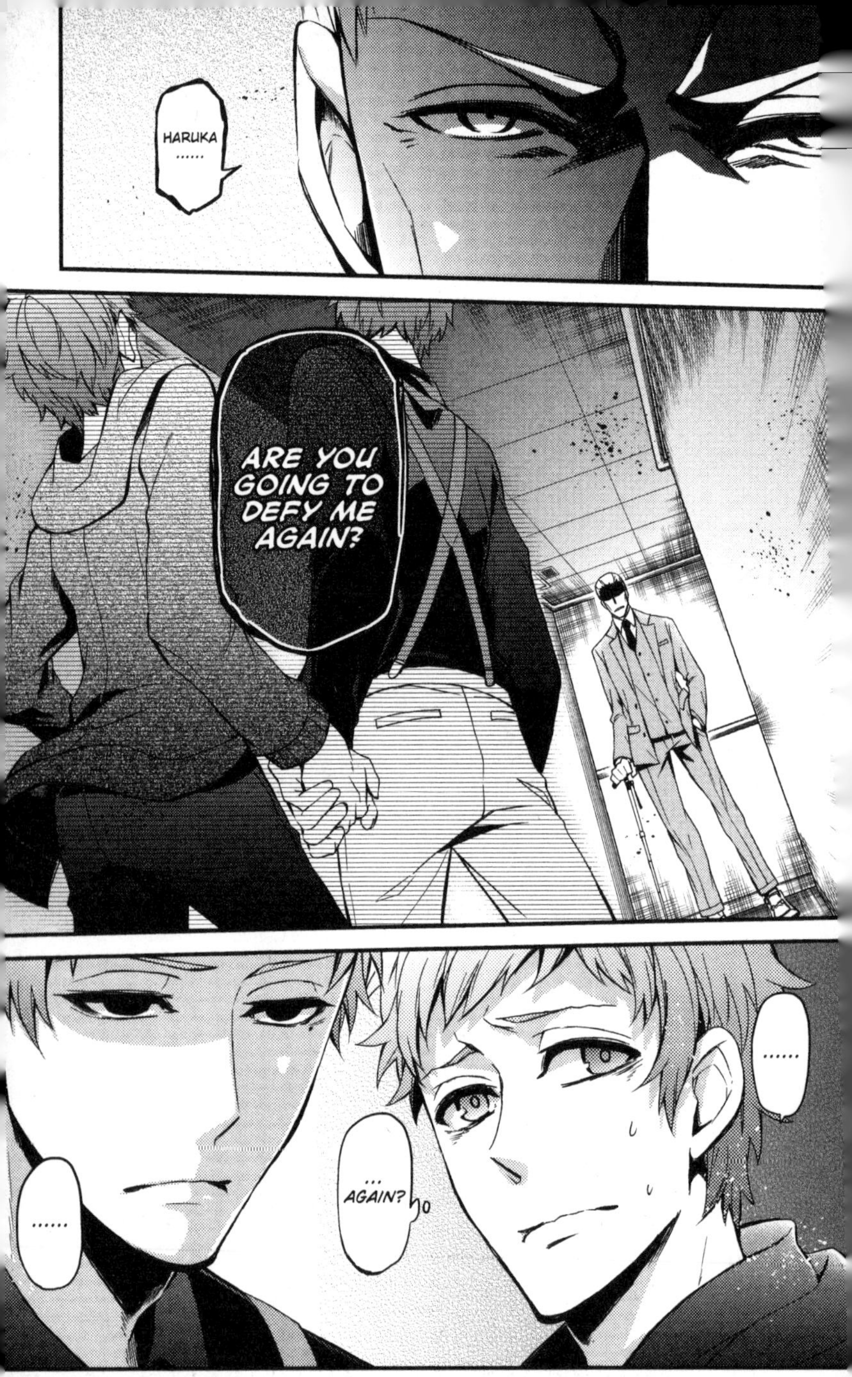

HARUKA ......
ARE YOU GOING TO DEFY ME AGAIN?
......
... AGAIN?
......

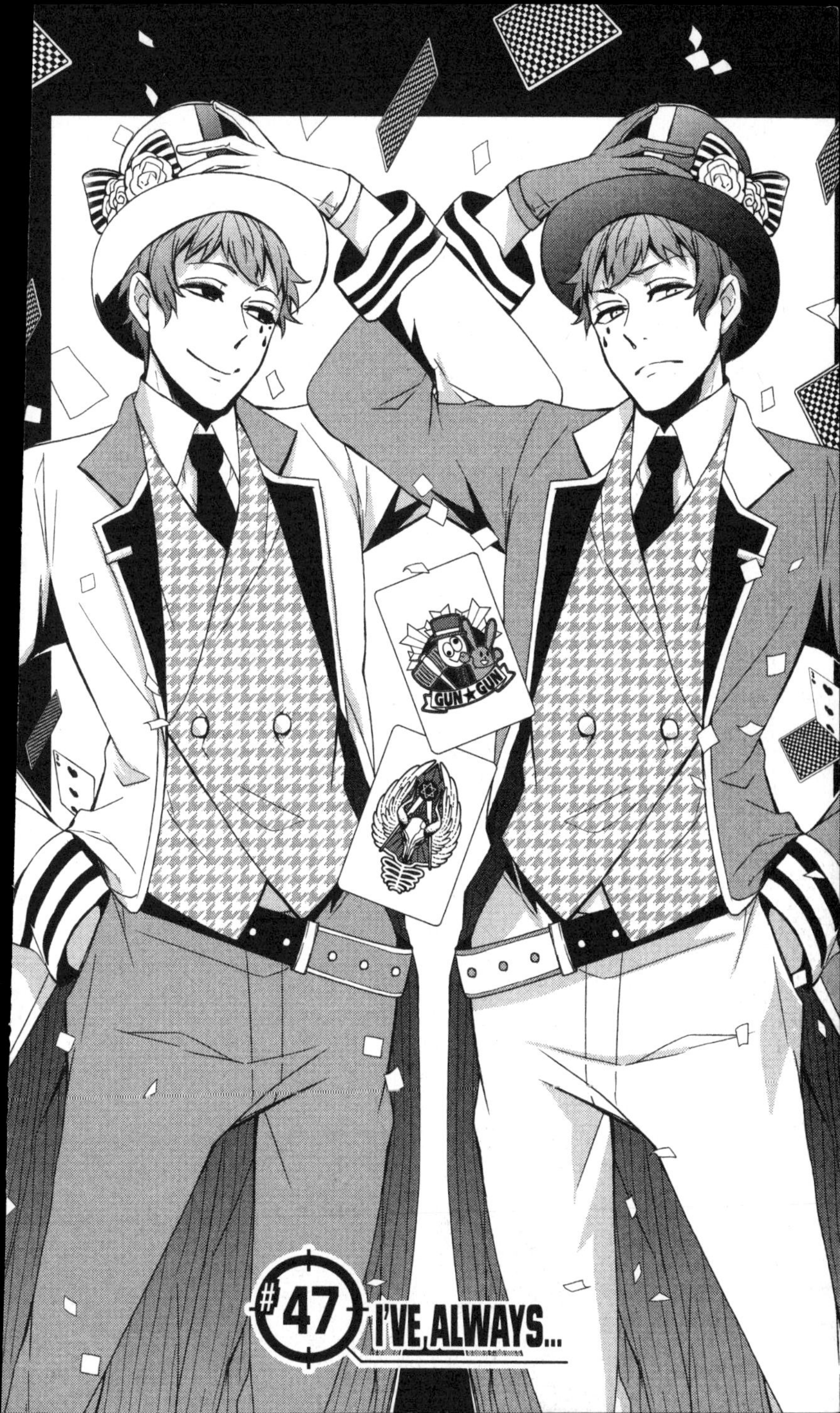
GUN★GUN
#47 I'VE ALWAYS...

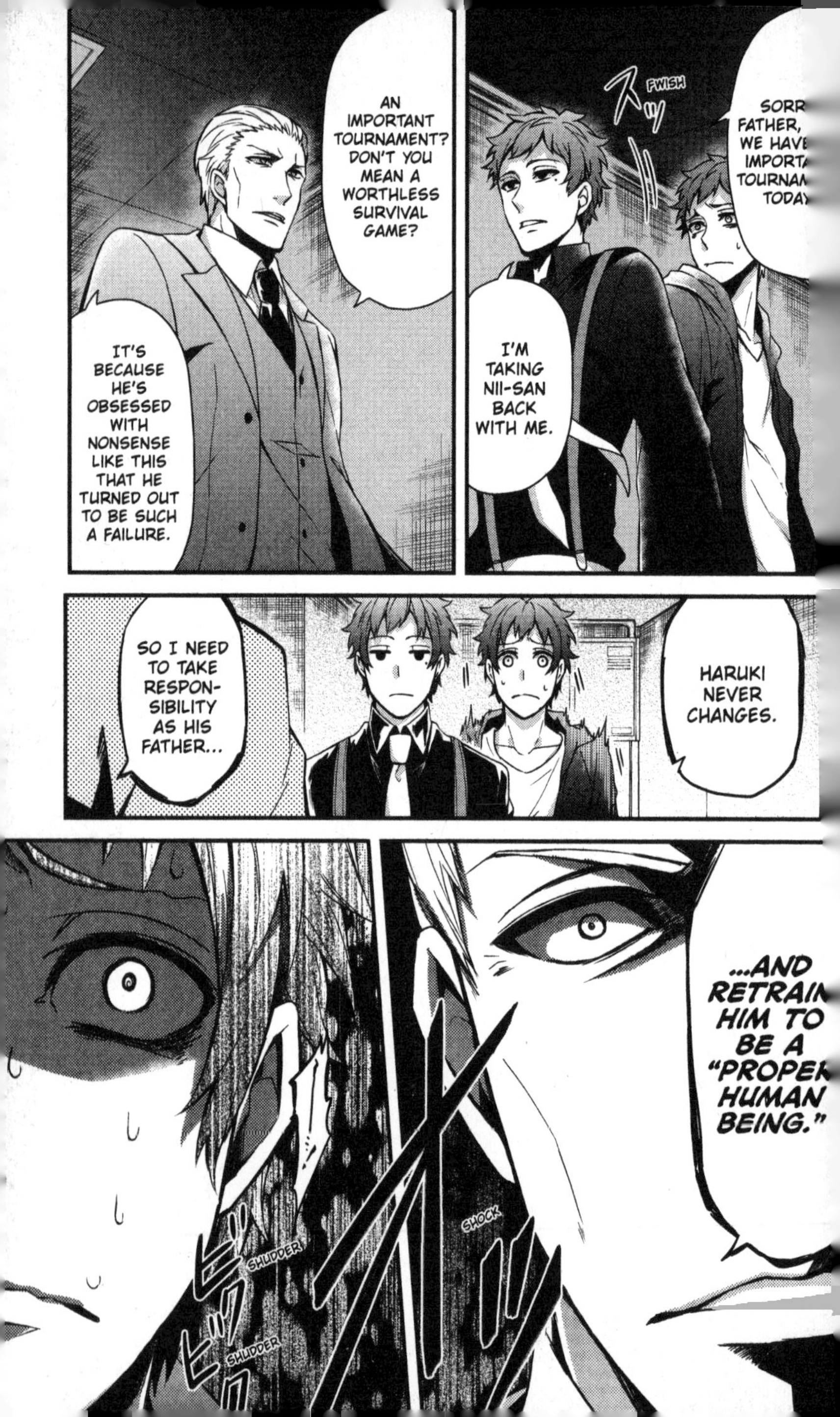

FWISH
SORR FATHER, WE HAVE IMPORTA TOURNAM TODAY
I'M TAKING NII-SAN BACK WITH ME.
AN IMPORTANT TOURNAMENT? DON'T YOU MEAN A WORTHLESS SURVIVAL GAME?
IT'S BECAUSE HE'S OBSESSED WITH NONSENSE LIKE THIS THAT HE TURNED OUT TO BE SUCH A FAILURE.
HARUKI NEVER CHANGES.
SO I NEED TO TAKE RESPON- SIBILITY AS HIS FATHER...
...AND RETRAIN HIM TO BE A "PROPER HUMAN BEING."
SHOCK
SHUDDER
SHUDDER

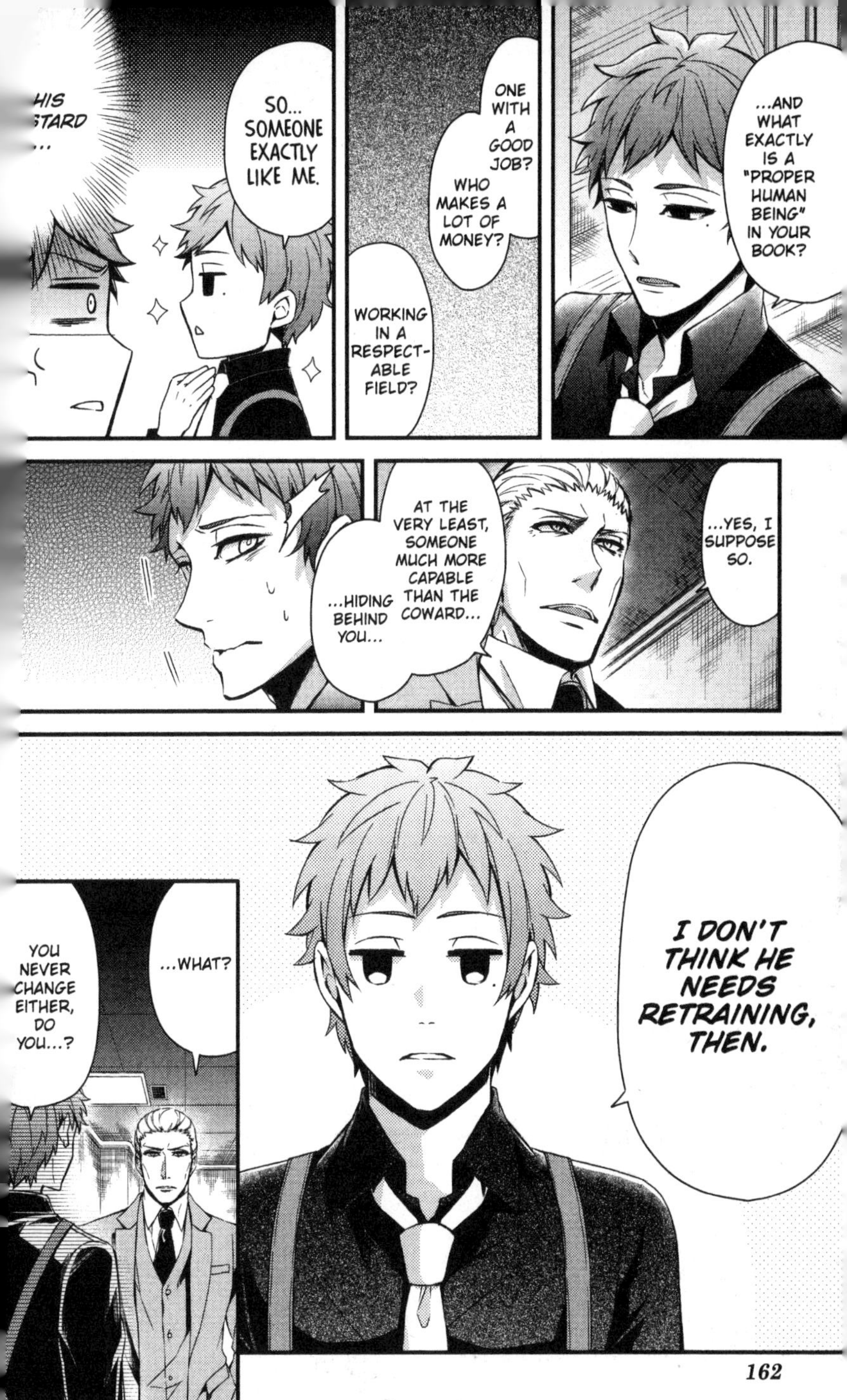
...AND WHAT EXACTLY IS A "PROPER HUMAN BEING" IN YOUR BOOK?
ONE WITH A GOOD JOB? WHO MAKES A LOT OF MONEY?
WORKING IN A RESPECTABLE FIELD?
SO... SOMEONE EXACTLY LIKE ME.
...YES, I SUPPOSE SO.
AT THE VERY LEAST, SOMEONE MUCH MORE CAPABLE THAN THE COWARD...
...HIDING BEHIND YOU...
I DON'T THINK HE NEEDS RETRAINING, THEN.
...WHAT?
YOU NEVER CHANGE EITHER, DO YOU...?

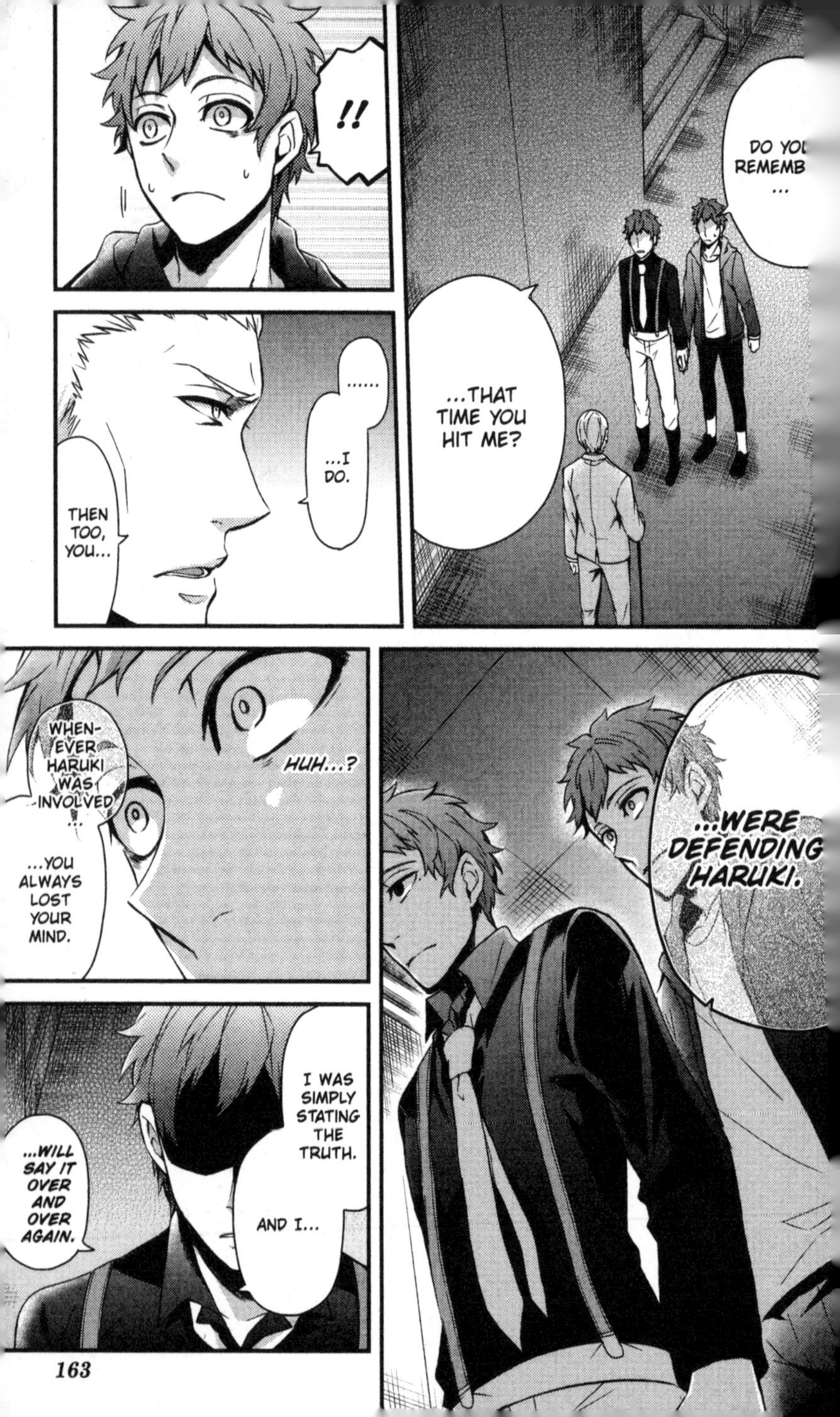
DO YOU REMEMB ...
...THAT TIME YOU HIT ME?
!!
......
...I DO.
THEN TOO, YOU...
...WERE DEFENDING HARUKI.
HUH...?
WHENEVER HARUKI WAS INVOLVED...
...YOU ALWAYS LOST YOUR MIND.
I WAS SIMPLY STATING THE TRUTH.
AND I...
...WILL SAY IT OVER AND OVER AGAIN.

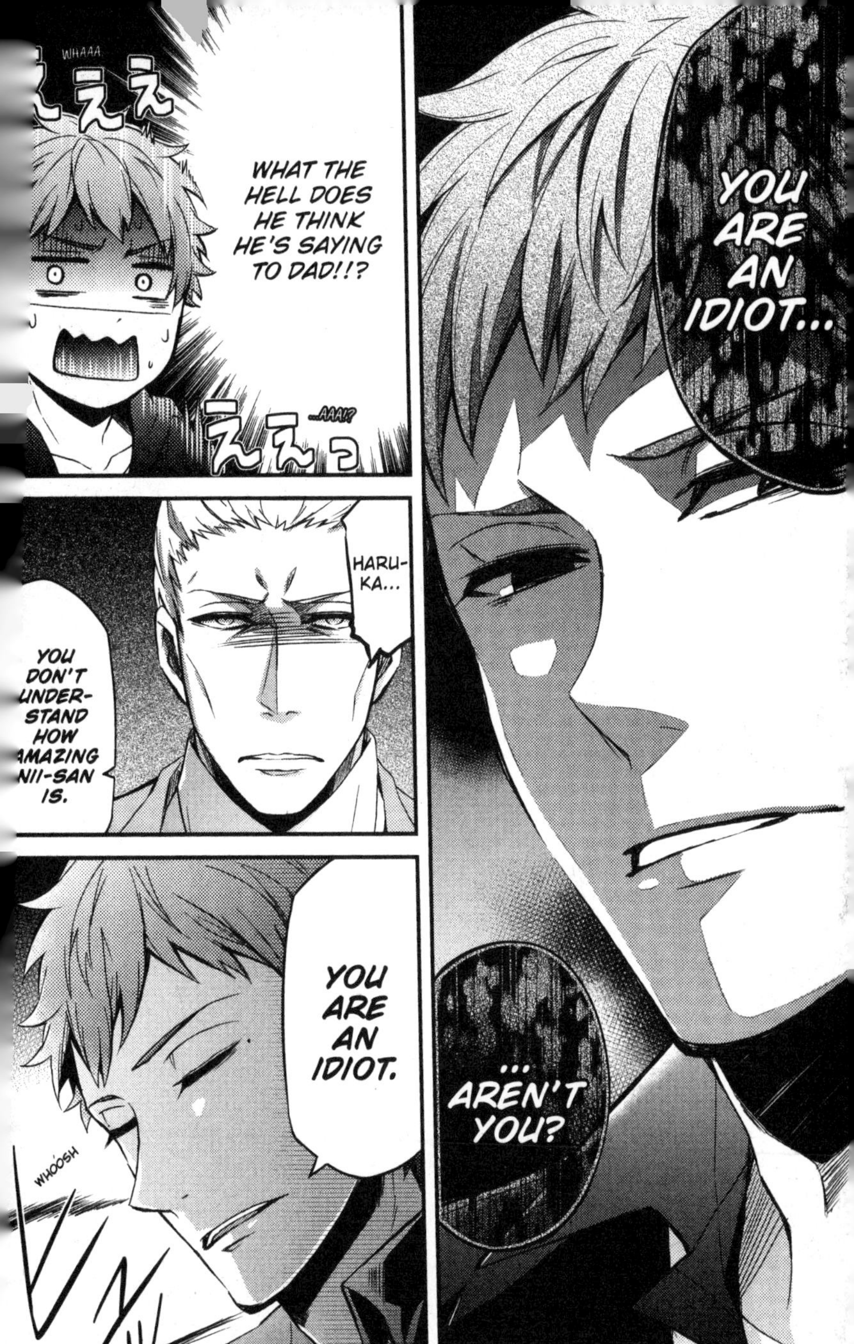
YOU ARE AN IDIOT...
... AREN'T YOU?
えええ
WHAAA
WHAT THE HELL DOES HE THINK HE'S SAYING TO DAD!!?
ええっ
...AAA!?
HARU-KA...
YOU DON'T UNDER-STAND HOW AMAZING NII-SAN IS.
YOU ARE AN IDIOT.
WHOOSH

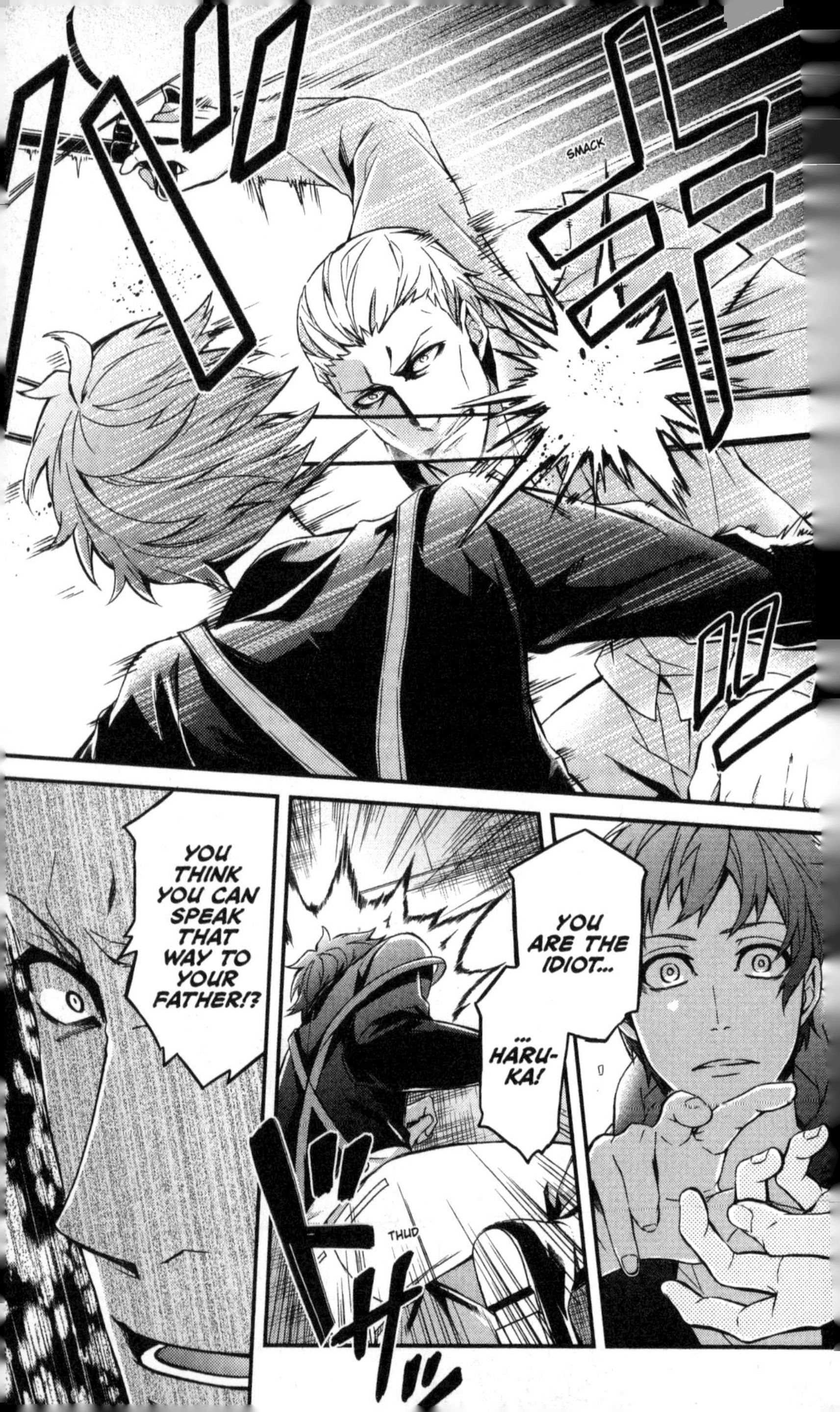
SMACK
YOU ARE THE IDIOT...
... HARU-KA!
THUD
YOU THINK YOU CAN SPEAK THAT WAY TO YOUR FATHER!?

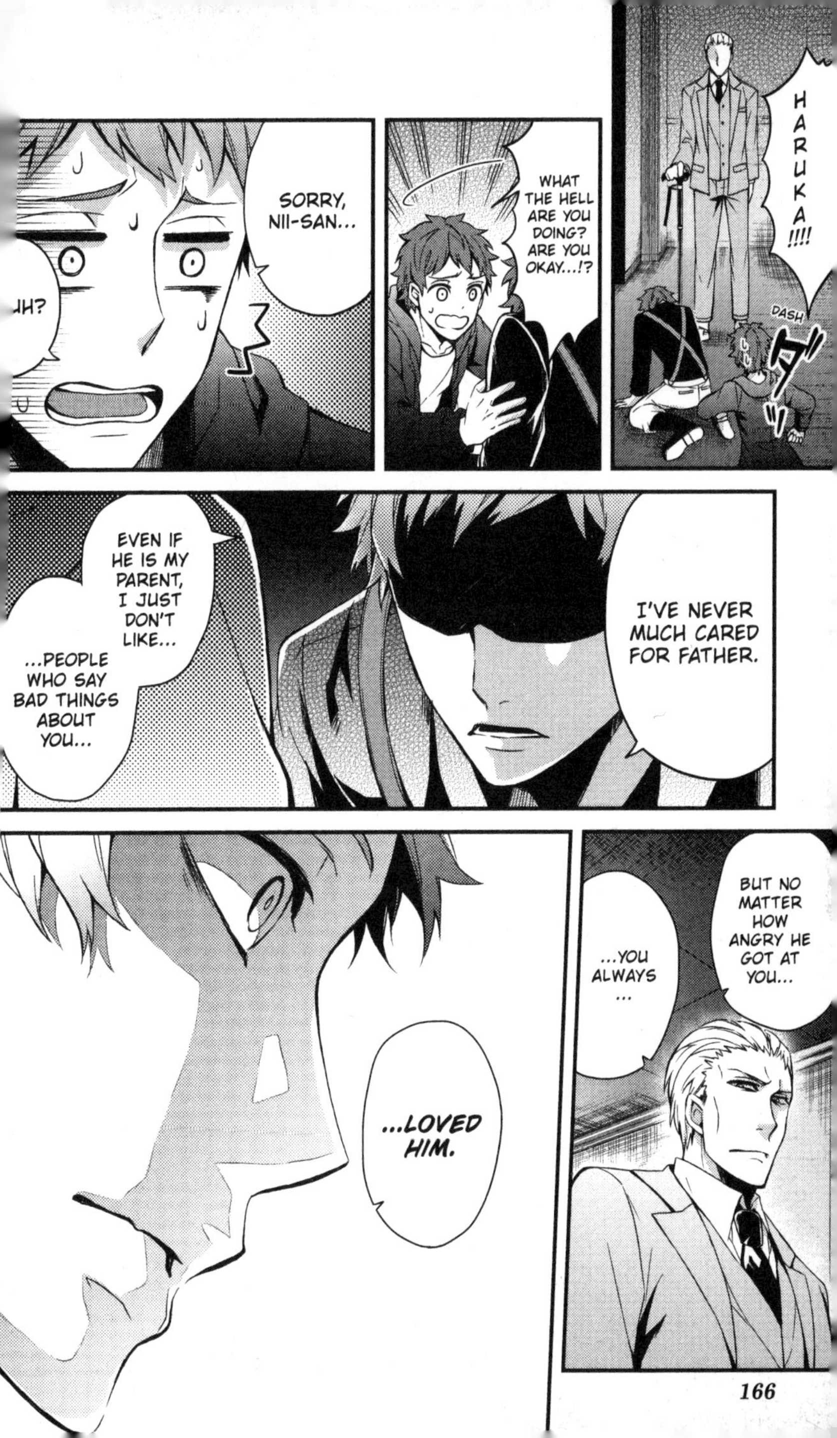
HARUKA!!!!
DASH
WHAT THE HELL ARE YOU DOING? ARE YOU OKAY...!?
SORRY, NII-SAN...
I'VE NEVER MUCH CARED FOR FATHER.
EVEN IF HE IS MY PARENT, I JUST DON'T LIKE...
...PEOPLE WHO SAY BAD THINGS ABOUT YOU...
BUT NO MATTER HOW ANGRY HE GOT AT YOU...
...YOU ALWAYS ...
...LOVED HIM.

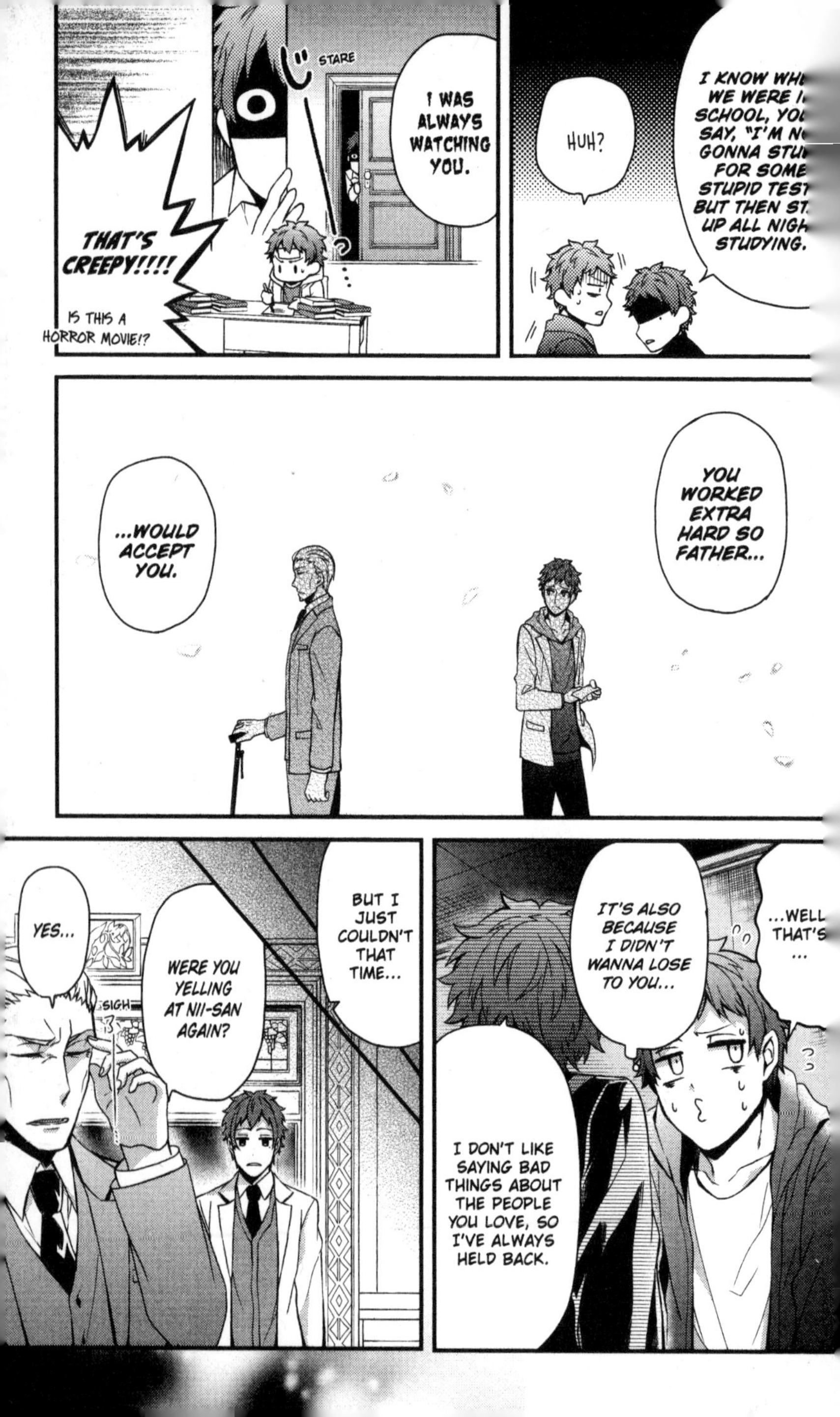
I KNOW WH WE WERE I SCHOOL, YOU SAY, "I'M N GONNA STU FOR SOME STUPID TEST BUT THEN ST UP ALL NIGH STUDYING.
HUH?
STARE
I WAS ALWAYS WATCHING YOU.
THAT'S CREEPY!!!!
IS THIS A HORROR MOVIE!?
YOU WORKED EXTRA HARD SO FATHER...
...WOULD ACCEPT YOU.
...WELL THAT'S ...
IT'S ALSO BECAUSE I DIDN'T WANNA LOSE TO YOU...
I DON'T LIKE SAYING BAD THINGS ABOUT THE PEOPLE YOU LOVE, SO I'VE ALWAYS HELD BACK.
BUT I JUST COULDN'T THAT TIME...
WERE YOU YELLING AT NII-SAN AGAIN?
SIGH
YES...

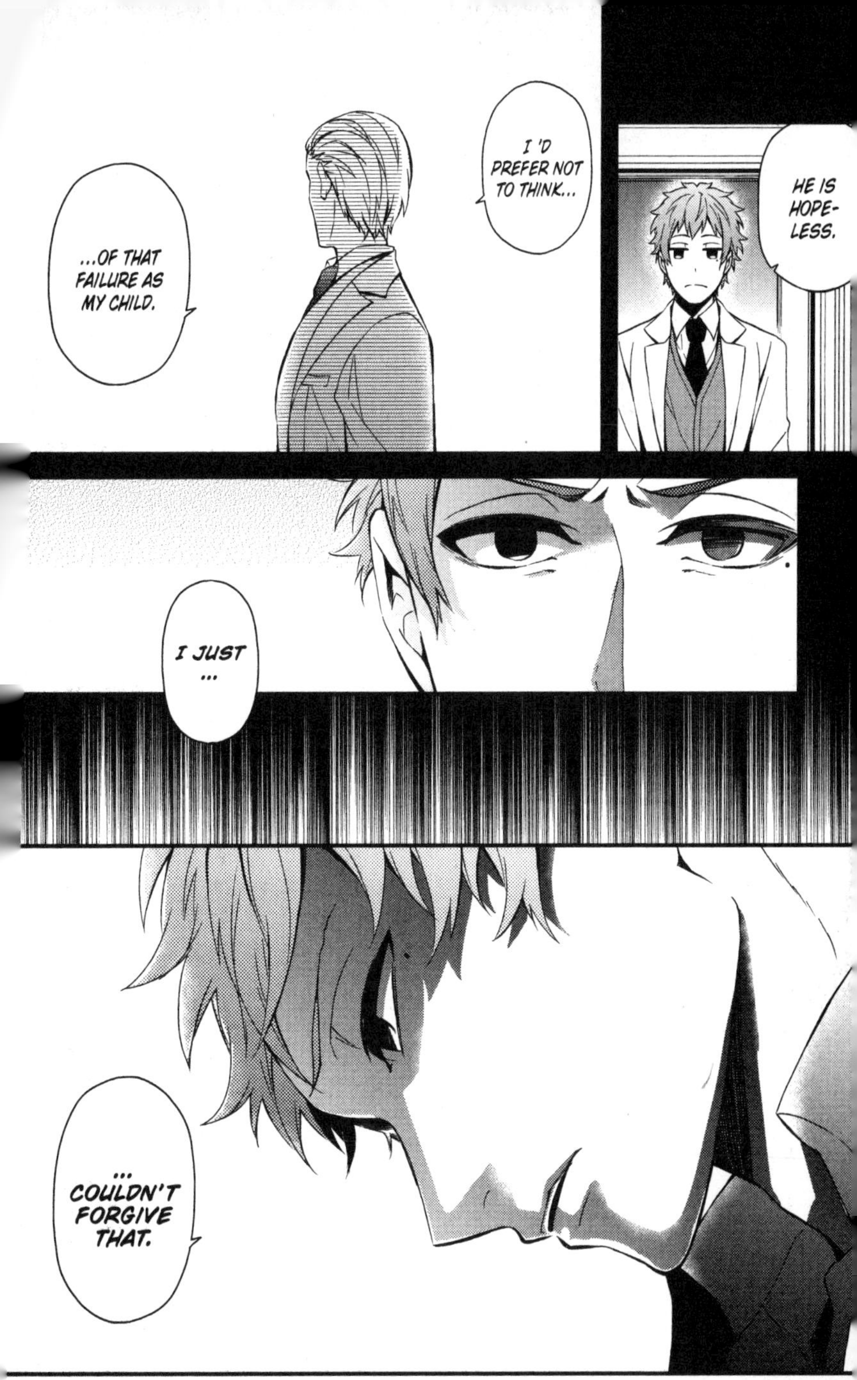
HE IS HOPE-LESS.
I 'D PREFER NOT TO THINK...
...OF THAT FAILURE AS MY CHILD.
I JUST ...
... COULDN'T FORGIVE THAT.

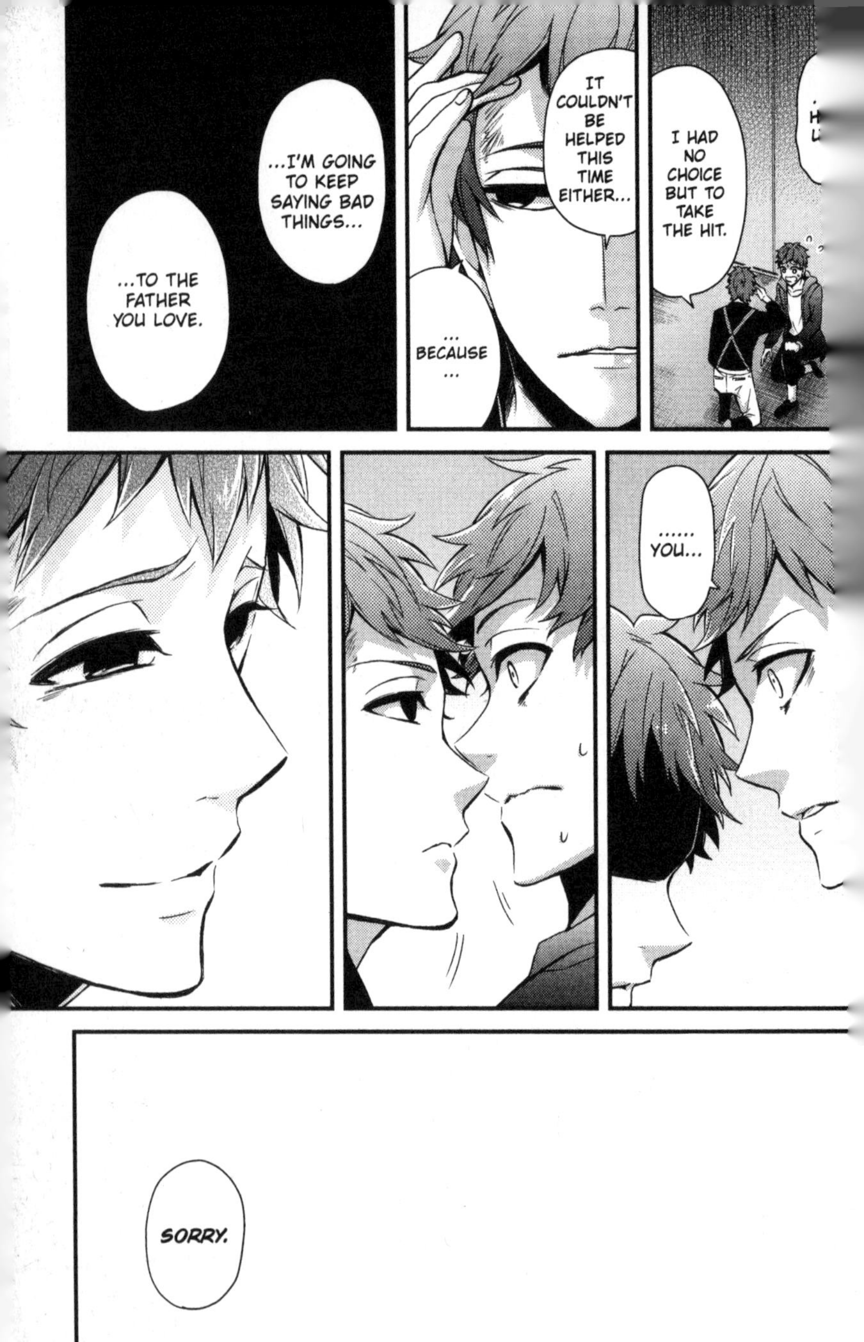
I HAD NO CHOICE BUT TO TAKE THE HIT.
IT COULDN'T BE HELPED THIS TIME EITHER...
...BECAUSE...
...I'M GOING TO KEEP SAYING BAD THINGS...
...TO THE FATHER YOU LOVE.
......YOU...
SORRY.

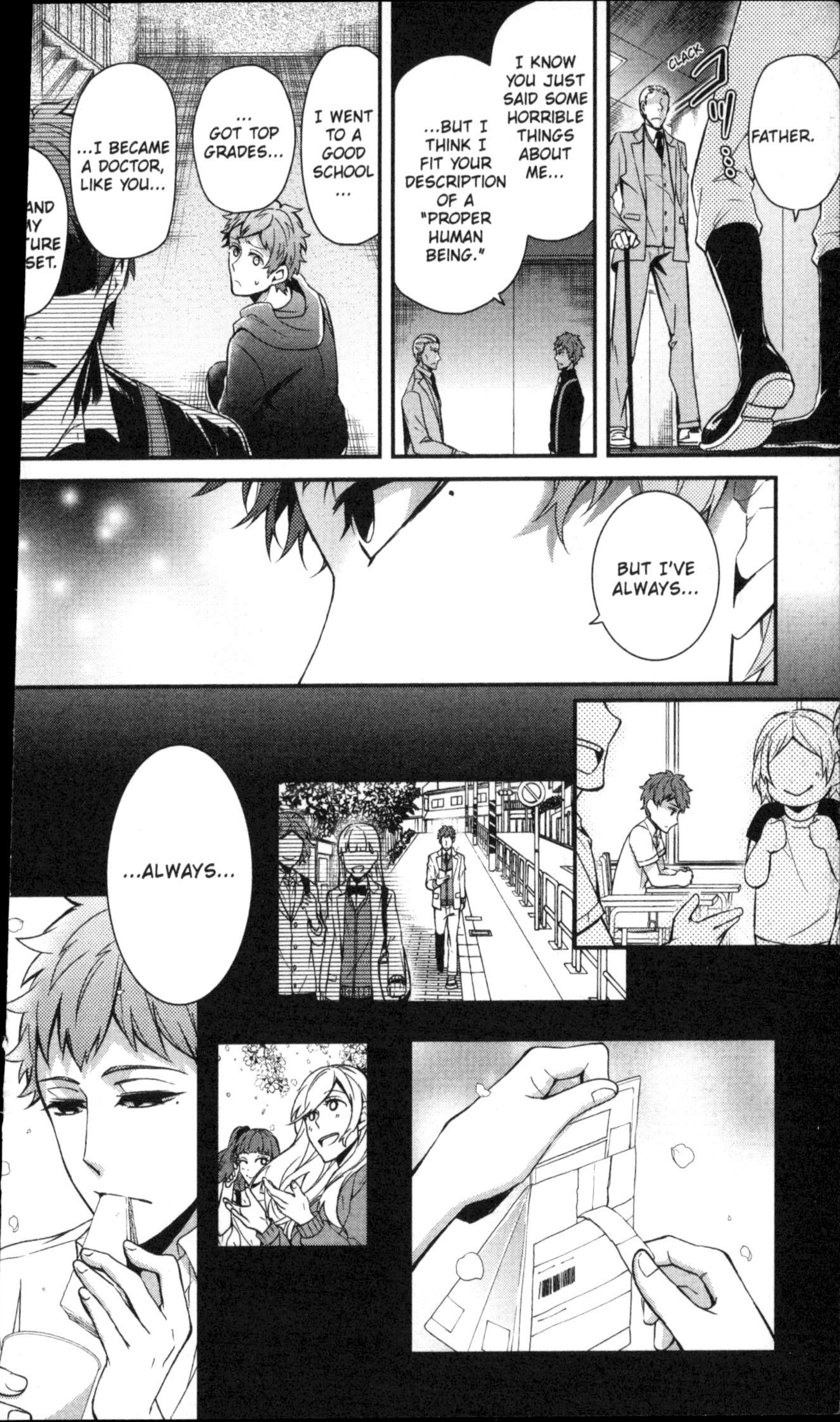
CLACK
FATHER.
I KNOW YOU JUST SAID SOME HORRIBLE THINGS ABOUT ME...
...BUT I THINK I FIT YOUR DESCRIPTION OF A "PROPER HUMAN BEING."
I WENT TO A GOOD SCHOOL...
...GOT TOP GRADES...
...I BECAME A DOCTOR, LIKE YOU...
AND MY TURE SET.
BUT I'VE ALWAYS...
...ALWAYS...

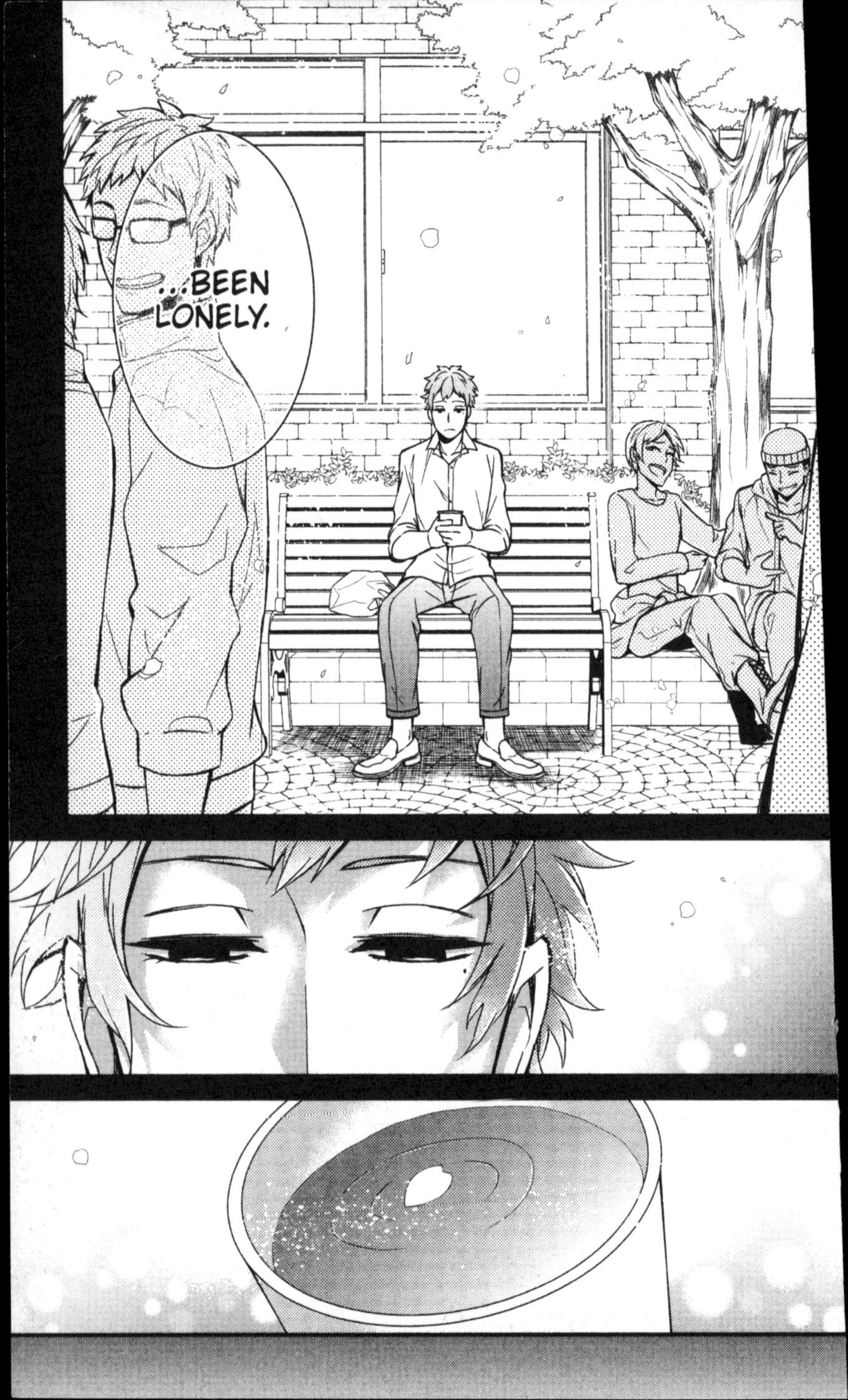
...BEEN LONELY.

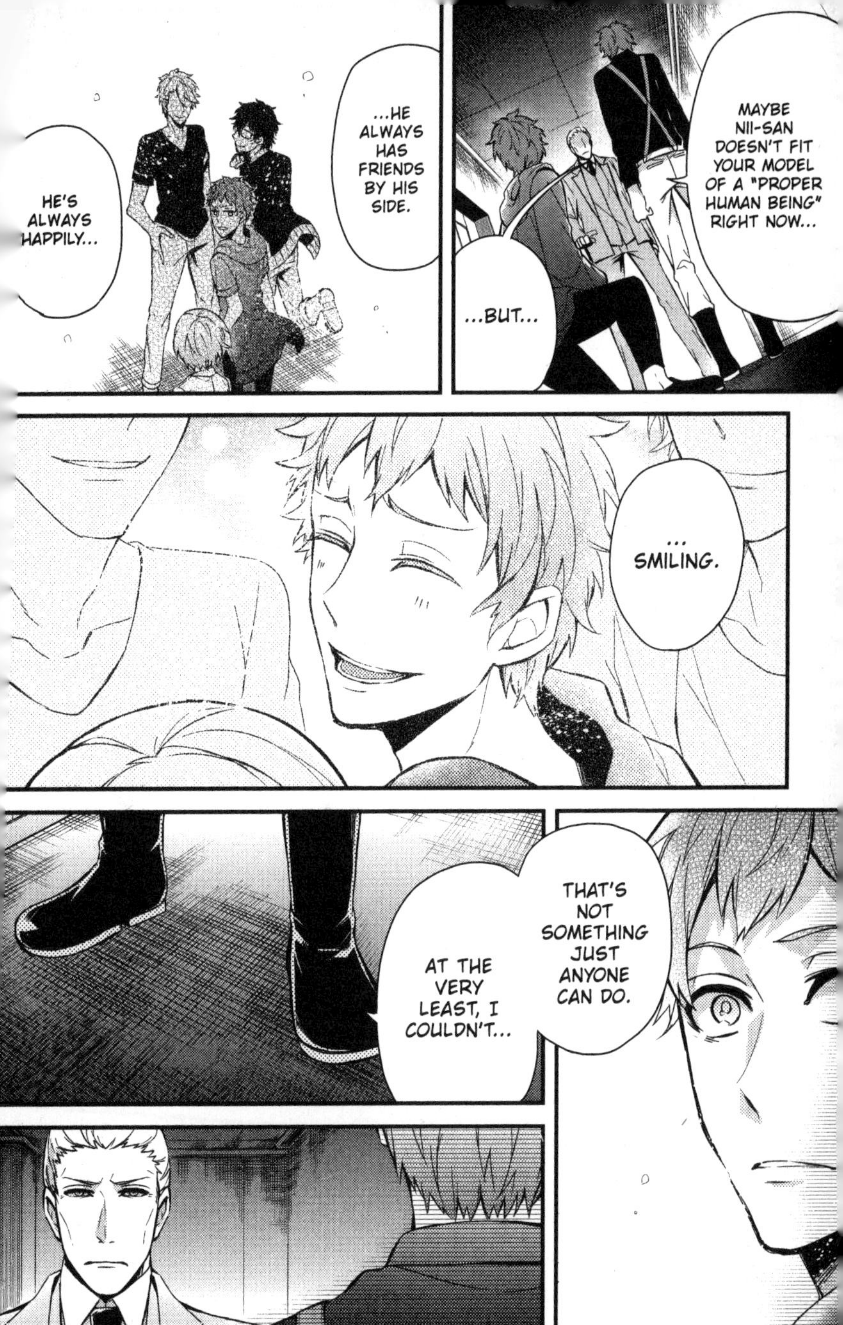

MAYBE NII-SAN DOESN'T FIT YOUR MODEL OF A "PROPER HUMAN BEING" RIGHT NOW...
...BUT...
...HE ALWAYS HAS FRIENDS BY HIS SIDE.
HE'S ALWAYS HAPPILY...
... SMILING.
THAT'S NOT SOMETHING JUST ANYONE CAN DO.
AT THE VERY LEAST, I COULDN'T...

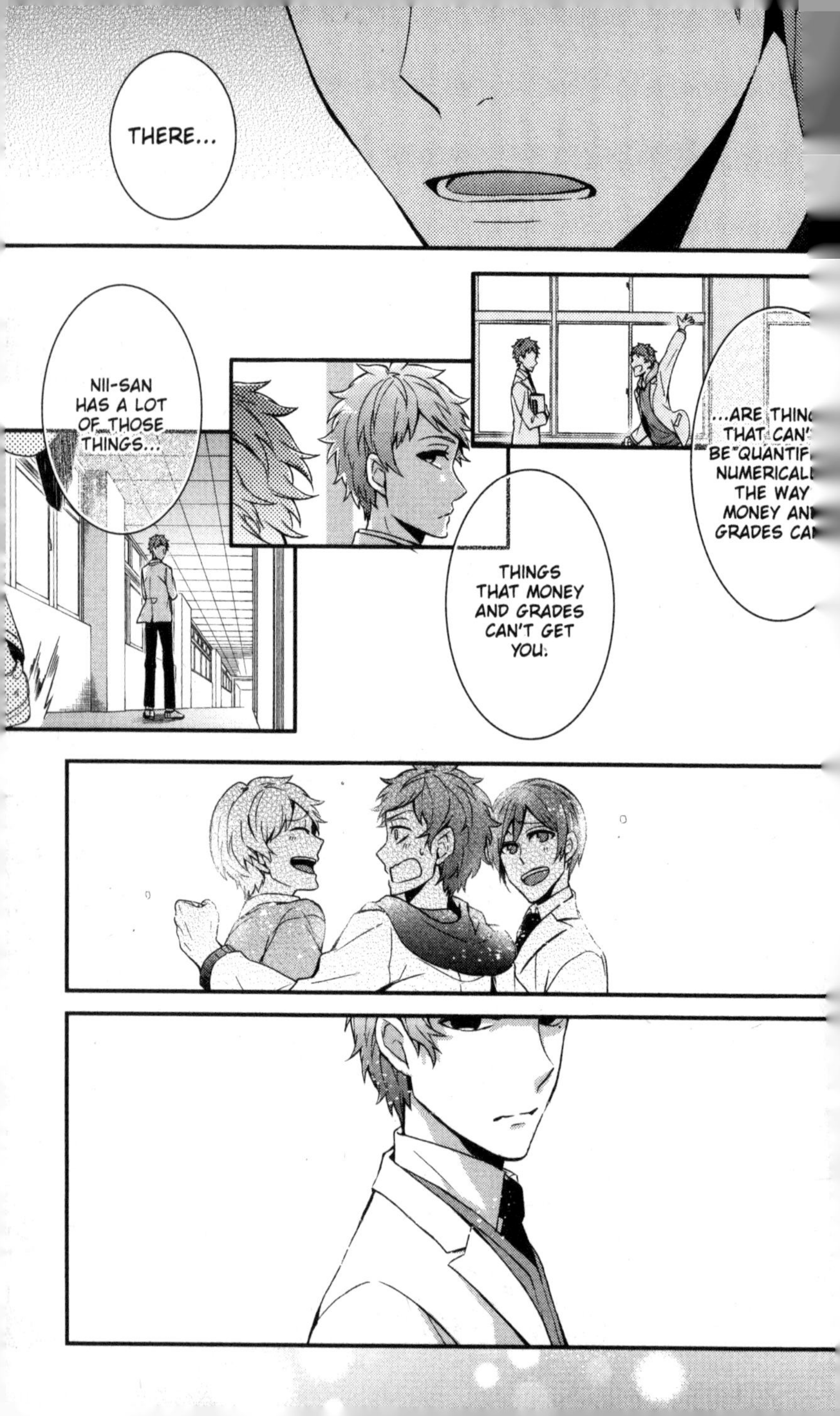
THERE...
THINGS THAT MONEY AND GRADES CAN'T GET YOU.
...ARE THING THAT CAN' BE QUANTIF NUMERICALL THE WAY MONEY AN GRADES CA
NII-SAN HAS A LOT OF THOSE THINGS...

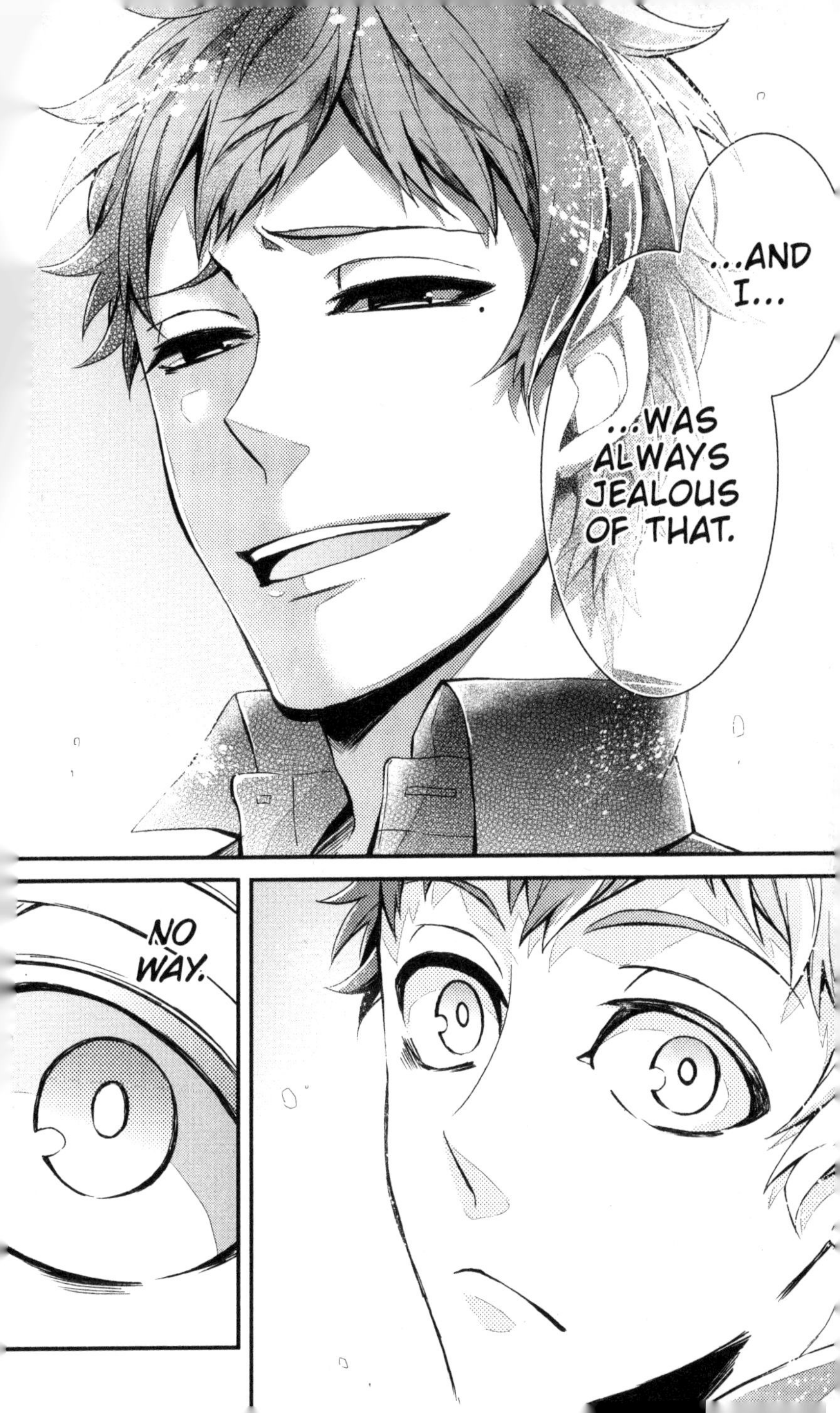
...AND I...
...WAS ALWAYS JEALOUS OF THAT.
NO WAY.

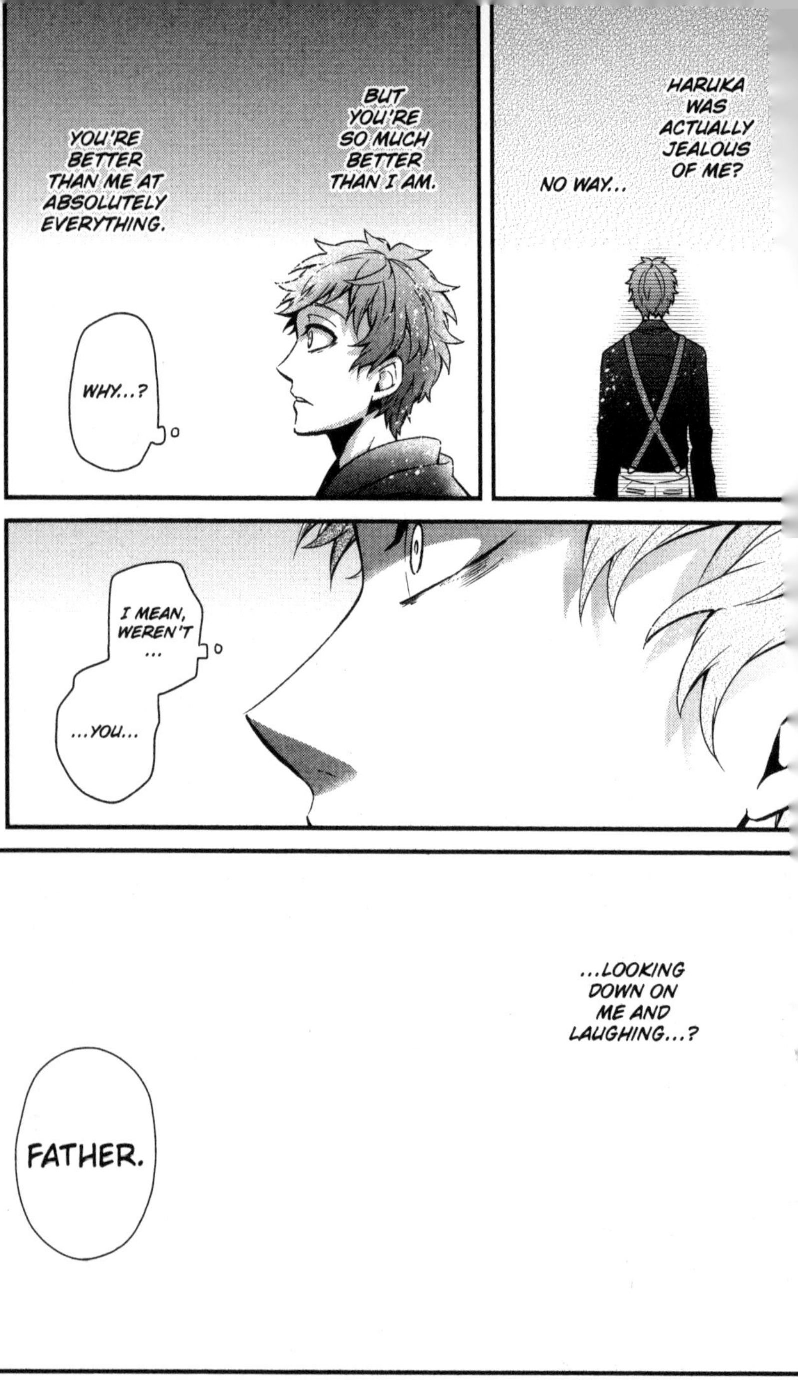
HARUKA WAS ACTUALLY JEALOUS OF ME?
NO WAY...
BUT YOU'RE SO MUCH BETTER THAN I AM.
YOU'RE BETTER THAN ME AT ABSOLUTELY EVERYTHING.
WHY...?
I MEAN, WEREN'T ...
...YOU...
...LOOKING DOWN ON ME AND LAUGHING...?
FATHER.

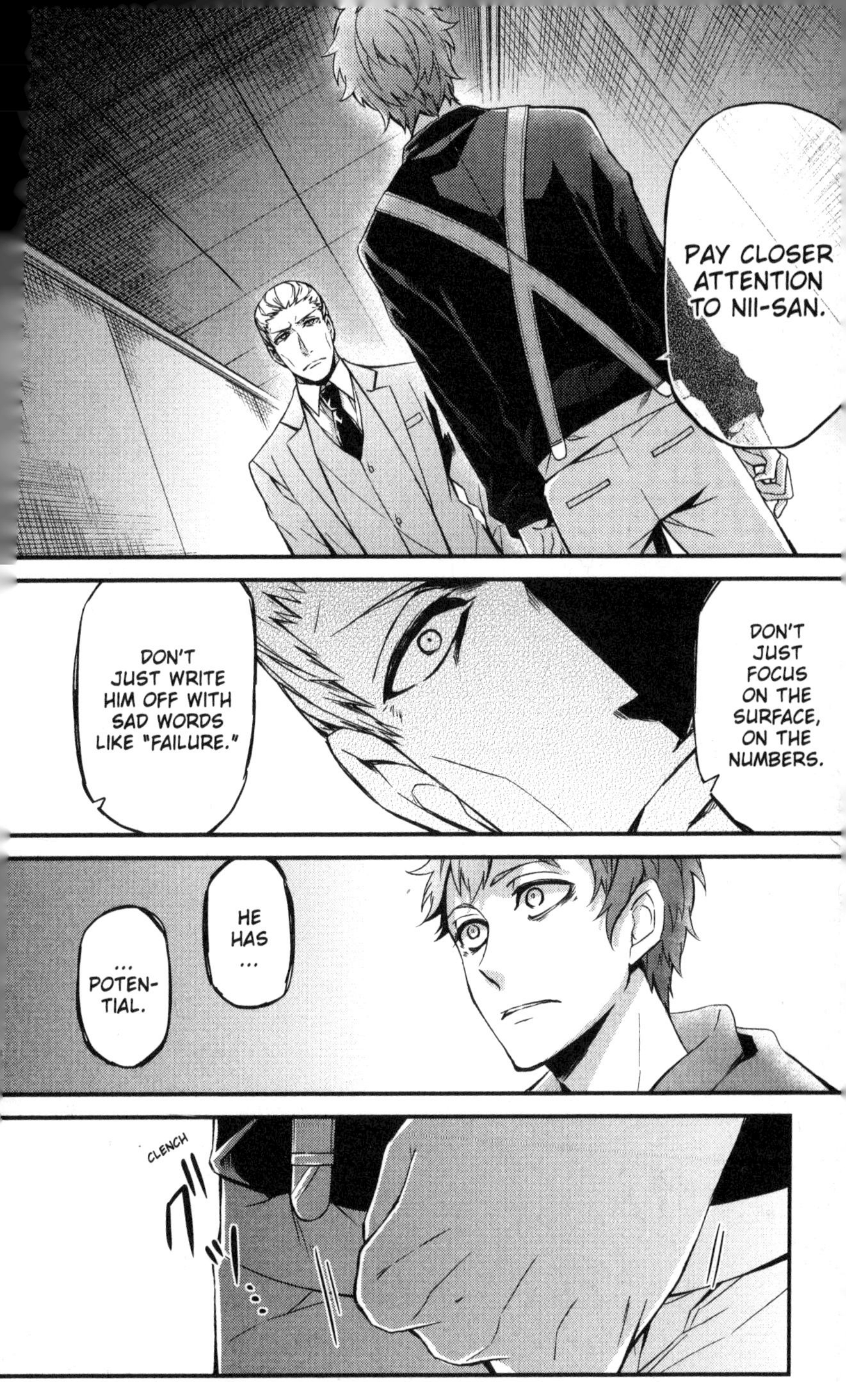
PAY CLOSER ATTENTION TO NII-SAN.
DON'T JUST FOCUS ON THE SURFACE, ON THE NUMBERS.
DON'T JUST WRITE HIM OFF WITH SAD WORDS LIKE "FAILURE."
HE HAS ...
... POTEN-TIAL.
CLENCH

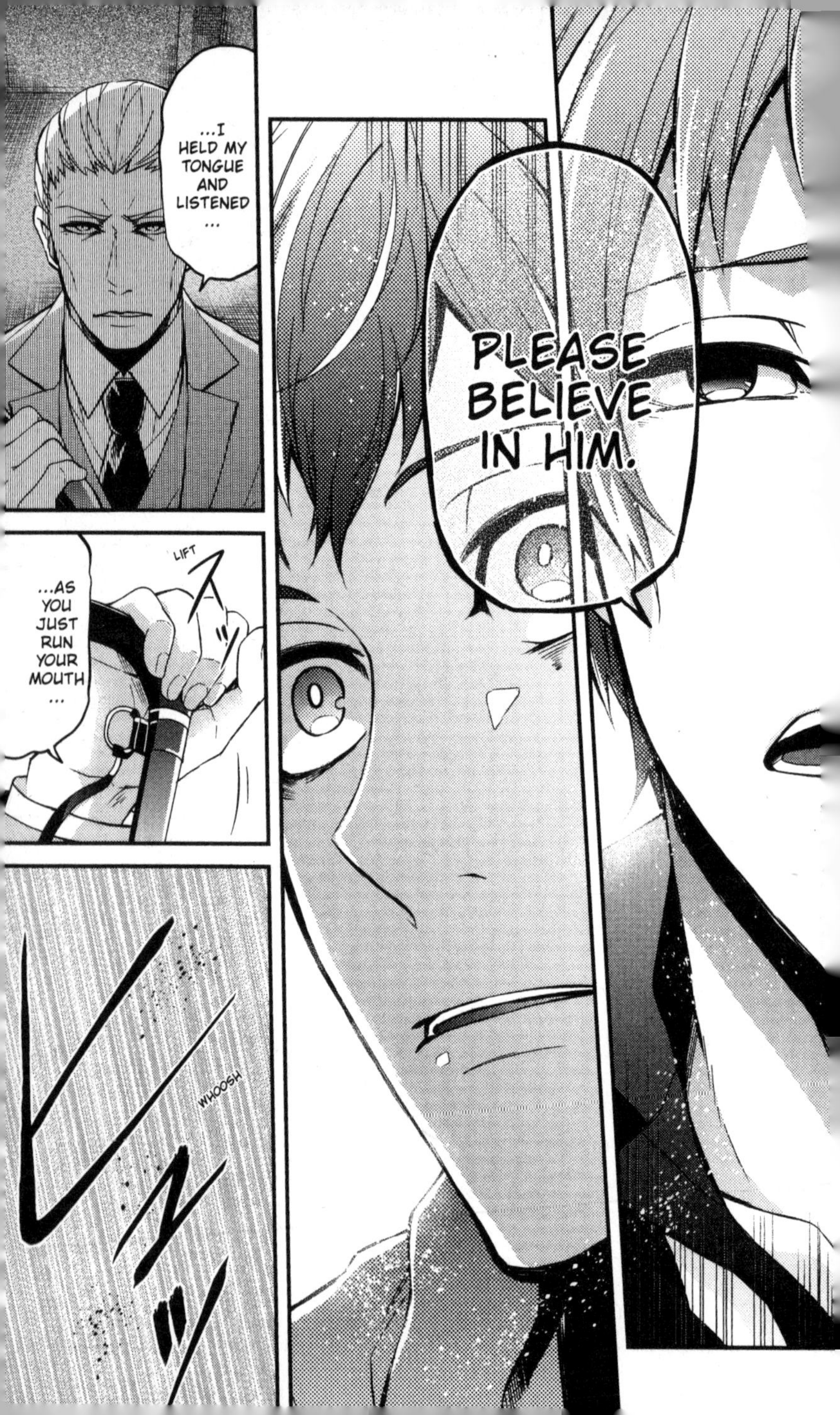
PLEASE BELIEVE IN HIM.
...I HELD MY TONGUE AND LISTENED ...
LIFT
...AS YOU JUST RUN YOUR MOUTH ...
WHOOSH

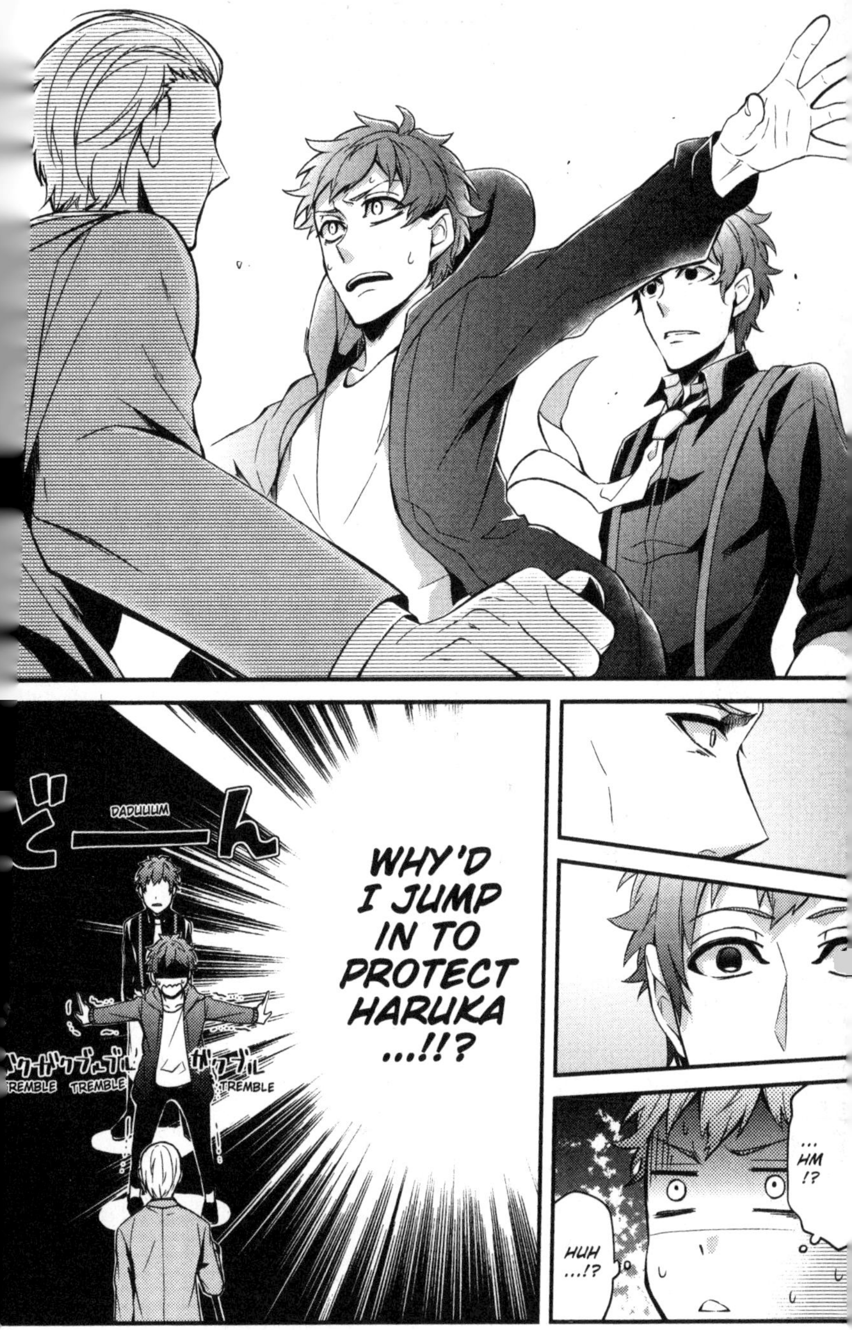
...HM !?
HUH ...!?
どーーん
DADUUUM
TREMBLE TREMBLE
TREMBLE
WHY'D I JUMP IN TO PROTECT HARUKA ...!!?

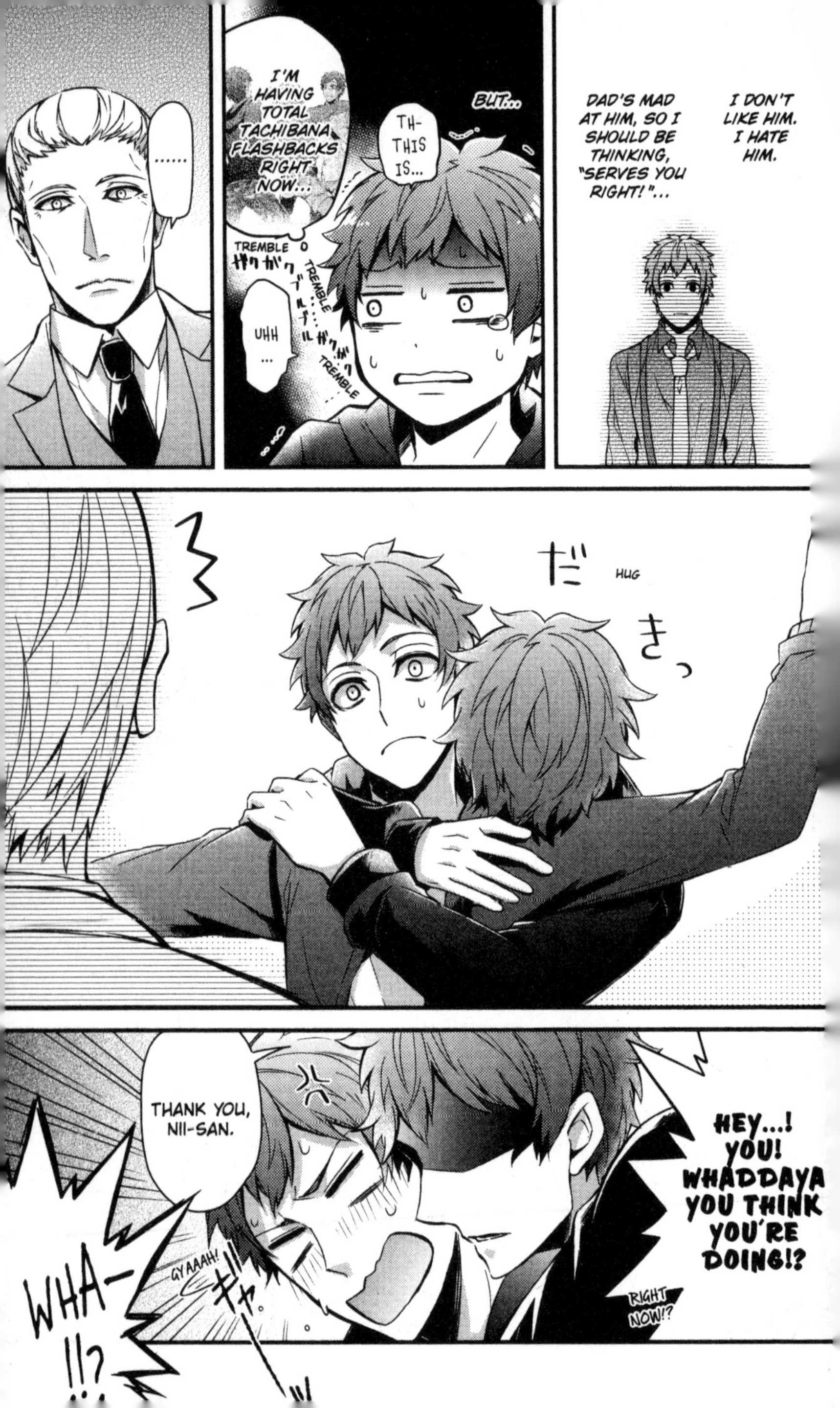
I DON'T LIKE HIM. I HATE HIM.
DAD'S MAD AT HIM, SO I SHOULD BE THINKING, "SERVES YOU RIGHT!"...
BUT...
TH- THIS IS...
I'M HAVING TOTAL TACHIBANA FLASHBACKS RIGHT NOW...
TREMBLE
ガクガク
TREMBLE
ブルブル
ガクガク
TREMBLE
UHH...
......
だきっ
HUG
HEY...! YOU! WHADDAYA YOU THINK YOU'RE DOING!?
RIGHT NOW!?
THANK YOU, NII-SAN.
GYAAAH!
ギャ
WHA-!!?

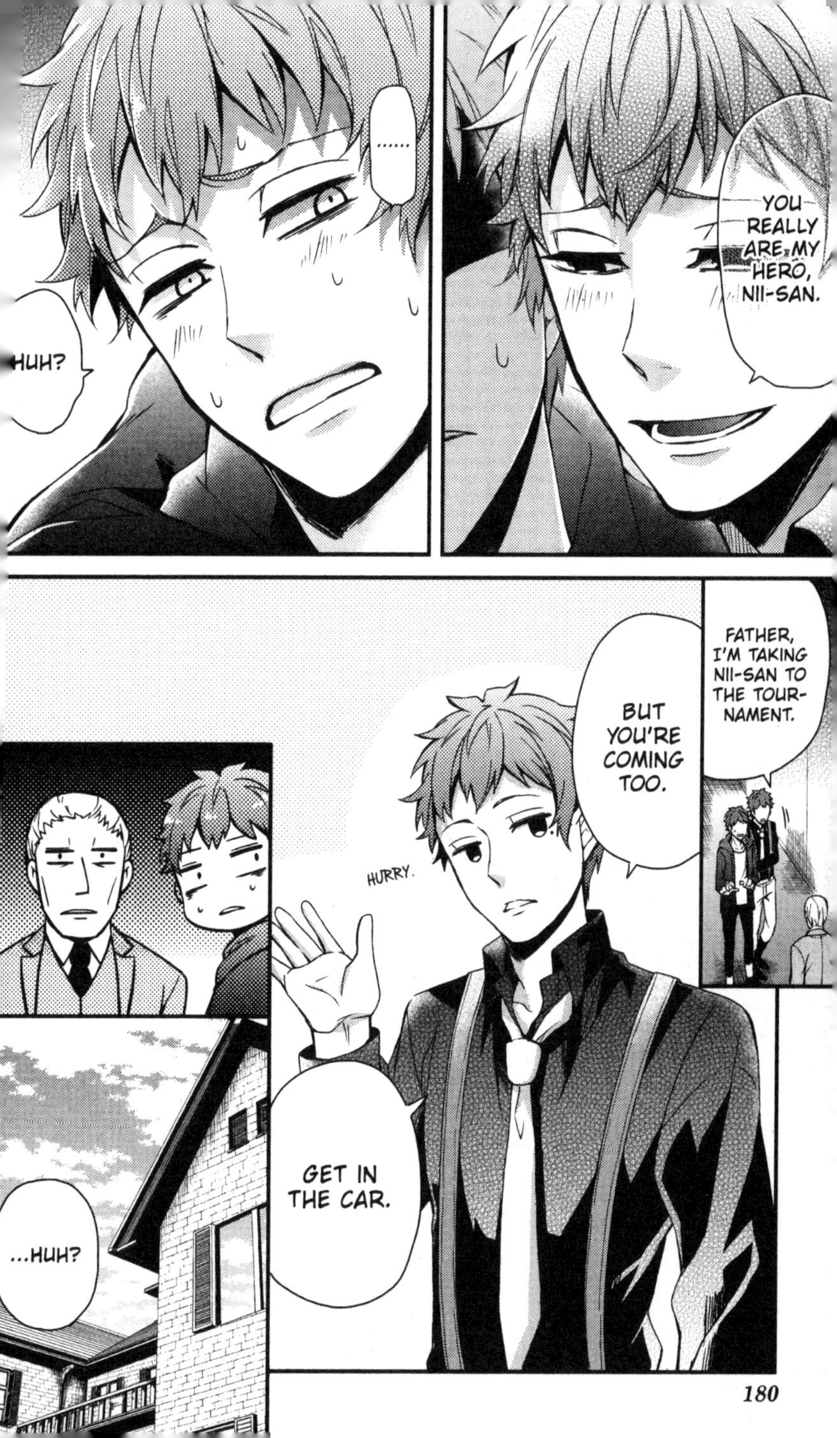
YOU REALLY ARE MY HERO, NII-SAN.
......
HUH?
FATHER, I'M TAKING NII-SAN TO THE TOURNAMENT.
BUT YOU'RE COMING TOO.
HURRY.
GET IN THE CAR.
...HUH?

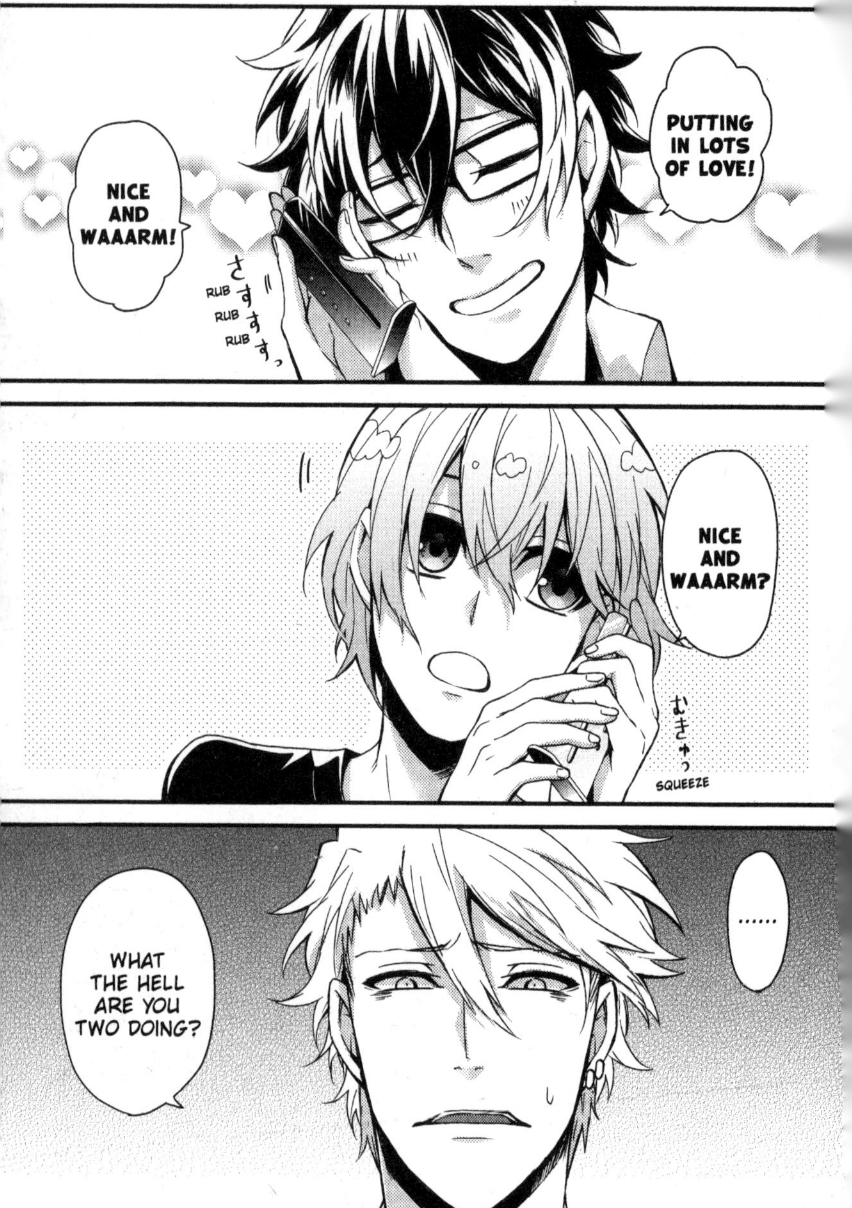
PUTTING IN LOTS OF LOVE!
NICE AND WAAARM!
さすすすっ
RUB RUB RUB
NICE AND WAAARM?
むきゅっ
SQUEEZE
......
WHAT THE HELL ARE YOU TWO DOING?

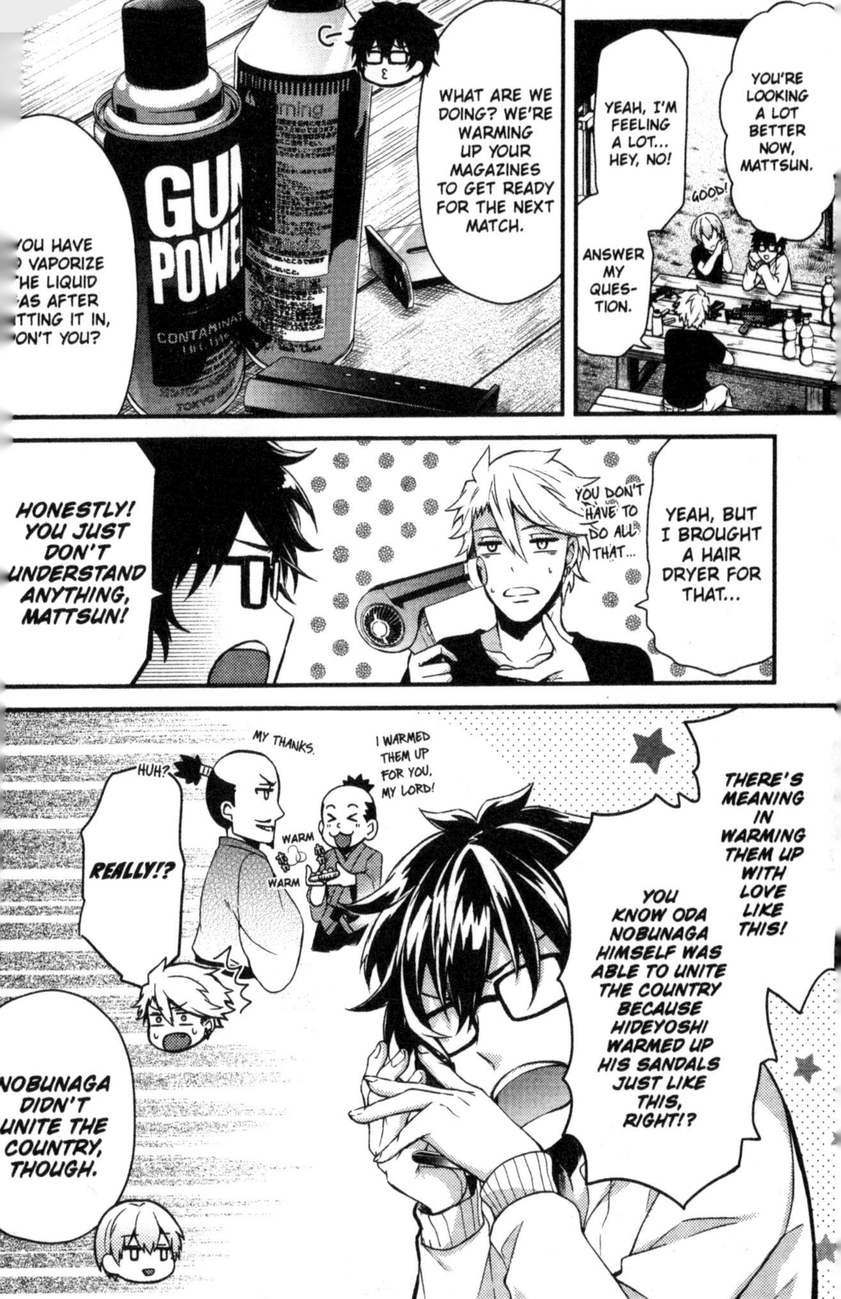
YOU'RE LOOKING A LOT BETTER NOW, MATTSUN.
GOOD!
YEAH, I'M FEELING A LOT... HEY, NO!
ANSWER MY QUES- TION.
WHAT ARE WE DOING? WE'RE WARMING UP YOUR MAGAZINES TO GET READY FOR THE NEXT MATCH.
GUN POWE
OU HAVE VAPORIZE THE LIQUID AS AFTER TTING IT IN, ON'T YOU?
YEAH, BUT I BROUGHT A HAIR DRYER FOR THAT...
YOU DON'T HAVE TO DO ALL THAT...
HONESTLY! YOU JUST DON'T UNDERSTAND ANYTHING, MATTSUN!
THERE'S MEANING IN WARMING THEM UP WITH LOVE LIKE THIS!
YOU KNOW ODA NOBUNAGA HIMSELF WAS ABLE TO UNITE THE COUNTRY BECAUSE HIDEYOSHI WARMED UP HIS SANDALS JUST LIKE THIS, RIGHT!?
I WARMED THEM UP FOR YOU, MY LORD!
MY THANKS.
WARM
WARM
HUH?
REALLY!?
NOBUNAGA DIDN'T UNITE THE COUNTRY, THOUGH.

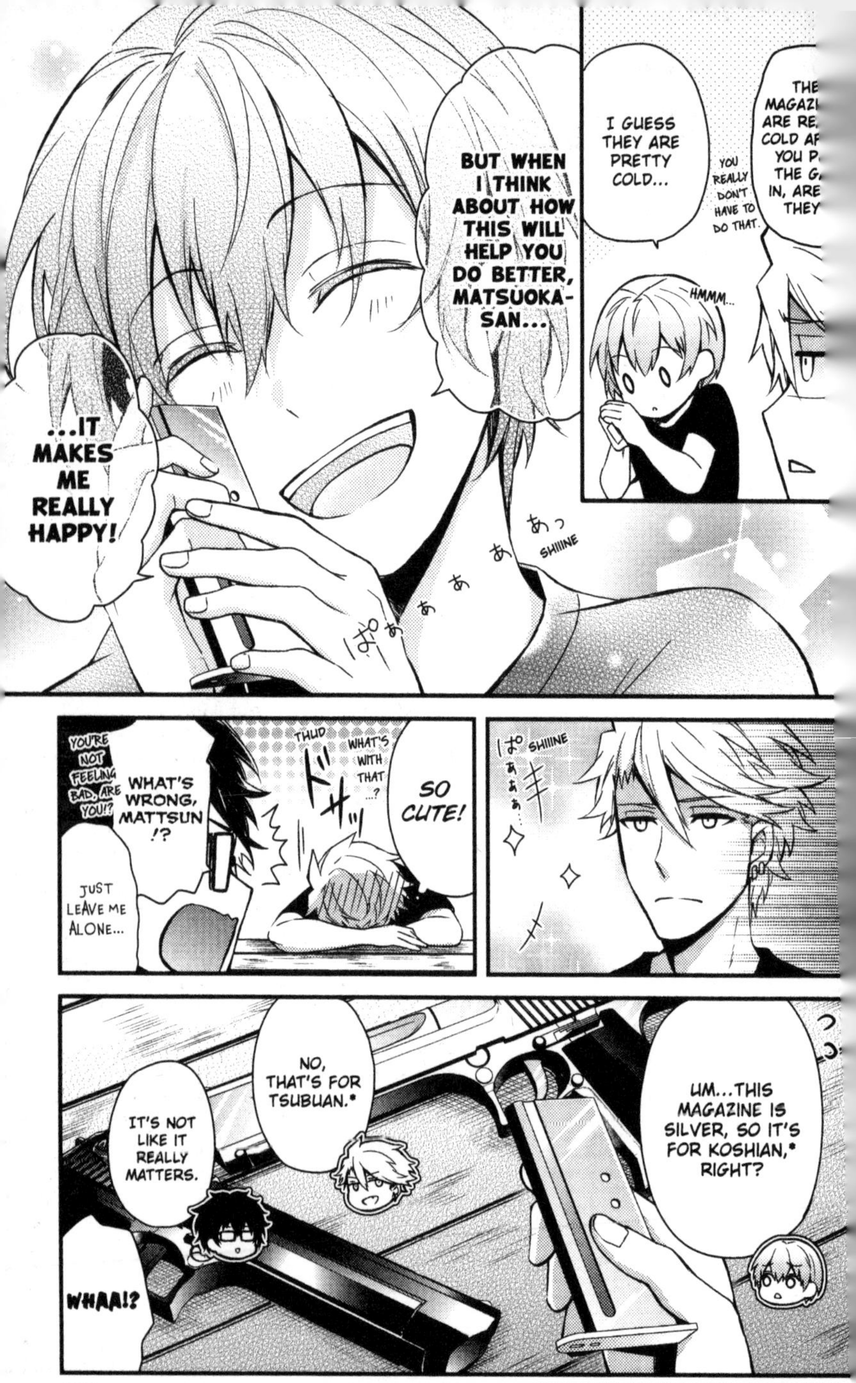
THE MAGAZI ARE RE COLD AF YOU P THE G IN, ARE THEY
YOU REALLY DON'T HAVE TO DO THAT.
I GUESS THEY ARE PRETTY COLD...
HMMM...
BUT WHEN I THINK ABOUT HOW THIS WILL HELP YOU DO BETTER, MATSUOKA-SAN...
...IT MAKES ME REALLY HAPPY!
ぱあああっ
SHIIINE
ぱあぁぁ...
SHIIINE
SO CUTE!
WHAT'S WITH THAT...?
THUD
ドサッ
WHAT'S WRONG, MATTSUN!?
YOU'RE NOT FEELING BAD, ARE YOU!?
JUST LEAVE ME ALONE...
UM...THIS MAGAZINE IS SILVER, SO IT'S FOR KOSHIAN,* RIGHT?
NO, THAT'S FOR TSUBUAN.*
IT'S NOT LIKE IT REALLY MATTERS.
WHAA!?

*SMOOTH AND CHUNKY RED BEAN, RESPECTIVELY.

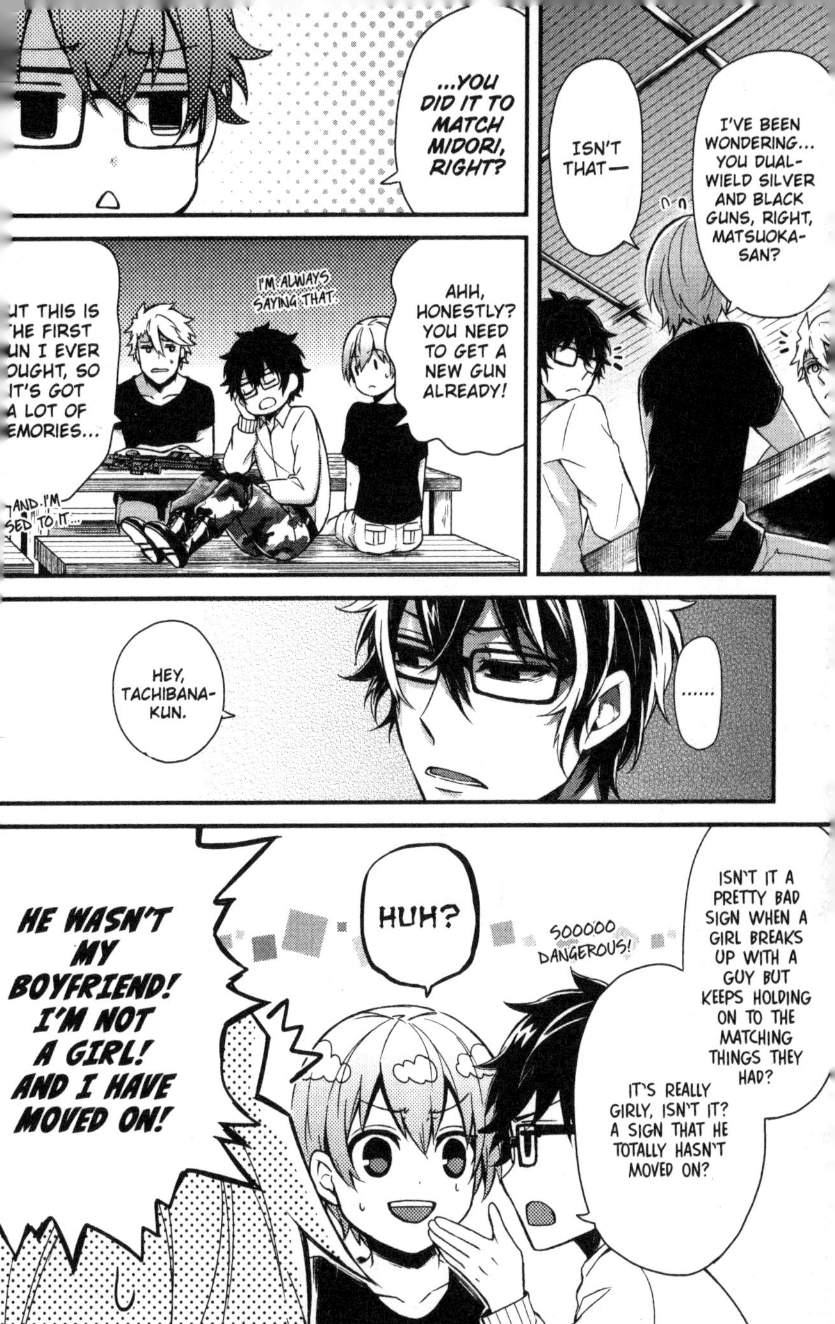
I'VE BEEN WONDERING... YOU DUAL-WIELD SILVER AND BLACK GUNS, RIGHT, MATSUOKA-SAN?
ISN'T THAT—
...YOU DID IT TO MATCH MIDORI, RIGHT?
AHH, HONESTLY? YOU NEED TO GET A NEW GUN ALREADY!
I'M ALWAYS SAYING THAT.
UT THIS IS THE FIRST UN I EVER OUGHT, SO IT'S GOT A LOT OF EMORIES...
AND I'M SED TO IT...
......
HEY, TACHIBANA-KUN.
ISN'T IT A PRETTY BAD SIGN WHEN A GIRL BREAKS UP WITH A GUY BUT KEEPS HOLDING ON TO THE MATCHING THINGS THEY HAD?
IT'S REALLY GIRLY, ISN'T IT? A SIGN THAT HE TOTALLY HASN'T MOVED ON?
SOOOOO DANGEROUS!
HUH?
HE WASN'T MY BOYFRIEND! I'M NOT A GIRL! AND I HAVE MOVED ON!

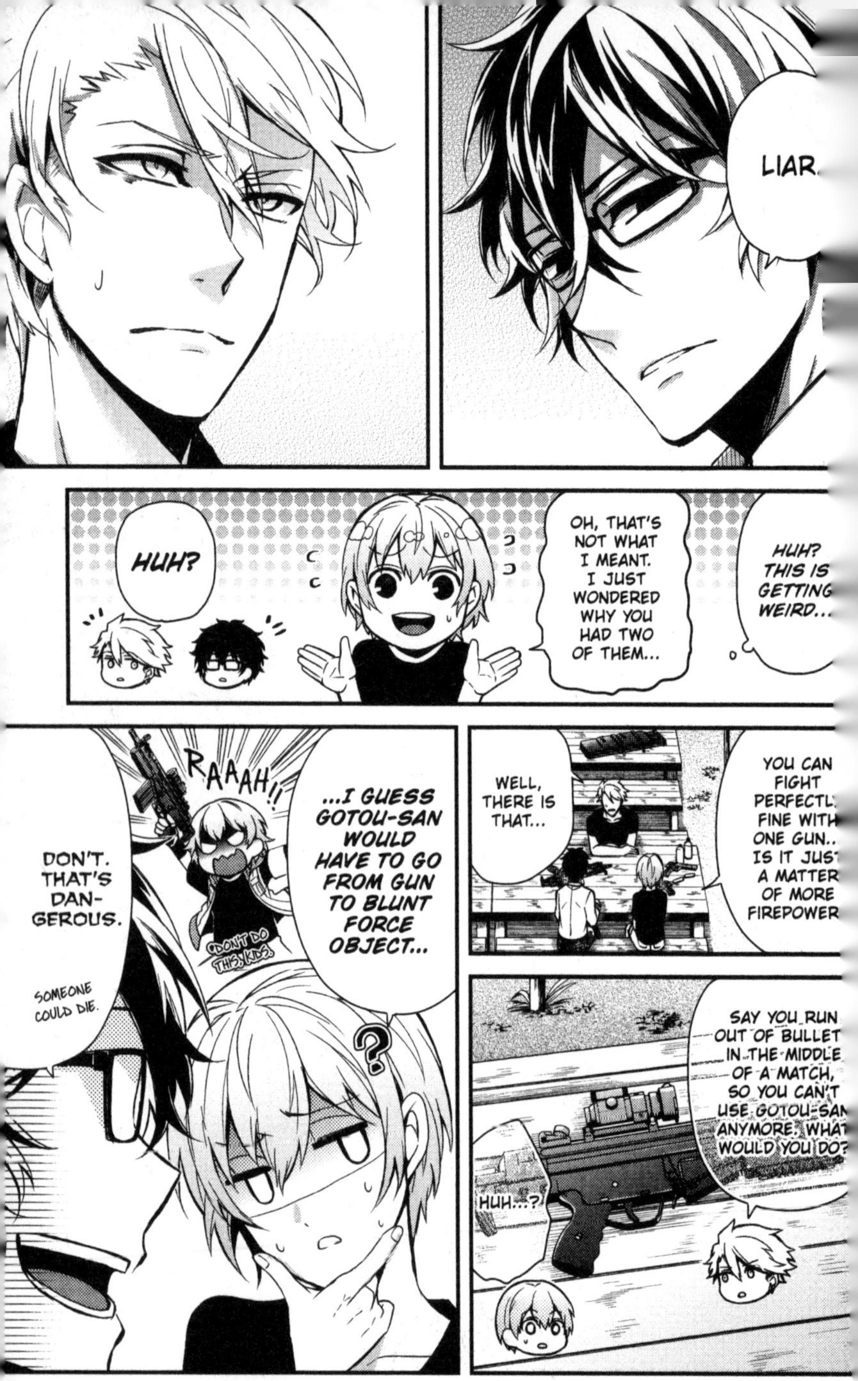

LIAR.
HUH? THIS IS GETTING WEIRD...
OH, THAT'S NOT WHAT I MEANT. I JUST WONDERED WHY YOU HAD TWO OF THEM...
HUH?
YOU CAN FIGHT PERFECTL FINE WITH ONE GUN.. IS IT JUS A MATTER OF MORE FIREPOWER
WELL, THERE IS THAT...
SAY YOU RUN OUT OF BULLET IN THE MIDDLE OF A MATCH, SO YOU CAN'T USE GOTOU-SAN ANYMORE. WHAT WOULD YOU DO?
HUH...?
...I GUESS GOTOU-SAN WOULD HAVE TO GO FROM GUN TO BLUNT FORCE OBJECT...
RAAAH!!
*DON'T DO THIS, KIDS.
DON'T. THAT'S DAN-GEROUS.
SOMEONE COULD DIE.

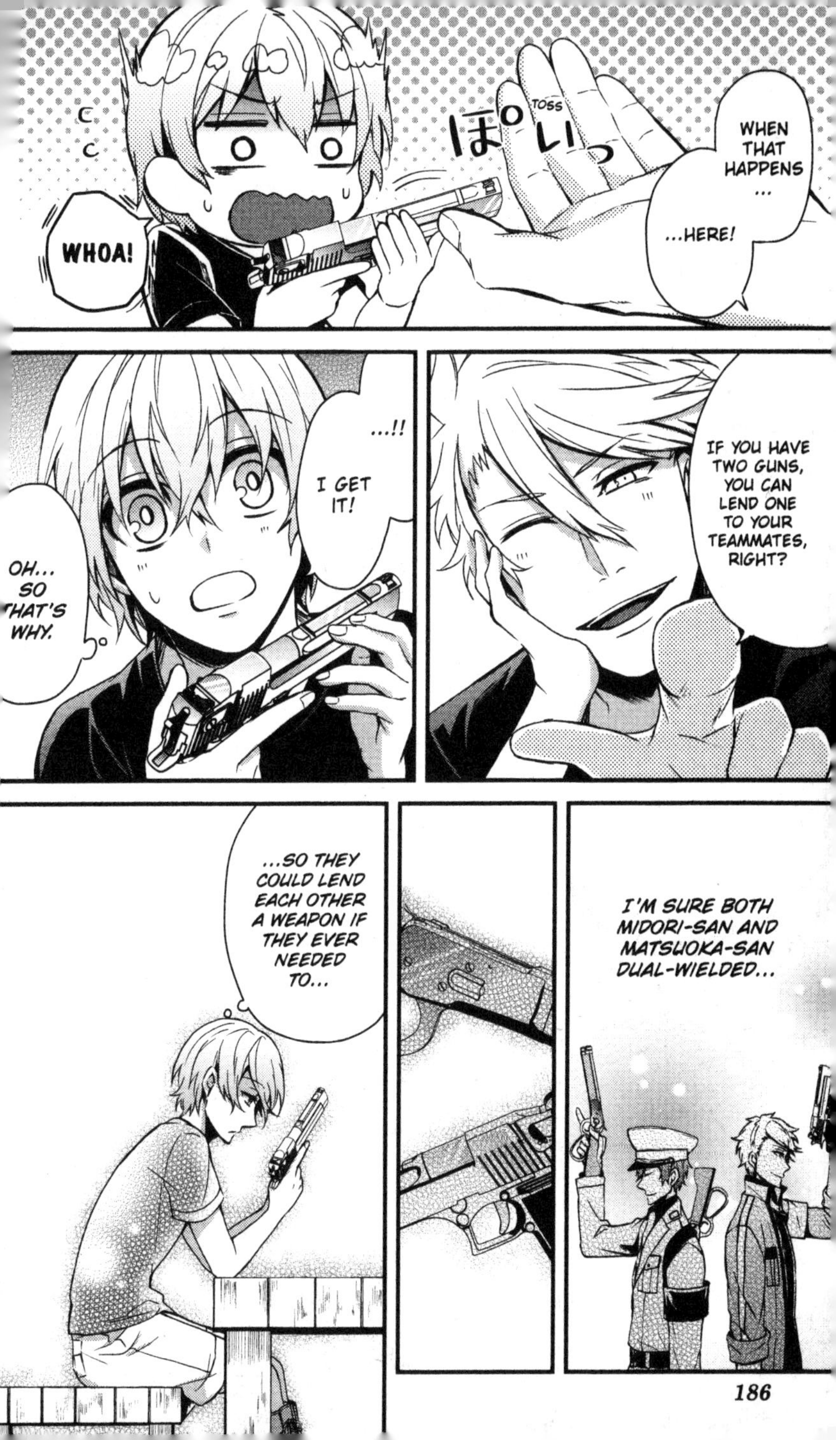
WHEN THAT HAPPENS ...
...HERE!
TOSS
ぽいっ
WHOA!
IF YOU HAVE TWO GUNS, YOU CAN LEND ONE TO YOUR TEAMMATES, RIGHT?
...!!
I GET IT!
OH... SO THAT'S WHY.
I'M SURE BOTH MIDORI-SAN AND MATSUOKA-SAN DUAL-WIELDED...
...SO THEY COULD LEND EACH OTHER A WEAPON IF THEY EVER NEEDED TO...

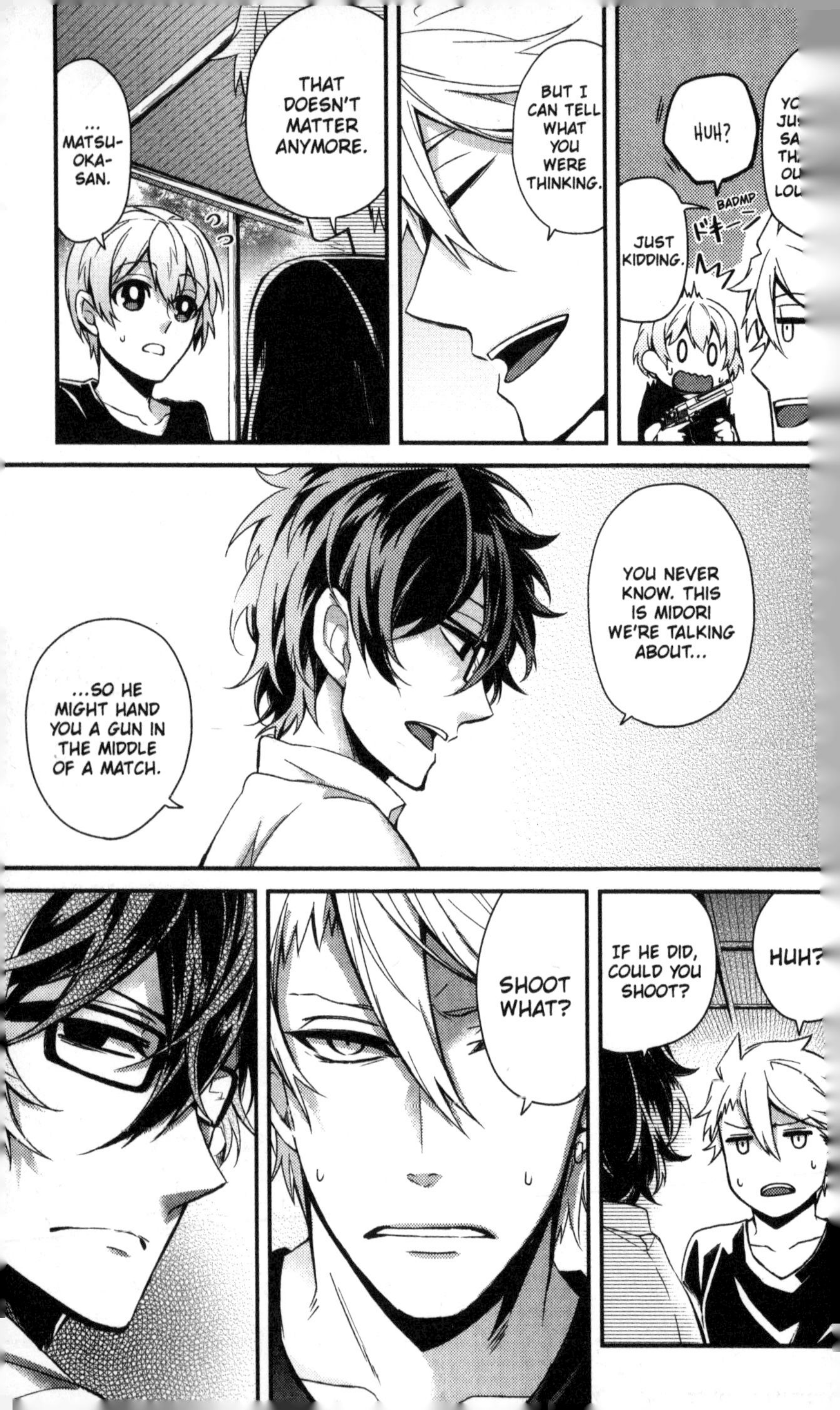
HUH?
BADMP
ドキー
JUST KIDDING.
BUT I CAN TELL WHAT YOU WERE THINKING.
THAT DOESN'T MATTER ANYMORE.
... MATSU-OKA-SAN.
YOU NEVER KNOW. THIS IS MIDORI WE'RE TALKING ABOUT...
...SO HE MIGHT HAND YOU A GUN IN THE MIDDLE OF A MATCH.
HUH?
IF HE DID, COULD YOU SHOOT?
SHOOT WHAT?

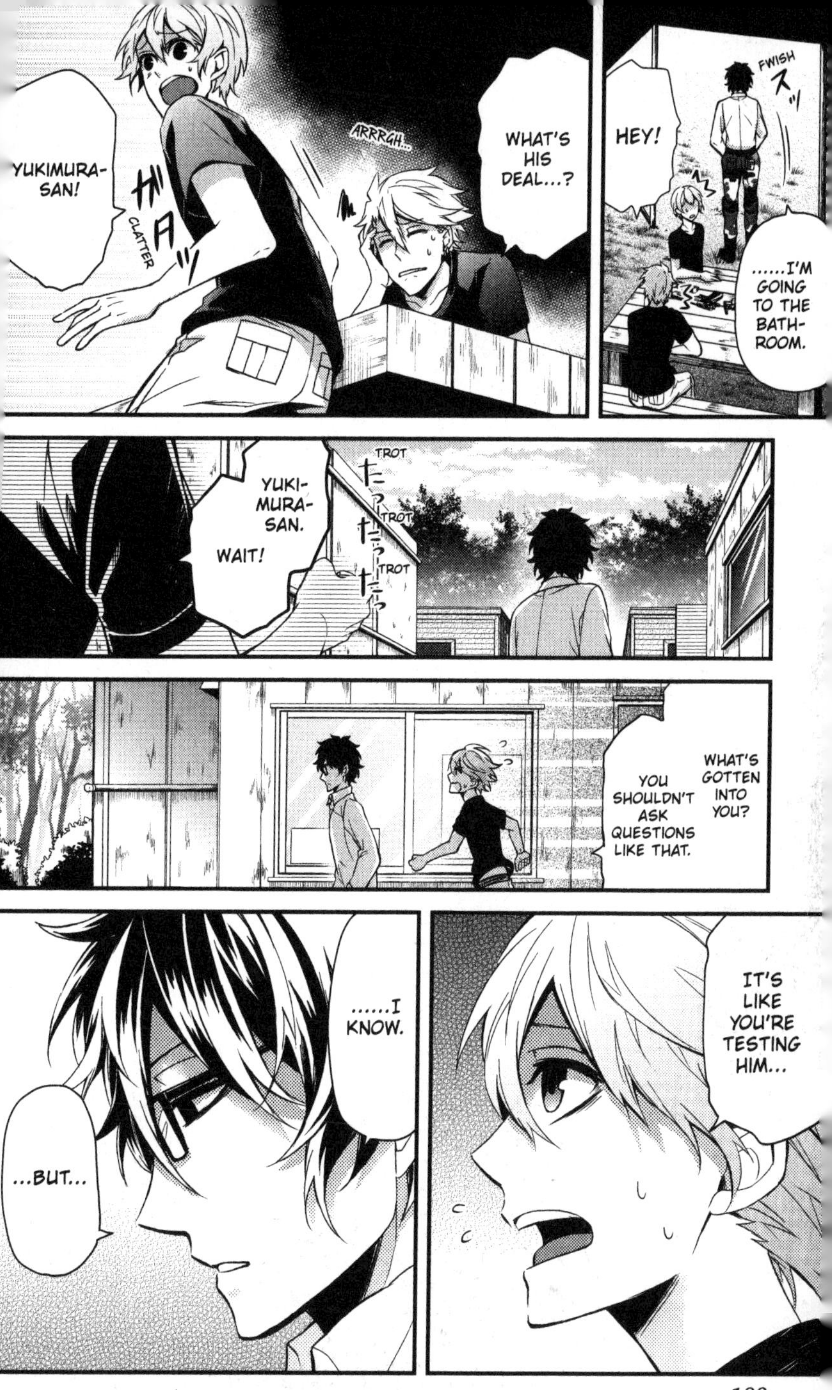
FWISH
HEY!
......I'M GOING TO THE BATHROOM.
WHAT'S HIS DEAL...?
ARRRGH...
YUKIMURA-SAN!
CLATTER
YUKI-MURA-SAN.
WAIT!
TROT
TROT
TROT
WHAT'S GOTTEN INTO YOU?
YOU SHOULDN'T ASK QUESTIONS LIKE THAT.
IT'S LIKE YOU'RE TESTING HIM...
......I KNOW.
...BUT...

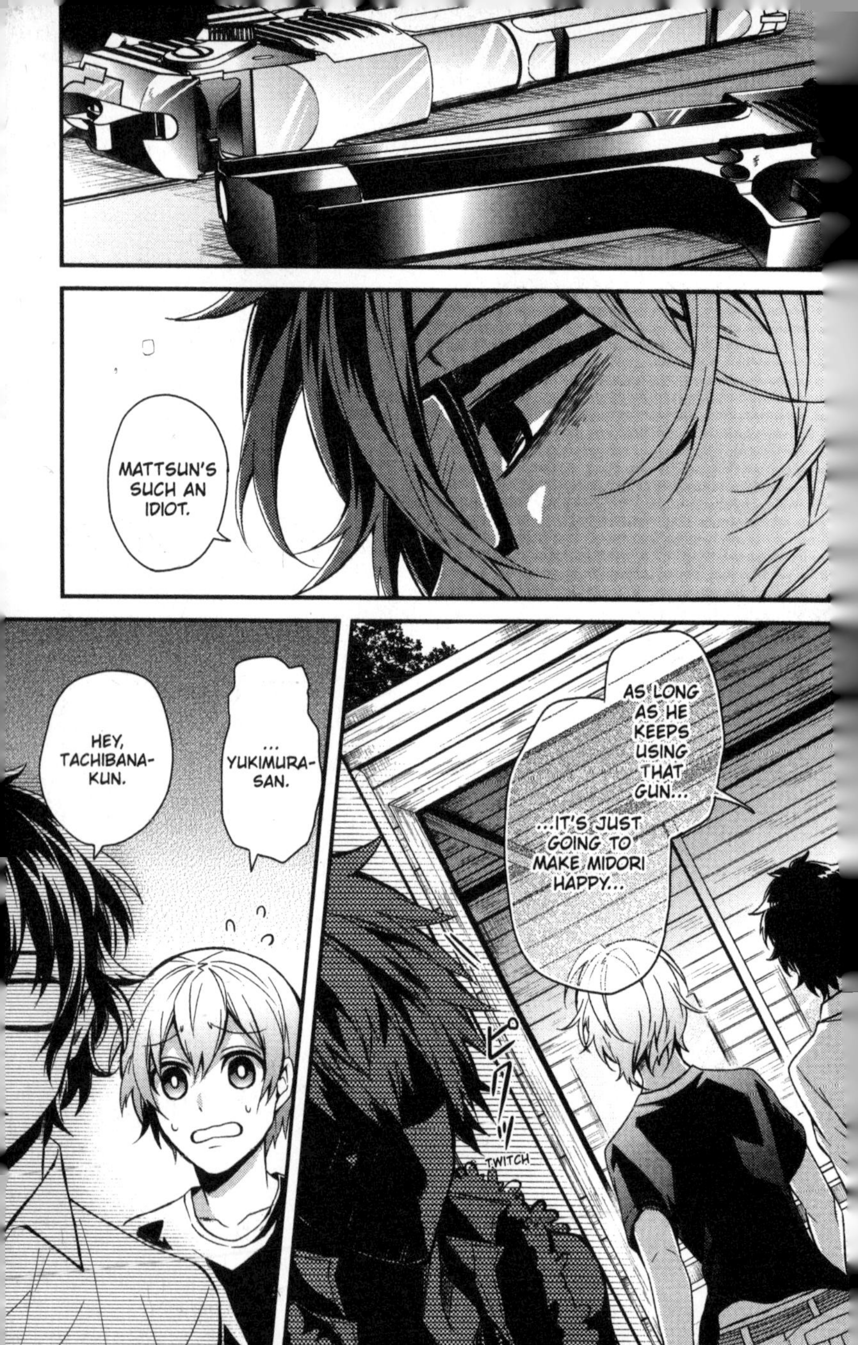
MATTSUN'S SUCH AN IDIOT.
AS LONG AS HE KEEPS USING THAT GUN...
...IT'S JUST GOING TO MAKE MIDORI HAPPY...
TWITCH
... YUKIMURA-SAN.
HEY, TACHIBANA-KUN.

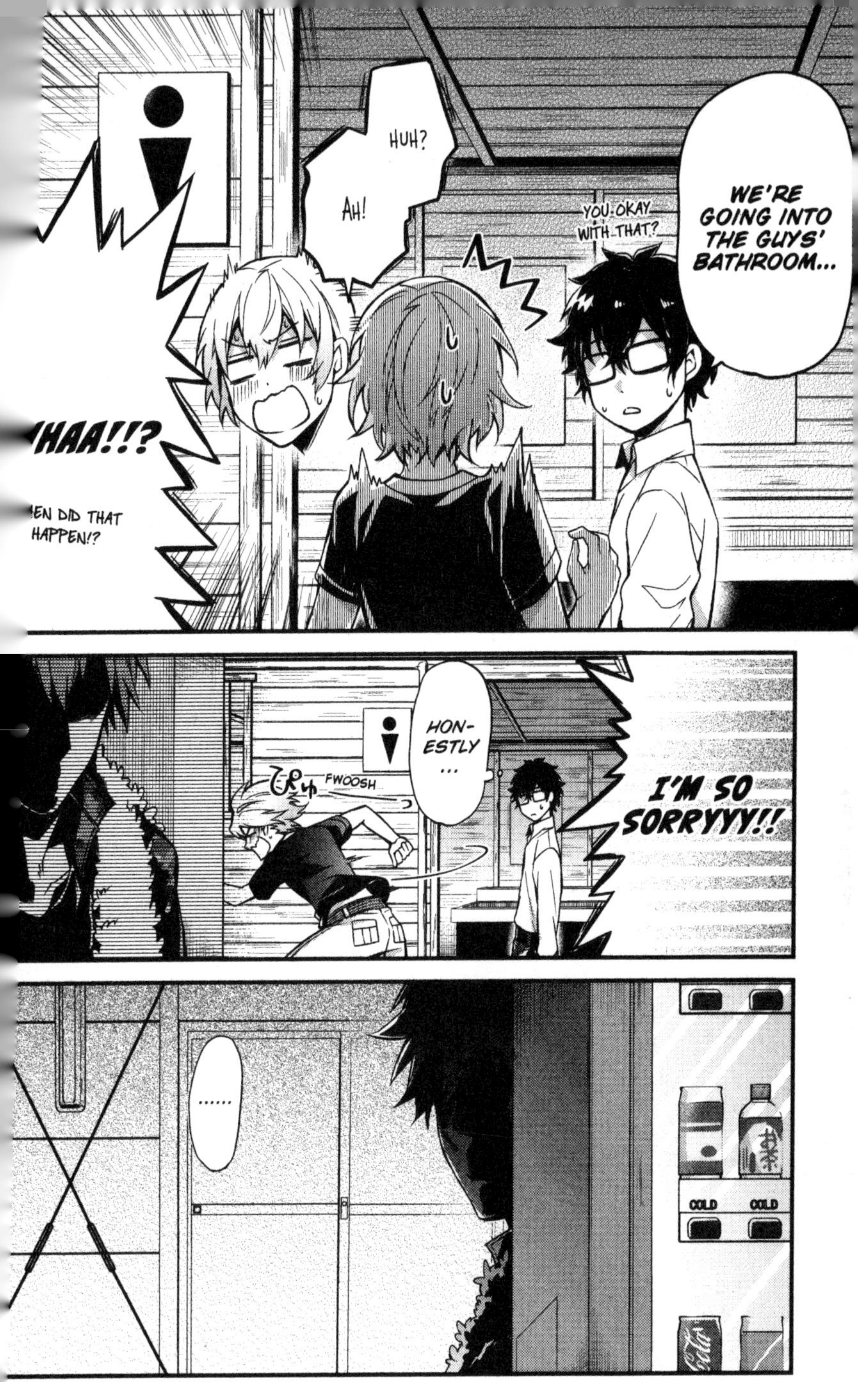

WE'RE GOING INTO THE GUYS' BATHROOM...
YOU OKAY WITH THAT?
HUH?
AH!
HAA!!?
EN DID THAT HAPPEN!?
I'M SO SORRYYY!!
HON-ESTLY ...
FWOOSH
......
COLD
COLD

SPECIAL THANKS

MY EDITOR, THE EDITOR-IN-CHIEF,
THE SALES STAFF, THE DESIGNERS.

TOKYO MARUI, DEKA SHIMAMURA-SAMA,
THE AKIHABARA BRANCH OF WILLYPEET, HIRANO-SAMA.

[HELP]
FRIENDLY FIRE-SAMA
#44 SHOOTING RANGER TARGET-1 AKIHABARA BRANCH

[EMBLEM DESIGN]
SHISHIHIME-SAMA

[ASSISTANTS]
WAKA SANADA (DOKUGANRYUU)-SAMA
SHIRASE (HITLER)-SAMA
YUUSUKE MURAI-SAMA

MY FATHER, MY MOTHER, MY BROTHER, AND YOU!

SEE YOU LATER!!

Naoe

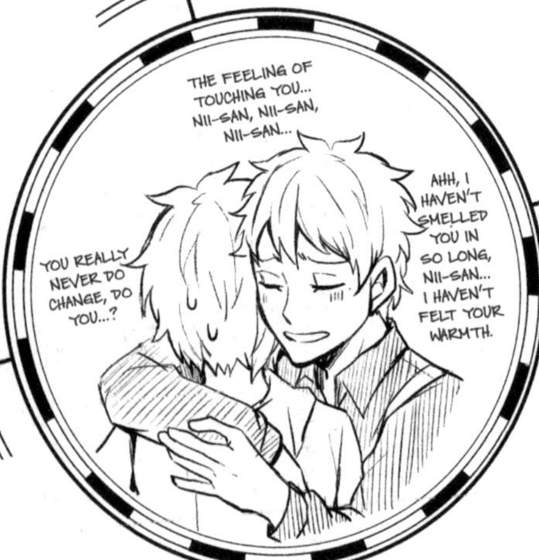
THE FEELING OF TOUCHING YOU... NII-SAN, NII-SAN, NII-SAN...
AHH, I HAVEN'T SMELLED YOU IN SO LONG, NII-SAN... I HAVEN'T FELT YOUR WARMTH.
YOU REALLY NEVER DO CHANGE, DO YOU...?

AOHARU×MACHINEGU

#46

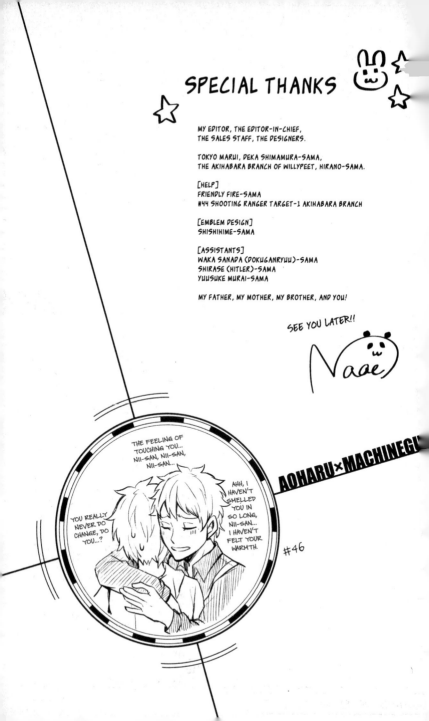

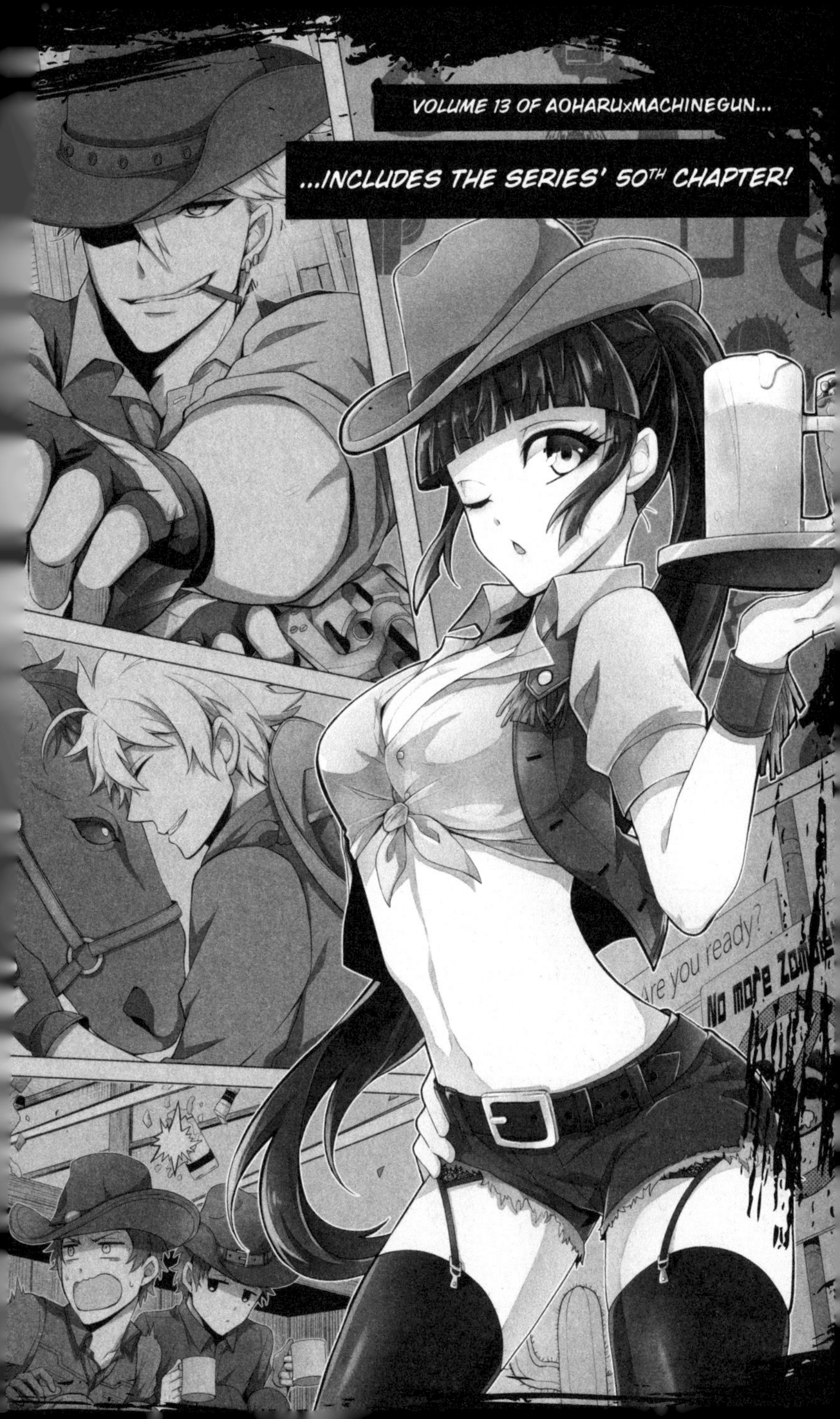
VOLUME 13 OF AOHARUxMACHINEGUN...
...INCLUDES THE SERIES' 50TH CHAPTER!
Are you ready?
No more Zom

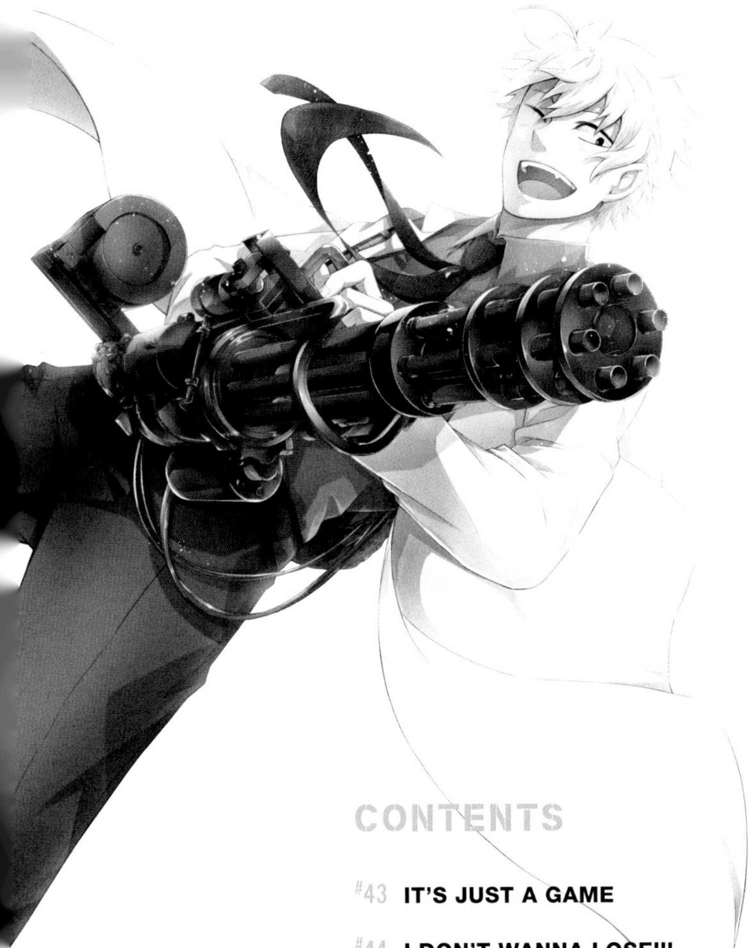

CONTENTS

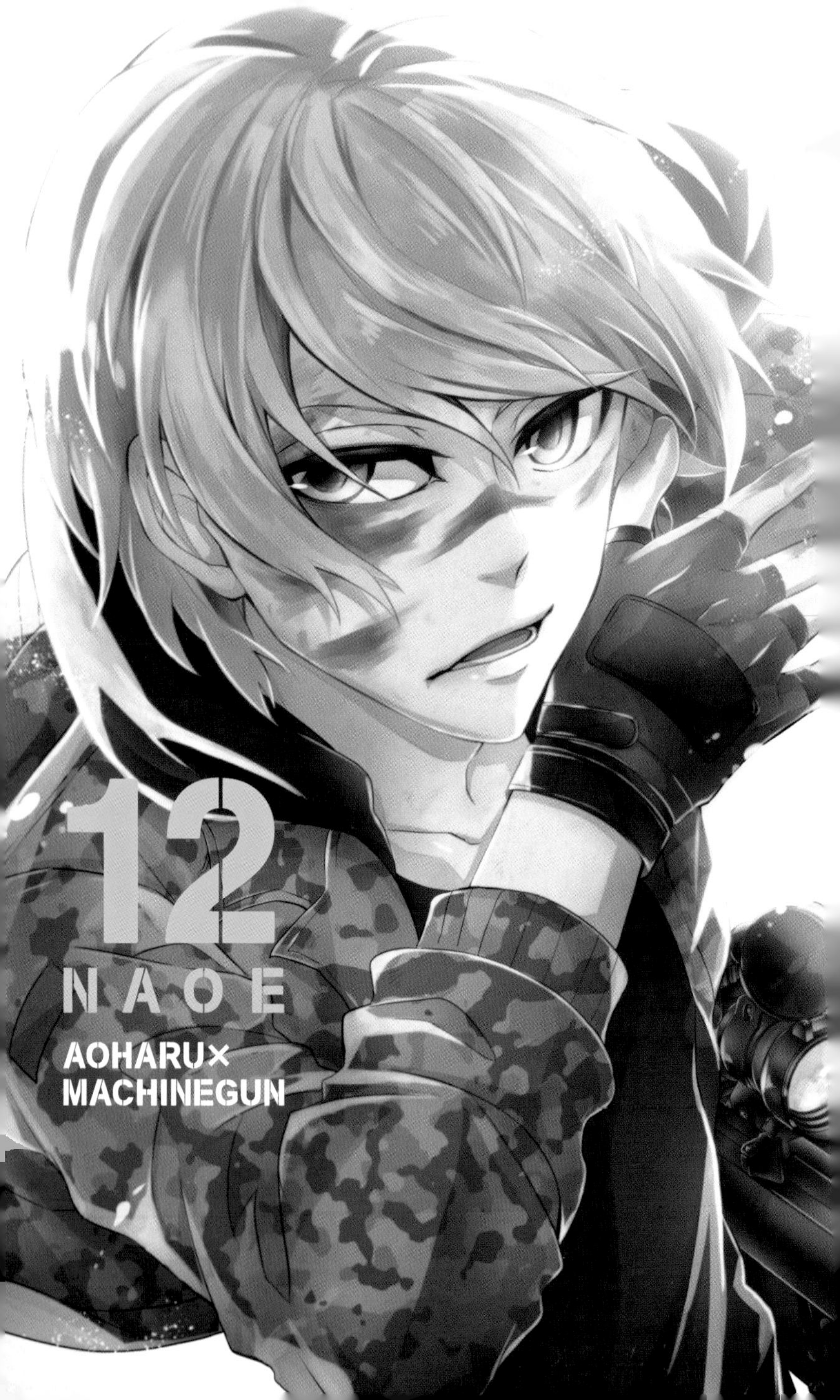
12
NAOE
AOHARU×
MACHINEGUN

GREAT TALENTS

The Story of

NEGRO LEAGUE BASEBALL

by Mark Spann

MODERN CURRICULUM PRESS

Pearson Learning Group

Who is the greatest home-run hitter in baseball?

You might say Babe Ruth. He hit 714 home runs. You might say Hank Aaron. He was the only major league player to break Ruth's record. Aaron hit 755 home runs in his career. Or you might say Mark McGwire. He holds the major league record for the most home runs in one season.

From left to right:
Hank Aaron,
Babe Ruth,
Mark McGwire

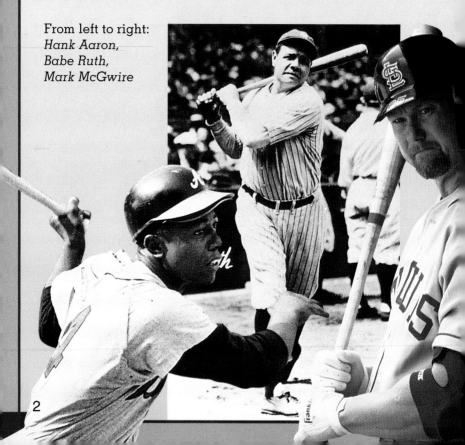

But the greatest home run hitter was an African American catcher. His name was Josh Gibson. He hit 962 home runs in all.

Have you ever heard of Josh Gibson? Most people haven't. That's because, as great as he was, he never played in the major leagues.

Josh Gibson

Before 1947, African Americans played baseball in their own leagues. They were called the Negro Leagues. Josh Gibson was just one of their many talented players.

There was a time in this country when some people thought that skin color made us different from each other. People who did not have the same skin color could not do things together. They could not even play baseball together.

Therefore, African Americans were cut from the regular teams.

It wasn't that way when the game began.

Baseball is an old game. People were playing it 150 years ago. Soldiers played during the Civil War.

Later, teams formed in the big cities. Anyone who was talented enough to make the team could play.

Many teams included African Americans. But some people did not like this idea. Soon African Americans were cut from all of the teams.

When this happened, the major leagues lost many valuable players. And African Americans lost the chance to play big league baseball.

The African American players did not let that stop them. They organized teams of their own.

The first such team was the Cuban Giants, from New York. Frank P. Thompson started the team in 1885. He was a waiter at a hotel. Most of the other players were waiters who worked with him.

Jud Wilson of the Philadelphia Stars scores a run against the New York Black Yankees, c. 1936-1937.

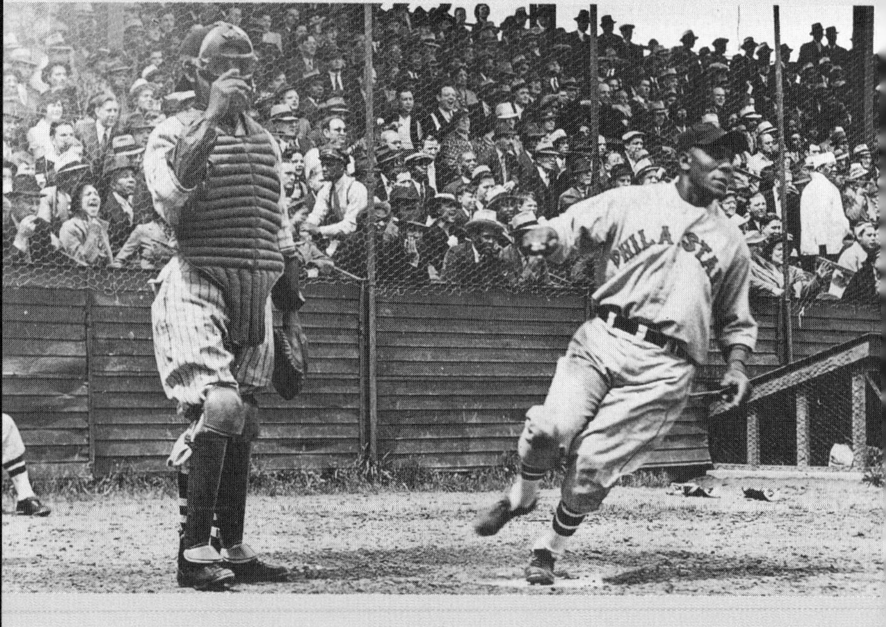
PHILA STA

The Cuban Giants played against the best teams in New York. They won most of their games.

At the same time, teams were forming in other cities. The teams played against each other.

— COLORED —
BASEBALL & SPORTS
MONTHLY

Vol. I - No. I NEW YORK, SEPTEMBER 1, 1934 Price 15c

C. THOMAS, C. JENKINS, C. SPEARMAN
Three Shining Lights in Colored Baseball.

THE ONLY PUBLICATION OF ITS KIND IN THE WORLD

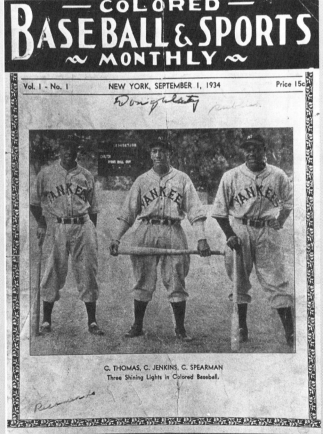

In 1920, Rube Foster formed the Negro National League. A few years later, the Negro American League came along. These were the biggest Negro Leagues.

Many of the teams had colorful names. These were names like the New York Black Yankees, the Atlanta Black Crackers, and the Page Fence Giants. They played all over the country. Often, they used major league ball parks.

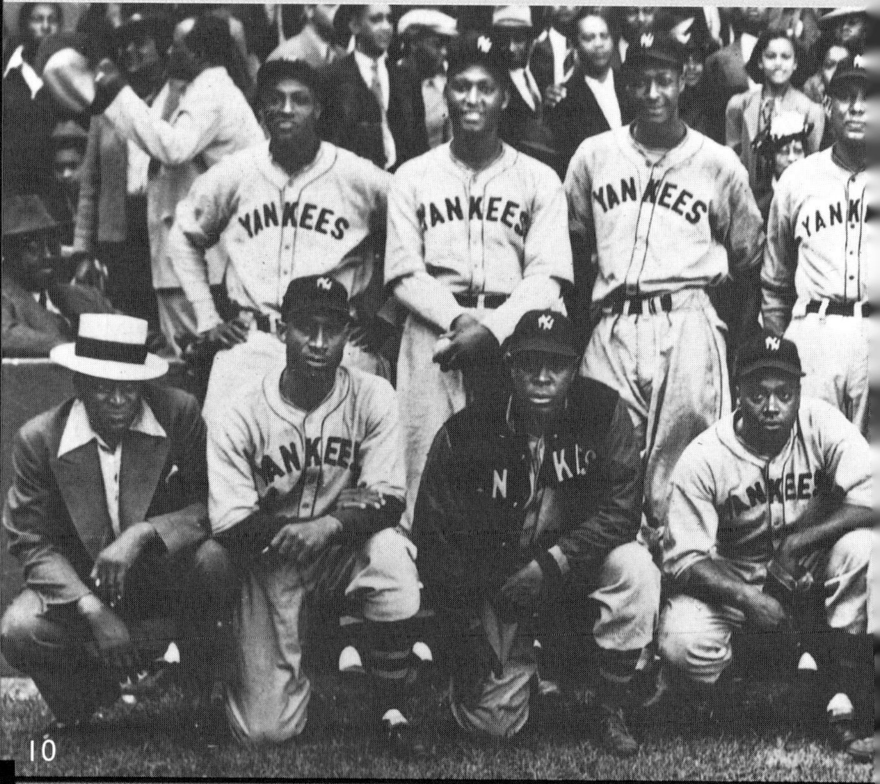
YANKEES
YANKEES
YANKEES

The Negro Leagues had their own World Series. They also had an all-star game. It attracted huge crowds. Sometimes the crowds at those games were larger than the crowds at major league games. People who watched knew the Negro Leagues had many valuable players.

The New York Black Yankees

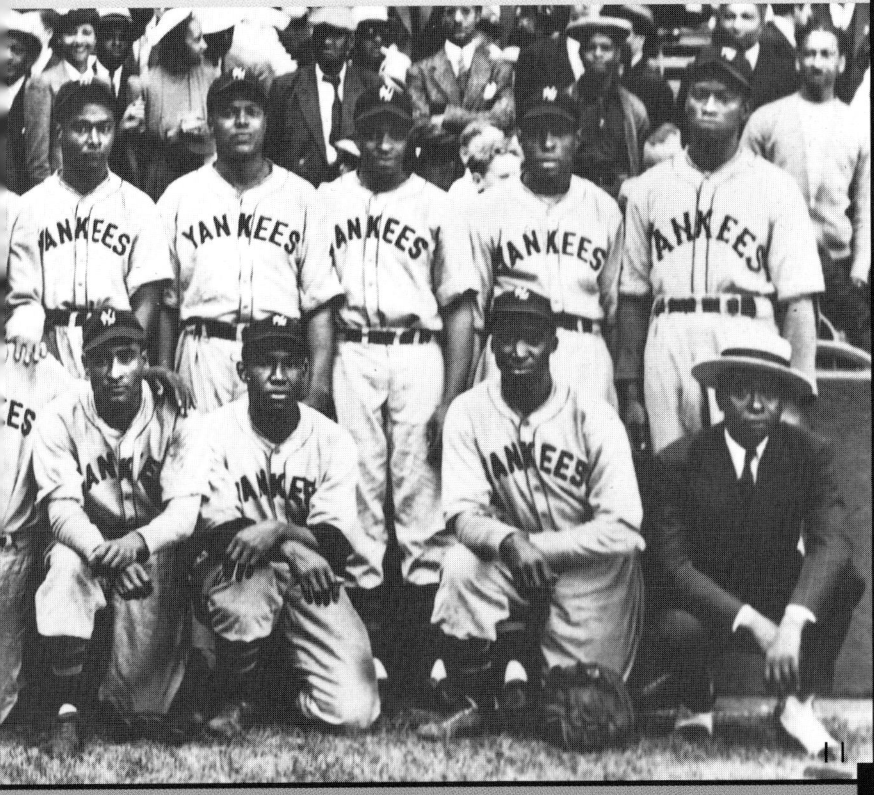
YANKEES
YANKEES
YANKEES
YANKEES
YANKEES

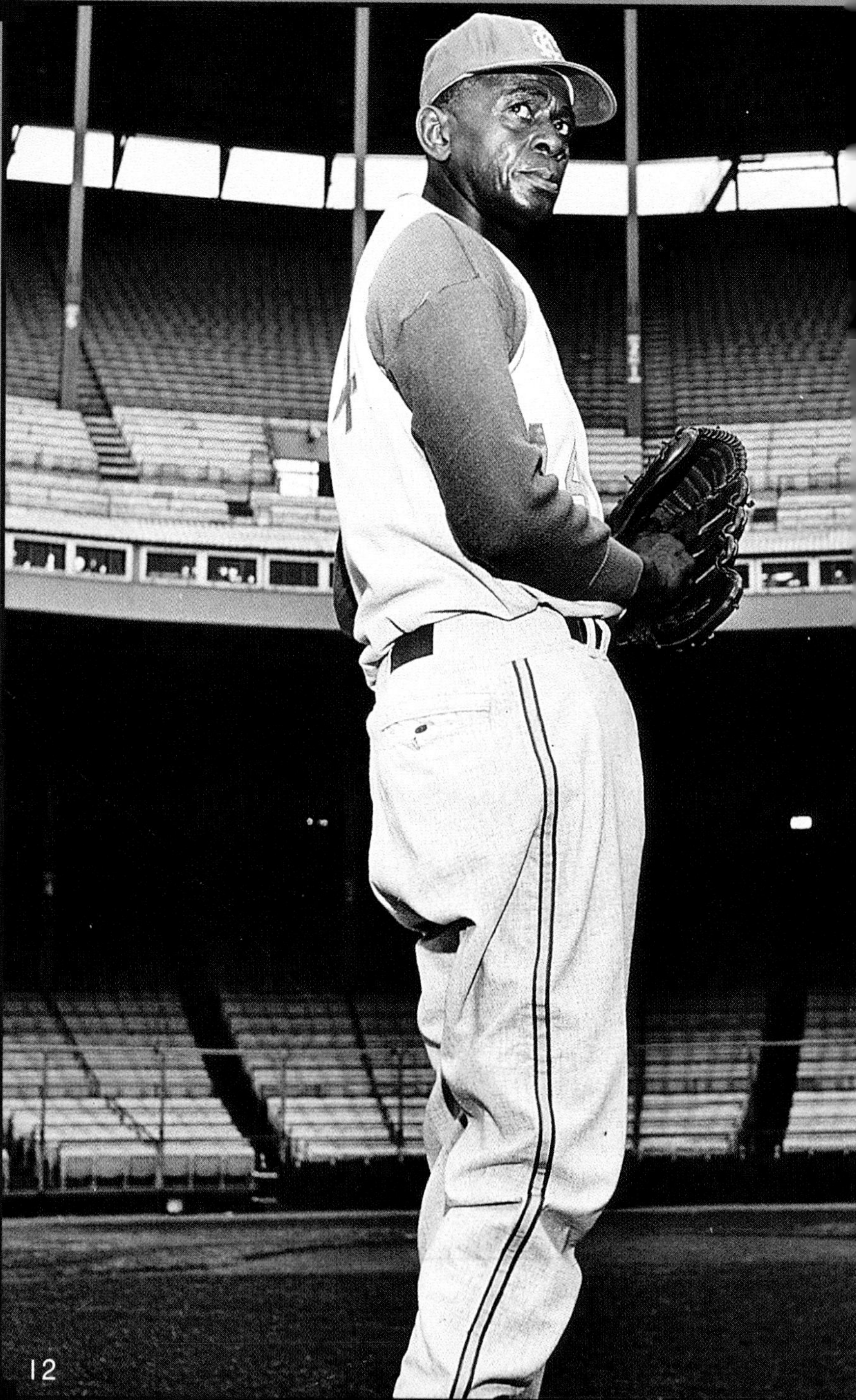

A pitcher named Satchel Paige was one of the most popular and valuable players in the Negro Leagues.

Paige later played in the major leagues too. Dizzy Dean, who was one of the best pitchers of all time, once said that he was not nearly as good as Satchel Paige.

Paige was twenty years old when he began playing baseball. He was tall and skinny. But he threw a baseball harder and faster than anyone else. There was always a big crowd at the game if Satchel Paige was pitching.

In the 1940s Paige and his all-star team played all over the country. They beat many major league teams.

In every city people saw how good the Negro League players were.

They began to think that it was time for these valuable players to play in the major leagues.

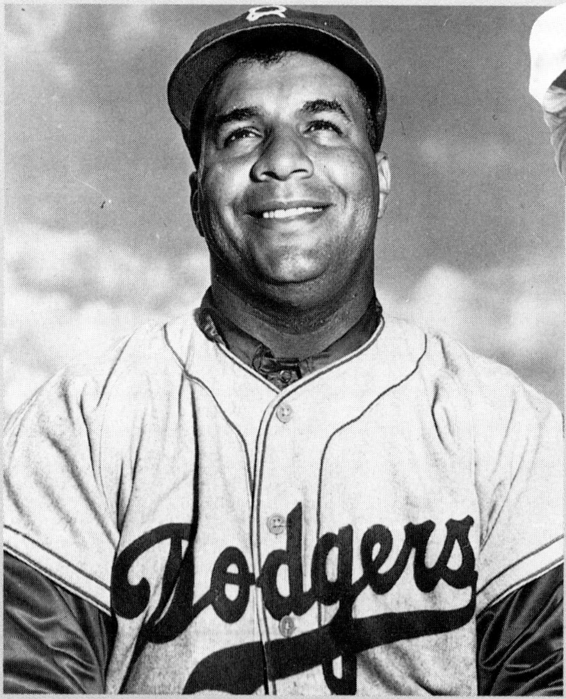
Dodgers

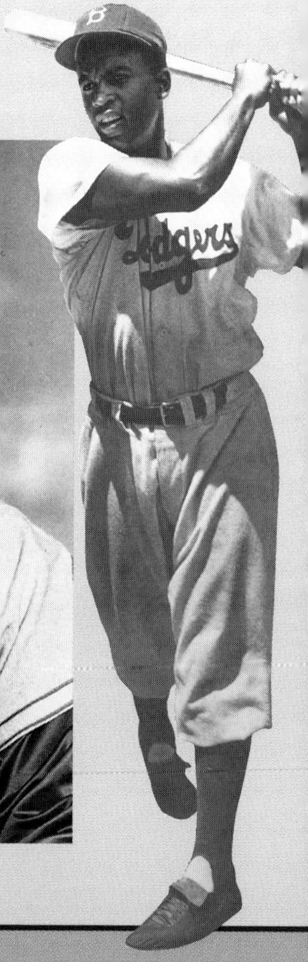
Dodgers

Left: *Roy Campanella*; right: *Jackie Robinson*

In 1947, Jackie Robinson became the first African American in the major leagues. Soon others, such as Willie Mays and Ernie Banks were asked to join.

Satchel Paige was invited even though he was in his forties at the time. Paige was so good that many teams wanted him to play for them. He pitched in the major leagues until he was fifty-nine years old.

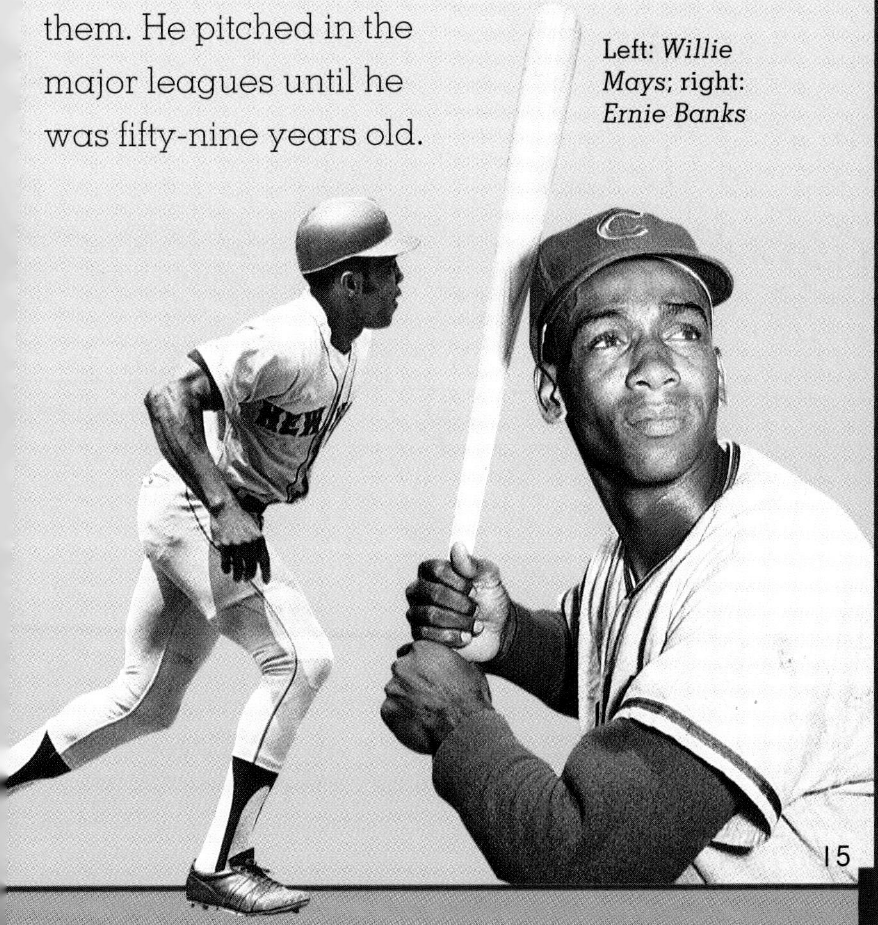

Left: *Willie Mays*; right: *Ernie Banks*

The Negro Leagues were less popular once the major leagues allowed African Americans to play. The last teams stopped playing in 1960.

Negro Leagues were an important part of baseball for over sixty years. They gave African Americans the chance to play the game. They also gave baseball some of its greatest players.

Josh Gibson